Monica Dickens was born in 1915 in London, the great-granddaughter of Charles Dickens. She was educated at St Paul's School for Girls, from which she was expelled. After a brief and unsuccessful career as a debutante, she worked as a cook and servant of all kinds for two years until she met a publisher, on whose suggestion she wrote a book about kitchen life, *One Pair Of Hands*, published in 1939. During the Second World War she worked in an aircraft factory and then for three and a half years as a hospital nurse. Two further autobiographical books followed – *One Pair Of Feet* and *My Turn To Make The Tea*. In 1951 she married an American naval officer: they live on Cape Cod, USA, and have two daughters.

Her recent novels include *Kate And Emma* and *The Landlord's Daughter* as well as a number of children's books including *Follyfoot* and the 'World's End' series. Monica Dickens wanted to write about the lonely misfits of modern society; she went to Chad Varah of the Samaritans and joined the group – hence her latest novel, *The Listeners* She still works for the Samaritans when in England.

THE LISTENERS

Monica Dickens

UNABRIDGED

PAN BOOKS LTD : LONDON

First published 1970 by William Heinemann Ltd.
This edition published 1972 by Pan Books Ltd,
33 Tothill Street, London, SW1.

ISBN 0 330 23230 4

Printed in Great Britain by
Richard Clay (The Chaucer Press), Ltd,
Bungay, Suffolk

To Chad Varah, Samaritan Number 1

'Homo sum: humani nihil a me alienum puto'
'I am a man: I count nothing human alien to me'
Terence, *c* 190–159 BC

ONE

On the sunless side of the hills, where the overgrown town petered out at last in dead grey blocks of flats chucked down on the waste land for people who were supposed to be glad of them, a woman was lying on a bed.

She lay on her back, her large head flung like a stone into the creased pillow. An ashtray rested on the front of her slacks. She had not taken off her boots. Exhausted boots, planting at the ankle, gum and something else on the soles.

It was a high wooden bed with cat-scratched knobs the shape of lidded chalices. The brown corduroy cover did not hang down far enough to conceal cardboard boxes and balls of fluff underneath. Because the whole building had settled slighly soon after it was slapped up twenty years ago, the wardrobe tilted forward, so that the bottom drawer hung like an underlip and the narrow door swung open when the children ran overhead. One night a body would fall out, toppling on to the linoleum with a gangster's hat and staring eyeballs.

The woman shut her eyes, but the lids were pulled back by the weight of the words behind them.

Don't be such a bore.

It's Thursday.

Well, Christ – do we have to stick to the same freakish routine till the end of time?

She would listen to the words for ever, licking them over and over, like a dog with a torn nail.

She stared at the cracked ceiling of the box within a box wherein she lay. There was a rough map of Ireland in the circle of light from the shade clipped on to the bulb of the lamp. The lamp stood on a powerfully ugly piece of furniture that might once have been a hospital locker. On it there was a dream book, half a glass of whisky, a telephone. Earlier, the telephone had still looked as if it might ring.

'Guess who?' Giggling. Drunk. 'Come and get me.' Time was.

She lifted her wrist to look at her broad watch. When she sighed, her diaphragm went in and out like a singer. She took a cigarette from the pocket of her shirt, and the ashtray tipped on to the bed as she raised herself on one elbow to light it. She swilled the whisky round the clouded glass and into her mouth and fell back heavily, her stiff beige hair striking the same dent in the pillow. The cigarette drooped between her top lip and her chin. Soon ash fell on her chest. Full breasts, naked under the shirt, were spread flatly backward by their own weight, the nipples out by the armpits. As the cigarette burned shorter, her eyes were full of smoke, but at some time after she had dropped the cigarette into the last quarter inch of whisky, they were not watering but crying, the corners of a gargoyle mouth pulled back towards the tears that ran into her hair, carrying mascara with them like river silt.

About an hour later, moving as heavily as a sleepwalker, although she could not sleep, the woman propped herself up again and groped for the telephone.

She had torn the advertisement out of the evening paper. Torn it carelessly, leaving the top words behind on the floor of the bus. '... desperate. If you are at the end of your tether.' The words were crumpled from her pocket. '*Samaritans.*' And the number to ring.

Who would answer? Nobody. Do yourself in between nine and six, dear, if you expect anyone to give a damn. She dialled the number, to prove it.

Although she had been a Samaritan for more than a year, Victoria was still not free of that tiny instant of panic when the telephone rang.

It was only a fraction of a second. Half a pulse beat, the beginning of a deeper breath. Her left hand was out before the second ring, her voice was speaking for her, the other voice made known, and she plunged like a diving bird into the grappling waters of speech.

'I can't sleep.'

'Oh ... how awful for you. Do you want to talk?'

'There's nothing to talk about. I can't sleep. I just lie like this and my heart pounds right up at the top of my chest. You know?'

'Mm-hm.'

'Like it will choke you. And the way you can't stop thinking. Over and over, I hear the same words over and over.'

'I know. That can be unbearable.'

'It's so bloody unbearable, I—' The woman on the telephone began to cry. Not gasping sobs, but small bleating moans, as if she were being physically hurt.

'Tell me. Tell me about it. It's all right, I won't ring off. I'll wait till you can talk.'

'I'm— oh shit, it's no good, I can't—'

'There's plenty of time. I'll wait.'

'What's the use?' The voice strengthened into a cry. 'You don't care. Why should you? Nobody cares. There's no one to talk to. Those shitty friends...'

'I care.'

Startled, the woman held her breath, then released it on a sigh. 'I don't believe that.'

'You can believe it or not.' Victoria put her elbow on the desk and leaned her ear on the telephone receiver. 'It's true.'

'I thought – well, I mean – aren't I supposed to say, "I'm going to kill myself"? That's what you're there for, isn't it?'

'We're here' – it always sounded a little mannered this, and yet there was no other way to say it – 'to try and help anyone who needs us.'

'Do-gooders.' The woman made the vowel sounds of a jeer. 'I've had some of that. I had one once – well, she was

9

a probation officer, if you must know. She said, "You ought to find some nice man and get married, that's what you ought to do." What do you think of that?'

'Well ... that's all right, I suppose, but nice men aren't all that easy to find.'

'You married, dear?'

'No. I'm not.'

'How old are you, can I ask that?'

'Thirty-five.'

'You a lesbian?'

'No.'

'I am. Does that shock you?'

Victoria laughed. She felt among the papers on the desk for a cigarette. 'You'll have to try harder than that. Let's talk about why you can't sleep. Why you're unhappy.'

When Victoria's voice became gentle, the woman gave a sort of strangled gasp. 'How could you sleep when the only person in the world you care about calls you a freak? Oh shit, you couldn't understand.'

Across the desk, Helen was talking into the other telephone. A homeless man who was waiting to be fetched by the students was a heap of old clothes by the wall, his broken shoes at a slack angle, as if they had no feet in them. His red-rimmed eyes watched the woman vacantly.

Victoria, in a thick white pullover and blue jeans, her long red hair tied back with a green scarf, elbows on the desk, shoulders hunched, hugged the telephone receiver like a harmonica and asked it fiercely, 'Why should you care what people say? What's wrong with being a lesbian?'

Helen, with her shoes off and a pencil stuck through her short wild hair, told her noisy telephone, 'That's enough, Jackie, that's enough. Knock it off now and go back to bed, there's a good boy. It's much too late for you to be up ... Yes, of course you can. Anytime. Yes, I'll be here next week ... Yes, I love you ... I've told you what I look like. I look like your mother. Does she? All right then, your grandmother. No, Amy's not here. Her husband's got flu. Victoria's here. She looks like your sister ... Well, if you did. Yes, yes, she loves you too. All right, love. You go to bed. Goodnight, dear.'

She put down the receiver, looked at the clock and made a note in the log book. Jackie was one of her steadies. On Thursday nights, he set his alarm under his pillow and crept down barefoot to the telephone so that Helen could chide him back to bed like the child he still was at twenty-two.

'Yes, do,' Victoria said. 'There's always someone here.'

'I'd rather speak to you though. No sense going through the whole bloody mess all over again.'

'I'm usually here on Sundays. My name's Victoria.'

'Mine's Billie—well, just Billie.'

'I'll give you the second number, in case the emergency line is tied up. I hope we can talk again, Billie. I enjoyed it.

The jeering vowels again, but with less energy.

'Try and get some sleep.'

'I'm going to have a drink.'

'Does that make you sleep?'

'No, but it makes me more enjoyable.'

Victoria put down the receiver, slid a hand under her hair and flipped it away from her neck. 'It can't be much fun being a lesbian if you have to feel guilty about it.'

'What did you tell her?'

'To go on loving. Was that right?'

'No good without.' Helen got up and went to pick up the slopped cup of tea from the floor by the keeled-over feet. The homeless man was asleep, snoring gently inside the long threadbare coat, a bubble of mucus blowing in and out of his nose.

Victoria, Helen had said. 'She loves me too?' Jackie shouted into the telephone. He always spoke too loudly. If your lips didn't close properly on the beginning and end of words, you had to shout to be understood.

The telephone was in his father's workshop, on the wall above the nailing machine. In the front part of the shop, his mother sold handbags and slippers and rain-boots and shoe brushes and polishes and dyes. Her hair was like a grey helmet. She wore a green smock to match the carpet, and her nails were shell-clean as she gave the change on to a little pimply rubber mat like goose-flesh.

His father did the shoe repairs on the trimmers and stitchers in the workshop at the back, whistling through an unlit match. Jackie did heels 'Wile-U-Wate', and the waiting women sat in the front of the shop like goods on display and read magazines and curled their stockinged toes and rubbed one foot over the other to get the bunions going.

Jackie got quite bored with the heels. He would much rather sit on the green plastic chairs and look at pictures in magazines, but it was very important for him to have a job and 'contribute to society', so that nobody would say he was childish. Jackie would not care if they did say it. He liked to be childish, but his mother did not like it, and his father liked what his mother liked, because she was better educated.

'All right, love.' Helen's voice was rough and friendly, like a blanket. The sort of voice his mother listed as common. The sort of voice that Jackie liked.

'Goo-ni, He'en. Goo-ni.' Jackie hung the telephone back on the wall, smiling and safe. Then he remembered that he had forgotten something. He picked off the receiver again and shouted, 'God bless!', but there was only the dialling tone, purring at him like a mechanical cat. He was going to dial again – his finger knew the right holes in the dark – when he noticed with a painful chill like frost on iron railings, that the door between the workshop and the stairs that led to the flat was ajar. He must have closed it so gently that it did not catch, and here he had been shouting and laughing as if he was alone in the building.

Would his mother be waiting at the top of the stairs with her 'patient' voice? Jackie sucked his lip. Got to risk it. He tiptoed up the stairs, holding up his pyjama trousers and watching his bare feet grab the carpet like sand. When he reached the top, her bedroom door was open, and in the light from the seven-watt bulb left on for young Malcom to go to the WC, Jackie's eye travelled up all the buttons of her dressing-gown to the round furry chin, small pink mouth, bumped-up nose, and at last to the eyes.

They were not unkind eyes, or frightening. They were blank. Clear blue like laundry bleach, not smiling, not glaring, not puzzled. They were as expressionless as Mrs Brady's glass eye, at the greengrocer's. It was a marvel to Jackie that anyone could see with eyes like that. Mrs Brady couldn't see you if you came up unexpectedly on her glass side.

'Hullo, Mum.' That was what he meant, but he knew, because Malcom's friend had made a tape-recording for him, that he said something like, 'Huh-o, Muh.'

'What were you doing down there? I thought you weren't going to talk to yourself any more.'

'I talking to He'en.' Jackie did not bother to lie to her.

'I see, dear. And what did Helen say?' Muh was always careful how she spoke. She said, 'And-a h-what-a did', especially when she was speaking to Jackie, moving her lips like captive worms, precisely.

'She told me about her dog. It bit a bloke was selling carpets.'

'It-a bit-a man.' Muh's forehead frowned, though her blue eyes showed nothing. 'I don't want you to go downstairs at night,' she said. 'You're too big a boy for playacting and games. Aren't you?'

Jackie nodded, looking down at her from under his thick forelock. She only came up to his shoulders, but she made it seem an advantage to be short.

'And-a there is no Helen, is there?'

Muh did not believe in Helen or Amy, or any of them he talked to at the Samaritans. One day, when he brought in some 'Wile-U-Wate' heeling jobs, the women were talking about a piece in a magazine which gave you the number to ring if you were going to put your head in

13

the oven, so Jackie had rung them up on Thursday night to see what they would say.

He had been ringing almost every Thursday night since, with the workshop door shut. Muh had caught him once before, but she thought he was pretending. So when she said, in her 'teaching' voice like that poor woman at the school who kept trying to make him read, 'There is no Helen, is there?' it was safe to say, 'Yes.'

Jackie yawned. Helen had sent him to bed, so he toddled in his drooping pyjamas into his room and manoeuvred his length into the tunnel of bedclothes.

'Good night, Jackie,' his mother called in a sanitary voice. She still tucked up Malcom, and read him stories about children called Rodney and Tessa who navigated space rockets. Jackie was allowed to eavesdrop on the stories, but not to be tucked up. Jackie was a man.

'Samaritans—'

Rapid electronic beeps from a call-box.

'Samaritans – can I help you?'

'I don't know. I saw your poster. I've nowhere to go.' A Tyneside voice, a broad flat statement, not asking for anything.

'I can give you some names of hotels and boarding houses...' Victoria tilted her chair back to reach for the folder.

'How much?'

'The cheapest you could get would be about fifteen shillings a night.'

A single-syllable laugh. 'I'm broke, sister.'

'Where are you? I can tell you where the Reception Centre is.'

'What's that?'

'A Government hostel, they'll give you a bed. Hold on just a minute...'

When she hung up the telephone, it rang again before she had taken her hand off it.

'Samaritans – can I help you?'

The beeps again, replaced by heavy breathing. A man.

'Yes? Can I help you?'

The breathing continued. It could be anxiety. It could be a joke. It could be a sex call. It could be fear or pain. Whatever it was, you waited. You never rang off first.

You tried to offer help without being officious. You tried to make contact, but if no one spoke, all you could do was show that you were there. That you were still listening. That you would listen all night if that was what they wanted. Friendship. Caring. Love. Your voice had to convey your heart.

And if you failed— 'Tell me what number you're ringing from,' Victoria said too anxiously, 'and I can ring you back if the money runs out.'

The breathing went on, harshening, quickening, until the beeps cut in again. Then nothing.

'Damn.' It was horrible when that happened. You didn't know. You didn't know that it was not your fault.

She made an entry in the log book. '22.00. *Phone-box call. Breathing only.*' An entry of Helen's higher up said, '*21.40. V. rude person who might be our old seagoing friend rang from what sounded like a public swimming-bath. So abusive even I couldn't answer back.*'

Helen was in the kitchen at the back of the old greening stone house that had once been a rectory, breaking the hearts of parsons' wives and their poor little maids, and was now the Samaritan Centre. The homeless man was still asleep by the wall of the small front room that had once been a study where the parson yawned over repetitious sermons, wearing mittens to save coal. Depressed, Victoria sat and twisted her hands in her lap, staring at the telephone. Please try again. She turned Robbie's ring round and round on her finger. When he had given her the little box, irritatingly glorified with shiny paper and bows, she put the ring on to her right hand quickly and casually, before he could suggest the other. The tiny jewel was absurd on her. Wanting her to be petite, Robbie invariably chose presents that were too small and too dainty. If the ring would not go back over her knuckle, she would have to be buried in it.

Please try again, she begged the unknown man who had breathed his fear and loneliness. Perhaps it had taken all the courage he had left to ring this number. Don't be afraid. I am afraid too. I lost you. I let you go. Give me another chance.

She heard Helen coming back down the hall. Victoria dug the corner of Robbie's absurd jewel into the flesh of her finger, and leaned over the desk where the telephone squatted like a black secret. Ring now. If Helen comes in here, I shall be coward enough to let her take the next call. She'll talk to you. Help you. Save you. But I want it to be me.

Although she had been passionate to join the Samaritans, and would have died if she had been turned down, Victoria was not really sure she should have been accepted. She had the wrong spirit. Selfish. Obsessed. The others were so balanced. So bloody nice. They accepted her as they accepted each other, and every last least lovable client, without judgement, without seeing how inadequate she was.

As she turned to smile at Helen, coming back into the room with sandwiches, the telephone jerked her back with a shock of nerves. She grabbed it, waited for the beeps. 'Yes? Oh – Billie. Hullo.'

'Just making sure you're still there.'

'Do you want me?'

'Me? No, but all those poor sods.'

'What sods?'

'Well, I mean ... ringing and ringing. Can't have that, you know,' Billie said sternly, and rang off.

'How is she?'

'All right, I think,' Victoria said, 'She's drunk.'

It seemed like a message sent direct to him.

If you are desperate, the poster said. *If you are at the end of your tether*. Well, if it could be the end of something that had never properly begun, that's me.

Tim was twenty. He had lived for almost two years in

this great conglomerate town of slums and university and factories and rich flowering suburbs and seaside trippery and reeling rows of new estate houses, eating up the salty grassland. He had come from the flat wet plate of an eastern county, where he was supposed to learn how to grow the flowers and vegetables that made their own frenzied growth out of the dark earth that was so frigging fertile, Mr Gregg said, it was like growing the poor buggers in straight manure.

That was not Tim's natural home. He had spent the first years of his life in some place like Harrow or Hendon that you could call a part of London if you liked. His third foster-mother took him to East Anglia, and after she sickened of it, and of Tim, he had lived mostly in a Children's Home, where the nurses came and went almost every month, since girls these days would not stand for all the washing.

At school, the boys from the Home tended to shun the others, to forestall being shunned. Once, Tim had been invited to tea with Adam Johnson, whose mother felt that we should all do what we could to help those less fortunate than ourselves. They had sardines on toast and Battenburg cake in a little house by a canal lock where Adam's father worked the gates.

His mother said, 'When Adam was a baby, all he wanted was sardines and pickles,' as though she were telling some event in history.

'That's right.' Adam's face spread into a hypnotized beam of self. 'And I'd lick the oil from the tins. They couldn't keep it out of my hair.'

'You couldn't remember when you were a baby.' Tim stared across the table at him. He could remember nothing of Harrow or Hendon.

'Mum tells me about it.' Adam made round smug eyes over a two-fisted mouthful of toast, and his mother, seeing Tim's burning face, had coughed into her finger-tips, spitting a crumb of toast on to her cheek, where it remained, and got up to fetch hot water to the teapot.

Later, Adam's father had let Tim spin the big cogged

helm to open the lock gates; but he would not go to tea at the lock cottage again, so Mrs Johnson invited one of the other boys, to satisfy her social conscience.

When he left the House of God's Angels (Tim had never been able to say the name of the Home, only the address) and went to work for Mr Gregg, people in the villages began to know him as the runty boy who came round with the truck of hyacinth seconds or subsize caulies that could not go to market. Quiet chap. Doesn't say much. But there was nothing to say, either to the housewives with their time-worn comments on the weather and the crops, or in the dormitory hut, where the floating population of Italians and Spaniards did not stay long enough to learn much English. It had taken Tim half a year to tell Mr Gregg that he was not going to stay either, and another five weeks to announce that he was going south, and another eight days after that to rehearse what he was going to say at the ticket office in the railway station.

Going through London and out again like a boy in a dream, he had thumbed a lift on a furniture van coming to this town and stayed here, drifting from job to job, sometimes drifting jobless, his tongue thick in his mouth like a parched desert traveller's, strangling himself with silence.

In the hotel kitchens, no one could talk against the volcanic clatter of the dishwasher. On the night squads, the vacuum cleaners shut out the world. In the factory loading bays the diesel lorries roared. On the building sites, it was too cold that winter to think of much more than knocking-off time and how quickly you could get your gloves back on after blowing your nose. On the roads, standing boot-deep in the spring mud of the sewer-pipe trench, everyone was in too sullen a temper to try to compete with the clatter of the excavators.

Most evenings he went to the same café and ate the same food.

'The same, dear?'

'Ta.' He sat by the fly-trap curtain in the window and

looked as if he was reading the paper. Sometimes people came and sat at the table without noticing him. Sometimes they asked for the sugar or the thick sauce.

'Live round here?'

'Darley Road.'

'Working?'

'Not this week.'

'What's the treacle tart like?'

'All right.'

'The trouble with these people down here, they make it with golden syrup. Now where I come from, where they understand good food, it's got to be black treacle, or they'd get it thrown back in their face.'

Tim listened, sketching the pattern of the formica with his finger-nail. If you listened to a man, he went away thinking he had had a conversation. But a girl ... It was not true that a girl only wanted to talk about herself, whether you listened or not. If you could not even answer a question like, 'All on your own?' she stared and giggled and said to her friend (they were always in packs), 'What's the matter with him?' as if you were a personal affront.

In his room, in the toppling terraced house where he lived half underground with the weight of a dozen or more people on his head, he listened to the beat of ground-floor transistors and thought of storming up into the night streets and doing some abomination, some unimaginable thing to a girl.

'You're mad,' Frank said. 'You don't want to be afraid of them. They're screaming for it.'

A lot of them looked as if they were. In the streets, on the buses, strutting in and out of the shops, they moved as if they were naked, except that they had a few clothes on. There was a smell of sex all over the place. The town ought to spray.

'Screaming for it,' Frank said. 'A lot of them won't drink or smoke, mind, but you're always safe if you offer them the other.'

But they look through me as if I wasn't there.

19

Even if Tim had been able to tell him that, Frank would not believe it. Frank believed there was only place a girl looked.

Frank was a lorry driver running to fat before thirty, with all his small features crowded into the middle of his face, as if it was warmer there. He drove for the paper mill, and he had a room half-way up the house in Darley Road, having left his wife, or she him. The others in the house – white, black, brown, men, women, pigs – were in twos or threes or more. When Frank came back from the Carlisle run, doped with the road, he occasionally talked to Tim, because everyone else was feeding children or making children or stretched out on the bottom rung of their spine, eating pies made of stewed mongrel dog and watching television.

The night that Tim saw the poster, Frank had come back from Nottingham with energy to burn and a couple of free passes for a dance hall in the South End that a man had given him in a lorry park in exchange for a packet of cigarettes.

Tim shook his head.

'Come on,' Frank said. 'Do you good, a young chap like you, hanging about with a face like a drain. What's the matter – you never been out dancing?'

'Yes, I have.'

A bristly girl like a boar who washed lettuces at one of the hotels where he worked had once asked him to go with her, and then not turned up. Tim had hung about outside the hall for a while with his hands in his pockets, pretending to be taking a door count. Then he had waved and grinned and raised his eyebrows at nobody in the distance. Then he had gone away. He did not go back to the hotel kitchen any more, so he never knew whether the girl turned up or not.

At the dance hall, Tim had thought that he and Frank would stand together and say things about the girls, but Frank went away with a person who even looked horrible from the back, shunting her off into the pulsing mob.

Tim stood as if his feet were nailed to the floor, his

hands hanging and heavy, a tight hot band round his forehead where the bumps would neither flare up to a head nor fade away. He could feel his pale hair rising from the back of his scalp in a stiff tuft. Sometimes he could actually feel his hair growing, sprouting out at strange unmanageable angles.

His Adam's apple was swelling like dough. He could not swallow it down. He wanted to unsnap the neck of his denim shirt, but he could not lift his hands. If he kept perfectly still, the two girls in matching pink-flowered pants, their bottoms carved like jelly babies, would go on looking beyond him at whatever was making them simper and whinny and nudge each other's fat little chests.

With a superhuman effort, Tim turned his legs and body on the pivot of his nailed feet, to show that he knew there was something ridiculous behind him, and they could all whinny at it together. Behind him were several piles of aluminium chairs, stacked like geological strata so that no one could sit on them.

He turned back with a clever smile to show that he appreciated the joke.

'Who are *you* laughing at?' asked the girl whose dry black hair had somehow been manœuvred up to ride her fat head like a bearskin. The other one, with slick orange hair like furniture polish, touched her friend for luck and said, 'What's eating *him*?'

When they moved on, propelled from behind by assorted bodies, Tim realized that the whole encounter, which had seemed like an hour's paralysis, had lasted only the less-than-a-minute that it took for the flowered pants to approach and pass.

Under the low ceiling, battered by noise, the crowd in the dance hall heaved like maggots. The lights swivelled the colours of death mercilessly over the faces, shrieking into each other's mouths. Disguised as a house detective, Tim put his hands in his jacket pockets and began to slip through the crowd, turning his narrow hips this way and that to avoid contact, hanging his head to protect his identity. The man without a face. His orders were never to mix, never to acquire personality. The man without a name. They had chosen him for his size.

He reached the bar undetected. Everyone had a half-filled glass in their hand, without any apparent way of getting it. Gimme a Coke, Tim's mind announced; but if he had been capable of forcing himself through the thorn forest of bodies between him and the bar, and then of forcing the words past the obstruction of his throat, there would be no problem about himself at all. He would be somebody else.

The problem now was to get out. It couldn't be helped, Frank. You walked off on me. I tried to find you to tell you I was leaving . . . well, I'm sorry you waited, that's all. Oh – and thanks for the ticket. I had a great time. Mm? Oh well, not bad. Have to take what you can get, don't you? And a wink, to show that he had observed and assessed the front view of Frank's girl as well as the back.

The designing of this conversation got him back into the crowd with a set jaw, butting with a shoulder, jerking up his elbows, raising his knees to wade towards the doors, which seemed to get farther away, not closer. No one was annoyed with Tim for shoving through. They fended him off and handed him past and pushed him on with an indulgent palm behind his head, as if he were a child trying to find his Dad in a football crowd,

'What's the panic?' a young man with a bear's pelt of hair stopped him near the doors. 'Your Mum want you home?'

Tim plucked at the fingers that gripped his sleeve, and drew his hand back with a cry.

'Ah,' said the bear thoughtfully. 'You want to be careful, sonny.' He held his hand close to Tim's face. The ring on the middle finger had a curved hook on it. Tim ducked through the swinging doors – lucky to escape with his eyes!

He ran through the entrance hall and out into the street. A handful of rain was thrown in his burning face.

He took off his jacket and was instantly icy cold, but he dragged his hand across his face and shook it out, to show why he was standing there with the wet wind from the sea whipping his shirt against his ribs.

Outside the hall, a posse of motorbikes browsed at the kerb, their riders camouflaged by moon helmets, a loose knot of girls admiring. Slinging the jacket over his shoulder, Tim walked away from them to where he could cross the street. An engine raced. A motorbike came at him with a dazzling eye, swerved, canted, screamed off down the hill.

Tim had jumped on to the centre island. As he stood there gasping for his breath, the traffic lights on the corner changed, and an armoured division came charging up the hill. At the same time, more cars and buses bore down on the other side of his narrow refuge, so that he was caught in a scissor of traffic. He clung to the lamp-post in the middle of the island until the lights changed and he could run for it, then sped down the hill to the bus stop, legs grown fleet as a spider, his breath sawing his throat.

In the chilly bus shelter, walled with corrugated green plastic that ended in a draught two feet from the ground, like a lavatory, a few of the dance-hall crowd were fooling about, guffawing, jostling, grabbing, the girls twirling away on to the pavement but wheeling right back when no one pursued them.

Tim stayed outside, hands in pockets, shoulders hunched against their laughter. If they reeled out and pushed him under a bus, arms outstretched as he pitched face forward, the passengers would all get out and stare, and the bus driver would be led away, grey with shock.

Who is it? He was not labelled. No one would know. Frank would go to Carlisle. The people in the Darley Road house came and went all the time. If Tim never came back to his room, they would give his bits of stuff to the Salvation and move someone else in. If anyone at the Employment Office missed him on Monday, they would only think: Well, there, you see. Shiftless. They all are.

It was getting late. As usual, a bus had just pulled away as Tim came down the hill. There was a long wait till the next. He went behind the bus shelter and walked along the hoarding that hid a row of condemned shops, looking at the pictures of crippled children and men in bulging underpants and the swim-suit girls with hair pencilled on their crotches.

He had walked by the small black and white poster without giving it any more attention than if it was a religious advertisement. When he passed it on the way back, he saw that it said: *If you are desperate*.

Tim stopped and turned to face the hoarding, which was made of dozens of old doors side by side, leading nowhere. *If you are at the end of your tether*. There was the name, *Samaritans,* and bold and black at the bottom a telephone number, 333-4000.

If you are desperate. Of course. The poster was a message sent direct to him.

Far down the road, the lights of a double-decker bus rode high over the traffic, an almost empty bus behind it, patrolling in pairs like scared policemen. The girls and youths burst out of the shelter and claimed the first bus for their territory, racketing up the stairs, the girls parading their thighs for the coloured conductor who did not notice. Tim went to the second bus. There was no one on top.

The conductress, with her cap tipped back on a nest of hair and penny-stained fingers said, 'If you're going up, I'll take the fare now.'

Holding on to the stair rail, Tim found a shilling and a threepenny bit in his pocket and gave them to her.

'Where to, dear?'

Dog and Duck corner was impossible to say, so Tim said, 'That', and nodded at the coins.

'One and threepenny? Don't bother saying so then, will you?' she said, taking automatic offence, and Tim ran up the stairs and fell into a seat at the back. He rode up the hill past the closed shops and banks and painted glass fronts of estate agents, the empty seats going ahead in pairs, his image riding beside him in the dark window.

I am desperate. How could he not have seen that before? Yes, I am desperate, and they know it.

Instead of getting off at the Dog and Duck, Tim ran down the stairs long before that and jumped off the bus as it slowed down for a corner by the station. In the archway of the station entrance, there were three telephone boxes next to the shuttered news-stand. In the first a man talked earnestly, with his hat square on. In the second a boy lunged, inspecting his nails, laughing occasionally, shifting his weight from leg to leg, from one wall to the other, bending at the knees to squint at part of his face in the little mirror, listening, contributing nothing, tireless. In the third box, a woman talked fast, like a foreigner, her eyes darting from side to side, her unheard mouth twisting wet and rubbery.

Tim's mind raised a gun and shot all three through the head, splattering the stones of the archway with glass and brains. The man in the hat finished talking, fussed with his collar, pulled his gloves with difficulty out of his pocket, put them on, refolded his newspaper and stepped out, staring straight ahead as Tim darted under his arm into the box.

333-4000. Tim had been chanting it to himself like a spell. What would they say? What would he say to them? He dialled quickly and pushed in his sixpence.

'Yes? Can I help you?'

A woman's voice. He had not thought about it being a woman. He tried to speak, but no words came with the breath that rasped through his constricted throat.

'This is the Samaritans. Please tell me how I can help you.'

Help me! Tim shouted without sound. Help me. I can't—

His fists were clenched. His jaw and neck were rigid with effort. For what seemed like hours, his whole body struggled, his chest like a bellows, his stomach drawn into a knot of anguish. He did not know whether he was fighting to get the words out or keep them back.

'Tell me,' she said gently. And he tried to tell her, tried to force something past the suffocation of his throat.

'I'll wait,' she had said. 'I won't ring off.' But now she asked him quickly what the number was. 'I can ring you back if the money runs out. Tell me where you are. What number.'

Fighting for breath, fighting for time, he could hear his own breathing, harsh and urgent in the sour mouthpiece.

'Tell me the number. It's all right. It's all right . . .'

Shrill and demanding, the beeps cut the thread that held them. Tim slid his fingers into his trousers pocket, felt a ten shilling note and crumpled it as he listened to the senseless beeps as if they were a voice. Soon they gave him up as a lost cause, and the dialling tone came smoothly in.

Tim stood and listened to it for quite a long time while his breath slowed and quietened. He could talk now. He would get his money changed and try again. The woman would say: Can I help you? and Tim would say: Yes. Help me. There's no one. Please listen to me.

When he put down the telephone and turned to go, he saw that the young man in the next box was looking at him, still laughing, contemptuously, his eyes far away, as if Tim were not worth a focus.

Tim pushed open the folding door and went through the black archway into the station, empty and dim under the high glass roof, a few people moving slowly or sitting inert, looking at nothing. On a bench in the pillared shadow beyond the parcels office, a heap of rags and newspapers was already asleep, with no head or feet. Tim went to the only window in the booking office that was not blanked with a board shaped like a gravestone.

'Change for ten bob?' He put the crumpled note on the ledge without letting go of it.

'Sorry.' The floor inside was raised so that the man could look down his nose at his customers. He had crinkled ginger hair and a moustache no wider than his nostrils. 'No change for the phone. Sell you a ticket, though.'

Banging against the curved wooden bottom of the ticket office, a stunted woman with a great wide broom as high as her chin was collecting unnamable refuse from the station floor. Tim put the ten shilling note back in his pocket and ran past her and out through the archway entrance against a funnelling wind that tried to drive him back in again.

SAMARITAN LOG BOOK. NIGHT DUTY.
23.00 Phone-box call. Breathing only. (Victoria, 422)
23.15 Billie again. Bit tight. Less miserable. (Victoria, 422)
23.20 Michael still asleep here. Rang students' hostel again about a bed for him. (Victoria, 122)

Some time before midnight, a young Spanish theology student with a ruffianly beard, and a beautiful girl with soft clean hair came in a little yellow van painted with daisy flowers.

'Hullo, Michael. I thought you were in the hospital.'

'I got out.' The homeless man woke easily, accustomed to napping where he could, and being moved on from anywhere that was warm and comfortable. He wiped his nose with an old bus ticket and put it back in his pocket.

'I'm afraid it will have to be the floor,' the girl said. 'That's all we've got left tonight.'

'Not a bed in town,' Helen said, 'except the Government hostel.'

'He can't estand that.' The Spanish student wore a skiing sweater and a pair of old Army trousers. His eyes were a clear tropical blue between his thick black hair and beard.

'I was at the Spike a couple of times. Camberwell.' The man bent down to arrange his shoes so that what was left of the soles was flat on the floor, and took the Spaniard's arm to pull himself more or less upright. 'They make you stay on in the morning and do all their work for them.'

'You scrubbed the bottom of my pans though, last time

you were with us.' The girl, who was in her first year at the University, had a lovely full-cheeked smile, which turned with completely honest kindness on the tattered smelly man. No, not as deliberate as kindness, Victoria thought. An effortless acceptance. God – in the unlikely event I had ever done anything for anyone at her age, I can picture my strained condescension, how I would have admired myself, and run afterwards to wash my hands and tell someone about it.

'That's something else, darling. I'd work my fingers to the bone for you people, if I had my strength.' The thought of it brought on a foul, waterlogged cough.

The girl took his other arm. 'You sure you shouldn't go back to the hospital, Michael?'

'Don't talk like that to an old man.' He hung on her arm and turned up eyes that swam rheumy and colourless between inflamed lids. 'Been through two wars. Pensioned off. Lungs all to bits. They don't care. Police State, dear, you mark me. Milk, give him milky feeds. Cut his rotten toe-nails off . . .'

Muttering, he let himself be shuffled towards the door on the feeble legs that somehow carried him up and down the kerb of Marsh Lane on their good days, announcing the end of the world to sinners only.

They got him into the front of the yellow van. The Spanish student got in beside him, propping him with his shoulder, and the girl climbed into the back among the boxes of sandwiches and meat pies and the cans of tea and soup which they would take round to the vagrant derelicts of the town.

Victoria and Helen switched the telephone through to the upstairs room that had once been the vicarage nursery, and lay down on the bunks.

'Who's on call?'

'Peter is Home Service all this month. You check with him first and if he thinks it's an emergency, you get hold of, let's see' – Helen licked her finger and ran it down the duty list – 'Paul's on Flying Squad tonight.'

'Which Paul?'

'401.' Samaritans were identified by Christian name and a number. 'Big man with a very deep voice. Teacher or something.'

'Oh yes, I know him. He's nice. Calm. Patient.'

'Going to read?'

'No.' Victoria turned out the overhead light, and Helen said, 'He was marvellous to me once. I don't know what I'd have done without him.' She waited, then added more lightly, 'Saved my life, to coin a phrase.'

'You?' Victoria looked across to the other bunk in shadow beyond the light over the telephones.

Helen laughed. 'Why are you so surprised? Everyone feels like slicing their bleeding throat some time in their life. Didn't you learn that in your training?'

'But you always seem as if you were – well, on an even keel.'

'A puff of wind could sink me. When my husband walked out, and I didn't know how I was going to keep the three kids, I sank.'

'What did you do?'

'I rang 4000. Told them I'd found myself in the garage with the engine running without knowing how I got there. They said come round and talk. I did. Brought all the kids, what a turmoil. Someone took care of them while I went into one of the rooms and talked to Paul.'

'What did he say?'

'Oh – I don't know. It wasn't that. It was just the thing of him listening. A man with problems of his own, I thought from his face, and here he is spending a couple of hours with a stupid, jealous bitch who couldn't hold a man and hasn't got the guts to get up and go to work to feed the kids she was selfish enough to have.'

'What did you do?'

'Only thing I knew. Taking care of people who are too stupid to take care of themselves. Housekeeper, they call me where I am now, which is an upgraded term for cook-general, I don't care. We've got our own flat, run of the garden, use the pool when it's too cold for *them*, free food, the lot. They're terrified I'll leave. Can't do enough for me. Even listen for the kids Thursday nights.'

'They know you come here?'

'I tell 'em I go on the streets, what the hell. It's not their business.'

Paul Hammond, Samaritan number 401, went out for dinner. When he came home that Thursday evening, his wife was out somewhere and he could not be bothered to cook anything for himself.

There was nothing to cook. He stood in the narrow kitchen of the flat, opening doors all round him without moving his feet. Nothing feasible in the cupboards, nothing in the middle, edible range. Baked beans, mulligatawny soup, half-used packets of semolina and prunes. Then jars of expensive unnecessary things like artichoke hearts, pine kernels, foie gras, lichees.

Mouse droppings round the boxes of stale cereal. Fermenting ketchup. A piece of honeycomb on a saucer stuck to the stained shelf. In the refrigerator, three bottles of milk with the cream drunk off, no eggs, some unwrapped bacon extravasating salt, sweated cheese, three doubtful sausages. and again the kind of things they could not afford, uneaten, unneeded beyond the placebo of their purchasing. Caviare, an avocado black and squashy, packets of frozen lobster and rum babas thrown in among the ice trays.

Paul took a piece of paper from the burgeoning wastebin and wrote, 'You have got to clean this place up.' He made a hole in the paper and pushed it over the knob of the cupboard under the counter where they kept the drink.

On the refrigerator door he wrote in pencil, 'Alice. Tomorrow, Friday is laundry day. No more clean shirts. Love P.' He licked his finger and rubbed out 'Love'. Then he took the pencil and wrote it in again. 'Give up,' his daughter had said. 'You're a fool to go on.' But he would go on trying.

From the fourth floor, he went down to the restaurant under the block of flats. It was twilit, with dusty plastic plants and a smell of curry hanging about the carpet. Some unidentifiable music seeped out of the walls like marsh gas.

'How's Mrs Hammond?' Phyllis, with a towering top-knot of Dynel scrollwork two shades lighter than her hair, could make a pretty good guess how Mrs Hammond was. Had seen and heard her in the restaurant on occasion and been moved, like many other people, to feel sorry for Paul. 'You drive me to excesses,' Alice accused him, 'so that other women will be sorry for you.'

'She's gone to see her sister.' Reading the appetite-routing menu, Paul smiled at the image of Alice's sister Myrna at the Capstan Club in one of the turned-up felt hats she had been wearing ever since she left school, twenty years ago.

'That's nice.' Phyllis took the smile for herself and made crescents of her eyes over her fat cheeks. 'You'll have the roast chicken, I expect.'

'I think I'll risk the fish.'

'No one's died of it yet.'

The restaurant was only half full, mostly married couples, eating the small dry tiles of bread for something to do, very polite, raking over stale items in their heads for something to say. A few men alone with a drink and the evening paper. Women alone, eating as guiltily as a dog with the cat's dinner, knives and forks making mimsy little packets of the food.

Each time Phyllis came back, with bread, soup, beer, the turbot, she and Paul exchanged the ritual small talk and Phyllis was quite pleased. She would tell her husband, 'Mr Hammond was in.'

What would happen if, instead of asking after her husband and being told that he went on much the same, Paul could ask, 'Is it cancer? Where? Is he going to die? Does he know?' and be told, 'He's got about six months and it's destroying me because I can't tell him'?

What would happen if, instead of asking after his married daughter and being told that she was all right, Phyllis could say, 'How could you let her marry a man

31

like that?' and be told, 'We thought she was pregnant'?

The food was tasteless because the fish was cut in a square chunk and the cabbage was an insulting wedge. Paul thought of the pleasing shapes of the food at lunch, the potatoes and carrots cut in olives, the diagonal beans exactly crisp and green, the thin expert strips of saddle of lamb, the cool dew on the butter, the good rough bread tossed in the basket with a haphazard success of textures and mealy colours.

It had been lunch in the dining-room of an electronics company, one of whose directors had had a son at Burlington when Paul was a housemaster there.

The week before, Paul had met him by chance in the street.

'Aren't you Mr Upjohn?' They were waiting for the traffic light on a windy Saturday morning corner.

'Yes – I know you, don't I?'

'Paul Hammond. Steven was in my house my last year at Burlington.'

'Good Lord, my dear chap.' The lights changed and they started across the street, were separated by a surge of people from the opposite side and came together on the other corner, exchanging grins and exclamations of surprise, while Mr Upjohn tried to cast back his mind – some scandal, what was it? Shot his wife or something?

'Alice and I are living at Singleton Court, out towards Haddington.'

Not shot her then, or a messy divorce ... homo probably. Must remember to ask Steven.

'I'm teaching at Butterfields Comprehensive,' Paul said, and Mr Upjohn had said, 'That's where our new plant is. Tell you what, love to have you up for lunch one day.' A gust of wind made an attempt on his hat. 'God, this weather! Ring me at the office next week. Love to fix something up.'

At first Paul had not meant to ring Unitech. Then he did, for some reason – all right, nostalgia for Burlington. More exactly, nostalgia for himself as a master at Burlington.

He sat in the middle of the table and did not get a chance to talk to the only woman at the lunch, a tall and gravely smiling person with calm eyes and grey in her brown hair, although her skin was smooth. When she was introduced as Mrs Frost, Paul had thought at first that she was a director's wife, but there was no Mr Frost. After the first drink, she went through a door in the panelling and came back with a man in a white steward's jacket and some trays, and Paul saw that she was a sort of hostess for the company, and had indeed cooked the beautiful lunch.

She helped the man to serve, and while he poured the wine, she slipped into her place at the end of the table, unfolded her napkin, and at once said something appropriately gracious to the guests on either side of her.

Because she was there (perhaps that was why she was there?) no business was talked at lunch. A young man with an idea to sell made some opening remarks, but most of the talk was about the New Town and the complexities of the huge comprehensive school, deferring to Paul, as if that was all he could talk about.

Afterwards, over coffee and brandy at the end of the room where great chairs like the tombs of Pharaohs overlooked the green and piney hillside, Paul thanked Mrs Frost for the lunch. They talked briefly about France, and then she caught the eye of one of the men, and left.

Paul got the message too and made his goodbyes.

'Oh my dear chap, must you really?'

'I got out of a class as it is.'

'Look in again any time. Love to see you.'

'Thanks. Remember me to Steven.'

He went out into the passage to get his coat. He turned the wrong way and found himself in a little spotless kitchen like a ship's galley, all stainless steel and white enamel, where Mrs Frost in a red butcher's apron was drying glasses.

'Can I help you?'

She smiled. Short locks of soft undemanding hair lay on her cool forehead. Her rings were on the back of the sink. 'Oh no, thank you. I've got plenty of time.'

She was somebody's wife. Whose wife? Paul wanted to sit down on the stainless steel stool and say, 'Tell me about your husband.' 'He's dead,' she would say, and Paul would wait until she had finished drying all the glasses with her clean expensive cloth, and they would go and have tea somewhere in the South End and walk on the raw beach among the dog-owners and lonely winter-people. He said, 'All right then. And thanks for the lunch.'

'I'm glad you liked the soufflé.'

Phyllis brought coffee in a narrow tube impossible to get the nose into or over. The coffee was slippery like soap, with flakes of curdling milk skin.

'How can you expect anyone to drink that?' he wanted to ask. But other people were tipping up the awkward little cups without reaction, either not knowing or not wanting to know. Mrs Frost's coffee had been burning hot, a fragrant drug, strong and stimulating.

Upstairs in the flat, he did various small things, automatically previewing Alice's reactions if she should come home at that point. Don't you read anything but books about the war? It's plebeian to make coffee in a saucepan. I thought you never watched television. I thought you had a bath this morning. If you're writing to Jeff, tell him I'll write soon.

At ten o'clock, she was not home, but Paul went to bed. He was on Flying Squad tonight. He had not been called out to an emergency for weeks, but there was still the chance that he might spend most of the night trying to help someone to see that destroying yourself was not the answer. And tomorrow he had an early class.

He was asleep when Alice came home. She banged into the room, turned on the light and said, 'What do you mean, got to clean the place up? I haven't *got* to do any thing.'

She was half drunk. Not very drunk. Quite a nice surprise. So Paul rewarded her by asking without opening his eyes if she had had a good time.

'Yes, it was rather gay. Bruce was there, and Roma and that man from Nicaragua – well, you don't know them, and you wouldn't like them if you did.'

Alice was still not bad looking, with short beige hair which she thought had kept its colour, having forgotten that it was once golden. She was thin and wide-hipped, a figure that looked better from the side. She had been drinking for so long that Paul had got used to the blurring of what had once been a neat round face, the slackening of the mouth, the slight protrusion of the eyes, as if the gin had backed up behind them.

'Have you had anything to eat?' He rolled his head round on the pillow and opened his eyes to see that she had bought a new dress. Why? It was bile-coloured, with bright stripes round the bottom of the skirt, well above her middle-aged knees.

'I forgot. Paul fry Alice eggs and bacon?' She sucked in her bottom lip and pouted the top one. The lipstick had melted out and down at the corners. There was a faint moustache of nicotine.

'Look, Alice, I must sleep. I've got an early class tomorrow and you know I'm on call.'

'Oh, God, is it Thursday? What a farce. The blind leading the blind. I hate it when you try to play Jesus.'

'I don't.'

'Jumping out of bed in the middle of the night with that glad crusading face, dashing out to put your finger on the artery of some poor bugger who isn't even allowed to die in peace—'

'Shut up, Alice, we've heard it all before.'

'Paul Hammond, Flying Squad. Tune in next week for another thrilling drama of life – and death.'

She went into the kitchen and banged about in there for a while. Something broke. She swore. Water ran. Ice cubes fell into a glass. He closed his eyes and turned away from the door, conscious of the slight downward shift of the flesh of his stomach and cheek that came with fled youth. Then she was standing over him at the foot of the bed with a drink in her hand, her mouth shaping greedily towards the glass.

'Damn you, there's nothing to eat.'

'That's your fault.'

She threw the whisky all over his head and face, and went out again to get another drink.

Tim went on running for quite a while after he left the station. He ran through some empty streets, over a windy bridge, round a square where a woman was walking two huge dogs like antelopes, across a main road without looking at the traffic, through a crowd coming out of a cinema, switching his face from anxiety to urgency so that they should think he was on a mission. Sobbing for breath, his stomach sucked in, he trotted on through back streets, looking for a place where he could get change for the telephone, but keeping away from the main thoroughfares where he might find it.

When he could go on no longer, he stopped and leaned against a wall. He liked the sensation of being quite empty of breath, his chest aching, his throat a desert, and then the gradual recovery, his lungs filling gratefully, the quietening of his frenzied pulse under his fingers. He could judge its rate quite accurately without looking at his watch. He often put his finger on the tender flesh beneath his wrist, and listened to the message from his heart.

It slowed to about seventy-five. Bit fast, but good enough for now. Tim walked on. He passed cigarette machines chained to shop doorways so that they could not be lifted bodily and staggered off with to a waiting van. They were full of sixpences he could not reach. He had seen a man on the pier, with two leather bags bulging with packets of nuts and chocolate bars. He unlocked a machine, shook out the money into a pouch, filled up the stacks with nuts and chocolate, locked it up and kicked his heavy bags along the planking to the next machine. When he had done them all, up one side and down the other, he heaved the bags into a little van outside the turnstile. and was carried away. Not a bad job. If Tim could get a job like that, he would be able to stick to it.

'Don't you ever stick to anything?' the woman at the Employment Office said, goggling through glasses as thick as bottle-bottoms.

I couldn't stand the hotel. There was a fry cook would have got me with a knife sooner or later. Dumbly he stared at her.

'I think I can get you on the pipe-laying.' She wrote an address on a slip of paper and pushed it across the counter. 'Go to the works manager and say where you've come from. Perhaps you'll do better in the open air.'

'Timothy!' She called him back, he turned round again. Her mouth was smiling, but her eyes were still staring pebbles. 'Stick to it for a bit, eh?'

Stupid cow. She was supposed to help you live your life, not tell you how to run it.

Somewhere north of The Broadway, he went into an all-night café. He had never been in here before, which was risky. In some places, you were to go to the counter and ask for what you wanted. In others, there was a girl in an apron longer than her skirt who came to the table, or a bald man in an apron half-way down his legs and tied round the middle with tape.

The few people in the café pretended not to see Tim coming in. He sat down quickly and scouted out the situation, rehearsing an answer in case someone asked him what he wanted. A ham sandwich. What if there was no ham? He read the list above the counter three times before he could concentrate on what it said. Ham sandwich was one-and-six. Tea was sixpence. That would be two shillings out of his ten shilling note, and they would give him four two-shilling-pieces and he would be no better off than he was before. If he had ham and tomato, it would come to two-and-seven, and they might give him three florins, a shilling and five pennies. But shillings were scarce. They might give him two sixpences, and then he would have a second one to put into the telephone if he would not speak at once.

When there seemed no likelihood of anyone coming to the table, Tim got up and went to the counter. Now was the time to have your voice vanish! He had had that happen to him too, don't think he hadn't. Oh, I've had everything in my time.

'Cup of tea and a ham sandwich.'

You see – it was no use. All he had to do was decide to ask for a ham and tomato and this was what happened. But why had it to be ham and tomato? At the table, it had worked out easily, but it was not clear now. A few figures wandered about his head, but would not line themselves up into sums.

The woman behind the counter, her bosom and stomach fused together in the middle of her blue overall, did not notice that he had made a mistake. She drew off a cup of tea. She lifted a plastic dome and gave Tim two triangles of sandwich. When he got back to the table and looked between the slices of bread and saw the grey liver paste that lay like a rubber doormat, tears rushed into his eyes and he had to pass his hand across his face.

You bitch! His mind jumped up and roared his rage. It leaped with clawed hands and reached for her grainy throat across the counter.

Three boys ate meat pies hungrily, devouring the thick whitish pastry and lumps of meat in three or four bites. An elderly couple sat side by side without speaking, as if they were at the cinema. A girl talked to a man, leaning her arms on the table, putting back her hair every few words so that it could fall forward again.

Tim drank half his tea. It was very hot. That was why his eyes were watering. He ate one of the triangles of dry bread, which was the top half of the hateful sandwich. As soon as he could get the idea to his legs, he went to the counter and put down his ten shilling note.

The woman's spying eyes flicked to the table where he had sat. 'Wasn't it the liver paste you wanted?' she asked kindly.

The whole café stared up. Eyes struck into Tim's rashly exposed back. The three boys, the girl with the hair, the couple.

'What did you ask for then?'

Ham, ham and tomato, two-and-nine, three half-crowns ... Tim's face was like molten pig-iron. His hair rose on end, dragging his scalp with it.

'I can change it for you, if you like.'

So that everyone can laugh? Give me my change! his mind roared. He said, 'It's all right.'

'Dreadful waste, dear.' Her mouth was a drawstring bag. She laid the ten shilling note on the ledge of the cash register so that he could not pretend he had given her a pound, and put down some silver coins. Tim grabbed them, turned at bay to face the enemy for a moment and escaped – God knew how!

Outside, he went this way, that way, like a fickle leaf. He did not know where he was. He started down the hill, saw by the window full of drums that this was the way he had come, swayed and went the other way, crossed the street, walked on until he was beyond the café, then crossed back and wandered on up the hill hesitatingly, as if he were walking in a fog in an unknown country.

He turned a corner and there were tall flat lights making day of night. He stood against the stem of one, although the spread of its light was universal, and pulled the coins out of the pocket of his jeans. He picked out a sixpence and ran to the telephone box which clung like a limpet to the building on the next corner.

The number rang in his head like his own name. He turned the dial round, letters, numbers, one after the other with the perfectly co-ordinated machine of his finger. At his command, rods fell into slots, wheels turned, lights flickered, a vast computer was agitated to his will. The beeps commanded his sixpence.

'Samaritans,' she would say, and, 'Can I help you?' And then what on earth would he say? He had nothing that could hold her. They don't care. You see – the conviction of it was almost a reassurance – they don't care.

On an endless hoarding, rushing into the perspective of nowhere, a black and white poster bulged in and out in the wind of fun-house laughter. *If you are desperate ...* But the telephone could not wait. The impatient beeps surrendered to the dialling tone, arrogant as a purring cat. Tim put down the receiver, put the sixpence back into his pocket, pushed out of the glass door and wandered away, wandered weeping through the lit, deserted streets.

At the Samaritan Centre, there were a few more calls after midnight. A woman quoting the Old Testament. A boy asking for help for a homosexual friend – but perhaps it was for himself. A man on the night desk of a London paper, looking for information about a missing girl. Whenever the call was from a telephone box, Victoria thought that it would be the man who had breathed so distressingly, and gone.

She was dozing when the telephone shocked her awake. Her hand went out before her eyes were open. 'Samaritans – can I help you?' The beeps answered her. She waited. Nothing happened. 'Please put in your money,' Victoria said.

'They can't hear you till they have,' Helen said irritably. The dialling tone started. Victoria put down the receiver and fell into a light dream, half involuntarily, half consciously imagined. Sam was in it, and she had shorts, and brown legs and feet, and they were still in the house in Spain with the donkeys rambling along the beach by themselves under mountainous loads of seaweed.

Paul had got up to run water over his head and take a clean pillow from his son's bedroom, but the sheets still stank of whisky. He could not sleep in another room, he could not even move to the dry side of the bed, because of the telephone.

He was falling asleep again when Alice came into the bed like an earthquake, jouncing the mattress, tugging at the blankets, her breath augmenting the reek.

'Why didn't you go and sleep in Jeff's room?' she asked.

'You know why.'

'Oh, dearest, I never knew you cared.' She climbed on top of him, knees and flat breasts and wild dry hair. He lay still on his back, and after a few feeble heaves and grunts, she passed out and he rolled her off him, and they both slept.

Frank had never been with an Indian girl. Would she step out of that long swag of coloured cloth, or would he have to unwind it, or find the opening, or what?

They were in a part of the Town where he had never been before, in a house full of people, some asleep, some awake – my brother, my uncle, my cousin – 'How do?'

Hours ago, in one of the clubs, he had swopped the big ugly girl from the dance hall for this one. 'You'll have to wake me at six,' he said sternly. You could order 'em about, you see, that's what they understood. 'And make my tea, mind.'

She had tiny brown feet like a field mouse. It was all very novel.

It was about the time when the first shadow of grey light begins to creep up from the bottom of the world, that Tim found himself again in the narrow hilly streets he knew. He was very hungry. He would go back to Darley Road and see if he could find something to eat. Frank always had beer and cake. Beer up the narrow chimney where no one could find it when he was on an overnight run. Cake in a mouseproof tin at the back of the cupboard.

A police car slid up beside him, the radio conversing in an unheeded monotone.

'Where are you going, lad?' A slow northern voice. What was it doing among these meaner vowels?

'Home.'

'You're out late.'

'Been out with my girl.' Tim managed a wink.

'Ah. What's your name then?'

'Tim Shaw.'

'Live at home?'

'With my mother.'

'Where's that?'

'14 Darley Road.'

'All right.'

The car moved on, the two men staring straight ahead.

Tim felt his pulse. Very good. He had not been afraid. He had talked right out to them, a boy going home to his mother's house from an evening out with his girl. If they had asked her name, he would have said, 'Rosie.' That had been the unsuitable name of the girl in the hotel kitchen.

He had managed that very well, very well indeed. He walked on smiling, and when he turned at the end of the street, the smile was still on his face, so that anyone who was round the corner would not guess that behind the smile there was neither girl nor mother, nothing.

The house in Darley Road tilted backward into the clouded sky, its round tile chimney pots like sawn-off arms. It was still too dark to see the door properly. He fumbled with his key, sensing, even before the door opened, the heady mixture of cooking and sewage that possessed the narrow hall.

Instead of going to the basement at the back of the house, he ran upstairs, and knocked on the door of Frank's room. No answer. He put his eye to the keyhole – darkness. He put his ear to the keyhole – no sound of breathing. Tim turned back to the stairs and went heavily down the hall, along the chipped tiles past the place under the stairs where the sink and toilet were, and down the dark bending steps to his room.

It was always fairly dark in here, but often in the daytime he did not turn on the light. He had trained his eyes to read comics in the half-light, sitting by the window with the bottom of the backyard dustbins on a level with his head, and the bed and the other bits of furniture in the room seen in shape rather than detail, more reassuring.

It was quite dark now, and he switched on the light, a boy coming home from a dance. Hullo, dear, had a nice time?

Yes, thanks. Anything to eat?

His room was square, with a low ceiling. There was a gas fire and a small rug and some pictures from magazines tacked up on the walls. Frank had been in here once or twice and had looked at the pictures that were of girls, but in the months that Tim had been here, nobody else, nobody at all, had been in this room.

He sat by the window and waited for Frank's feet on the steps of the house, or the sound of the front door. He was terribly hungry. There were some biscuits in his cupboard, but the weight of his misery would not let him get up to cross the room. He sat with his feet on the chair rung, leaning forward as if he had cramps, his arms wrapped round his ribs, rocking, staring at nothing.

After a long time, although his eyes had not seemed to close, he must have rocked into sleep, for he woke in a panic of fear and jumped up. The air was full of a dirty grey dawn. He must have missed Frank.

He ran upstairs and knocked on the door again. When there was no answer, he began to beat on the door with his fist and shout.

'Frank! Frank, let me in!' A door across the passage opened and an unseen person threw a shoe at him as if he were a cat, and banged the door.

Tim went down to the little lavatory place under the stairs. He ran water into the dirty glass and drank, staring at himself in the mirror over the corner basin. There's a nice looking boy, who is he? Oh, don't you know, that's Tim Shaw. No, I don't know. Holding the glass, he put the tip of his fourth finger against the artery of his left wrist. He could not find the pulse, so he turned over his hand and let it hang slack, counting the gentle thread of his heart.

If you are at the end of your tether. Watching his

aghast face, he broke the glass in the basin and drew the sharp edge deeply across his wrist. Blood sprang out before the pain. He looked down and saw it, welling into the basin as if his soul was emptying away. With a sob, he pulled the towel off the hook, wrapped it round his arm and ran out of the little place, down the hall, out of the front door and down the steps to the street.

Will I die – will I die? He thought of all the people in the house surging down under the stairs and shouting round. They would be horrified, disgusted, blood all over the place – get the police. Holding the towel round his arm, feeling the blood beginning to soak through on to his right hand, he was running down the echoing street towards the main road, running for his life.

The telephone clamoured in Victoria's ear. She grabbed it and spoke before she was awake enough to think.

'It's done . . . I've done . . .'

'What is it?' Victoria sat up. Helen woke and got quickly off the bunk.

'I'm going to die.'

'What's happened?'

'Help me. It's all blood . . .'

'Where are you?'

'In a phone box.'

'Where?'

'Near where I live. I ran out. I can't stop the blood.'

'Where?'

'Near the waterworks – Flagg's Hill. Oh, come and help me, I can't—'

'Stay there. Stay where you are. I'll try and get help. Hang on,' she said, 'hang on, it's all right.' But there was a clattering noise, and then nothing more.

Paul woke, and reached for the telephone without turning on the light.

'Near the waterworks on Flagg's Hill.' Helen told him. 'Victoria thinks he may have collapsed. He dropped the phone. She's hanging on in case.'

'Suicide attempt, is it?'

'Looks like it. Peter thinks I should call an ambulance.'

'All right. Then try and trace the call in case I can't find him.'

He got out of bed, quickly into some clothes and out of the flat without waking Alice, buried in sheets and pillows. Downstairs, he ran through the hall and out of the side door to the yard in the middle of the buildings. He got into his car and drove towards the north, weaving through the first traffic that was beginning to drag the cold grey streets to life.

Near the top of Flagg's Hill, the old brown brick water tower rose crenellated above the labyrinth streets. Around it, a high sooty wall bristled with spikes like a tiger's cage, befouled by dogs and artists of the obscene chalk stub. On the corner of a small street behind the wall, Paul found the ambulance waiting by a telephone box outside a public house. There was some blood on the floor and smeared across the coin box and the glass of the door. One of the ambulance men was on the telephone talking to Victoria.

'Yes, he's here now. All right, miss ... well, we may do. All right?' He came out of the box, looking at the ground. 'I found the phone hanging where he'd dropped it,' he told Paul. 'You'd think we could trace him by the blood. There's some here, look, by the wall.' He brightened up. 'At least it's not another practical joker. Now where?' He cast about on the pavement as if he were divining water. 'Must have found some way to stop it, or someone came by, more like, and helped him.'

'We've got to find him.'

'Probably already on his way to hospital.' The ambulance man shrugged.

'I'm going to have a look round,' Paul said. 'Will you stay here?'

'Not all morning.' He was an ungracious man, with a cold eye and a defensive way of speaking, on guard against public effrontery. His mate, more rubicund, his uniform less sharply fitted, was at the side of the public house, talking to a man with a raincoat over pyjamas who kept a hand on the edge of the door as if ready to slam it. At a window above, a netted woman looked out, chewing on her gums.

'I told you – nothing,' the man was saying. 'I'd have known if there was any trouble. I know everything that goes on round here. Blood in the phone box – that's nothing to wake people up for. Always cutting each other up, they are in these parts.' He shut the door. The woman kept the window open until Paul and the ambulance men, searching the ground, moved out of her sight.

'Better not be another false alarm,' the defensive man said. 'I was out last week to a chap who was supposed to have taken thirty nembutal, and found him in bed with his landlady. Gives your lot a bad name.'

'I don't think so.' Paul disliked him on sight. 'I think it's the other way around.'

'Suit yourself.' The man did not like Paul either. 'Ten minutes, Jim,' he said to his mate, 'and that's it.'

He went down a passageway behind the public house. The rubicund man crossed the rood, and Paul went down the hill, looking in shop doorways, trying side gates, scouting the yard outside a garage. At the corner, there was blood again. Behind a broken wall, on a demolition site strewn with bottles and rubbish, he found the boy, his white ghost face half in the mud, his left arm bundled in a denim jacket wet and sticky with blood. Paul knelt down to him and shouted. The red-cheeked ambulance man came running, the other more slowly, with a face that had seen everything.

The morning shift of Samaritans had arrived. In the bunk room, Victoria had changed into a dress, and was trying to make something out of her face in a two-inch square of mirror propped on the bookcase. Long greenish eyes that looked sleepy until half-way through the morning, her grandmother's nose, which had been the only classy thing about her, a pale mouth that looked sad if she caught its reflection unawares.

'You look as if you knew this had to end,' Sam had once said. 'Do you?'

'No.'

But she did. They had both known. Sometimes now when she caught herself looking sad in a shop window or in a mirror at the turn of the cinema staircase, she noted: There is a woman who has lost her love.

Andrew, who was a student at the University, put his shaggy head round the door. 'Someone called Billie wants to know if you're still here. Are you?'

'Oh yes.' She had untied the green scarf and she went downstairs with her hair hanging round her shoulders. 'How are you, Billie?'

'How do you expect?'

'Didn't you sleep?'

'Yeah, but there's such a thing as a hangover, dear heart.'

'Oh, I'm sorry.'

'Serves me right.'

'Are you going to the cafeteria?'

'After a night like that? Hell, no. I'll tell you something, Victoria. I had a full bottle of aspirin in the drawer by my bed.'

'So have lots of people.'

'You know what's very annoying about you? You won't get excited. I was going to take the lot.'

'I'm glad you didn't.'

Billie's jeer, a noise between expectoration and vomit.

'I'll be here on Sunday. Why don't you come in and have a chat?'

'Might. Might not. I'll see what – you know – what develops.'

'Good luck.'

'Ta.'

Victoria went back to the mirror on the bookcase.

'Why bother?' Helen came in with her coat on. 'Aren't you going home?'

'I'm going to get some breakfast and then go to work.'

'No sleep?'

47

'It's press day.'

'You told me you needn't go to the paper this morning. Why?'

'Oh – I don't know.' Victoria told quite a lot of lies, sometimes to fend off solicitude.

'If you'd told me, I wouldn't have asked if you could do the extra night duty,' Helen said.

'I know.' Victoria gathered up her long sandy red hair and began to wind it smoothly round her tired head. 'That's why I didn't.'

'Yes. I see.'

They felt easy and honest together after their shared night. To work as a Samaritan was an intensification of the focus of living, direct and clear. You knew what you had to do. You knew why you were there. Could even sometimes begin to grope towards an idea of who you were, as the pretence and defences fell away before the urgent truth of human contact.

Paul stayed at the hospital until the boy's arm had been sewn up. He had severed a tendon, and they put the arm in plaster to the elbow. A splint was bandaged to the other arm where the needle of the blood-drip went in. After they had taken him up to the ward, Paul waited outside until a staff nurse with a waist girthed in between bosom and swinging hips came out and headed for the kitchen, mouth working importantly.

'The boy with the wrist – could I see him for a moment before I go?'

'In the middle of my bedpan round? You must be mad.' She went into the kitchen and poured tea out of a great metal pot that stood stewing on the stove.

Paul wanted to ask, 'Can I have a cup?' but she had her back turned, looking out of the window in a sudden daydream, the calm eye of her storm of early morning activity. Through the glass of the ward door, Paul could see nurses panting round with shrouded bedpans. A few patients shuffled about in dressing-gowns collecting bottles from old men who drew them brimming forth from under the bedclothes where they had secreted them all night. By the far wall, the boy lay on his back under the drip bottle, his suffused face turned to one side, his arms stretched stiffly out beside him.

'Tell him I'll come back this evening,' Paul said, as the staff nurse headed out of the kitchen again and through the ward door, twitching the curtain all the way across the glass to stop him looking.

TWO

I T WAS A TOWN that had everything. Old, new middling architecture, pleasing to the eye, unremarkable, appalling. Shops, factories, seafront, slums, University. A satellite New Town full of disoriented families who would not think of it as home until the next generation. Floodable bungalows along the estuary where people pottered through the end of their lives. Esplanade hotels where ditto, but more lavishly.

Peter Wallace, Samaritan number 100, who was the Director of the branch in this town, lived at the unfashionable end of the seafront, disguised as the proprietor of a small, comfortable hotel where families came back year after year and found their odd lost sandal still at the back of the cupboard. They knew that he worked somewhere else, since his wife seemed to run the hotel and he was not much seen in the daytime. They knew that he had an attractive, reassuring way of making you feel that the hotel was for you, instead of you and your cash for it. They knew that he and their children enjoyed each other, that his wife sang in the kitchen and that they somehow kept staff year after year. They did not know that he had studied for the priesthood until he saw that his ministry must be larger than the church. They did not know about the Samaritans, unless they happened to ask.

Beyond the Wallaces' Baytree Hotel, at the mouth of the small sluggish river was a pier, and a clutch of bothies where you could drink and dance and see a film with whips and snarling women, eat batter with a little acid fish inside, feed money into machines with flashing lights and belting music, and wander past bland wax figures of

Princess Anne and Mao Tse-tung and Lyndon Johnson (Nixon not yet ready).

On the other side of the river was the New Town, name of Butterfields, not a cow in sight, spreading like a brick psoriasis over the downs and meadows. It boasted an elementary school, and a big comprehensive school where older children could learn anything from computer programming to fitting pipe-joints. In the comprehensive school, Paul Hammond, Samaritan number 401, was in the English department, not its head nor ever would be with that public-school-housemaster background, although the staff were willing to condone it, since he had had the sense to get out.

Most of the Butterfields children could walk or bicycle to school, as their parents could walk or bicycle to the factory estate where great names of industry were taking root, company flags flying, storm-driven sea-gulls beating round the plate glass towers and concrete chimneys. It was in one of these shining towers that Mrs Barbara Frost had cooked lunch for Paul and the directors of Unitech Electronics. It was in the vaunted Butterfields shopping centre, where you could stroll without getting yourself or your pram run over, and chill sea winds swept through the holes in the pseudo-Moore statuary, that Jackie's parents plied their trade in leather and plastic and Jackie did his Wile-U-Wate heels in the back workroom.

Out to the west on the other side of this great conglomerate town, the richer people, who had moved away from its terraced streets as the town grew too crowded, had turned the outlying villages into suburbs. In the twenties and thirties, they had built timbered granges and brick mansions and stucco villas with red tiles in the back hall and a room with wicker furniture for the maids. They had set out lawns and borders and tennis courts and blue-grey conifers, and roses which they had to prune themselves now that all the old men of earthy aphorisms had been killed off by Welfare.

In one of the half-timbered manor houses, with feather designs stamped in the plaster and unnecessarily latticed windows which she only cleaned when no one could see out any more, Helen, Samaritan number 434, lived with her fatherless children in a flat behind the kitchen and sustained a mutual love-hate existence with her employers.

The tall terraced houses in the Victorian part of the town were now mostly cut up into flats and government bureaux and day nurseries and clinics and offices where social workers kept a one-bar electric fire under the desk, the heat not quite reaching the visitor's chair. On the edge of these streets, strategically placed to catch those who fell through the holes in the passionless sieve of bureaucracy, the Samaritan Centre offered unconditional welcome. You did not have to fill in a form. You did not have to categorize your problems. You did not have to have a problem at all if what you wanted was to sit and be at rest in the comfortable warm room which ran from the jungle of the front garden to the wilderness at the back, and had once been the vicar's parlour, with a paper fan in the fireplace and brown paper to keep the sun off the carpet.

Above the Samaritans' square stone rectory, Commercial Road deteriorated upward through the mazes of Flagg's Hill. Half-way up was Darley Road, grim grey housing for the artisans of the early factories, now warrens where luckless families and loners like Tim and Frank paid four or five pounds a week for a peeling buggy room without heat or water.

On the flatland beyond Flagg's Hill were the austerity flats built after the war and never improved, the ground trampled as hard as the cement yards where children shrieked and fought and bloodied their grey knees. Billie had a flat in Block C, a prison address for a prison building, the stairway open to the rain and snow, the lift stinking of urine and vomit, even when it worked.

On the mornings when she could face it, Billie put on her green cafeteria overall and hauled herself across the river to the other side of the valley where the University had kept part of that opposite hillside green, with a park and playing fields that dropped in terraces to the river and the boathouses. Upriver, the raw orange brick of the hospital where they had taken Tim, belching forbidden smoke as if it had a gas oven instead of a mortuary. Downriver, the old factories, spewing forbidden ullage. Many were defunct, all their dirty windows broken, their yards piled with rusted junk. One of their old office buildings, condemned but not yet demolished, was the house run by some of the University students for derelicts like old Michael who drifted in and out of town, and sometimes died there, from crude spirits, or drugs, or pneumonia, or starvation, or simply because they stopped living.

Lower down towards the sea, the busy town-centre clustered on either side of the river, old and new unpatterned, shops and offices and municipal buildings. On the second floor of an old structure that rocked perceptibly when the presses ran was the office of the bi-weekly local paper, where Victoria, Samaritan number 422, was receptionist and secretary to the editor.

Behind the *Courier* building, wandering like a colon through the main part of the town and somehow ignored by the planners who dreamed of their city resurrected clean and white, Marsh Lane still held the miasma of its name. It started with the suspect Station Hotel where no one would choose to stay because of the noise, and petered out in an abandoned coal yard off Commercial Road. Somewhere near the middle, where Marsh Lane crossed the main shopping street, old Michael could be found off and on hobbling along the gutter, yoked back and front with boards that hectored, 'Repent Brethren, for the end of the world is tomorrow.'

There were three town bridges over the polluted river, two railway stations, cinemas, theatres, traffic jams twice a day, hundreds of places where you could drink or eat, and a famous little old seagoing village where chestnut trees grew out of uneven brick pavements and artists real and quasi set up easels in the leafy summer streets.

It was a town that had everything, although chunks of

53

it had nothing much. Singleton Court, where Paul and Alice Hammond had lived for the two years since he had been allowed the charitable chance to resign from the Cotswolds school, had not much to do with the town, the suburbs or the countryside, its flats designed with nothing much in mind but housing bodies. It was full of people like Alice who had nothing much to do but get through the day, and people like Paul who had not much choice but to survive their marriage, and hope for something better for their children.

'Where have you been?' When Paul went home for a shave, Alice was in the sitting-room, cutting her toe-nails on to the fireplace rug.

'I left you a note.'

'Can't read.'

'I was called out about five.'

'Did somebody, as we say, "put an end to it all"?'

'Almost. I think he'll be all right. He lost a lot of blood.'

'Why?'

'I don't know yet. I'll try and talk to him this evening.'

Alice sighed. 'Are you going to make some tea?'

When Paul came back with a cup for her, she was sitting hugging her knees, her bare feet yellow, the toes distorted by the pointed shoes she had continued to wear after they went out of style, because it met some neurotic need in her to walk painfully.

'Darling.' She was staring at the fire which glowed and flickered through logs whose metal mesh foundation was wearing through the painted bark. They had inherited it from the last tenant. 'Darling, you know, now that the children are off my hands,' (they were twenty and seventeen) 'I ought to have some purpose in my life.' She said this about once a week. 'I might try the library, or get a job in a boutique. I'd like to take a course at the University. Sometimes I think I'll join the Samaritans. Would you sponsor me?'

'We don't "sponsor" people. Either you are the right type and they take you, or you're wrong and they don't.'

'I feel I could offer so much to people who were plumbing depths, because I've been there myself.'

'You said that when we started in A.A.'

'Oh, them. I'm not an alcoholic, that's why it was no good. And I don't like coffee in paper cups. And everyone being nice to each other, and jolly.'

'And not being able to have a drink.'

'Right, as usual. Darling,' as Paul went to the door, 'the tea is too hot. I can't drink it.' She was whining like her own daughter, a dozen years ago. 'Get me a little short one, will you? Just to set me up.'

'Help yourself.' Paul went out yawning. Alice went into the kitchen, poured something, and had to be sick in the sink because Paul was shaving in the bathroom with the door locked.

'One to bring up, the next to keep down,' she chanted like a nursery rhyme, sitting red-eyed on a counter stool in the tiny kitchen, clutching a glass while Paul made toast and ate it quickly. When he went to get his jacket, she followed him and stood in the bedroom doorway, so that he had to move her aside to get out. Her shoulder under the torn frills of her birthday negligée (he should have bought something that was easier to wash) was a bony knob.

'One day,' she called after him when he was at the front door, 'you'll be killed in a car crash or stoned to death by the children, without kissing me goodbye.'

He came back to kiss her and she bent her head to rub the dry colourless hair under his chin.

'I couldn't have married anyone but you.' She put a sob into her voice.

'Have I made you happy?'

'So very happy.'

Sometimes they played at being closely married, to disguise the possibility that under the misery and disgust and disappointment, they still might be.

Hungry and with a headache, a little sick from sleeplessness, Paul drove to work through the thick morning traffic in the little red car which was mutilated with

Alice's dents and scratches. He crossed the river by Royal Bridge where he had sat and talked one night to a girl on the parapet, both of them dangling their legs over the black water. If you jumped in the river, it was said, you would be poisoned before you drowned.

Turning north where the older factories squatted under the hill that hid the University from the town, he skirted the new factory estate, and saw the electronics plant where he had lunched yesterday, the executive building landscaped with readymade grass and pools and little trees, the huge window of the dining-room flashing an acknowledgement back to the sun. If there was to be a big lunch with things that took a long time to cook, might Mrs Frost be in there already, her small diamonds on the back of the sink and flour in her wedding ring? If Paul were to turn into the car park and go up to that floor in the silently chuckling lift, she would make him a cup of coffee, and he would be late for his first class.

Another half-mile of wide white road brought him to the chainlink fence of Butterfields Comprehensive, a model modern school complex fantastically equipped and furnished for two thousand children. He parked his car, walked under the granite pillars that held up the gym, and pushed through the swinging doors whose original glass had been replaced by a sandwich of glass and wire netting. Feeling older than fifty, he went up to his classroom with his hand on the rail, while multitudes of boys and girls in mulberry uniforms and shoes that sounded like clogs surged past him up the stairs as if he were not there.

Mumbling and muttering, dropping heavily from stair to linoleum stair in his new leatherite walking shoes with simucrêpe soles, young Malcom sulked off to school from the flat over the shoe shop.

'Bye!' Jackie called from the top of the stairs, his toes on the edge like a diver; but Malcom would not turn round or answer. Jackie shut the door of the flat and shuffled back to his breakfast, clapping a spread hand over the yawn that would make his mother say, 'And-a no wonder. Play-acting downstairs with the phone half the night. Pick up your feet.' His mother was at the sink, plunging plates into hot sudsy water almost before you had finished the last corner of fried bread. She never let the washing-up wait. She always left a shining sink, even if it meant opening the shop late or missing the start of the evening news.

'Malcom don't want go a school, Muh,' Jackie chuckled.

'Doesn't want,' Muh said. 'He didn't finish his homework last night, so he'll have no one but himself to blame if he gets a wigging.' She turned back to the sink. She was always careful to face Jackie when she talked to him, as if he was deaf.

Malcom was thirteen. He bicycled every morning from the shopping centre down Cherry Tree Avenue, up Holly Rise, round the long curve of Meadside and past the football grounds to Butterfield Comprehensive School. At four-thirty, he bicycled back, grubbier and more rumpled, was inquisitioned about marks and placings, and sat down to a brain-building tea of eggs or herrings, with vitamin complex stirred into his milk.

Malcom was clever. Malcom was in the 'A' stream. He read the newspaper and did electrical experiments on the end of a bench cleared off for him in the workshop. Malcom was clever. He got it from his mother, who had been to college for two years, never forgotten. He was nine years younger than Jackie. No need for Muh to say why she had waited so long for a second child. It was there in her neat pink face when she turned it from Malcom to Jackie.

But Malcom was not the only one going to school today. Jackie was going to school too. His mother belonged to the Association of Parents of Special Children, and Friday was her day to help at the Play School. Jackie was much too old to play, but he liked the music and the cheerful company, and he had learned how to take the little ones to the You-know-where. So Muh usually took him with her, leaving Miriam to take care of the shop, and no instant heeling done that morning, unless Dad had time, which was unlikely, with the perpetual pile of soleing and stitching with which he never quite caught up. Butterfields was very hard on shoes. All the walking on pavements which had been made with some kind of hard sparkling stone in them. Very good business for *some* people, the customers joked, drawing shoes from among the boxes of soapflakes and cornflakes in their shopping bags.

'Keep them going for just a bit longer.' Like taking an old dog to the vet, they brought out dreadful old favourite shoes, and pretended they were only for gardening.

'Yoo hoo – yours truly reporting!' Miriam had some rather common mannerisms, like shouting up the stairs, but she knew the business of the shop, and Muh did not have to pay her too much, being a cousin. 'Hello, love!'

Jackie went clattering down on his big feet which had to go sideways on the stairs, and she hugged him fondly, smelling of armpits and cigarettes.

'Huh-o Mim!'

He went through into the shop with her, and she showed him what she had brought, a marvellous little man on a tricycle, whose bell rang as his legs went round. He was seamed down the middle from front to back. Jackie pulled him apart – 'Mind what you're doing, that cost money!' – and cleverly clipped him back together again, to show Miriam how it could be done.

'Ah well, another day, another deed.' Miriam began to pull the dust cloths off the permanent displays, and to bring out from under the counter the handbags and the better-quality shoe buckles and bows that were put away each night.

'Good morning, dear.'

Jackie's father came through from the workshop in his apron, a beam on his shiny red face, which went right on over the top of his head. He was going to have Miriam here all morning, popping into the workshop for a cigarette when the shop was empty. 'You got here then.'

'No, I was run over crossing the Broadway. This is my

ghost.' Miriam's laugh was an open-mouthed shriek. Muh frowned as she came in through the front of the shop with her gloves on, rainboots over her shoes, and a top layer of transparent plastic like a cake cover over her orange felt hat. She had gone out at the side entrance and in again at the shop door like a customer, to see what Miriam was up to.

'Aren't you coming, Jack?' He was watching the little man tricycle down the counter.

'Yeh.' He looked up, open-mouthed. Of course he was coming.

'Then put-a on your galoshes.'

'No.' His mouth closed with the lips tucked in.

'It's starting to rain.'

'What's the matter, can't John put on soles that don't let water?' Miriam laughed and so did Jackie and his father, all throwing back their heads, and a customer who pushed open the door at that moment (da-*doing* on the musical chime) looked embarrassed, as people do coming into a jolly group.

'Have you got any black shoe polish?' There were stacks of it, but she had to say something. She said it to Jackie's mother, but because it was Friday and she was in her outdoor things, she pretended she was a customer too and would not answer.

Miriam began to show black polish, and Dad backed into the workshop like a kitchen hand. He had not shaved the bottom half of his beefy face, because he was not supposed to be seen in his working apron. Only Jackie went in and out between the customers and the workshop, shutting the door on the elves.

When he came back wearing huge galoshes like rubber life-rafts, the customer had gone and Muh had the little tricycling man on the palm of her hand like a butterfly.

'Malcom is much too old for toys,' she chided kindly. 'You shouldn't spend your money.'

Miriam winked. 'It's for Jackie.'

He had known it would be a mistake. Although Muh often treated him like a child – wipe your mouth, let me

59

see your hands, only dirty boys make that noise – he must not behave like one. He had to go to cunning extremes to hide toys and picture books and furry animals from her, because she turned out wardrobes and drawers at every change of season and flipped over his mattress once a week. A blue wool monkey was dangling on a string alongside the drainpipe outside his window, puzzle books were in the holiday suitcase on top of the linen cupboard, and a vast store of bubblegum that he had stolen from Woolworth's was buried in a box of coloured leather scraps under the workroom bench. Only Helen knew where the gum was. He had told her one night, and she said she liked it too.

His mother put the toy into her handbag – would she give it to one of the special children? – and they went out.

The play centre was in the basement of St Barnabas Church on the other side of town. Jackie and his mother walked there in the drizzle. It was quite a long way, but Muh did not like the bus. She could not be shut in anywhere. On the rare occasions when she would go to see a film, to be able to say it was no good, she had to go out and stand outside at least twice. When she came back in, she could not find where the family was sitting, so she made Jackie go with her, since Malcom refused to get up.

The windows of the flat were always being flung open. 'It's stifling in here!'

'It's the change of life, dear,' Miriam said.

Muh went pink like a geranium. 'I'm not anywhere near that, thank you very much. The whole place reeks of your vile cigarettes.'

She flung open the windows and Miriam turned up her collar and said, 'If you're still smoking at forty, you've got lung cancer anyway.' Muh would *die* if she knew that while she was out, Jackie and Miriam had been smoking away like twin chimneys, lighting each cigarette from the stub of the last, desperately inhaling. They had let young Malcom have a go too, to stop him telling.

If Jackie shut his window on a frosty night, she would

come in after he was asleep and sneak it open. 'You can have another blanket,' she said if he complained that he woke up cold, but all the blankets in the world would not save you from Muh's idea of a little healthy fresh air.

She walked briskly through the clean wet streets with Jackie beside her, his long disorganized legs skipping occasionally, hopping between the pavement lines, but she laid her hand on his arm and said, 'Easy fellow,' as if he were a horse.

They might meet someone they knew. They did know quite a few people in town, because of the shop, and Muh being on the Parent-Teacher committee, and a member of the Butterfield Culturettes, who read poems to each other and made a little thin music with whatever they could play, even if it was only a comb and toilet paper.

Jackie and Malcom sometimes listened outside the window of Mrs Devon's large sitting-room, where the meetings were held.

'Ill met by moonlight, proud-a Titania,' declaimed Muh, and, 'What,' said Miss Larkin, 'jealous Oberon! Fairies skip hence.'

Jackie and Malcom fell into the flowerbed in stitches.

Butterfields had grown to such a size that the people you knew were only a tiny speck among the whole crowd. You could go for days without a familiar face coming into the shoe repair shop or into other shops in which you were buying. You could walk, as Jackie was allowed to ('Have you wound your watch? What-a time did I say be back? And six means six and not half past') for hour after hour among the doll's-house streets and never see a face that opened to a smile or a hullo. It was not like the pictures in the leaflets where women called and waved to each other over their flapping laundry, or a man with a pipe and a pullover leaned on his spade to talk to a grandmother and a little boy over the garden gate. Butterfields people kept themselves to themselves. Muh joined things because she said she must give of herself, but there were many women who saw nobody when their husbands were at work and the children at school. Last month, one of them had been found dead of sleeping pills.

Malcom had read bits of it to Jackie out of the local paper. 'She was such a quiet girl we never hardly saw her.' The neighbour on the other side, a certain Mrs Digit, world-famous now with her picture in the paper wearing a flowered overall like a bolster cover, had said, 'How should I know? I don't poke my nose into everybody's business.'

The body, Malcom read, had been lying on the bed for about eight hours. 'Phew, what a ponk—' The story disappeared with a rattle as his mother snatched the newspaper away.

The Play School was in the basement of St Barnabas Church which stood behind the recreation hall and the bowling alley and one of the public houses where a man had once staggered out as they were going home from the cinema and almost knocked little Muh over. 'Here, here,' Dad had shouted, and rounded his fists, red as a tomato, and the man had laughed and gone back into the pub. The church was built on a slight grassy rise so as to poke its spire as close up to God as possible. There were only a few gravestones in the fenced plot, but 'Another winter like this,' Mrs Manson said, taking off her scarf and shaking raindrops out of the front of her hair, 'and it will be standing room only.'

They had caught up with her on the path that led round the side of the church to the basement door, running from her car with her little boy whose hair clung in spikes whether it was raining or not.

'Huh-o-, Char-ie.' Jackie crouched down and grinned into the child's face. The dark eyes looked neither at nor through him. They did not look at all, but that did not discourage either Jackie or lively Mrs Manson, who had five other children and looked like her eldest daughter.

'He knows you, you see!' She put Charlie's hand into Jackie's, where it neither pulled away nor clung. Jackie took Charlie down the steps and over to the pegs at the end of the big noisy basement room. As soon as you let go of Charlie's hands, he put them in his mouth, working them round and round inside the wet reddened lips, so that he left strings of saliva on everything, including Jackie as he unfastened the little boy's coat. At home, Jackie knew, because he had been there to tea, Mrs Manson went about with an old towel tucked into her waist and wiped the doorknobs and chairs and tabletops without noticing she did it.

The floor of the long low room was littered with toys, pedal car, blocks, tricycles, a small slide and a climbing frame where a little girl hung upside down by her heels, red in the face if she had not been black to start with. In one corner, three or four children were cooking at a sand table, banging toy saucepans about and throwing sand into each other's eyes. Jackie led Charlie to the slide and put his limp pigeon-toed foot on the bottom rung of the ladder, but as soon as he took away his hand, the foot slipped off.

'Ugh-gh-gh! Gurr-r-r!' Charlie roared like an unknown animal. His meaningless eyes stared at nothing over his hands, working and turning inside his mouth.

'Let's leave him alone, Jackie, and see what he'll do, shall we?' From six years of living with Charlie, Mrs Manson put everything as a bright question, rather than an order. 'Yesterday, Harriet almost got him to clap his hands. It was marvellous!' Jackie laughed an empty kind of laugh ha ha, to match her eagerness.

Harriet was especially good with the children who stayed in a shut-in world. She rolled on the floor with them and came up dusty on her large behind. She tickled them, pinched them, sang into their uncaring eyes. 'Anything to make contact!' she cried to the other helpers, crashing herself down on the mattress where a child lay with his arm curled defensively over the back of his stubbly head. Jackie thought she was a little touched.

Feeling suddenly blank and without a notion of who or where he was, or what for, he mooched over to the low tables and unfolded himself into one of the small chairs. He pretended he was helping the fat girl with the jigsaw puzzles, so that he could collect them in front of him and do them himself. Fat Mara shrieked and her face collapsed in exaggerated sobs. Jackie pinched her rubber thigh under the table and she fell off the chair and ran to a grown-up. She ran to a girl Jackie had not seen here before. She was standing awkwardly in a corner with her hands hanging, as if she did not know what to do or how she got here. She looked as if her mother had left her at a railway station and forgot to come back for her. She had thin straight legs in white stockings sticking yards out of a very very short skirt – Muh wouldn't think much of *that*! She had short straight hair cut raggedly, and great eyes with lashes painted round them like a doll.

When the fat girl ran at her legs, she reeled, then dropped quickly to the floor to hug her, glad of something to do, burying her face against the child's. But old fatty Mara never stayed with anything more than a minute. She pulled away, thumping the girl's arm to make her let go. The girl got up and stood again, watching.

Jackie put his tongue between his teeth and went on with the puzzles. Most of the children were playing quite busily. His mother was in the kitchen-space behind the hatch, opening a tin of biscuits. Harriet was at the gramophone with a small group, waving her arms and singing, head going like a mad bobbin. At the far end of the room, the sand table was deserted. Charlie was standing by it with his toes turned in and a naked slice of back where his trousers were dropping over his narrow hips. One hand was in his mouth, the other was on the edge of the table.

Looking round, Jackie saw Mrs Manson watching Charlie as if there were nothing else in the room. His hand trailed in the sand, stopped, and picked up a little pie pan. He was just scooping up sand like any other child when Jackie's mother slipped open the hatch and, seeing that everybody was happily employed, clapped her hands like a pistol shot and cried, 'Snack time, everybody.'

Charlie, with his hand raised to dribble sand delightfully back on to the table, let it drop and wandered away, scattering sand on the floor and letting the pie pan roll away without noticing.

'Come along, everybody! Come on then, Mrs King, you're not doing anything. Now is when we have our snacks. Oh no—' as the girl in the long white stockings, glad of a job, pushed a chair towards one of the tables. 'We all bring our own chairs.'

'We,' Jackie wanted to tell the girl, means the children, not her and you.

'Now then, Jack, come along, look lively! I thought it was your job to fetch the milk. Harriet – come, it's table time.' She switched off the gramophone and it died with a groan and a wail from Tommy to add to the shrieking of the chairs as the children dragged or pushed them across the floor.

Those who would came and sat round the tables. Charlie had gone to the side of the room and was sitting with his arm over the back of the chair, the hand dangling, his head on his arm like a tired old man. Jackie's mother picked him up chair and all, and put him at one of the tables, where he turned sideways and drifted away again with his arm on the back of the chair.

Muh wiped strings of saliva off the front of her Play School washable dress and called again, 'Come along, Jack, sharp's the word! The milk won't grow legs and walk in, you know!'

'Ha, ha,' said Harriet, trying to make the children laugh by force.

Jackie said a very bad word. He was fitting the last few pieces into the sailing ship puzzle. 'Fuck,' he said, and the girl with the painted eyelashes heard him. Her brown eyebrows went up and her pale mouth pulled down into her chin as if she would cry, but she was laughing really. Jackie uncoiled himself from the chair. 'Want come fetch a mi-uh!' he shouted, to make sure she understood. Harriet did not always understand him. She pretended she did, but she bobbed her head and said 'Cheers' when he told her he had a cold.

The girl understood. She nodded and let the smile break on her face. She put out her hand and said her name was Sarah. Jackie took her hand as if she were Charlie and led her towards the kitchen.

'Darling? Darling, is that you?'

'Who else were you expecting?'

He sounded rather cross, but Sarah threw herself down the dark little hall and flattened herself to him, cheeks, breasts, stomach, the front of her white mesh thighs, as if she could pass right into him like an astral spirit re-entering its earthbound body.

'Oh, I love you, I love you. You smell like my husband.'

'What kind of man would he be, Madam?' Brian pushed her away gently and took off his coat. He was not tall, but square and muscular under the sharp grey trousers, the double-breasted blazer with the monogram FRH.

'He's the junior assistant to the assistant manager at the Front Royal Hotel,' Sarah said. 'I've just made him a martini, but you may have it.'

'Thank God.' Brian went up the staircase, which was no wider than a ship's ladder, and fell into a chair with his legs stuck out in front of the glowing mouth of the little iron stove. Their house in Salt Street in the old fishing village part of the town was so narrow that there was only room on each floor, kitchen, sitting-room, bedroom, with a bathroom hanging on at the back like a papoose.

'God, I'm tired,' Brian groaned. 'We've had a hell of a day. Everything blew up at once.'

'Tell me.' Sarah gave him his glass and sat on a stool by the stove to stare at him. They had married three months after they met – couldn't wait, now or never, whichever way you saw it. She still could not at all get used to him, with his fair glinting hair and lazy spoiled blue eyes and his hands and the alien smell of his shoes, and his continuing presence in her life. She watched him constantly, trying to understand. Sometimes, sitting opposite while he ate, or watching him at the mirror tying his tie or narrowing his eyes conceitedly with his head turned to smooth the side of his hair, she panicked: I don't know you! What have I done?

He did not know who she was. She dressed the way she always had, big sweaters, tiny squares of skirt, coloured tights, her boots the most expensive thing she bought, her hair carefully ragged, ten minutes to outline her startled eyes and paint lashes one by one on her cheeks. She had looked like that since he knew her, except for the painted lashes, which was a brief fad that had almost run its course as disguise. She was disguised as Sarah King, and he was Brian. How long did you have to live together before you could be honest?

Pouting a little, sipping his gin, his fingers holding the glass in just the way his father did, he told her of the hells and calamities that always chose to break loose when he was on the reception desk. Of the two men with the same name, one an actor of whom he had never heard, of the epileptic liftman, the couple in Suite Four, the woman with the giraffe coat who had moved to three different rooms and finally out and away to the Grand, the taxi driver coming back to Brian for his fare. Of the colossal muddle of next week's American convention. 'Twenty more than we expected and not a cupboard left to put them in and everywhere else jammed for the boat show – why the bloody boat show *now* of all times? I've got to go back in a while and start trying some of the smaller hotels.'

'Do you want to have dinner now?'

'God, no. I couldn't eat. This is all I want.' He lifted his glass. 'Perhaps some biscuits and cheese.'

The biscuits were stale. She could put them quickly in the oven? Oh *God*, she had used the last of the Cheddar on the fish! It was not that he was demanding or critical. He had not had a hard-cooking mother, nor been married before to some smooth-haired girl who washed out her dish towels. He was undomestic, product of nomadic, cruising people, unaware of things that Sarah did when he was not there, which gave them, for some reason, extra neurotic importance.

His stomach, hard and flat as it was under the hotel blazer, was quite a worry to her. Sometimes he wanted no dinner, but would be ravenous for her to get up and fry bacon and eggs at midnight. Sometimes he would come home at some odd time in the middle of the afternoon and expect to smell beef roasting as he opened the yellow front door. There was no way of knowing what to cook or when.

'Why? What's the matter?' He looked at her. She sat hugging her knees, her head on one side, wondering what she could do with the rotten mistake of the fish pie. 'Had you cooked something?' He screwed up his fine healthy face which had a golden fuzz on it like fruit in the sun. 'I don't smell fish, do I?'

'Oh no.' She was not going to be caught. 'Well – Mr Dobbs gave me a whiting for the cats. I haven't made anything, honestly. I was going to see how you—'

'Lousy, that's how. I tell you darling, I don't know how much longer I can stick it. There are people in that hotel ... and as for Dick Rattigan, that little pock-marked scab – "Brian, old boy," coming at me with a sheaf of papers as big as your head, "this seems to be your balls-up. Perhaps you'd straighten it out like a good chap before you go home? Won't take a moment. Yes, I know the girls are going off, but you can type, can't you?" Looking at me with those eyes like poached testicles...'

Sarah sat and hugged her knees and smiled at him and got up to fetch the martini jug when his glass was empty, and sat down again and drank Dubonnet and waited. She was bursting to talk about her day, but she waited. The women's magazines were right. If you did not let them tell their story first, they would not listen to yours. One of the flat surprises of marriage was how many people had been there before.

'You're a lovely girl,' Brian said contentedly. He sat up and she went to kneel in front of him. When they stared into each other's eyes, they were in love.

'Should we go to bed, do you think?' Sarah asked. 'Would you – I mean, would there be time?'

'Later, love,' Brian said. 'I promise you later.'

'Can't wait.' She kissed the hand that rested too placidly on her small breast. She was supposed to be now in a fervour of expectation for what he would vouchsafe her. But since in her limited experience – one fumbled affair with a physics student and one romantic two-nighter in an Austrian ski lodge – the man often seemed to get the most out of it, why was it the girl who was supposed to be grateful?

'About the cheese?'

'Oh yes.' She ran downstairs and up again with what there was. She put a piece of wood into the stove and while she was kneeling there, he said, 'What did you do today?'

He yawned even before he stopped saying it, but she rushed in. 'It was marvellous – really the best day I've had for ages.'

'At the men's sauna?' The health food shop where she worked part time was called The Men's Sana, but he always called it the men's sauna. (There couldn't be anything marvellous about stone-ground senna and macrobiotic olives.)

'I don't go today, you know that. But you remember I answered that advertisement from the Society for the Handicapped, asking for helpers? They rang up this morning and asked me if I could go out to Butterfields and help with a sort of nursery school. Only it wasn't a nursery really, some of them were quite old. Oh, Bri, it was fascinating. There was a mongol boy, terribly inter-esting, and some of the children, they were completely, you know, withdrawn, no expression, no reactions, you can't get at them. This woman called Harriet, when I came in – I was late, of course, because I got lost – she was rolling on the floor and I thought, hullo, she's in a bad way, but she was trying to get this little boy to notice her. When he put out a finger once and touched her, she cheered like a football match.'

'What did you do?'

'Well, nothing very much. There was this woman, you see, she was sort of running the show, at least I don't think she was supposed to, but she did anyway. She's one of those people, she knows it all, you know the kind. When she talks to the children, it's very slow and me-ti-cu-lous, as if they were daft – well, they are, I suppose, but you don't have to talk as if they were.' Sarah talked in rushes, in gabbles with breathy gasps. She could not keep still when she was enthusiastic. She got up and moved about the small room touching things while she talked, leaning, falling over a claw foot of the table, while he watched her over the rim of his icily misted glass.

'And she knows all the names of everything, it's too sickening. When the children are doing something ordinary like playing ball, she says they are motivated, or relating. She didn't like me because I didn't know what autistic meant.'

'What does it?'

'I don't know. She didn't tell me, She didn't like me being there. They didn't need anybody, but the Society had sent someone away. First, she wouldn't let me do anything, and then she kept telling me what not to do. "Oh, we don't get seconds of milk until we have wiped our mouths, Mrs King." There was this poor boy with his ears taped and his face all pulled back as if a hand took hold of the skin at the back of his head and pulled it tight. He had spilled two mugs of milk in a rage, but then I had got him to drink some and want more. Why should he wipe his mouth? Oh, I hate her. She talks like this: "We don't-a-get-a seconds of meelk..." She imitated the neat sterile woman with the cheese-paring mouth and the sliced-bean nostrils, and Brian laughed.

'That the end of that craze then?'

'Oh no. I might not have risked going again, not unless I could find out when she wouldn't be there, but then I made a friend. This woman – the Don't-a-get-a meelk woman – she's got a son, he's about twenty, but he has the brain of, let's say about eight, because it was injured before birth, or during, or something. I don't know. She

70

looks as if you'd need a tin opener to get in or out of her. Jackie, his name is. He's sweet. He hates her. Then she said it was circle time. "Circle Time, everybody!" ' Sarah clapped her hands and put on the clear carrying voice.

'All these poor little things, they sit round in a circle. I sat too and Harriet and the mongol boy's mother, and we sang songs about windmills and teapots. I didn't know what to do, but the girl next to me, very solemn, pushed my arms where she thought they should be, and when I didn't know the words, she took hold of my hips to make them work. Then Jackie's mother sings, in that sort of voice that puts you off going to church, "Good morning to Johnny, good morning to you, good morning to Johnny and how-do-you-do?" And at the end bit, they're supposed to stand up and bow. And they do. Some of them get right down and knock their foreheads on the floor. The withdrawn ones, who don't really know if it's Christmas or Easter, somebody stands them up and pushes them in the middle to make them fold over, and their heads flop and their arms dangle, like puppets. "Good morning to Mara" – she was so fat she could hardly bend, but she put her legs apart and squatted down somehow with her hair hanging on the floor. If that meelk woman hadn't been there, I would have cried. Then of course Jackie wanted to be in it too. His mother shook her head at him. She treats him quite austerely, though really he likes to be cooed at like a child, and so I, God help me, sang for him "Good morning to Jackie" – and he stood and bowed. He's about six foot tall with feet like barge boats, but the other children clapped and so did the mother of the mongol boy, but Jackie's mother just got up and went away.

'And now this was what was so odd. I talked to Jackie for a bit, because his mother had all the children lying on the floor – "Come along people, rest-a-time!" – and he kept talking about someone called Helen, who is his friend. Helen, who's Helen? And he told me a telephone number that he rings up at night. It seems to be the Samaritan place—'

'Where they help suicides?'

'Yes, but you can ring if you just want to talk, and they listen. "I taw to He'en," Jackie said – that's how he talks, with his mouth open, not making any consonants. And then he suddenly clamped it shut and went blank because his mother was approaching on dreaded feet. And then – this was what was odd – you know when you hear something interesting, you almost always hear about it again the same day? Well you do. Listen, this was such a coincidence. On the way home—'

The dolphin knocker pounded on their yellow front door. Sarah went down, jumping the last four stairs as you had to, because of the momentum of the steep narrow treads. The flap of the letter-box was up and a hand was groping. Theo – she recognized the bitten nails. She slapped the hand and opened the door. Theo and a girl with hair down to the hem of her skirt.

'Brian in?'

'Didn't you come to see me?' But she did not like Theo too much, so why the automatic archness?

'Yes darling, if I was alone, but I've got this positive limpet hanging round me. Anna, this is Sarah. You see what I mean?'

'Yes, I do see.' Anna had a slight foreign accent and a long perpendicular nose modelled unsuccessfully on Edith Sitwell. What did she see?

'Brian's upstairs.' Sarah turned her back and went ahead. 'Come on up.'

Anna pronounced the house charming. 'That's a relief,' Brian said. 'We were afraid you wouldn't like it.' Four people talking at once, pouring drinks, inspecting the bookcase, cutting wedges of the waxy Dutch cheese, made quite a turmoil in the small low-ceilinged room. Brian's voice, which he was training to be urbane and reassuring for hotel work, was always louder for friends. Sarah often heard herself a little shriller, trying too hard. She did not like all Brian's family or friends, but they must all like her. What did they want her to be? What did Brian want her to be to make them envy him?

'Tell us about the coincidence.' he said. 'Go on. Sarah was all steamed up about what happened today among the mongols—'

'What mongols?'

'Oh nothing.' She was not going to tell Theo about the play school, and certainly not Anna, who would tell her what Krafft-Ebing said.

'But you said, on the way home – what was so odd?' He wanted to have her standing on the bright rug in front of the stove with her long white legs and her angular poses, telling an amusing story.

'It was only just that I went to get some oranges, and Mr Lox was telling a woman in the shop about his cousin's wife who had tried to kill herself. She thought she had an incurable disease, but it turned out it was only an ovarian cyst. "Ah," the woman said, "we had one of those once in our family, and they thought it was a false pregnancy." '

'Why false?' Anna's black eyes arrowed down her nose.

'Because she was eighty.' They laughed, and Sarah went on embroidering the story about the smell of gas and the window stuffed up with socks and how Mr Lox and his cousin dragged her out like dead on to the scullery roof, red as a cherry. Lo – listen everyone! If you are Sarah, going to the greengrocer's can be a tragi-comedy, with Mr Lox and the customer as jesters. Whereas really the whole conversation had been dead serious, and Sarah had been not an audience. but very much at one with them, sharing Mr Lox's distress, like the warm interest of the customer, who had a country face and a contented child who leaned against her.

'We never knew,' Mr Lox had said, 'That's the pity of it.'

And Sarah had said, 'How terrible to think of someone being so alone and desperate that they could do something like that.'

And the country woman had said, 'She ought to have got in touch with those people who try to save lives, the Samaritans, they call them.'

That was the odd coincidence. Sarah had not heard of them in this town, and now today, twice within an hour ... but Brian and the others were talking about something else by this time, so she did not get to the point of the greengrocer story.

Theo and Anna would have stayed all evening and might even have granted asylum to the fish pie, but Brian turned them out, since he had to go back to work.

The rain had stopped. To the right, where their cobbled street tipped down to the little walled harbour, thick with masts and flags in summer, a D-shaped moon stood high over the cold flat sea. 'Come with me,' Brian said. 'I think I'll go round to some of the smaller hotels instead of telephoning. Then if the Rat says I have to go and personally ensure that the rooms are good enough for our guests from overseas, I'll be able to say, sucks, I have.'

In the car, he ate one of the chlorophyll pills supplied to all the hotel staff along with the monogrammed blazers and ties and the instructions about hair. They drove up Salt Street and turned at the top round the public gardens with the shuttered restaurant and empty paddling pool, along the sea-front, past the new expensive flats with bushes swaddled in sacking on the roof garden, past the old white houses which had once stood alone along this coast, past all the big hotels, the Grand, the Ivor, the Front Royal, the Paramount, the Queen's Ship. Towards the estuary, where the Esplanade narrowed and the pavements were common coloured instead of impressively terracotta, they turned among the back streets where ten thousand boarding-houses and guest-houses (no difference) kept off-season hibernation. Several of the small hotels were open at weekends. They stopped at the Glenalmond, the Essex, the Victoria, the Marbledown, the Bristol, the Baytree. Sarah sat in the car while Brian went inside, and came out checking his list. At the Victoria, he came out smelling of beer, and at the Baytree, he leaned across Sarah to open her door and said, 'Come on, there's a nice little bar here.'

The bar was closed, and the hotel would not be open until the week before Christmas, but the owner, a friendly man with a head like a lion on powerful shoulders, gave them a drink and said in his surprisingly gentle voice, 'Americans? All right, we can probably open a bit early to help you out.'

Feeling important to Brian, Sarah went up with the wife to see the rooms. 'They're so attractive,' she said when she came down. 'I hate to say this, but if I was an American insurance man, I'd rather be here than at the Front Royal.'

The owner laughed and said, 'If I can't get my staff back early, I'll send for you.'

From the Courier, *Friday Evening. YOUTH FOUND STABBED.*

Early this morning, a passer-by answered cries for help from a disused area on Flagg's Hill. An unidentified youth was taken to University Hospital for treatment of what are thought to be stab wounds.

Sammy 'the boy' came up from the press-room with the first run of the Friday edition and tossed one on to Victoria's desk as he slammed into the reporters' room, like a bicycling newsboy in a small-town American film pitching the newspaper on to the front porch. Victoria looked through it, and identified the story about the unknown youth as the suicide attempt that Paul had rescued. The old cliché about nothing you happened to know ever being reported quite right was especially true if you worked on a newspaper.

Uncle Willie's light glowed, a startling innovation, sole upshot of a Time and Motion man's untimely sweep through the office. She picked up his telephone. 'Come in here will you, Victoria? I think Curly and I are being brilliant, so you'd better take it down while it lasts.'

'Yes, Mr Fisher.' She rang downstairs for Margot, then got up and offered the paper to the young man with the folder of drawings who had been waiting for an hour under the window-sill, with Victoria's sun-starved *impatiens* straggling into his hair.

He had been day-dreaming. 'Mm?' He looked at the ink-smelling newspaper as if it were the last thing he expected to find here. 'Oh – no thanks.'

'There's a rather clever cartoon—'

He blew into his upper lip, as if he knew his were cleverer.

She put the paper on the table. 'I don't think he'll be much longer.'

'God, I hope not.' He ran his hand through his hair, and some *impatiens* leaves fell out.

'Are you all right?' He looked pale and limply damp, like the first copies of the Friday edition.

'It's OK.' His young face locked its secret.

You must be a Samaritan all the time, not just on duty. Easy to say.

One night last week, Victoria had sat upstairs on a bus, alone except for a woman who sat behind her on the back seat, weeping.

What's the matter ... Let me help you ... Tell me ... By the time Victoria had found courage to get up, the bus slowed and the woman had stumbled down the stairs. When Victoria went after her, she was already gone somewhere down the dark street.

'Getting off?' The conductress looked like a mother of six, attacking housework and laundry after work with copper-tainted fingers.

'I wanted to ask that woman – she was crying, wasn't she?'

'Best not to turn a stone,' the conductress said. 'We see it all, in this game.'

Margot came up with her hair all frizzed out like a Kalahari bushman, and Victoria went into Uncle Willie's inferno of an office, where fat steam pipes clanked like the engine room of a ship and the waste-paper basket was often on fire. When Victoria had to call Margot up to Reception, Mrs Watcher, who refused to be alone on the Classifieds desk, rang through to Circulation for Bridget, and Circulation made a pot of tea and would not finish Bridget's work, even to catch the post. It would have been simpler to hire one more girl, but the *Courier* could not thrive that way. It had to be lop-sided, stop-gap, stumbling every Tuesday and Friday hairsbreadth on to the streets.

When Victoria came out of the editor's office, a reporter who was sitting on the corner of her desk got up to go, and Margot said, 'There was a phone message for you.'

'Who?'

'They wouldn't say. A private call, they said. I wrote the number somewhere.' She riffled through bits of paper, licking her finger.

'It's all right, I know it.'

'Ho ho, a man then?'

'Yes, ho ho, a man.' No one at the *Courier* knew that she was a Samaritan. When Margot had gone she dialled the Centre. 'This is 422. Do you want me?'

'Oh yes.' Betty's soft Welsh voice. 'Can you ring Jean? She said she must speak to you.'

Jean answered the telephone in a defensive moan. 'You may not believe it, but I went out. I did go out, and I thought, well, Victoria will be pleased anyway, even if nobody else cares one way or another. I was in a shop – I actually was, and it was all right, until that woman had to speak to me. I hardly knew her. Why couldn't she leave me alone?'

'Did you talk to her?'

'How could I? I was terrified. I ran home like a rabbit. That was ages ago, and I've been here in the bedroom ever since, feeling so dreadful. I tried to get hold of you. Where were you?'

'I'm sorry. I'm at the office.'

'Victoria, I must talk to you. Please come and see me. Can't you come in your lunch hour?'

'Oh, Jean – I've had that.'

'When you get out then. *Please.*'

'Well, I—'

77

'Look, you're the only one who cares. If you let me down, I don't know what I'll do.'

'Did you see Dr Hunt last week?' Victoria had her hands round the telephone talking softly. The pale boy with the folder had gone off with Curly, but there were other people passing in and out.

'It's no use. He doesn't help me. He doesn't tell me anything.'

'Would you like me to make another appointment?'

'I couldn't get there.'

'Even if I went with you?'

But when Jean was like this, her mind slithered away from anything practical or positive. 'Can't you come here? I know you don't want to. I know I'm a nuisance to you . . .'

Don't whine, Victoria wanted to say, but she said, 'All right. I'll try and be there about six.'

'If no one is home, there's a key buried under that little bush the dogs killed. I can't come down.'

When Robbie fetched her for a family weekend in the next county, driving patiently round and round the old brown newspaper building because there was nowhere to park, Victoria kissed his cheek briefly, turning away from his quickly searching lips, and said, 'I'm sorry, Rob. I have to stop and see someone on the way. Could we go out by Newton?'

He groaned. 'Through all that traffic? Victoria, I wish you—'

'All right, I'll get a taxi. You can meet me somewhere later.' Anger was in the car with them even before she had rolled down the window to exorcize his thin cigars.

'Don't be stupid.' He reached across to push down the lock of her door. 'Of course I'll take you. Who is it?'

'A client.'

'Why didn't you say so?' His voice grew dutifully considerate, as if the Samaritans were a crank religion. 'Newton – oh, it's Jean, is it?'

'Yes. I don't know what to do about her. She isn't getting any better. I don't seem to be helping her much.'

'I'm sure you do,' Robbie said, too dotingly. 'I think it's marvellous what you do. I only wish I had the time to be a Samaritan myself, but I'm afraid I'd get too involved.'

That's the point. Victoria did not say it. You have to.

At ten that morning the telephone woke Billie from the drowned, snuffling sleep into which she had fallen after she talked to Victoria. She raised her face an inch from the pillow. Morna? She never rang from work, even when Billie begged, 'Just to say hullo, that's not much to ask when someone's got flu.' There's no phone in the laundry,' Morna said. But you could bet old Sister Speculum could ring down any time and say, 'I'm short two drawsheets.'

'Oh sod off.' Billie collapsed again, but the telephone went on ringing. *Bad news* was the rhythm with which it rang. When it was evening, and Morna's squeaky voice might say, 'There's a *fantastic* picture at the Odeon,' the ringing drummed out *Good news.*

Billie rolled over, reached out and jerked the telephone to silence. '*What* is it?'

Bad news was right. 'That's what I want to know,' Mr Fettiche snapped. 'I need you down here, worse my luck.'

'I'm ill.' Billie lowered her voice an octave from its normal baritone. 'Really ill this time. I ache all over. There's a lot of polio about, you know.'

'Not since the vaccine,' said Mr Fettiche cruelly. 'You get down here by ten-thirty, or I'll see you sacked.'

'You'll not get another counter hand to work the hours I do.'

The student committee is talking of running the cafeteria,' he said, 'unless the service improves. That means you, Camilla Cripps.'

'Oh shit.' She said it after she heard him ring off. She was not ready to lose the job. Not yet.

Hots on Friday were ham and beans, lamb stew with a papery white skin on it, macaroni and cheese for the strapped, baked haddock for the children of Mary. In her green overall which had big pockets below counter level for slipping buns and sugar lumps into, and squares of cheese for Thing, Billie ladled out hot lunches gracelessly, like the Trusty with the dinner wagon in *Birdman of Alcatraz*.

'Where's your cap?' Mr Fettiche stood at the board behind her on tiptoe, changing the plastic letters that spelled Swiss Roll to Trifle. That meant the Swiss had gone stale. 'I said where's your cap?' He had had the inspector down last term, lifting lids and recoiling from the roller towels.

'In my pocket.' The caps were only stiff green bows, but still technically a head covering. Billie pulled hers out, shook off biscuit crumbs and pinned it somewhere on the back of her head without letting go of the ladle.

Colds were the usual. Ham, galantine, Scotch eggs, sardine salad and egg mayonnaise – they had it soft, these kids, but they did nothing but grumble, passing sideways with their bent-up trays, their hair a scandal, trailing in the butter the fringes of shawls that Billie's grandmother would not have given attic room to, leaving wiry beard hairs on the jelly as they bent to sniff.

'What is it?'

'Lemon-lime.'

'It looks like spawn.'

'Is it the fish that's off, or what?'

'Man,' they said to each other, 'I was hungry before I saw this.'

Anyone would think they had eaten real food, where they came from. In their skinny jeans which bent at the knees like broken drainpipes, skirts to the crotch or trailing in the dirt like stuffy old women, parting their hair to get a cavilling look at the haddock – most of them looked as if they had never had a decent meal, nor a home to eat it in.

The stew ladle in one hand and the fish slice in the other, Billie caught a vision of Morna with her bubbly hair and baby strap shoes, and felt suddenly faint.

When Helen got home to 'The Maltings' after Samaritan night duty, her children had gone to school, leaving messages all over the kitchen. 'Out of peanut butter. Please iron my blue dress. Good a.m. mother with love from Danny.'

Mrs Weinberg had been in the flat. The door to the kitchen sighed shut as Helen untied the cross-eyed dog from the boot scraper and came in from the garden.

'Looking for something, Mrs W?'

'Oh hullo, Helen.' Mrs Weinberg was in a jutting pink overall with a strand of thick pink wool round her new Egyptian haircut. Must be Incurables library day. She hardly needed any civvies, since she was always dressed in Ranger Guide uniform, or WRVS green, or a doggy white coat for the PDSA, or the tricorne and starch of St John's Ambulance, the Maltese cross so far out on the apron front that she could hardly get the smelling salts to the noses of the fallen at the Whitsun fair.

'I was just going to see about breakfast, as you weren't back.'

'That's funny, I thought you'd been in the flat. The beer is mine, in case you wondered.'

Helen said more or less what she liked to her, or to Mr Weinberg or any of the family. They pretended that they thought it amusing, but sometimes they talked about it. 'You must say something to her.' 'She might leave.' 'Let her.' 'But I'll *never* get another!' 'If you didn't run about all the time disguised as a Christian, you wouldn't need anyone.' And etc., and etc. Helen had heard them at it through the back of a bookcase which used to be a window before the flat was built on.

'Had a good night, dear?'

'Yes, love.'

'Any casualties?' As a first-aider, Mrs Weinberg was always interested in overdose or haemorrhage, though with a hint sometimes of jealousy. If a person was in danger of hanging himself or opening a vein, what could the amateurish Samaritans do that St John's couldn't do better?

'Not to speak of.' Helen began to bang noisily about the kitchen in the motions of making breakfast. 'There's this man comes in and says, "Is this the place where they stop people killing themselves?" "That's right," I say, so he pulls out a pistol and drills himself, right there on our carpet.'

'You're joking.'

'If you say so, Madam.' Helen put on her underdog drone, beaten stupid by years of service. She bent to pat the dog as if he were her only ally, then she made up a few more Samaritan clients to keep Mrs Weinberg happy while she watched Helen fry eggs. She did not tell her about Jackie or old Mike or the homosexual librarian, or the boy with the slashed wrist who would by now have woken from the anaesthetic to find himself alive, with what? Relief? Disappointment? Had he gone bleeding to the telephone because he did not want to die, or because he only wanted someone to know? When Helen had woken choking in the garage, the terrifying thing was how easy it would have been.

Tim's bed was opposite the ward door, with the television set on the wall above his head. Everybody stared his way, but he could not see the picture.

After tea, fed into him through a small teapot by a nervous boy in a white coat who seemed to be learning, they took the needle out of the inside of his arm and put on a piece of plaster.

'There! Good as new,' But it was not good as new. The skin was bruised and the arm was a heavy ache. He held it bent up with his fist to his shoulder, as the nurse had told him. His other arm, the plaster one, lay outside the covers, palm up, as if he were asking for something. It did not hurt him as much as the one they had put the needle into.

He could not remember how much it had hurt when he had come down on it with the piece of broken glass. Perhaps it had not hurt at all? He remembered almost nothing except the terror of the blood. In the telephone box, he had pulled off his jacket and wrapped it over the soaked towel, but the blood came through. It was everywhere, his fingers slipping in it as he fumbled with the dial.

'Hang on.' Unseen, she had been joined to him in fear. 'Stay where you are.' He remembered the panic of pushing blindly out and falling on the pavement, a stunning smack in the face. Somewhere, a man's voice shouting. The grip of hands.

Some time that evening – the clock was behind his head by the television, and although several people, nurses and patients, had spoken to him, Tim had said nothing to anyone – faces and waving hands began to gather on the other side of the ward door. Two nurses hurried round straightening the bed covers. Don't touch it! Tim cried silently, as the darker one lifted the dead weight of his left arm so that the other could smooth the fold of the sheet. The Sister, a little person in dark blue with a winged cape like a bird, fussed round the men who were sitting in chairs, tying pyjama cords, tweaking dressing-gowns across gaps, pushing down the awful handkerchief that sprouted from an old man's pocket.

'It's gone seven, Sister!' someone called out, and the swing door took courage and moved very slightly, as if in a draught.

She looked round her kingdom. 'No one is coming in until this ward is straight.' But if you had your girl waiting out there, what would she care if the black nurse and the brown nurse had made those sharp folded corners at the bottom of your bed, lifting and tucking and creasing down with swift, pale-nailed fingers?

The draught that moved the door strengthened. Each time it swung, it opened a little farther, until all at once the Sister pulled it open and a horde of people spilled into the ward, tracking out immediately in different directions, eyes fixed towards one bed.

'It's the hardest time of day.' The chubby man in the next bed rolled his balding pink head on the pillow to look at Tim. 'Don't you have anyone either?' Tim shook his head. 'Cheer up,' said the man. 'Some of the frights I see coming in here, makes you glad you got nobody.'

Through the tears on Tim's lashes, the crowd of bodies that had burst in began to resolve itself into individuals. A lank-haired girl sitting with a man's hand in hers, staring, saying nothing. A woman whispering behind her hand, eyes darting. A boy in work clothes, dried clay on his trousers, the Sister looking at his boots. A mother in a merciless hat, bringing forth chocolate, nuts, a toilet roll from a bottomless bag.

'My old lady came once,' the fat man said. 'But I told her if all you're going to do is complain about Dad, you'd best not trouble.' But he held his eyes on the door, which kept opening again as people came in late.

A woman with curly fair hair, her arms full of bundles, laughing, dropping an orange, the low chatter pausing for a moment as people turned to watch her hurrying to Tim's bed.

Hullo, Mum.

Hullo, dear. Feeling better?

A tall solid-looking man with dark grey hair whiter at the sides came through the door, stood looking lost, then spoke to the Sister, smiling down at her as she sat at the centre desk. She nodded and pointed, and the man turned the smile towards Tim and came over. He had very large feet, with rubber soles that squeaked on the polished floor.

'Hullo.' He stood by Tim's bed looking down. Although he was still smiling, he looked serious as well. 'How are you feeling?'

'All right.' It was the first thing Tim had said since he woke up and found himself here. The words came out in a croak from his dry lips, swollen where he had grazed them falling.

'I wasn't allowed to see you this morning.' The man looked round for a chair, but there were none left.

'Sit on the bed,' the fat man said, interested. 'What's it matter?'

'Better not risk it.' the tall man folded his arms and turned slightly to block the fat man without being noticeably rude. 'Did you get my message?'

84

Tim shook his head.

'What a pity. I said to tell you I'd be back tonight. I didn't want you to think we'd abandoned you.'

A policeman? He did not talk like one, but that was the thing. You didn't know. Tim lay with the back of his head pressed into the hard pillow, his eyes fixed on the man's friendly face, shadowed round the mouth and chin. He could feel his heart pounding under the tidy bed-clothes. Would the man notice that as a sign of guilt?

'My name is Paul.' He had a very deep voice that came out of his throat, not his head, like some people. 'Do you want to tell me yours?'

Oh, no. *Oh*, no. You don't trick me that way, mister. He had stubbornly refused to tell anyone his name since he had woken with a headache and vomit in his mouth, and the nurse had said, 'What's your name, dear?' before he had finished chucking up.

The man thought for a moment, then he looked at the plaster, and asked, 'How's the arm?'

'All right. Had a bit of an accident. Nothing much.'

'Yes. I know. I hope it doesn't hurt.' After another pause, his face creased into a smile again, and he said, 'You don't remember me, do you?'

Tim shook his head.

'You don't remember then – last night. The Samaritans? You rang our number, 333-4000. Do you remember that?'

333-4000. He could feel the holes of the dial, slippery with his blood. 'It was a woman. She spoke to me.' 'Help me,' I said. 'I can't stop the blood.' 'Where are you?' They had been joined in a secret fear.

'You asked for help,' the big man said, 'and so I went to try and help you. Near the old water tower on Flagg's Hill. I found you behind that broken wall. But it's not surprising you don't remember. You were bleeding very badly.'

'You – you were there?'

'Yes. I'm still here, if you want me. Don't worry, I know you can't talk now. You've been through a pretty rotten time. I'll come back, if you want. Would you like me to?'

Tim could feel his face growing hot and swollen. The tears were on his lashes again. He blinked and a tear fell, wet on the side of his nose, salt in his mouth.

'My name is Paul,' the man said again. '333-4000. The Samaritans. If you want me, you can get Sister to ring us.'

'I wouldn't cry,' the chubby man said, after the bell had emptied the ward and the nurses were carrying out the flowers. 'Was that your old man? I say, was that your old man?' Tim would not look at him, but he knew that he was turned humpily on his side, staring with his sticky eyes.

Tim put the back of his good wrist across his eyes, as if the light hurt. My name is Paul ... My name is Tim. All right, I mucked it up. That's it then. *If you are at the end of your tether* ... Under the stairs, with his dream face staring in the mirror, and the thing done. But even that I couldn't do. Even that I mucked.

WHAT I WANT FROM NEXT YEAR. D. GERALD BRIGGS

Next year I leave and get my car licensed. Next year I go forth as it's said to meet the world with equal terms, except that for my generation it will never be equal to them who have got it made while we were still too young to know.

At home on Saturday morning, Paul was correcting essays. Alice answered the telephone in the bedroom, and came to the sitting-room door with white grease on her face and her hair back-combed straight up from her scalp. 'St Peter's on the line. They've got a throne for me in paradise and want to know if you're good for the fees.'

'I've got a policeman here.' Peter was speaking from the Samaritan Centre. 'He's asking about the boy you went out to on Thursday night. 200 says you saw him in the hospital yesterday. Do you know his name? Not that I'd tell the copper, but it would be useful to know.'

'He wouldn't tell me anything. Poor kid, I think he's terrified.'

'He would be. I'll keep the law off his neck, and you—'

'Do you think I should go again? He didn't seem to want me.'

'Look Paul, he asked for our help. Let's try and give it. Go back today and try to get through to him, will you?'

Visiting hours on Saturday were from two to six. Paul could go to the hospital on the way back from taking his son out to lunch. Jeff was still at Burlington, the school where Paul and Alice had once lived in a faded, comfortable house with trellis on the brick for roses, and twenty boys perpetually clumping up and down the bare wooden stairs and the dormitory passage.

At the time of the scandal ('She's nothing but a drunken nymphomaniac'), the school had offered half-heartedly to let Jeff stay out his four years, not expecting that he would, since every boy, master, wife, maid and local tradesman knew about Alice and the Assistant Head's wife's Australian cousin. Paul had wanted Jeff to leave, but he could not insist without seeming unwilling to pay the full fees, which would be charged now that he was not on the staff.

'Don't let him stay,' Alice had begged, in the drying-out clinic where Paul had taken her. 'How can you want to, Jeff?' she wailed at her son. 'After the things that bastard said about me!' But the boy had set his mind to it, sticking out his lower lip, crusted with impetigo at the time. Outside, he told Paul, 'I'm not going to let her spoil my life, or you because you can't handle her.' Frighteningly, he had grown up, grown away. Paul could not talk to him. Somehow he managed to find the extra money, and Jeff had stayed at the school.

Alice would not go there, not this Saturday, or ever, so

Paul went off alone. It was a long drive, through country that became increasingly familiar and dear to him as he went farther inland. Here had been much of his life. The grammar school in the quiet Cotswold town which never grew larger or smaller. The rivers and hills and tunnelling lanes, the misted forests of childhood. The stone farmhouse where he had found his father sitting on a sack in the grain shed the night after they slaughtered his infected cattle. They had moved away after that, his father glumly caring for another man's stock, but many years later, after the war. Paul had jumped at the chance to go back.

Ten years at Burlington, seven of them in Archway. The chunky brick house which had been built on at the end of the main building had been the favourite home of his marriage. Until everything went wrong.

'And if we're raking up the past,' Alice said sometimes when they were not, 'you were doing your share of the boozing at Archway, in case you forgot. If those damn boys had been less unconcerned, you'd have got kicked out long before.'

Paul drove in at the back gate, past the beech hedge, the tarred toolsheds, the neglected orchard where the grass was never cut because of the daffodils, and where Alice would have hung her laundry if she had been that kind of woman. There was laundry there now, small children's things and the home-washed shirts of a thrifty young wife.

Paul drove through the brick arch to the paved yard where there had once been stables, now sheds for bicycles, sports gear, mowing machines, the pottery shop with the zig-zag chimney which had been built for a wash-house. He stayed in the car for a minute or two. He had hoped that Jeff would be watching for him and would come out. Which was more stupid, for Paul to be a coward at fifty, or for Jeff, at sixteen, to be unaware?

Paul got out of the car, put his foot on the familiar granite step and went into the back hall, which still smelled of linseed oil and the red scouring soap the school had always used, oblivious to the advent of detergents. Two boys in sweaters and running shorts, jumped down the last flight of stairs and pivoted round the pineapple newel post as boys had done for years, the carving almost obliterated by squeaking palms.

The boys were not familiar. 'Excuse me, sir.' They edged past, their legs white and knobbly.

'Is Jeff Hammond up there?' Paul asked.

'No sir, I don't think so.' The boys went on, but as they opened the door, one of them stopped for a glance back and then jumped out over the high granite step to be able to tell the other, 'Hammond's father – *you* know.'

The present housemaster's wife was in one of the front rooms, hair pinned up but coming down, an air of small children about her: pins stuck into the band of her skirt, a mess like baby's dribble on her blouse, a torn book in her hand.

'Oh, Mr Hammond, how *nice*.' She had been the new geography master's wife when Paul was here, living down in the village, invited to the duty sherries, but not the *intime* parties where Alice would get stoned and Paul would forget that he must be up at seven to shout his boys into the showers. 'Is Jeff expecting you? He went up to the library, I think. Do come in and sit down, though it seems silly inviting you into your own house, doesn't it? I hope it doesn't make you feel dreadfully sad,' she said, kindly deciding that this was a better approach than pretending to know nothing.

She produced the inevitable sherry, which Paul had learned in ten years to live with, if not to like, and presently Jeff knocked and came in, poking his head owlishly round the door, his shoulders rounded, a pile of books in his long arms.

'I didn't know you were here. Sorry, Dad.' He invariably started off with an apology, which caused Paul, as now, to solicit one.

'I did say twelve-thirty. I haven't got too long.' And that was unfair, since it was not until this morning that he knew he must be back in time to go to the hospital.

'I'll just take these books up,' Jeff said in his gentle, immature voice. 'Am I OK?'

'What else have you got?'

'Nothing much.' Jeff was wearing rubbed corduroys and a sort of Western leather jacket with remnants of fringe and the nap worn off the shoulders like the back of a baby's head. Paul knew better than to suggest the school's regulation grey suit. 'Do you want me to change?'

'Look, it's not what *I* want – it's what you think you ought to do. You're sixteen. I don't have to tell you to breathe.' Why did they irk each other so, they who had always been allies against the tough sufficiency of Laura, the catastrophes of Alice?

When Jeff had trotted upstairs in the grubby yellow sandals he wore over thick sweat socks, Paul turned with a laugh and spread hands to the housemaster's wife, sorting socks in a laundry basket. 'You wouldn't think we loved each other.'

'I think he's very fine,' she said. 'He thinks a whole lot of you, you know. He talks a lot about you, what you write to him, what you and he did last summer.'

'Does he?' Paul eagerly believed it.

When he had got Jeff in the car, he said, 'What's the matter with your eyes?' The housemaster's wife might have thought it odd that he did not know.

'Nothing.' Jeff grinned and took off the round wire spectacles and held them in front of his father's eyes to show they were plain glass. 'Do you want me to – sorry.' He started to put the glasses back on, looked at his father, and folded them and put them in his pocket.

'God, it's good to get away from here.' He leaned back and sighed as they drove under the archway.

'Things are all right though, aren't they?' Jeff did not write letters, though he occasionally telephoned, reversing the charges.

'Oh yes. Great. Mark's pretty good, if you care about that.'

'Friends?'

90

'Some. They're all right.'

'What about games? Any football this year?'

'Oh come on, Dad,' Jeff said irritably. 'I've been here long enough to know how to get out of *that*.'

Crossing the front of the school buildings to go out of the other gate towards the hotel, Paul allowed himself a little treat of nostalgia for the round pancake of lawn, the coloured glass crests in the library windows, the broad oak where his poetry class had sprawled, sucking grass, in the first shimmer of June.

Facile. It was possible to be nostalgic about anything past, even a prison camp, since it represented a part of your own precious life. When he and Alice left Singleton Court, as they would have to eventually, or die, no doubt he would occasionally think fondly of the artificial fire, the bathroom view of other people's bathroom window-sills across the yard.

Out of the headmaster's house came the familiar cinnamon tweeds, the patch of freckled skull like a tonsure, the pigeon-toed lope. As always, the little start of recognition, of surprise that he had the nerve to come, before the sincere grin and the double handshake. 'My dear Paul!' He had both arms in through the window of the car. 'The nicest surprise. Have you got a moment? Sheila would love to see you.'

'The hell she would,' Jeff said when they had driven on. 'It must be hell for you coming back here – I mean, it must be hell.'

'It's the only way I can see you till next year when you can get weekends. I'm sorry,' Paul said, as they got to the road, 'I should have asked you if there was anyone you wanted to bring to lunch.'

'No thanks.'

Jeff was fairly uncommunicative at lunch. He drank beer, and Paul kept some sort of conversation going, but his questions about Jeff's news brought only monosyllables, and his news of himself was clearly of little interest. Some parents and boys from the school came into the hotel restaurant, and Jeff put the spectacles on again. He was rather waxy and pale, the pinkish scars of the impetigo still staining the skin of his mouth and chin.

'Sick of school?' Paul asked casually, getting out his wallet to pay the lunch bill, higher on term-time Saturdays since there was nowhere else to go.

'No – why?' Jeff looked up through the fake lenses.

'Oh, I don't know. I wondered if you ever regretted your decision. At the time you had to make it, you were under a pretty bad strain. We all were.'

'I told you then,' Jeff looked at the middle of his father, not at his face. 'I wasn't going to let my mother spoil my life.'

There was nothing to do after lunch except sit in the cinema and watch a second-rate film. Paul dozed and Jeff fidgeted and muttered and groaned as the film got worse. But when Paul woke, looked at his watch and saw that he must go, Jeff was quite sullen, although he had been throwing himself about in his seat and complaining: 'I can't stand much more of this.'

Paul did not get to the hospital until after six, but he went up to the ward anyway, hoping that he might find a nurse he knew.

The ward was closed for the Saturday night concert. From the corridor, Paul could hear some basic guitar chords and pleasant young Anglo-Saxon voices singing that 'De Lawd He know 'bout all de hungry chillun.'

He looked into the office. Good luck, Nurse Drage was in there, sneaking a cigarette. She was an intense, impulsive girl with her hair scraped back behind enormous ears and her stiff cap riding her forehead like an American sailor.

'My God, you scared me.' She jumped up, with her cigarette inside her hand, even more like a sailor.

'Where's Sister?'

'At supper. I'm in charge here.' She stuck out her apron front and put on Sister's voice. 'The ward is closed, my good man.'

'I know I'm late, but I promised that boy – the one with the wrist – that I'd come back. Has he told you what his name is?'

'I don't think so. He's been asleep since I've been on. Is he one of yours?'

Paul did not answer. Nurse Drage put out her cigarette, dropped the stub in her pocket, wiped the ashtray with a square of gauze dressing and put that in her pocket too. 'Sister's got another twenty minutes,' she told him, and then as De Lawd ended to no clapping, she took a quick look down the corridor and said, 'Quick – sneak in before they start again.'

The next song was beginning, but all the men and boys in the beds and chairs turned like a theatre audience to look at Paul coming in. He raised a hand in apology to the two serious boys and the singing girl with the sweet triangular face, and tiptoed round the side of the ward from bedrail to bedrail, as if the middle of the floor were a torrent.

The boy by the end wall had his eyes shut and was either asleep or pretending to be. He was very young, perhaps not yet out of his teens. His light hair, badly cut too long ago stuck up at odd angles on the pillow. His face was narrow, with a small delicate nose like a girl and fair flushed skin that could not need much shaving. The grazes on his mouth and cheek made him look victimized, the outflung arm a plea for mercy.

As Paul sat looking down at him, he opened his eyes, frowned, closed them again and then opened them and opened his mouth as if he might say something.

'How are you?' Paul asked, when he did not.

'All right.' The music was loud enough for them to talk without being heard by the chubby man, propped on a thick elbow to listen. 'I didn't think you were coming back.'

'I'm sorry I was late. I had to go to Oxfordshire. My son's at school there,' Paul said, for something to say, not expecting the boy to care, but his eyes brightened and he asked, 'How old's he?'

'Sixteen. Bit younger than you. Where did you go to school?'

'Not much of a school. I didn't mind it. Does your son?'

'Not too much. The work's all right, but he hates games and he seems to be a bit of a loner. He doesn't go round with gangs of friends.' Paul was feeling his way, trying to keep the boy's interest.

The boy nodded. 'What's his name then?'

'Jeff.' Paul talked a bit more about his son and the school and the lunch and the film they had seen. People in trouble usually wanted you to listen and not talk about yourself, but this boy seemed to want it the other way round. He wanted more about Jeff, perhaps to keep from having to talk, perhaps because some drift of fantasy was making Paul a father?

At the end of the song, the boys and the girl waved and called out. 'See you next week!' and took their guitars and their healthy youth away. The girl kissed a very old man by the door, and he chuckled and made a grab at her thigh.

'You off?' the boy asked, as if Paul had only come for the concert.

'I'll have to go before Sister comes.'

'Yes.' He had lowered his voice when the music finished. Paul had to lean forward to hear his murmur. 'She's like when I was a boy.' He smiled a little and shook his head as if it were a very distant memory.

'Someone strict?'

'Yup.' No more.

Paul let that go, and asked casually. 'What's your name?'

'I've not told them.'

'Why not?'

'Because of the police.'

'It won't make any difference. Anyway, I don't think the police will bother you.'

'What I – what I done ...' His pale-lashed eyes flicked to his arm.

'Was that why you went off and hid, after you rung us?'

'I don't know.' He had to keep his arm still, but the rest of him moved restlessly on the bed. 'I don't remember. I don't remember nothing about what happened. It's all so confused all the time. I don't know what to do...' His voice went wandering away, and Paul said again, 'What's your name?'

'Tim.' His eyes came back to Paul as if in surprise that he did not know. 'Tim Shaw. I live up Darley Road.' He added without being asked, 'Got a room there.'

'A job?'

'Oh yes, I've got a job but – I don't know if I'll stay. It's not much,' he pursed his mouth in a businesslike way. 'Not my kind of thing really.'

Paul did not ask what it was, nor whether he should get in touch with the employer, because the boy seemed to have made it up. The door crashed open wide as if an army were coming through, and the birdlike Sister marched into the ward, buttoning her cuffs and looking round for trouble.

'I've got to go.' Paul got up quickly. 'Goodbye for now, Tim.'

The boy neither answered nor seemed to notice. He had withdrawn from behind his face. Paul put back the chair and was starting off with a conciliatory smile for the advancing Sister, when there was a nudging tug, like a child, at the edge of his jacket.

'Will I see you again?' the boy asked anxiously.

'Of course.' Paul steamed out of the ward in a glow of elation that frizzled Sister's outrage and caused Nurse Drage to grumble, 'There's *some* people have to work on a Saturday evening...'

Alice was not in the flat. That was not unusual, at drinking time. Not that she favoured any one particular drinking time over another, but the evening was when she wandered off to her favourite pubs and bars, or the Capstan Club down by the harbour.

Tonight they were supposed to be dining out, but once gone, Alice was not likely to remember. Paul went on his own, and his friends accepted the excuse of Alice's flu as if they had not heard it before, and not as if they were quite relieved. They were, because they had invited a strange couple, and with Alice, you never knew.

You never knew when she would come home either. Paul got back to the flat at midnight, and paced about undressing and muttering to himself, 'If I had a pound for every night I've had to worry about her ... If I had five quid for every time I've been fool enough to call the police and ask about accidents...'

His pacing eventually led him into bed. He turned on the lamp to read, and saw, stuck into a book he had finished and would not have been reading, a note from his wife.

She had gone to stay with Hazel Rencher, a stoical friend from days long past who had always been 'good' to her. Hazel thought that Paul was a bad influence on Alice, and traced her drinking directly to him.

On Sunday, before he went to the Samaritan Centre, he rang Hazel's number in a town farther along the coast, which Alice disliked even more than this one.

'How's Alice?'

'She's all right.' Implying, why wouldn't she be, since she is with me? 'She expected you to ring up last night.'

'I went out to dinner. She was supposed to go too.'

'She was lonely with you off all day. She got on a bus and came here. She didn't want to be alone.'

'She could have gone with me.'

'To *Burlington*?'

'To see her son.' The conversation was getting too righteous on both sides. 'Let me talk to her.'

'She's asleep,' said Hazel triumphantly and rang off.

'Vicky. How nice of you to come.'
  'It was nice of you to ask me.'
  'I expect you'd like a drink.'
  'Thank you very much, I—'

96

'You and Robbie are rather late. I expect you'd like to go up and dress first.'
'Thank you very much.'

The weekend with Robbie's parents near Maidenhead had been no more stimulating than usual, though not completely a weekend since Victoria came back on Saturday evening.

Robbie's parents were afflicted with an anachronistic title, which was one of the reasons why she could not marry him. There were others – he was shorter than she was, she needed a couple of drinks before she could enjoy his hand on her, at the Bank he wore a braided Edwardian waistcoat and half glasses and was irascible with the melancholy trainee girls – but it was enough to tell him, 'I couldn't possibly ever be called Lady Roundswell.'

'I don't see why not.'

'I'd have to pay for everything in cash because I wouldn't be able to say my name in shops.'

'Would you marry me if I gave up the title?'

'That would kill your father.'

'If I was Lord Roundswell, he'd be dead anyway.'

The white house was beautiful, the garden falling in terraces to the river. If she married Robbie, this would eventually be theirs. What would they do with his mother? She was not the kind you put in a flat over the stables. Not likeable, she made it difficult to dislike her by giving you no cause. She was passive, placid, dull as bottled water, demanding so little of life and of herself that she did not appear to notice what was lacking. She was a stiff awkward shape, in dressmaker, not couturier expensive clothes, with a mass of grey hair piled haphazardly above a face blessed with a wild-rose skin from not drinking or smoking. She called Victoria Vicky although she had been asked not to, and thought she was not quite top drawer and had knocked about too long without a husband, but might do for poor ridiculous Robbie who had made such a fiasco of his first disastrous marriage. She did not remember that she had originally favoured it; only that he had muffed it.

She was fairly inarticulate, from caution and lack of ideas rather than shyness. His fat, silly Lordship was so uncomfortably shy that you automatically checked the exits if you found yourself alone in a room with him. When Robbie was at home, he dropped back into their habit of clearing his throat and emitting little Hms and Wells and small nasal sounds to fill silences. Victoria was no great hand at small talk, but nervously she tried, and succeeded only in sounding garrulous.

The two couples who came to dinner on Friday night were more or less untitled versions of the Roundswells. Everyone stood round with drinks, giving out little moans and hums from up in the nose, while his Lordship went 'Ha ha, well', and 'Well, ha ha' a few times, and Victoria wished they could all sit down and read magazines till dinner.

The food was marvellous and the wine was good. Victoria looked across at Robbie's nice polite face under the short fringe he had started to wear after he saw Richard Harris in 'Camelot', and tried to imagine eating with him at this table her own food that she was not allowed to cook. Why could she not throw everybody out of the kitchen? And have the guilt on her soul of Ethel Mobsby, whose whole life was here? And Robbie's mother would move pointedly from the end of the table, though nobody asked her to, and watch Victoria trying to be Lady Roundswell; or sit stuffed into her Paisley, picking at the pheasant, because the Hon. Robbie had had himself demoted to Mister. Though if he did, they would not get this house.

Sometimes Robbie went wild and heaped on Victoria exhilarating ideas of an island in the Hebrides, a boat in the south seas, a plunge to Australia. She joined in the heady plans, but when he pressed her, 'Is that the adventure you want? Is that the kind of marriage you'd like to have?' Victoria could not answer, because she could not say, 'But it wouldn't be an adventure with you.'

Before they went home, one of the couples, who had

not seemed to enjoy themselves at all, said with surprising warmth. 'You must *all* come round to us for drinks tomorrow.'

'Oh I say.'

'Oh splendid.'

'Oh jolly good.'

That would be tomorrow taken care of then. 'Well now. Ha ha, yes.'

Victoria said, 'Thank you so much, but I have to be back in the evening.' But they meant drinks before lunch, bloody Marys, gin and bitter lemon. Ha ha, jolly good. She and Robbie would not be able to take the long walk across the hills and lunch at the Lamb and Flag.

Afterwards when the Roundswells had gone up – there was a bed in his Lordship's dressing-room, but Victoria could not guess whether he used it, and Robbie did not know, didn't *know* whether his parents slept together! – he sulked under his fringe and said, 'You didn't say you had to go back tomorrow. I was taking you to a party.'

'I'm sorry, Rob. I must get back. I have to be on duty by eight on Sunday so that Kathleen can get to Mass.'

He groaned and tutted and swung his head about. He was not so enthusiastic about the Samaritans when they interfered with his plans.

Victoria would not let him drive her back. She took a train and went straight from the station to a cinema, dropping into her seat in the darkness with the familiar drugged satisfaction, alone, unknown, craving the safety of the dream.

When Billie rang up on Sunday, opening defensively, 'You said to ring,' she had been to the cinema too.

With Morna. 'That's the name of my friend, I told you. Morna, her name is. Short for Maureen that her mother called her, but she spelled it wrong and they put it on the birth certificate as Morneen. Silly, you know, but then.' Billie sounded very chirpy.

'I'm so glad you're feeling better.'

'Well, I'm better than when I rang you Thursday night, I'll say that much.'

'I know. Poor Billie. Things are all right now, are they, between you and Morna?'

'I don't know about *all right*.' Billie would never have everything roses. 'She's not really the sort of girl you can trust. A bit tricky, you see. Sometimes she won't answer the phone, to make me think she's gone out. I never quite know who she's with. But Saturday lunchtime when I came back from work – oh, you should see my feet, the standing is criminal – there she was at the door, pushing a bar of chocolate nougat through the letter-box. So in the afternoon we went to see *Twisted Nerve* and we got a bit of supper and then went down to South Parade and saw *Rosemary's Baby*.'

'How is it?'

'Smashing. All those old bags standing round without a stitch on, I had to laugh. And there's poor old Mia Farrow stretched out like a stewing chicken, not a bit of flesh on her, and you see the devil doing it, right there before your amazed eyes, you ought to see it. Or are you prudish, Victoria? Funny, it's as if I know you quite well, but I don't know anything about you. You're thirty-five. Old maid. Not a lez. Right? So you're a prude.'

'I don't think so.'

'It's all orgasms now though, isn't it, the films, all orgasms. I get a bit sick of it. *Tereese and Isabella* – I don't know. Morna and I started to laugh, and pretty soon we had the whole house in fits. "It wasn't like that when I was at school," someone said, and it started everybody off again. In *Twisted Nerve*, where poor old Billie Whitelaw is off to the woodshed, there was a woman giggled. Nerves, you see. She was still sniggering when he smashes that hatchet down on her forehead and all blood and stuff comes out. How do they do that? Like that bit in *Psycho* where the dick is coming up the stairs and Anthony Perkins puts the knife into his face. I've seen that picture three times.'

'I've seen it four.'

'My God, you're as bad as me, Victoria. Do you see everything?'

'Except the surfing ones.'

'I go all the time. That's how I met Morna, as a matter of fact. It was *The Americanisation of Emily*. A person like an elephant came and sat down in front of me, so I moved my seat and there she was. Someone had finally got Julie Andrews into bed.'

'James Garner.'

'You're right, I'd forgotten. It's what they call a merciful oblivion.'

When Victoria put down the telephone, laughing, Paul raised an eyebrow. Apart from bare facts in the log, you could tell or not tell about telephone conversations. No one would bother you.

'Isn't it nice when people ring up to say they feel better, instead of worse?' she said. 'I wish I knew what to do about Jean – you know, the agoraphobia woman I'm befriending. She's terribly depressed. It just seems that every time she gets up the nerve to go out alone, something happens to panic her, and so she's even more afraid to try it the next time.'

'Is she married – what's the husband like?'

'Oh, he tried, but it's been going on for so long, he gets a bit sick of it, you can't blame him in a way. Their doctor told him it was nerves and she should pull herself together, and so he was against the idea of a psychiatrist from the start. That's perhaps why Jean stopped going. I tried to persuade her on Friday, and said I'd go with her. She's all right when we're together. I thought at first that I was really helping, but now she's afraid of that too, because she thinks she *ought* to be going out by herself. So what do I do now?'

'That does happen,' Paul said. 'People feel guilty about some problems. They ask for help and then when they get it, they begin to feel guilty about needing the help.'

'So should I go on nursing her along or encourage her to try and be tough?'

Samaritan befriending seemed so clear when you were instructed in your training that what was needed of you was simply a caring, accepting friendship. Then when the clients were real people instead of hypothetical examples, it was not so clear. Jean was so sad, so difficult, quick to see the snags and slow to see the joys in anything. Victoria usually felt depressed when she had been with her, hearing Jean's view of life where everything was a threat or a burden. 'She's difficult to help,' she told Paul, 'because she doesn't seem to want to hope.'

'But don't forget,' he said, 'that if she wasn't difficult, she wouldn't need befriending. Why don't you have a word with Peter when he comes in?'

'I hate to bother him all the time.'

'It's not bothering. We can't run this thing with a bunch of amateurs like you and me. There have to be the experts behind us.'

One of them, a youngish man with a Christian name so intolerable that he was known simply as 200, came into the long reception room, where Paul and Victoria were at the desk in the bay window at the back. He held the door for a frail-looking girl, pregnant and down at heel, a huge red-faced child so heavy in her arms that she could hardly walk in her miserable shoes.

'This is Judy,' 200 said. 'Will you look after her for a while? I'm trying some addresses.'

Victoria tried to take the child, but he screamed and clung to his brittle childlike mother, who seemed to have no substance but her pregnancy. 'He won't go to anyone else,' she whispered.

'Sit down then, Judy.'

She sat down with her double burden, and sighed. Victoria went out to get her a cup of tea. When she came back, Paul was talking to a middle-aged man and a boy who both looked furtive. Which one was the client? The man had brought the boy – no, the boy had brought the man, who was just out of prison.

'Your son?'

'No.' The man laughed and pulled at the boy's hair. 'He's what you might call a neighbour. "Here, what do you want, keep bothering me," I tell him. "I'm going to see you don't get back inside," he says. 'What do you think of that?'

The boy giggled and ducked his head to flick back his hair, and the man rumpled it forward again. The pregnant girl watched apathetically, her flat anaemic eyes moving from face to face without interest.

Paul took the man upstairs to talk in private. The boy settled down with a comic. A new young Samaritan called Ronnie came back from buying buns and was sent out again to drive Judy and her child to the address in the country which 200 had found for her.

200 sat down by the desk with Victoria, an oldish young man with a high domed forehead and a slow, thoughtful way of looking at you intently and then suddenly relaxing into a deep, sweet smile. Victoria had known him for a year, because he was at the Centre almost every day, but it was not until she ran into him one evening in a corridor of the hospital's new clinic, that she found out that he was a psychiatric nurse. He knew a lot about the other Samaritans but they did not know much about him, except that he was a strong, refreshing mixture of wisdom and naïveté, experience and discovery.

'How was the weekend?'

'All right. I stayed with Robbie's family.'

'What are they like?'

Victoria shrugged. 'They can't help it, I suppose.'

'As bad as that?'

'They don't bend in the middle, and they go ha ha and rub their hands.'

'Not going to marry him, are you?' 200 asked anxiously.

'I shall if I want to.' Victoria tired of the joke. 'It's too easy to jibe at those sort of people.'

'The whole country's turned on them,' 200 said. 'Backbone of England, they used to say. With fused vertebrae.'

People came in and out. A boy in a tight leather jacket with the sleeves half-way up his arms, who looked as if he was on drugs. A regular called Nancy who had been dropping in several times a week since she had been hauled out of suicidal depression last year. A professor from the University to ask if the Samaritans would help one of his students. 'Only if he will come in, or ring us himself.'

Eric, who was a police sergeant for the rest of the week, was at the emergency telephone in the little study across the hall. Ronnie came back. Peter arrived with a box full of clothes and toys, crashing the front door open with his shoulder. The Samaritans did not hand out money, except to tide over an emergency, but Peter always had jerseys, coats, socks, dolls in the corner of his office. Where did he get all the stuff he gave away? 'He steals it off the hotel guests,' Helen said.

One of his clients, a smart pretty woman in a fur coat was waiting to talk to him. The boy in the leather jacket was waiting for 200, head in hands, feet tapping a bored rhythm. Nancy was in the kitchen washing up. A girl with a white skin and big dark blue eyes fringed with unlikely lashes opened the door and stood childishly for a moment, head down and stomach out, the toes of her white boots turned in. Ronnie, who was still new enough to try not to be responsible for a client, looked round the room, saw that the others were leaving her to him and ambled up, swallowing. 'Can I help you?' He was as nervous as the girl.

'I don't know.' She pulled in her stomach and lifted her small chest in a bright red coat like a military tunic. 'I – well, the trouble is—'

'Won't you sit down?' But they remained standing. 'Well, look, tell me.' Ronnie took the plunge. 'What's the trouble?'

'Oh.' She smiled and shook her head. 'It isn't that. But thank you.'

From the sofa where she was talking to Peter's client, Victoria heard them conversing like a minuet, with the very serious and courteous attention that the young reserved for each other.

'I don't know if it's right, to just come in like this without an appointment.'

'Of course it is.' Ronnie waited. She looked at him as if

he were her confessor, and then got it out. 'How do you become a Samaritan?'

Coincidence number three! ! ! First Sarah's friend at the Play School, Jackie with the awful articulating mother, who stole out of bed to ring up his friend Helen. Then the customer in the shop, talking to Mr Lox about his cousin's wife, 'red as a cherry'. And then – when Brian was on the hated Sunday shift and Sarah wandered like a somnambulist up to the address in Church Grove, reading the names of the seedy old houses behind bulging walls and dilapidated hedges – *then*, the man manœuvring himself out of a small dusty car outside the stone house green with creeper stains was the owner of the Baytree Hotel, who had said to her, 'If I can't get my staff back early, I'll call you.'

Was he in such desperate straits that he sought help? He had not seemed to be. Oh God – her mind flew loyally to Brian – what if this man shot himself in front of the American insurance brokers? Carrying a big grocery box of what looked like clothes, he went through the gateless gateway that had 'St George's Rectory' carved into one stone pillar and a board on the other that said, 'Samaritans. Please come in', along the mossy path and up the two front steps. The door was unlatched. He pushed it open with his shoulder and disappeared inside.

'My name is Paul,' the man said.

'I'm Sarah King.'

'Let's go upstairs, Sarah, where we can talk. We like to find out a bit about you, and tell you a bit about us. Then if your application goes through, and you still want to – that's very important – you can start the preparation classes when the next series begins.'

He was a tall solid man of about her father's age, with lines round his eyes, and hair that he was allowing to go greyer than Sarah's father. Not good looking – she was suspicious of good looking middle-aged men since the shocking realization that her father still thought of himself as about thirty-five – but nice looking. Very *nice* looking. And strong. Friendly. Yes. She saw herself coming in desperately pregnant. Deserted. Riddled with cancer. Shot her mother. Been caught shoplifting in Weinberg's. Yes, she would be able to tell him.

He took her out of the reception room and across the hall into a small room like a study, with tall empty bookcases and a wide desk with a peeling leather top, its missing foot replaced with the 1926 edition of *Who's Who.*

'Eric is on four thousand – the emergency number.'

Eric, in a grey seaman's sweater, was reading the *Sunday Express,* effectively at ease, awaiting a call that might mean life or death. Don't ring now, Sarah told the telephone that sat on the scarred desk like a time-bomb. I'll feel I shouldn't be here. I'll be in the way. I won't know what to do. It will be either right to listen and learn, or wrong to eavesdrop on something that I am too shallow and immature to ever be allowed to make my business.

'Eric, this is Sarah. She hopes to join us.'

Although he looked rather embattled and cynical Eric did not jest, like the man at the youth club when she asked if she could help. 'You must be as big a mug as I am.' He nodded and said, 'Good, Sarah.'

She jumped as the telephone shrilled. '333-4000. The Samaritans. Can I help you?'

What now? Drama? Tension? Crisis? As Paul took her out, she heard Eric say mildly, 'Yes ... yes ... we do if we can. Yes of *course,* tell me about it. It's all right, love. Take it easy. There's plenty of time.'

In the hall, Sarah turned to face Paul. 'How can he sit there and listen so calmly to some disembodied person who's desperate?'

'He's not so calm really. But grateful.'

'You mean because he didn't have enough to do?'

'No. We're pretty busy most of the time. He's grateful that someone gave him the chance to listen to them.'

The stairs at the back of the house, broad and shallow, curved upwards with a beautiful S-shaped line of banister. Below, what used to be the kitchen was now an office with desks and filing cabinets and an archaic sink where someone called Nancy was filling what looked like the first electric kettle ever made. Through the half-open door of a smaller room like a pantry, Sarah saw the man from the Baytree Hotel listening, nodding, 'mm-hm,' the telephone tucked between cheek and shoulder, looking through a folder with one hand, scribbling notes with the other.

'He's the Director of this branch,' Paul said. 'There has to be a boss, for the clients' sake, because mistakes or confusion could mean someone's life. But it's not like most organizations. There's no jealous hierarchy. No scrambling for promotion. No rewards or penalties. There are rules, but we – sort of discipline each other.'

He told her this after they had gone upstairs and into one of the small rooms divided out of the high cold bedrooms. The end where Sarah sat with Paul had the fireplace, a bitter narrow grate which would have held about three lumps of coal. There was an electric fire now, and comfortable broken-down chairs. Ashtrays on the floor, a switch by the door to turn on a red light so that no one would come in. Here you would sit, if you were desperate, and feel secure, at least until you had to go back out into life. Outside the window, an old lady was led by a rumpled dog. They stopped every few yards along the wall for the dog to ruminate clues while the old lady patiently dreamed.

They sat down. Sarah was not afraid. She almost wished she could be, to give the episode more drama. For two days, since she had heard about the Samaritans, she had felt within herself a surging tide of excitement. Coming here today she had been afraid, and almost turned back. If they said she had nothing to offer, if they turned her away, then the tide would go out and the excitement die like yellowing sea foam.

This man was quiet and easy. He watched her, but without judgement. He asked her to tell him why she wanted to be a Samaritan, and then he listened carefully while she tried to answer. The fear was gone. The excitement remained. Should she be more relaxed? She sat at the edge of the chair with her bony knees together and her toes on the floor, clasping her long hands, tensely making faces to try and produce the words to explain a desire that was more instinctive than reasoned.

'I knew, you see,' she said. 'I just knew it was something I must do. I never felt so sure of anything in my life. Do you think that's too impetuous? I was afraid I would be thought too young, but that boy I talked to downstairs – he's younger.'

Paul looked at her for a while, leaning back and swinging a foot. 'I've got a daughter about your age,' he said. 'How old are you, Sarah?'

'Twenty-two.'

'Laura is not quite twenty, but she looks older than you.'

'Oh dear.' Sarah laughed. 'I do work on my face. Is it a failure?'

'It's a great success, as far as I can see. I like you, Sarah.'

'I like you too,' she said eagerly. 'I like people you can talk to in a real way right from the start, without having to skirmish round with small talk, like dogs. Sometimes I talk too much, because I don't know what to say. I suppose here it's mostly listening, isn't it?'

Paul nodded. 'Listening to people telling you things that no one else will bother to listen to.'

'Do you think they would take me? I talk too much. I don't really *know* anything. My father thinks I'm practically illiterate – he's a professor at the Law School. I started at a College of Design in London, but then I met Brian and we got married. My typing is pathetic. I don't even cook very well. I have this stupid sort of job part-time, selling in a shop. I can't really do anything useful.'

'But being a Samaritan doesn't depend on what you know or what you can do. It's what you are. Look Sarah, if you join us, what will be asked of you will be to go on being yourself.'

Sarah sighed. 'I want to so much. I've known for ages that there was something I ought to be doing. That's why

I tried the Youth Club, but they only wanted men who were tough enough to stop the place being broken up. That's why I went to the Play School, where I met the boy who rings up here at night.'

'To compensate for something that's missing in your life?' Paul asked suddenly.

Did he think that? 'Oh no. I don't think so. I think it's to add to what I already have.'

'But if you do become a Samaritan,' he said, 'it won't all be rewarding. It can be frustrating too. You make mistakes with people. You can't get anywhere with them. Your friendship isn't enough. It can be depressing. I've been a Samaritan almost two years, but I constantly feel I've no right to be here. Then something good happens, and you – for instance, I'd been trying to get through to a very unhappy boy who had made a suicide attempt.' He began to tell her something of the story. Sarah leaned forward, her eyes on his face. 'He shied away from me like a deer. I was afraid to make a move to help him. He had asked for our help because he was afraid of what he'd done. Then afterwards he couldn't accept it. He wouldn't talk to me or anyone. He's so withdrawn, some terribly deep underlying unhappiness, but he wanted no part of me. And then yesterday at the hospital, just when I was thinking I might have to give up since I was getting nowhere, he put out a hand and tweaked my coat and said, "Please come back." '

'Oh – how marvellous!'

They smiled at each other.

'Yes, it was. It was marvellous. You see that. Good.'

Paul got up. 'Come down to the office and you can fill out an application form.'

'Does that mean you'll take me?'

'For the preparation classes, yes, I think so. It's not my decision, but I think so.'

He had not said: What use are you to us? He had not asked her: What do you know about the world or life or people and the terrible things that make them want to kill themselves?

Ronnie came into the hall as she was putting on her coat. 'How did it go?'

'All right, I think.' It was only with people of another generation that you had to underestimate.

'I'll see you again then.'

'I hope so.'

She had said the right thing about the boy in the hospital who seemed to mean so much to Paul. He had said, 'You see that. Good.' And Sarah swaggered out into the cold wet Sunday afternoon as if he had pinned a medal on to her red coat.

THREE

ONCE HE GOT used to it – and having lived for twelve years in the House of God's Angels, it seemed almost familiar – Tim quite enjoyed the hospital. There were always things going on and other people doing them. He could watch without having to take part. He occupied one whole day rehearsing how he could ask one of the nurses (not the Sister, no fear) if he could sit out of bed and watch the television. At first he had thought he would get the fat man in the next bed to ask for him. The man kept staring at him and saying things like, 'Lost your voice?' and, 'Cat got your tongue?' and, 'Give us a hallo then, come on,' as if he were a trick dog. Tim made up his mind to whisper across the polished floor between them, 'Please ask the nurse if I can get up.'

But as soon as the breakfast trays were gone, they had come and routed the fat man out of bed and into his clothes and sent him away with a pickled old lady who did not look as if she were glad to have him back. So Tim spent the rest of the day rehearsing. Several times the words were up in the place where his throat met his mouth, ready to be said, but the nurse had moved by him before he could get them out. After tea, the black one who was called Henriette and was always laughing came up to his bed with a big white grin as if Tim were the greatest joke in the ward. Before he could gabble 'Can I get up?' she said, 'Come on, lazybones, you'd better get up before you lose the use of your legs,' shook out a long giant's dressing-gown and had him up and into a chair among the old men before he could say, 'I don't want to.'

Paul came in later and talked to him while he was

trying to watch the television. After a bit he said, 'Take off those headphones, Tim. I want to tell you something.' Tim took off the headphones, though his eyes kept wandering up to the screen of their own accord. 'I've talked to your doctor,' Paul said. 'The one you saw yesterday.'

Tim nodded. The doctor had asked a lot of questions and had gone away unperturbed that most of them had not been answered.

'The thing is this,' Paul leaned forward with his arms on his knees and looked at Tim as if he really cared about him. 'He thinks you should have a bit more help. Not the wrist. That's all right, though you'll have to keep the cast on for a while. I mean some kind of psychiatric help. You've got problems – well, who hasn't? – but yours are perhaps harder for you to cope with than most people's. Would you like to go somewhere where they can give you the kind of help you need?'

'Leave here?' Tim's eyes forgot the demented figures on the screen, mouthing silently and flailing their arms. Just when he'd got safely settled in? He had only allowed himself to think once or twice about Darley Road and the woman at the Employment Office. 'I'd rather stay.'

'There is a clinic attached to this hospital, but you don't need that kind of intensive treatment. He thinks you would benefit from being in a place where you could make friends, do some jobs in the workshop, sort of get you going again among other people. From what you've told me, you were pretty lonely before. It can't have been much fun.'

'What place do you mean?'

At the little stinking zoo down by the estuary, Tim had seen a sort of small wild dog who had lain pressed against a wall, its yellow eyes travelling round the confines of its prison. He had recognized immediately in that dog, himself. Now at the familiar feeling of being trapped, he shrank against the confines of the wicker chair, although his body did not move.

'Highfield,' Paul said. 'You may have heard of it. It's about ten miles out in the country, a rambling old-fashioned place, they're always talking about rebuilding it, but they never do. There's a farm there and a nursery garden. You could do the same kind of work you've done before.'

'A nut house, eh?' They didn't fool Tim. 'I'm not mad.'

'No. The rest of the world may be. That's why it's difficult to live in. You don't have to go to Highfield anyway. It's your choice.'

He sounded casual. 'You don't want to bother with me no more.' Tim scowled, but Paul smiled as if he had given him a compliment.

'I'll go on bothering with you whatever you do, if you'll let me. We can work something out.'

A job, Paul was saying. Decent lodgings ... 'I want to stay here!' Panic spun into Tim.

'They need your bed.'

'I'll go to the other place.'

'Highfield? All right. I'd still be able to see you. I could drive you out there, if you like, if you really decide to go.'

'OK.' A girl in a sparkly dress as long as a shirt was singing on the screen, cuddling the microphone as if it was a man. Tim's hand reached out for the earphones.

'Is there anyone you'd like me to get in touch with?' Paul stood up. 'Someone who should know where you're going? You didn't – I mean, your mother's still alive, isn't she?'

Tim put on the earphones and began to tap his foot to the beat of the song. Paul laid his big hand on the back of Tim's good hand, pressed it and went away. The warmth of his firm grip stayed on Tim's hand, while the girl sang. 'Take take take, I said-a take take take.'

Paul drove Tim out to Highfield the next Sunday. The boy sat in the car with his cast supported in a sling, looking very pale, his hair, which had been washed before he left the hospital, sticking up from a small boy's cowlick at the back of his head. He affected to be intensely interested in the scenery, turning for a longer look at cows, churches, war memorials, so that he would not have to talk. It was going to take a long time to discover him. Perhaps no one ever would. 'Stick with him,' Peter had said. 'I think you should go on befriending him, since he seems to want it.'

After Tim was installed at Highfield, where a quietly smiling woman in a blue overall had shown him his bed and where to put his things, and a friendly man in the day room had immediately approached with a cigarette, Paul said, 'Shall I come out one evening this week?'

Tim nodded. He sat very stiff and awkward by the wall, like a shy stag at a village dance. All of a sudden, just as Paul was turning to go, he began to talk very fast, gabbling and partly incoherent. Paul found himself crouching down in front of him to shield him from the others, for the boy was beginning to cry.

'Don't leave me leave me because I done it to myself. I didn't mean to. I wanted to be good it was no good no good there's no one.'

'There's me.' Paul gave him a handkerchief and the boy passed it over his face and neck as if he were drying himself after a bath. He sucked up a shuddery liquid sniff, then looked at Paul and shook his head in a melancholy way.

How on earth to leave him?

'Come on now, Tim old chap, let's see that cast.' The male nurse in charge of the ward came up, loose face like a gun dog, clean freckled hands that picked up Tim's arm with impersonal care. The chubby man in the other hospital had written 'Goodbye old pal' on the plaster before his mother took him away. The nurse murmured to Paul, 'Better go now.'

In the corridor, where the doors of narrow bedrooms were open, thank God, with the old boltholes puttied over and the spy windows boarded up, Paul was heavy with guilt. Selfishly, for it would do the boy no good, he wanted to rush back into the day room and grab Tim by the good arm and say, 'Come on, I won't leave you.'

And take him back to Alice?

And take him away, away somewhere to a hill village in the sun where he could sit all day in the dusty square and be the village simpleton if that was what he wanted, going to the back door of the bakery when he was hungry, gathering flowers for the processions.

In the car, thinking of Tim beleaguered there among the terrifying assortment of faces and voices and feet shuffling on the swabbed linoleum, Paul realized that he was reliving his feelings of years ago when he had left Jeff at his first boarding-school.

'Better go now, Mr Hammond.' The kindly master, nodding with his chin pushed up into his smile, as if he had seen it all. 'Parents don't believe it, but they're always better after you're gone.'

As a schoolmaster, Paul had known that was true, but now he was discovering the parent's angle. The pain of abandoning a boy no bigger than a child – pushing him off or giving him his best chance – mixed with jealous resentment against whoever was taking over.

At Singleton Court: 'I'm getting a bit sick of the bloody Samaritans,' Alice yelled, loud enough to make herself cough.

'That's nothing new.' Paul came down the narrow hall painted in someone else's colour choice, smelling faintly of bacon fat, hung with Archway House group pictures. Paul in the middle with his dog, Jeff with a cricket team, almost obliterated by huge white pads, a gap in the wall where Alice had thrown a pie-dish (with pie in it) at the school picture with the headmaster's wife in a dirndl and flowered braces. 'You've been sick of them ever since I joined.'

'Joined. Went in there one night half sloshed and got hooked by an evangelist. Where have you been? I can't get my zip done up.'

Alice was sitting before the mirror with her dress falling off her bony shoulders, a large gin keeping company with the pots and crusted bottles on her dressing-table.

Well, all right, who didn't need a drink before they went out to dinner? Paul made one for himself, although he had heard that the inevitable drink while dressing was one of the signs of potential alcoholism.

The dinner-party was at the house of a couple Paul had met through the school, a mixed group of people, mostly familiar, not University, but in some capacity close enough to its fringes to talk as if they were.

The host brought Paul a whisky and something for Alice that looked like ginger ale.

It was. 'Take it away, John.'

'I thought you—' He had been pleased at the nicety of his tact.

'Stupid, I've been through with A.A. for ages. Liberated. Cured. Stop being so delicate.'

John's wife had started to drink before she finished cooking, so there was a long wait during which the guests drank enough to lose interest in whether she ever got the meal on to the table. Paul was worried about Alice, although she appeared to be holding her head above the gin. She had amazing powers of maintaining a coherent dam, but it could suddenly, disastrously, be breached. He sat on the other side of the room and drank slowly, feeling himself rather stiff and stuffy, bored with the endless argument about the last student riot, the ill-formed opinions salivated through beards, the puny, acquired radicalism.

Griselda, the wife of one of the wet-lipped beards came to sit on the floor by the fire. She sat near Paul's feet, her bare brown back exuding health and a permanent animal need to be caressed. 'Don't you get sick of it?' she asked, knowing that he was. 'I try to make Henry see that the students wouldn't want him on their side anyway, but it gives him the illusion of youth. So.'

'Jeff says that what sickens him most about what he calls Older People is that having forced the young to create their own society, we haven't even the grace to stay out of it.'

'What do you know about what Jeff thinks?' Alice

116

who had been quiet for a while, suddenly called quite loudly from across the room. 'He puts on an act for you.'

'I don't think so.'

'He pretends to be whatever you want him to be. Don't listen to him anybody. He doesn't know what he's talking about.'

When she reached this stage – and the next would follow if that idiot Sybil did not soon bring on some food – Paul could either tell her to shut up, which would make two of them shouting, or take her home, or pretend it was not happening. He turned his back slightly and leaned forward to push the end of a log back into the fire. Griselda had moved nearer to his legs when Alice attacked him. As he leaned forward, she leaned back, her long too-girlish swatch of someone else's glossy hair falling on his thigh.

At dinner, it started again. Alice brought her gin glass to the table, and when it was empty, asked John to refill it.

'Aren't you going to try my wine?' But they were all slightly afraid of Alice, afraid of what she might do or say, but without the guts to help her not to. John took the glass back to the drink trolley and refilled it.

The dam was still holding. Although she ate very little, Alice laughed and talked and appeared to be managing quite well on her side of the table, but when Paul made some comment about a new book, her voice rasped through the conversation as if she had been waiting for this chance.

'Listen to him.' She rocked back a little in her chair. 'He hasn't even read it.'

What could he do? Bark across the table, 'I have'? (He hadn't.) Throw wine in her blurred face? Ignore her?

'Don't you recognize the review he's quoting?' Alice was no fool, even when she was drunk. 'Not an original thought in his head, pontificating on while those poor deprived children have to sit for hours masturbating under the desks.'

'Alice, please,' Sybil said mildly as she got up to clear plates.

'Yes, Alice please. Leave poor Paul alone. Poor badly used Paul – why do you think he doesn't say anything? Because it suits him to get all the women on his side.'

'Oh come on, Alice,' Griselda said. 'That's not fair.'

'No, it's not, my dear. It's not fair at all for you to sit rubbing yourself against my husband like a little pussy-cat in heat while he sits there with that noble suffering profile.'

'Come on.' Paul got up. 'We're going home.'

'I don't care.'

Paul took her out. 'Sorry, John.'

'Sorry my wife got drunk again.' Alice could hear anything, even when she appeared to be in the unaware asterisms of booze. In the car, hunched into her last year's coat with the fur collar matted from sponging, she said almost soberly, 'It is true, you know. You play for the women's sympathy. Poor Paul. Horrid Alice. That's why you don't hit back, isn't it? Isn't it?' She leaned her head in front of his to peer at him.

'For God's sake.' He pushed her back and swerved round the island that appeared just ahead. 'Do you want to get us killed?'

'Yes.' She huddled in her coat like a bedraggled tropical monkey exposed to the English climate.

At lunch hour on Monday, Paul went to the open hooded booth outside the staff room and telephoned Unitech Electronics. He could not get the right extension. The girl at the switchboard was as unhelpful as if she were deliberately trying to make it difficult. Eventually he was through to Mr Upjohn's secretary. What if she had told Upjohn? Let her.

'Oh yes, thank you. That, er – that lady—' His mind was sponged out like a blackboard. 'She cooks – serves the lunches. For the directors. Could I speak to her if she's there?'

'Mrs Frost?'

'Yes. Mrs Frost.'

'Just one moment.' Paul collected himself to speak, for the secretary's voice sounded as if it would add, 'I'll put you through,' but it added, 'I'm sorry, she's not here at the moment. She's on holiday.'

'Could you please give me her number at home?'

'Who is calling, please?'

'Mr Hammond.'

'How are you spelling that?'

Good God, suppose I was called Strzemsky? 'H-A-double M-'

'Hammond, yes,' said the secretary, as if it were her idea. 'I haven't got Mrs Frost's number listed. I'm sorry.'

Paul went down to the lunch-room. It was his week to take a table.

'Did you have a nice weekend, Mr Hammond?'

'Thank you, Amanda, very nice. Did you?'

If Mrs Frost had been at Unitech, if she had been less prudent than she looked and had agreed to meet him – tea, drinks, dinner, anything – would it have ended up with Paul milking her for sympathy?

It was true. With Alice always wrong and Paul in the right – admit it, Paul, you hypocrite, you like it that way. You want to seem a martyred hero to Griselda, to Sybil, to that silly little woman in the celery earrings. You like that. Yes. You hear them say, after you've made your triumphal exit. 'Poor Paul, he's so patient and good.'

'And then, you see, there was this man,' Amanda said, through what Butterfields Comprehensive called fried plaice. 'No, not the one in the helicopter, the one they thought was the spy . . .'

Samaritan? You Pharisee.

'Is that the Samaritans?'

'Yes. Can I help you?'

'I want to speak to Victoria.' Careful, Billie. Neaten up your vowels.

119

'I'm sorry, she's not here at the moment. Could I—'

'This is Thursday, isn't it?'

'Yes, but – that's right, she was here a couple of Thursdays ago.'

'Why not now? She been fired?'

A laugh. 'Not yet. This isn't her regular duty.'

'Oh shit.' Billie surged into a sweat of anger. What was the good of Victoria if she wasn't there when she was needed? 'Give me her number at home then.'

'Sorry, I can't do that. If you give me your name and phone number, I'll get hold of her in the morning and ask her to ring you.'

'Do it now.'

'It's awfully late.'

'I want her now.'

'Who is it?'

'It's Billie.'

'Oh yes, I know.'

'What do you know?'

'I was here when you talked to Victoria. My name's Helen.'

'What did she tell you?'

'Nothing much.'

'She been discussing my business all over the do-gooders?'

'She doesn't do that. None of us do. What's the matter, Billie? You sound upset.'

'Upset – ha!' Billie barked like a seal. 'I'm pissed, if you want to know.'

'How about talking to her tomorrow when you're sober?'

'Afraid she'll be shocked? Listen Helen, you can't shock that old girl. I've fucking tried.'

'You can't shock me either.'

'I wouldn't waste my breath trying...'

While she waited, Billie ambled into the cupboard that called itself a kitchen and refilled her smeary glass. Thing roosted on the tiny stove like a hedgehog, all paws concealed. Billie trod in the bowl of fish. She rubbed her bare foot against the flabby white calf of the other leg – veins, a crime at your age – and went back into the bedroom. She sat on the side of the bed and observed herself in the mirror which hung over the tilting chest of drawers. One of the nails was pulling loose from the plaster of this hovel and the mirror hung slightly crooked, so that you had to tip your head to make your reflection fit. Billie raised her glass to herself without enthusiasm. She always looked the same, except when Morna had just cut her hair, so why bother with the mirror?

Morna put all sorts of stuff on her face. It took her hours in the morning. She was always late for work, and they had missed the beginning of *Bonnie and Clyde* – Billie would never forgive her for that – because at the last moment she had stripped a whole new face off and started it again.

Billie occasionally coated her short stiff lashes with some black stuff in a box she spat into, but mostly she rubbed a flannel over her rugged features as if she were polishing an apple, banged at her head with a brush and pulled on clothes as she was wandering about the two small rooms trying to find things, trying to remember what she was trying to find.

So that proved it. Ring me any time, Billie. But I'll not bother to ring you.

The telephone sat on the locker by the bed, some of the holes on its dial full of grey dough from the scones Billie had made for Morna, since the girl was half starved for want of nourishing starch. Billie's mother was always baking. Baking, baking, that's all she did. Constantly at the oven with that broad bo-hind sticking out. It was a wonder Dad didn't take a running kick at it.

When Victoria rang . . . but she wouldn't. That Nellie, Helen, whatever her name was – 'Can I help you?' but underneath, her voice was more Billie's kind and could probably give as good as it got – she wouldn't wake Victoria for someone like Billie. And if she did, Victoria would say. 'Oh her. She isn't going to kill herself.' She hadn't believed it about the aspirin. 'I'll ring in the morning.'

The phone would ring and ring, the bell shrilling out over the lifeless corpse. *Too late. Too late.* The police would have to break down the door with an axe and Mrs Groot and Olive Peace would stare from the corridor, their children peering round their legs and sucking their filthy thumbs.

Then you'll be sorry.

Billie opened the locker drawer. Christ, there weren't more than half a dozen aspirin in the bottle Morna had given her. Never had been. Old Morn ate them like sweets, but Billie had always been scared of drugs.

The telephone rang. As Billie snatched it to her ear, she noticed that her hand was trembling, the palm hot and sticky.

'Is that Billie?'

Suffer.

'Billie – are you there?'

Billie almost put down the telephone. Now that she heard Victoria's voice, it did not seem so important any more, what she wanted to tell her.

'I can hear you breathing,' Victoria said, either crossly or anxiously. 'What's the matter?'

'Hullo,' Billie said gloomily. 'I suppose you're angry because I made them wake you up.'

'No, I'm not, really.'

'You said ring any time I felt rotten. Well, I feel rotten now.'

'Oh dear, why?'

'Well look, it's that bloody Fettiche. My boss, I told you. I'm going off this afternoon, gone four, very late as it was, and don't think there's any talk of overtime when it takes so long to clear up after those tramps. "Back at six, Camilla Cripps," he says, "don't forget." "What do you mean?" "You know as well as I do it's Committee night," he says. "I don't." "You do." "If I do, I don't want to." Back at six to do the sandwiches and coffee. What do they think I am? Are you there? Victoria? What do they think I am?'

'I don't know. Is that what you wanted to ask me?'

'Don't be sharp, dear. You know it's Thursday. Morna's half day. She goes to the shops and as soon as I'm off, I go round to her place and get the supper started. She's not much at cooking, see, it's our regular thing. And we go to the Odeon, whatever's on, because that was where we met.'

'What is on?'

'Victoria, you're not listening. That's not the *point*. The point is I had to go to work. On a Thursday. And you ask me why I feel rotten. We were going to a party last night, me and Morna. Some of her friends from last summer. She said she'd go anyway.'

'Mm-hm.'

'Oh, it's not that I don't *trust* her, don't think that.' Billie went on for a while, watching herself in the mirror, lips squirming in the ugly way lips did when you looked at them on their own, not as part of a face. Victoria murmured, and once she yawned. 'You're not interested, are you?' Billie said. 'You don't care.'

'Yes I do, really.'

'Fat help to me.'

'Well God, Billie.' Victoria's voice woke up. 'What do you want me to do?'

'Sorry, sorry.' It was always enough to have goaded her to answer back, as a real friend would. 'It's just that I can't sleep, and when I do, the dreams I have, you wouldn't believe. Tonight I dreamed there was an old man begging in the street. He hadn't got any legs, just a sort of tray on wheels and he pushed himself along with his arms like a monkey. Well, you know what that means, it means someone is telling lies about you. So I got up and got a drink and here I am.'

'Worried about Morna?'

'No, I *trust* her, I told you. But she's got a lot of friends, you know, and – I don't know – the girls where I work, they're either married and dumb, first baby coming, or old grans with knitting patterns falling out of their bags, you know the type. And the people in these flats, dear, you wouldn't credit. I'm going to have to look for another place. Morna and I are talking of sharing, if we can find what we want. You seen *Faces*? Where they keep walking down those passages with the walls coming at them, that's the sort of flat we could have. Where she chucks up in the shower. I cried for her.'

'So did I. Let's go to the cinema some time, Billie, you and me. Shall we? It would be nice to meet.'

Billie stared at the tilted mirror, and the Billie that Victoria would meet stared glumly back.

No fear.

'*Dear Mrs King, ... should like you to attend the first preparation class at the Samaritan Centre at 6.30 ...*' *The date had hung before Sarah like a prize, foreshortening the days between.*

'Where are you going, my Sarah?'

'I told you. It's the first preparation class.'

'Is that why you're wearing a gym tunic?'

'It's called a jerkin. Can I have the car?'

'Yes, darling.' Brian clutched her. 'Don't go.'

'That's not fair. Wait till I get home.'

'What makes you think I'll still want you?'

'You'd better.'

They talked like this about sex. It wasn't very real. But it was better than people who never talked about it at all, just did it.

The class was held in the big downstairs room at the Samaritan Centre. Clients who came in that evening had to go upstairs, When Sarah went in, the wide hall was full of people in coats, all ages and types, looking confused. You could not tell if they had come for the class or to get help. Two girls were taking chairs into the big room, and presently everyone was in there, about a dozen people facing the desk at the back, where a youngish man with receding hair was looking carefully over the group as if it were a cattle auction.

'Is it a meeting?' whispered a young man who had come in with the others from the hall and sat down next to Sarah.

'It's a class for volunteers. Are you one?'

'Well, actually.' The young man desperately tried to find one tiny piece more nail to bite. 'I'm supposed to be seeing someone called Ralph. I talked to him on the phone yesterday. Ralph, 255, he said.'

'We could ask him.' Sarah nodded to the man behind the desk, who was waiting while people scraped chairs and took off coats and lit cigarettes and were extraordinarily polite to each other, like examination candidates not knowing yet who would pass and who fail.

'I am one of the deputy directors of this branch of the Samaritans.' The man at the desk stood up. 'You can call me 200. We use Christian names and numbers, see, but with a name like mine, I just use a number.'

Sycophantic laughter from a perpetually smiling lady with her head on one side. If she thought that would get her into the Samaritans . . .

The young man looked anguished, so Sarah stood up and explained.

'Ralph? Oh yes, he's upstairs.'

'Shall I take him? I know the way.'

'Thanks. That would be fine.'

Sarah took the young man out, and handed him over to a Samaritan at the top of the stairs. Sarah King? Oh yes, that's the girl who was helpful her very first day. Good sign that.

She went quietly back into the room. 200 had started to talk, head back, reading the ceiling for words. He did not notice her come in.

'If you want statistics,' he said, 'you can look them up. I can't be bothered with them. They don't make pictures for me, and I don't suppose they do for you either.' He brought his eyes down and set them on a restless woman in a sleek fur jacket like a labrador, without apparently seeing her. 'People kill themselves. For some reason – well, for obvious reasons, I suppose, seeing what a mul-

125

lock we've made of the world – suicide is increasing. A thousand a day, they reckon. And about eight thousand try it.'

The lady with her smiling head on one side shook it gently to show she cared.

'And that's an underestimate, because it often gets hushed up and reported as something else. Heart attack. Cleaning his gun. Took the wrong medicine bottle. Coroners are human too.' He had a slow simple way of talking, the easy unhurried accent of a countryman, the consonants soft, no pinched city sharpness in the vowels.

'In a big mixed-up town like this one where you get all kinds of people doing all kinds of things in all kinds of conditions, there are all kinds of reasons why some of them come to the end of their tether. We rank about fifth or sixth in Great Britain in that department. All right.' When he smiled, his long thoughtful face shifted into engaging new angles. 'I said I wouldn't bother with statistics. I won't. Give you just one more though, in case you want to know how the Samaritans got started. About twenty years ago, the man who founded it, the Reverend Chad Varah, heard that there were at least three suicides a day in London. Ought to do something about that, he thought, and he hit on the idea of an emergency telephone service for the desperate, like you can dial 999 if your house is on fire or you trip over the cat and break a leg. It had to be that sort of easy number that people could remember. Something like 9000. Mansion House 9000, since he was going to run it from his church, St Stephen's Walbrook, in the City. It had been damaged in the Blitz. Under the rubble somewhere was a telephone. When the rector dug it out and wiped off the dust, it already had the number he wanted, Mansion House 9000. Yes.' He nodded to the murmur that came from his audience of about a dozen men and women, the youngest Sarah and the two girls with waterfall hair from the University, the oldest a bald grandfatherly man in a tweed suit like market day. 'It was a miracle, you could say. That's how it started. There are more than a hundred branches in this country now. This is one of the biggest. And the best, of course,' he added, meaning it, not smiling.

'Number 100, Peter, he's the Director of this branch. You'll meet him next week. He and Ralph, 255, and myself, 200, we act as counsellors, with consultants, psychiatrists, doctors, lawyers, social workers behind us. But the main thing of the Samaritans is – the Samaritans. People like you. Ordinary people. That's where the need is. Ordinary people who know about love and tolerance and friendship. It's the reaching out of one human being to another. A sharing of – well, love is what it is if you want it in one word.'

He watched the faces of his audience. They watched him. The lopsided lady had relaxed her smile. The restless young woman with the black fur jacket and short black hair was still, her foot not swinging, her hands clasped round her knee.

'No problem,' he went on, 'can be solved completely. But if there is love, you see, each problem can be tackled and dealt with, perhaps in some ramshackle way that's better than nothing. Better than going under. We can't run people's lives for them. But we can try to put them in the way of doing it a bit better themselves. We try to give them back themselves. By being here. By paying attention. By listening. Those of you who get accepted as Samaritans' – his eyes moved from one to the other as if he had decided already: you, not you, perhaps you? – 'you will learn that there's only one thing you have to learn. All the rest follows. You listen, that's all. All you have to learn, my dears, is just to listen.'

The 'my dears' was not affected nor irritatingly folksy. It was natural and comfortable. How could Sarah ever explain this man to Brian? Should she even begin to try?

How can I make it sound like this? If I can't, he won't understand. He might even – yes, if he's wanting to be funny and cynical, he might even ... scoff.

The stab of guilt with which she thought that of him

was almost as if she had wished him dead.

'Any questions at this point?' 200 rubbed his eyes, pinching them at the corners and stretching his face as if he had just taken off glasses.

The labrador girl lit a cigarette and blew a stream of smoke at him from her determined underlip. 'What do we do? I mean, what are the duties? It's all so vague.'

'I know. Sorry, Meredith, I'm a lousy lecturer. The thing is, it's hard to explain it, but it all gets quite clear when you start to work here.'

'*If* we start,' one of the college girls put in, without looking up from her knitting, a brown mass of something like a muffler which even her lover surely would never wear. 'How do you pick who you pick?'

'We just sort of – know.' He spread his hands. 'Some people are natural Samaritans. It sticks out a mile. These classes are not only for instruction. They help us to find out about you.'

Some of the people tried to make their faces look kind.

'There'll be a test at the end, a faked distress call to see how you answer. But don't panic. Even if you mess that up, you'll get taken, if you're the right kind.'

'But what do we *do*?' Meredith asked again.

'Easiest thing is to explain what you *don't* do. With clients, either on the phone or when they come in here – let's see.' He ticked off his fingers. 'You don't judge. You don't get shocked. You don't talk about yourself: "Oh yes, my aunt died of that last February." You don't sit round and gossip with other volunteers. It's hard enough for someone in trouble to come through that door. If he finds a jolly group of people coffee-housing in here, he may go out and never be seen again. What else? You don't probe. You try to find out what you can about a client, but not third degree. Name, address, black, white, co-habiting, have you been vaccinated. If he wanted that, he'd go to a government agency. He doesn't want it. That's why he comes to us. You don't preach. You don't criticize. If he says, "I just raped my stepsister," you don't say, "Oh how dreadful, you shouldn't have done that." '

'What *do* you say?' From a man at the back of the room.

'Nothing really.' 200 sent him an innocent smile. 'You go mm-hm, or, "Tell me about it," or something. Show him that you'll listen if he wants to talk about it. He probably does. That's why he's here. Because he can't tell anyone else. And when it's told, you don't give instant advice. You don't say, "If I were you, I'd do so and so." He's not you. If he were, he wouldn't be in his particular kind of trouble.'

Meredith ground out her cigarette into the coffee-jar lid she was using as an ashtray. 'You've told us a lot about what we don't do,' she said aggressively. 'But you still haven't said what we do.'

'You listen.' 200 remained unprovoked. 'You listen and you try to—'

'Anyone can listen.'

'They can't. You're not listening to me now.'

'I am, but it's all so negative.'

She was heating herself up like an automatic kettle. Perhaps it was the only kind of conversation she ever had.

'They won't take *her*,' Sarah said to the man next to her, under cover of general questions and answers, punctuated by some semantic quibbling from the girl.

'You never know.' He had sideburns that would have been a beard if they had met in the middle of his chin. 'Sometimes that sort turns out to be a better Samaritan than some of them who just sit and soak it all in like sphagnum moss.'

'How do you know?'

'I'm doing this class as a refresher. I am a Samaritan, David, 520.'

'Oh – you lucky.'

'Yes. I don't know why they took me.'

Hullo, is that the Samaritans? Sarah saw herself in her little room at home, leaning over the back of the sofa to clutch the telephone. Yes, this is David, 520. And he would listen quietly while she babbled, I'm a failure, a wretched rotten failure. I'm a cheat and a liar and I don't

know what love is and I don't know how to find out ...
Horrified, she clamped down the lid on the dark secret
snakes that could never be let out. Never given freedom,
even in her own thoughts.

Unable to make a dent in 200's composure or logic,
Meredith buttoned her labrador jacket and left to catch a
bus. When the class was finished, Sarah and the knitting
girl made coffee for everybody, and David, 520, drove her
down to the Front Royal, since Brian was there for most
of the night.

The American insurance men were on the last lap of
their convention. They had had their lunches and their
conferences and their film presentations and their
speeches and their awards and their golf. The hardier
had trotted down the pebbled beach to the grey sea,
gorilla-legged, throwing punches at the air. The joggers
had jogged in their thirty dollar jogging shoes up and
down the Esplanade under the uncommitted gaze of the
old men sent out to sit in the shelters 'and don't come
home till lunch', who were more accustomed to the heel-
and-toe regulars in creased cotton shorts and black gym
shoes with galvanic Adam's apples and corks in their
fists.

The wives of those who could or would bring them
across the Atlantic had shopped for antiques and seen
castles and had their hair done every day, for you could
not step out of the Front Royal in December without
being set upon by the wild wet demons that funnelled
through the portico between the hotel garden and the
veranda where the residents measured status by how long
their jigsaw puzzles monopolized the card tables.

On this last night there had been a banquet, with
speeches and dancing. Most of the permanent residents
had gone to bed like huffed turtles. Some of the Americans who had neither a wife nor one of the leggy casual
girls who had been driving cars and handing round
drinks all week were in the hotel bar. It had been en-
larged and newly landscaped, but was now so dark that
you could not see the expensive knots in the panelling,

the graining of the padded plastic leather that edged the bar like a safety dashboard. Sarah found Brian in there with a group of men. Anyone personable in Reception or Management was constrained to socialize at conventions.

'Come and meet my husband,' she had said, getting out of David's loose-jointed car whose back seat was full of tools and coils of wire. 'Come in and have a drink.' And been sorry to feel relieved when he declined. Brian only liked people in cheap shapeless clothes if he had discovered them first. When he stood up, fair and smiling in his dinner jacket and white Italian polo neck, to signal to her across the dim smoky bar, she could imagine how his brow would have come down – Who the hell? – if David had been beside her in the doorway with his thick spattered spectacles and his green jacket that bagged like a smock.

'How was it?' Brian kissed her on the mouth.

'Marvellous.'

She said, tell you later, with her eyes, was introduced to the people at the big round table, and sat down next to a man who held on to his glass and drank sombrely with the corners of his mouth down, as if it was physic.

He was staying at the Baytree Hotel. When Brian was called away by an urgent porter, muttering and jerking his head forebodingly, the American said, 'No offence to your nice husband, but it's made the convention for me, staying in that little place. There's been only half a dozen of us there, and the Wallaces – well, they have this knack of letting you alone, but being around if you want them. I'm coming back. I'm going to come back this summer. Got my room all set. Up under the roof with a dormer you can sit in and look at the ocean far off without seeing the beach or any of these mausoleums.'

'Are you going to bring your wife?' Sarah instantly regretted her random shot, but he nodded into his glass and said, 'Yeah, yeah, I'm going to bring Anne. No kids. Just us.'

'Have you got pictures?' Sarah was not a hotelier's wife

for nothing. He brought out his wallet in the dark and showed her laminated snapshots of which she could see not much more than the teeth.

'Yes, sir.' He shook his head at the picture of the woman. 'I've got to show Anne the Baytree. You know something, Sarah? You want to know something about my wife?' He tapped the picture. He was fairly drunk, with a not very likeable smell somewhere about him, either his skin or his clothes, but Sarah bent forward to listen, imagining herself a Samaritan, accepting, listening without judgement. 'My wife is a very strange woman...'

One of the bar waiters had come up in his red monkey jacket and striped waistcoat. Drinks were ordered. The people got up to leave. Someone across the table began to talk to Sarah. She did not immediately get the chance to turn back to the man and ask, 'What were you going to tell me about your wife?' When she did, his wallet was put away and himself with it. She said, 'I'm sorry, what were you going to say?' but he shook his head without looking at her, as if he did not remember or care.

When Brian came back, she had to leave at once because one of his All Hells had broken loose and he would have to come in early tomorrow to start straightening out the bloody mess. He said that to the Americans at the table, who smiled politely, because he was a nice young Britisher, childishly flushed with petulance, although they knew as well as Sarah that he should keep quiet.

He fumed in the car, telling her about the Assistant Manager and the politician's party in room 119. His profile sped young and beautiful past the Esplanade hotels, the balconied flats, the dark cut hedges of the white mansions.

'Don't get so upset, darling,' Sarah said. His personality was all wrong for hotels, but he had committed himself for five years, although he threatened every month to set light to his contract under Mr Rattigan's nose. 'It wasn't your fault.'

'My fault! Of course it wasn't my fault. How was I to

132

know that bloody man was a reporter? If the Rat thinks I'm going to go grinning round with flowers and fruit to that tart of Fergusson's to cover up for his gross, his crass, his crude . . .'

He grumbled on, sticking pins into a mental doll. Sarah stopped listening, and Brian did not listen properly to her when she talked about the Samaritans.

'Glad you liked it,' he said.

'But you would too. I wish you —'

'I've got the Rat to rescue. Keep him from being throttled by dissatisfied customers.'

'Perhaps you would be a natural Samaritan. That's what they say about people who are right for them. Do you think I could be? A natural Samaritan. If you are truly that, this man said, you could end up as a Samaritan Companion. They're the heart of the organization. The élite, he called them.'

Brian swung the wheel to turn down their steep little street where the houses stepped down one by one like a child going downstairs, then lifted her hand and kissed it. 'That's my good girl. Always go right to the top.'

'No, it isn't that, but . . .'

He gave her back her hand and she kissed where he had kissed, dreamily. 'A company of Samaritans. It sounds so . . . heroic.'

At the next lecture, given by a psychiatrist, Meredith was surprisingly there, this time with no make up and a scarf whose colours had run in the rain, to show she did not care.

Sarah, with opposite tactics, had spent longer than usual on her eyes. Before she got her ragged crop, hair had been her fetish. Then it was boots. She still could hardly run down to the corner for milk without them. Now it was eyes. Without the artistry of shadow and liner and lashes, she would have felt naked before anyone, including Dr Harold Greiff, who was technical enough to satisfy Meredith's impatience, but not too technical for Sarah and the anxious man at the back who kept shooting up his hand like a schoolboy and saying, 'Would you repeat that? I want to be quite sure I'm getting this perfectly clear.'

'Don't worry too much, Mr – what was your name? – Richard Bayes. Don't worry too much, Richard Bayes. A Samaritan must have some psychology, that's obvious, but you don't have to know it all. The client doesn't want you to have all the answers, don't you see? He wants you to be human, fallible, on his level. Otherwise, how can he tell you the despicable things, the stupid, shaming things? For the answers, there will always be the experts behind you. And all the very practical agencies, like A.A., Alanon, Synanon, Gamblers Anonymous, Weight Watchers – no, that's not funny. Perhaps you didn't know that overeating is often related to depression?'

'Everyone knows *that*.'

It was a loud enough mutter. Dr Greiff lowered his peppery eyebrows towards Meredith and asked, 'And do they also know that it can be a form of slow suicide, the same urge to self-destruction as alcoholism or drugs or smoking, hainh?'

'And dangerous driving?'

'And dangerous driving. That can be a very quick way.'

'My name is Peter. My number is 100. I am the Director of this branch of the Samaritans.'

He was a burly man of about forty-five, with tawny lion's hair, although his eyes were not reincarnated cat, but brown and calm and concentrated, like the kind of dog that has been reincarnated from a man, a good lost friend. When Sarah had met him at the hotel, he was in old clothes, terrible wide-cut trousers of a style long gone. He kept pulling them out and up, as if he had recently lost weight, and was proud of it. Now in a dark suit, he was not much more stylish. He had the kind of shape and movements that break clothes in to their own requirements, like a saddle.

He spoke rather softly, sitting behind the desk and

fiddling with a pencil, but everyone could hear him, because everyone was quiet.

Meredith was still there, although last week when Sarah had said, 'See you on Monday,' she had answered, 'If I come.'

She was in slacks this evening, the collar of her white sweater high up under her determined chin, her shiny black hair newly cut with geometrical sideburns. She was attractive in a bright, glittery way, her teeth very white, her lips smooth and wet, her eyes like green glass on a sunny beach.

'People in our society,' Peter said, 'are supposed to know what it's all about. They know who they are, because the State has slapped labels on them. Homemaker. Educator. Computer Programmer. White Collar. Blue Collar. Law Enforcement Officer. Student. They are trained in what are called Skills, and they either have jobs or things with names like Earnings Related Supplements to Flat-rate Unemployment Benefit, from the Department of Employment and Productivity, which used to be the Labour Exchange.

'They move like a restless wind back and forth in cars and buses and trains and planes. They know where they are going. They know they are going towards death, but they don't think about it much, since the angels and thrones and cherubs aren't there any more. They know what they want in shops. They have to, since there is nobody to ask, "Have you got any chutney?" or "What's the pork like today?" They know what they want in marriage, having been sleeping together for a sensible period. They paint up a flat and eat paella and drink wine out of pottery mugs, and their children are called Tanzia and Melody and all speak slightly cockney, whatever the class of their parents.

'The State has everyone in a plastic shopping bag, and it's pretty sickening for our masters that there are still so many people who fall through holes and get lost among the broken cabbage leaves and crumpled grocery lists. That there are people who can't be neatly classified, except as Layabout. Failure. N.F.A. People who don't fit in anywhere. Who won't go along with the master plan. They are drifters, rejects. They can't cope. They have nowhere to go and no one to love and no one who will listen to them any more – if they ever did.

'Some of them have been like this since they were children. Some of them started out quite promisingly and then gradually everything went wrong. They are lonely because they are not very acceptable, and the more they are alone, the less acceptable they become. A vicious circle, sometimes subconsciously deliberate (that's not a contradiction in terms) to back up their slogan: Nobody loves me. In the same way that teenagers will make themselves unlovable, in order to be able to accuse parents, "You don't love me." '

He paused for a moment, and looked at the reflective smiles of the older people who were seeing their teenage children. Sarah was seeing herself, hiding behind her hair, rejecting her father's knowledge, scornful of his social antics, impatient with her mother's patience, sadistic to everyone but her animals.

'And so you see,' Peter went on, turning the pencil over and over, tapping the desk first with the point, then the end, 'it comes about that life has no place for these people. They drop out of school, of college, of jobs, of social groups, of marriage, of anything that emphasizes their own inadequacy. They don't like their lives, or themselves. They are confused, rejected, lost. They will end their lives. Why not? You can't live if you don't like yourself. You can't love anyone unless you can love yourself first. So if you hate yourself and your life and you have nobody to turn to – absolutely nobody, consider that – you kill yourself. That isn't the answer, but it seems like the only answer, when the world has left you for dead.

'But at the last moment, because you are a human being and self-preservation is your second strongest instinct, sometimes at the last moment, you send out one more cry for help.' He laid his hand on one of the telephones on the desk. 'And it is answered. At the last moment, because you can't bear to go unnoticed into your final act, you ask someone to listen to you. And they listen.

'And then?' He shrugged his broad shoulders. 'Perhaps you still kill yourself. Perhaps you don't. The Samaritans will never physically prevent you from taking your own life. They'll try to show you that it could be worth while not to.'

He sighed and leaned back, passing a large brown hand across his face, pushing back his springy hair.

'I hope I haven't bored you,' he said politely. 'I do so much listening that I grab at a legitimate excuse to talk. Listening. Befriending. Counselling. You have been told by now that this is the main work of the Samaritans. Those of you we choose—' He looked round the room as 200 had done, as if he were deciding now (what sort of face was best to make?) – 'will learn to listen and to befriend, both on the telephone and face to face with clients. I don't like that word, but it's the only one – patients, customers – there's no other. English has more words than any other language, but it lets us down there.

'I can't give you a typical Samaritan client. There's no such thing. I could sit here all night giving you example after example, each one different, and then your first call when you're alone on 4000 will be something you never heard of or even imagined in your wildest fantasies. What's the basic rule?'

'Listen,' someone said.

'Yes, that of course, but how?'

'Tolerantly.'

'And?' He lifted his chin.

'Not be shocked?' Sarah wanted to sound mature, but her voice came out naïvely high, as if she would run screaming at her first four-letter word.

'Right.' He did not seem to recognize that he had seen her before. 'You'll get sex calls. Filthy sex calls. You'll have to listen while people are masturbating in phone boxes, and you can't hang up. Ever. You'll hear foul abuse. Crude things about yourself and what might be done to you, but you hang on, because behind it is probably a cry for help. It's not a hoax. It's never a hoax. It may be some of the vilest words to get your attention before the real problem can start to be told. In any case, if it's masturbating in a phone box, that's a real problem in itself. If that's the only kind of sexual satisfaction someone has, then he surely needs help.

'I'll give you an example. One of the Samaritans, a middle-aged lady, very respectable, her husband was mayor or town clerk or something, she was walking in the park and she saw a man with his trousers open. He was wanking. That's a word you'll hear on the telephone. You may as well get used to it.

'The Samaritan lady, instead of screaming and running for the police, said to the man, "Look here, my dear, it wouldn't do for anyone to see you doing that. Better step back a bit behind that bush." She stood guard until he had achieved his orgasm, then asked him in her kindly motherly way if he felt better.'

He stopped and said suddenly to one of the college girls, the fat one with the bad skin, 'What's the matter? You're shocked.'

'No, I'm not.'

'Yes, I can tell. And a client would be able to tell right away, even on the telephone. Sometimes that's all it takes to scare them away. The first impact of your voice is crucial. It could make the difference between saving a life and losing it. Don't be embarrassed. This isn't a personal attack, I'm only making a point.

'Were you shocked?' He nodded to a comfortable country-veined woman with a bright blue fur felt hat of the kind made only in England and worn only by English women.

'You couldn't shock me, my dear.' She sat with her knees apart, feet planted square, from years of making a lap for children, and because her legs were too fat to cross.

'All right. I'm a client. I say to you, "I'm screwing my pet dog every night, and before that it was sheep." How would you take that?'

The woman smiled, her outdoor cheeks forming red balls. 'I was brought up on a farm.'

'What would you say?'

'I don't know. "Oh yes?" I suppose, or something like that.'

'And you?' Peter looked at Richard Bayes.

'Let me think.' He blinked and twitched and sniffed his nose to get his glasses up.

'You can't think in silence. You must say something to let the poor chap know you're still there.'

'How long has this been going on?'

'Too severe. You?'

The knitting girl said innocently, 'What kind of dog?'

Meredith did not laugh. She shifted on her hard neat bottom and asked, 'What *are* we supposed to say?'

'Not much. Just be interested. Murmur encouragingly. He wants to tell you, so let him tell you. I'll give you another one. A woman rings up. She says, "I'm forty. I'm not attractive. I've never had a man. What's wrong with doing it to yourself?" People don't always use technical terms.' He pointed to Sarah. 'What would you say?'

'Nothing. I mean' – Don't blush, Sarah, he'll think you're shocked – 'That's what I'd tell her. "Nothing." '

'Was that right?' Richard Bayes asked.

'Didn't you think so?'

'Well, it doesn't seem to solve anything for the poor woman.'

They visualized, this assorted group of all ages, classes and types, the plain ungainly spinster on her virginal bed.

'That's the point,' Peter said. 'You're not supposed to give instant solutions. You can't. It's very humbling to be a Samaritan. Everyone thinks they can change people. A Samaritan knows he can't. He can only support and listen and reassure them that they are not alone. If you can't learn that, we can't take you.'

139

Someone asked, 'When will we know?'

'We'll have the telephone test after Christmas. Then we'll let you know.'

'How many do you take usually?'

'About one in five, one in six, or something like that.'

'You mean only two or three of us will get in?' They looked at each other in consternation.

Sarah wished that she had not told Mrs Wrigley, at the Mens Sana, about the Samaritans. Mrs Wrigley had said, 'The young are so dedicated,' chopping nuts for banana loaf. 'If they don't take me, I'll ring them up and say I'm going to kill myself,' she told Meredith.

'Quite honestly,' she said, 'it all sounds so difficult. I don't think I could cope with it anyway.'

'Oh you could.' Sarah grabbed at the sycophantic talisman.

'Do you really think so?' The shining lips parted on the white teeth in a smile of genuine pleasure. She wasn't really aggressive at all. Why had she pretended?

Peter came up to them. 'How were the Americans?' he asked Sarah.

'I didn't think you recognized me.'

'Not everyone looks like you.'

He looked at her like a man, and Sarah said, 'Thanks. The Americans were fine. They liked being at your hotel. I talked to one man who said he was coming back in the summer.'

'Mr Reynolds. I hope he won't be disappointed. He seemed to be ... chasing something which he thought he had found here. How's Meredith tonight? Still think you want to be a Samaritan?'

'No.' She grinned with her mouth closed, denting her chin. 'I never did. It was you who said I wanted to.'

She lived outside the town. Sarah drove her down to the station. In the car, Meredith asked, 'You know Peter then?'

'I met him once, with my husband. He's at the Front Royal.'

Meredith made a face. 'Ghastly place.' She would have

said it anyway, if Brian had been the owner or the manager. 'That why you volunteered?'

'No. It was other things. Coincidences. A bell rang in my head, you know?'

'I try not to listen to mine. It usually tolls doom.'

'Why did you volunteer?'

'God knows. No – Peter. Don't confuse the two.'

'Do you know him well?'

'Mm-hm.' Meredith nodded, her chin cupped in the neck of her sweater. 'Too well. Hours and hours of battle.'

Sarah tried to keep her face incurious, but Meredith said in her clipped defensive voice, 'It's all right. I don't care. When you've got that tube down you sucking your guts out, you don't care about anything. He's seen me at my worst anyway. You could say that.'

FOUR

Mrs Olive Barrow, a dark plump widow with a shadow of moustache and trotting feet in small soft shoes, was a Nursing Assistant on the ward at Highfield where they put Tim. From the start, she was the one who focused for him the complicated hospital scene.

When he arrived, stiff and speechless, she helped him to put away his things and showed him his island of property – bed, rug, locker, chair – in the long dormitory. She took him into the day room and introduced him to Mr Gilbert, the Staff Nurse, who for days was only freckled hands and buttons on a white coat to Tim, who could not raise his eyes. She told him the names of some of the other men and which were the warmest places to sit and what time dinner would be. She fussed about in a bunchy blue overall with her hair piled up under a crumpled cap, exuding warm female sweat and kindly stock phrases, both comforting.

Tim could have died when Paul left him alone among thousands in this place which looked like a mad giant's castle outside and a giant anthill within, but after Mr Gilbert had left him too, Olive Barrow had come and said, 'Ah now, lovey, don't carry on. It's not as bad as that. Turn off the taps, there's a good boy, and you can come and help me set the tables for dinner. One hand will do the work of two, I'm sure. Keep busy, that's the ticket. Here's Uncle Fred, he'll show you the ropes. Uncle's my right hand man, aren't you, Uncle dear?'

She was there in the morning for breakfast, filling up mugs from the huge tin teapot, handing out the bacon and fried bread. 'Tomatoes! It must be Thursday already. Where does the week go?' She was there when Tim came back from the workshop, clattering the metal covers on the kitchen trolley with a noise that spoke of dinner. She was there at tea, her fingers smelling of bread and butter, and when she finally knocked off after helping the maid and some of the men with the washing up, she always looked for Tim to say, 'I'm off then, Timmy.'

'See you in the morning.'

'If I'm spared.'

Tim went every day with a batch of others to the carpentry workshop that was part of the Industrial Therapy unit. A male nurse went with them and they went in file, not like soldiers, but to keep out of people's way, tromp tromp down the long branching corridors, through doors and up and down stairs. Highfield was not locked, but if you were brilliant enough to find your way out, you did not need to be shut in.

After a week, they had taken the cast off his wrist to show the raised scar. Did I do that? A cramp clutched his stomach at the thought of the glass going in. They asked him what work he would prefer to do.

He shook his head. 'Nothing.' He kept his hand in his pocket now. When he had to take it out, he held it turned down.

'There's not much outside work at this time of year,' the doctor continued as if Tim had kept silent. Perhaps he had? Sometimes he thought he had spoken when he had not.

'There's the small parts assembly where we put together bicycle valves and things like that. Or the carpentry shop might be the place for you. Are you any good with your hands?'

Tim shrugged, spreading the fingers of his good hand and examining it back and front.

'What sort of jobs did you do?' the doctor asked quite casually, but if he expected to catch Tim by pretending to look for something on his desk, he was not as clever as he would like to think.

Kitchen porter, builder's labourer, roadwork – it would

all get back to the lady with the bottle-bottom glasses at the Employment office, and she would sink him, nothing less.

Tell nothing. This doctor did not seem to mind any more than the darkie one at the other hospital had minded getting no answers to his questions. So why did they bother to ask them? There was a Chinese one here, nice young chap, nervous, learning – they all learned on you – very polite.

'Tell me what you remember, Tim. Let's talk about when you were a little boy. Don't think. Just tell me anything that comes to you.'

It was very easy to switch yourself off like a wireless. No bother at all.

Tim went off every morning with Alec and Uncle Fred and Mr Podgorsky and Arthur Callaghan and them, and in the barn of a workshop that smelled so sweet of shavings and oil and hot grinding wheels, he learned how to make bread boards and chopping boards for women to chop on in their kitchens, and at twelve o'clock he went back to Olive Barrow with the cabbage and overdone meat smells, like any boy going tired to his mother after work.

On the first Friday when they gave him his pay envelope, he took it to her and asked her to keep it safe for him.

'You can't trust any of them.' He glanced at stupid Alec, and Nobby all hunched over the table with that string of saliva down his chin, and poor wurzel-headed Dick, giggling in his wheelchair, legless for all anyone knew under the plaid rug. Gang of thieves, the lot of them. There were footsteps every night in the ward. If you woke and yelled, 'What's up?' they would say, 'Got to go to the toilet again,' nastily, as if their weakness were your fault.

'I'll put your money in the hospital bank for you, dear,' Olive said.

'No, you keep it. You can give me the money for fags and that.'

'You can draw out of the bank any time. You must fill out a slip.'

'What slip?'

'The one they'll give you.'

He did not go to the bank. He did not know where it was. He gave his money to Olive each week, and cadged cigarettes off smarmy people like Ernie, whom nobody liked because he messed his trousers; or took them out of people's lockers, and sometimes off the trolley shop that the whistling lady in the yellow overall pushed round. You asked her for a magazine she had not got, and when she bent to the bottom shelf, it was easy. She whistled like a canary, it was marvellous to hear it, down the corridors to announce her coming.

Highfield was full of men and women, old, young, sick, well, mad, sane, doctors, druggists, keepers of mice, nurses, maids, stooped old men with sacks who picked up litter on the grounds and might or might not be patients. Tim wended carefully among them, avoiding contact, shrinking from Bob Bamber in the carpentry shop when he leaned over to check a measurement, safe only when Olive Barrow was about with her loose-powdered skin and her busy hands and feet and her warm flesh smell, watching for the evenings when Paul would come treading solidly into the day room, telling Tim stories about the pupils at his school, bringing books, sweets, cigarettes.

'I don't smoke.'

'You used to. Given it up?'

'Yeah,' Paul was his friend, but he might still be a spy for the lady with the trolley shop.

There were girls in the hospital, hundreds of them, patients, nurses, secretaries, girls in white coats who did nothing but go up and down the corridors very fast, to make their bottoms wag. There were thighs under tiny skirts, the inside flesh wobbling as the foot came down. There were big tits and little tits and sharp ones and blunt ones and clubs and concerts and dances where you could get close to them, because here it was not like the outside world where girls stared and pushed each other and said, 'What's the matter with *him*?'

'Go on, go tonight,' Olive Barrow said. 'Meet a nice girl.' But after she had gone home, Tim was always in the toilet when the lady with the beads came round: 'Who's going to Activities?'

And then one day, one bright and dreaming day with clouds like fluffs of whipped cream and a sky like the tune the yellow trolley lady lady trilled, Bob Bamber told Tim to take a nine-by-five bread board to the Domestic Science unit.

'I don't know where it is.'

Bob, who was very patient except when you dropped something on his foot, walked the length of the shop with Tim and took him outside and pointed to a brick building with white paint and chimneys. 'Across the grass, down that path, the door is round the corner, and be sure to make them sign the slip.'

The sun was out and the air was full of the sea, vigorous and cheerful from beyond the hills. Although it was not yet the end of December, the ground was ringing hard, with an icing of the snow that had drifted down half-heartedly at breakfast time. Olive said it would be a white Christmas. She was quite excited about it, although she had seen fifty Christmases, she said, and many of them lean ones.

Yesterday they had started to make chains of coloured paper cut in strips and pasted through each other. Tim had been quite good at it, working swift and clean, although it would be a long time before the fingers of his left hand were a perfect machine again.

'It's my hand.' He had whined a little to Olive, showing her the hand which no one was interested in now that they said it was healed. 'It pains me, but I didn't stop working. Look how much I done.'

'Oh, the poor hand.' She stroked the back of the fingers as if it was a dog's paw, but he did not snatch it away as a dog would have done. She bent to pick up the colourful paper chains that swirled about the bottom of his chair.

'Look how much Tim's done, Norman, and here you are all over paste, stuck to everything.' Norman's fingertips were all over bits of grit and fluff out of his pockets where he had kept putting them in to get the sodden pieces of sheeting with which he fought the day-long battle against his nose.

Olive took him away to wash. 'Christmas is coming,' she sang gently, like – who was it? – Auntie Ruth, it must have been, when they lived in that house under the railway bridge where the stove blew up and took off all her eyebrows. 'Christmas is coming, the goose is getting fat.'

Bob Bamber had told Tim to put on his overcoat for the trip to the Domestic Science unit, and he had reached the brick building before he realized that he had forgotten to take off his carpenter's apron. He had been working on a packing case with Stewart, one of those people who abounded at Highfield, who you were not quite sure whether they were a high grade patient or a low grade instructor. The apron was a silly looking pocket full of nails and screws which tied round your waist with tapes. Before he went round the corner to the door of the building, Tim tucked the bread board under his left arm to button his coat across, but all the buttons except the top one were off, so he wrapped the coat round him as far as he could. It was someone else's, a boy's, too small even for skinny Tim.

Outside the door, he realized what he was in for. Domestic Science. Cooking and laundry and that. He was entering a purely female world. He would have turned and gone back, but you did not go back to Bob Bamber without completing the mission assigned to you. If Bob Bamber said, 'Square that corner,' you squared that corner if it took you till dinner time.

The door was open, like all the doors at Highfield, except for two closed wards which were not much spoken about. Mr Podgorsky told him horror stories about other places where he had been, either prisons or nuthouses, it was all the same, because, 'All you hear is the jangling of keys, Timothy, and the shrieks of poor souls in torment.'

So when he and Tim were really browned off with the situation, they told each other it could be worse, and planned how they would go into the little town one evening and have some beer.

Tim went inside and stood warily in the shining hall. A woman was pinning notices on a cork board. 'Hullo,' she said, and smiled. That was the remarkable thing. Where on earth else did people smile and say Hullo before they even knew who you were?

'I brought the bread board.' It was still under Tim's left arm, the hand in the pocket of his coat.

'Oh lovely, for the cooking school. How very kind of you. It's that door at the end.'

When Tim went through the door, all he could see was women. There were cooking stoves along one wall, pans, sinks, what you would expect, but there must have been twenty or more women doing whatever they were doing, in flowered aprons.

Some of them were girls. A lot of them would pass as girls, at least. Three or four of them round a table in the middle of the big room began to neigh and giggle, taking courage from each other, pushing each other with floury hands, bumping against each other, just like girls in the world. Another girl who was not bumping stepped back, dusting off her hands as if she were going into a fight.

'All right, girls,' Tim heard her say. 'This one is mine.'

She came towards him. She was rather a bony sort of girl with long thin legs and an angular way of moving under the flowered apron, which went right up her front and round her long white neck, on top of which her small head was tipped a little to one side, smiling at Tim.

'Hullo.' When she got to the door where he stood, she lowered her eyes, pretending she was shy.

'Hullo.' Tim's right hand clutching the front of the skimpy brown coat, swelled instantly up like a crimson balloon, the pulse throbbing like a sore. The blush swept up his face so fast he had to blink his eyes. His scalp prickled. Surely she must notice? She had raised her eyes now without raising her pointed chin. They were rather

148

protuberant, dark like treacle, with smooth rounded lids. Her lips, which were smeared with pale lipstick, did not quite close, as if the short nose pulled the top one open.

'It's the bread board, Felicity,' a lady in a white overall called from the stoves. 'Get it thoroughly scrubbed up and take it to Mary Dale so she can start the sandwiches.'

The girl held out her hand for the board. Tim drew it out from under his arm. Everything seemed to be happening in slow motion, the girls watching from the table with their mouths agape, the board passing from Tim to the girl, the falling open of his coat and her eyes staring as she saw the perishing apron.

'Come to join the cooking class?' The softness of her Hullo had become a hard bright flash, a dart thrown at him. 'Move over, girls.' She stepped aside to show them. 'There's a new pupil in the pastry department.'

The slow-motion dream was dashed into a whirl of noise and movement as she spun away from him, holding the bread board like a shield, and the girls sent up a barnyard cackle.

'Wash the board, I said, Felicity,' the instructor said without turning round from the stove. 'Clean tools, good eating, you've heard me say *that* before.'

The girls went off like shot guns, clutching each other, getting pastry dough in their hair. It was some kind of private joke. Felicity, the ringleader, whispered to them as they bent round the table again, their eyes sliding off towards Tim, standing paralysed by the door with the coat wrapped round him again, his right hand clutching the top of his rigid left arm.

'Thank you, young fellow.' The instructor's voice set him in motion. He was out of the door and almost out of the building, pursued by shouts of, 'Shut the door!', before he realized that what his bad hand was clutching in his pocket was the slip he must take back to Bob Bamber.

Undecided, he stood in the hall, looking first at the front door, then at the door at the end of the corridor which someone had shut with a derisive crash. He took tentative steps first this way, then that, but there was really no choice. On feet that clung to the tiled floor as if it were a mud furrow, he went back into the cooking school.

'Don't look now,' someone said. 'It's back.'

'Now girls.' The instructor came to save him, but when she went for a pencil to sign the slip, the girl Felicity was there.

'Can't keep away, eh?'

'The slip.' He jerked his head.

'Quite sharp, aren't you, finding an excuse to come back and see me?'

How he got out of there he would never know. Somehow he must have gone back to the bench in the carpentry shop and then back to the ward when the twelve o'clock bell rang. He remembered nothing afterwards except the sallow pointed face of the girl, the creamy pink lips apart, the eyes sparkling with some kind of wet light like leaves in the rain at night. She had laughed at him like all the others, and yet – this was what had blocked out the memory of what had happened after – when the bread board passed from one to the other, it had been as if a message passed between them.

At Christmas, there was a big dance. The Art unit had decorated the assembly hall with cut-outs from old Christmas cards pasted on to coloured cloth and fashioned into great bows and swags, festooning the walls. Glittering stars hung from the lights, a spotlight all different colours swept constantly over the crowd, turning faces red, blue, purple, as it whirled over the whirling dancers.

Tim had not wanted to be there, but Olive Barrow insisted. She came to the dance in a green silk dress and brought her married daughter who was going to have a baby. Between them they swept Tim and Alec and even Norman down the stairs and along the main corridor to the hall, laughing and chattering like children.

Olive steered Alec out on to the floor, pushing him like a pram, and Tim danced with the daughter. There was no help for it. It was more her dancing with him.

'I can't dance,' he said, but she did not mind him stepping on her feet and did not seem to feel the heat that rose in him at terror of being bumped by the crowd close enough to feel the swelling of the baby that pushed up the front of her dress.

After, he did Lily of Laguna with Olive. That was easy. He had one arm round Olive's soft waist and the other round a big strong girl with a roaring laugh and they swung him back and forth, legs kick *up*, legs kick behind, while the hundreds of voices swung the dragging melody up into the rafters of the pitched ceiling, and the maniac spinning light whirled them round like the spokes of a wheel, colouring lips blue, cheeks green, setting hair on fire.

'I-know-she-loves-me,' *stamp*. 'I know she *loves* me,' *stamp*, 'Because she *said* so. She is my li-lee of Lagoo-na,' *kick*. 'She is my—'

Across the hall, head back, mouth open, eyes wild with fun, the whirling light hit in a white blinding second Felicity's face.

He had not thought about her being here. Or had he? The Chink shrink had talked to him about what he called fantasy, telling lies to yourself like you would to other people, although he did not call it lies. He did not seem to know that was what it was.

Tim had been afraid of the dance, half because she might be there, half because she might not.

After Lily, he and Olive went to have a drink of lemonade. There were sausage rolls, sandwiches, cakes, biscuits. A lot of the people just stayed near the food tables and ate their way through the evening. The staff and patients were all mixed up, as was usual at High-field, and with everyone in dresses or ordinary suits, no uniforms or white coats, it was harder than ever to tell who was who. The face of a perfectly serene-looking woman who might be a doctor suddenly crumpled into wailing sobs. A flushed girl, with a horse tail of shining hair down her back and her skirt too short to look, put an arm round her and led her away with a nurse's professional comfort.

Felicity was sidling round the outer edge of the crowd. Her hair was braided into a pigtail tied with a big red bow which she swung back and forth. She wore a bright red dress and her lips were painted the same colour, parted and breathless, as she pushed between a talking couple and came to Tim.

'Hullo.' She put out her hand. He put out his. He had never shaken hands with a girl. He had grabbed, clutched, squeezed, rolled over behind the straw stacks with Molly and her wicked little sister, but he had never solemnly shaken hands.

Felicity's hand was warm and damp, but light and trembling to the touch.

'Introduce me to your friend, Timmy.' Olive was smiling at his side.

'Er – this is er—'

'Felicity Gretch.' There was a sort of laugh under her voice, as if she were out to fool you. 'Gretch, I said, not wretch. Aren't you going to dance with me, Timmy?' No one would have known it was the first time she had heard or said his name.

'I didn't know you had a girl-friend.' Olive looked pleased, but Tim knew that underneath she was upset because he had not told her. 'Go on, dear. Dance with Felicity. I must go and find Norman.' That showed she was jealous, that she couldn't just tell him to dance. She had to say a man's name, even if it was only Norman.

Still holding Felicity's moist hand, pitying Olive's silly smile, Tim felt his heart lift and swell with a surge of elation and power.

'Come on.' Felicity pulled him away, but not towards the floor. 'You don't look as if you would dance very well,' she said in her rude Felicity way. 'I know a place where we can put on records.'

She led him through the usual baffling riddle of corridors and odd-angled stairs, and they came to a small room with a sofa and armchairs.

'It's the students',' she said, 'but they don't mind. I was in here once with one of them.' She dropped her voice excitingly. Oh, she was a wild girl, all right. Why was she interested in someone like Tim? In a dream of adventure, he did not let himself wonder. He watched her as she crouched on her long legs to switch on the electric fire, her knees sticking far out, her bare flushed heels coming out of her shoes. He watched her go to the gramophone and slide a pile of records about impatiently.

'Do you like the Ninnies?'

'I don't mind.' Tim liked all the groups, but on the ward if someone turned the wireless up, Mr Gilbert would put his head out of his office and yell, 'Not so loud!' as if he did not know that it was no good any other way.

Felicity had the record nice and loud, and she and Tim sat on the sofa side by side, not touching, while the sound beat over them, like being in a lovely hot water shower with no one tweaking at the curtain and saying, 'My turn.'

When the record was finished, she turned it over and sat back again and sighed. They could not have talked if they had wanted to.

After a while, Felicity took Tim's left hand out of his jacket pocket and turned it over. Tim kept it still in the lap of her dress while with a long light finger, she traced the scar. Then she brought her own left hand over and laid it next to his, palm up. Two narrow white scars and a thicker one, mauvish pink and not so neat. In silence, while the electric guitars battered them about the ears, they sat and looked down at their stigmata, side by side in the lap of Felicity's red wool dress.

They managed to meet quite often. Some afternoons they put on coats and scarves and Felicity's red rubber boots with the bells she had stuck on the toes, and walked on the Highfield paths, sometimes talking, sometimes silent, sometimes quarrelling, sometimes friendly, sometimes deliberately misunderstanding. Felicity was very good at that.

When it was too cold or wet, they sat at a corner table in the library, and Mrs Fletcher brought them illustrated magazines which she thought they read, because they turned the pages over whether they were talking or not.

One dark January afternoon, with a dirty rain weeping down the tall windows, Tim found himself stammering into the memory of the night he went to the dance hall with Frank. Hesitantly, ready to clamp his mouth if she threatened to mock or yawn, he told Felicity how he had wandered in fear and despair through the town, and how at last he had rung the Samaritans.

She had never heard of them. Nor had Tim before he saw the posters, but he said, 'I thought everybody knew their number. 333-4000.' He would never forget it.

'Enough to give anybody ideas, I should think,' Felicity said, disregarding that. 'You mean it was seeing that poster gave you the idea to cut yourself?'

'No, Fliss.' She invariably managed to turn what you said into something different. 'I'd had it on my mind. I tried to do something once before, with aspirin, but I brought it all up. No, it was seeing that poster, it was like – well, someone telling you they cared whether you lived or died.'

Felicity did not like sentiment. She blew a raspberry, quietly because of Mrs Fletcher, and said, 'Why?'

'Because it said they did.'

'Why?'

'I don't know. I don't see why they should.'

'I mean why did you want to do it?'

The doctors had not asked him that yet. Paul had not asked him. In some way, it seemed as if he did not need to ask, but if he knew anything, it was not because Tim had told him. How could he? He did not really know himself.

Paul had come on Christmas Eve and taken Tim out to lunch in the little market town where the newcomers were afraid of Highfield people and the old-timers were used to them. He had given Tim a blue pullover, brightly wrapped and tied.

Tim gave him a quilted chintz toaster cover from the

hospital gift shop. 'Have you got a toaster?' he asked anxiously. The gift had taken long deciding.

'Oh yes. This will be just the thing. My wife will be delighted.'

'What's your wife like then?'

'She's very nice. You'd like her.'

One day Paul would invite Tim to his home to sit down with his very nice wife and his schoolboy son and his daughter who was married to a man twelve years older. Warmed by the glass of sherry and the steak pie and the thought of Paul's family lifting off his quilted cover to make toast in a white-painted kitchen with nasturtiums on the window-sill, Tim was led to tell Paul that his own father and mother had died when he was a baby and that his foster mother had died too ('There I was without food or warmth for two days alone in the house with Aunt Posy before they found me'), and that was how he came to be in the House of God's Angels.

To Olive Barrow, who questioned quite directly because she did not think about people having anything to hide, he admitted that he thought his mother might still be alive.

'I don't remember what she looks like,' he said. 'I wouldn't know her if I saw her, I suppose. Funny, innit? You might be my mother and I wouldn't even know.'

'I'll *be* your mother, Timothy.' He was helping her to make beds, and she leaned across and pulled him forward to hug him, so that they almost fell together on to Mr Podgorsky's shameful rubber sheet. 'I'll love you, dear.' And she had glanced over her shoulder, as if she had done and said more than she should.

Tim used to help Olive wash up the teas, but now he had something better to do at five o'clock recreation time.

When Olive said to him, stacking plates, 'Come on then, sonny Jim, no rest for the wicked,' he mumbled, 'I've got something to do,' and got up and went off in the opposite direction from the kitchen. He did not look back, but he was sure that Olive would be standing holding the plates to her soft chest, looking after him like a dog left outside a butcher's shop.

He did not tell Felicity much about Olive Barrow, or Paul, or anything, because it was not often he could get her attention to talk about himself. She told him many things of her own, murmuring on for ages under cover of the library door squeaking open and shut, and people dropping books, and the dishwasher fan outside the window going off like Vesuvius after the staff cafeteria teas. She told him about her big family, her father a builder, her mother who had never had time to take a job because she was always on her back, either having kids put into her or taken out. About the brothers and sisters she hated, the whole bloody lot of 'em, teachers' college, training to be an officer, who does he think he is, giving orders to men who wouldn't give him their used toilet paper? About Janice who went to Business, and Dottie who had won scholarships all along the line and left school two years early. About Mark who was in cameras, who had married a dreadful classy girl called Harrie the Whore.

They had visited her over Christmas in bulk and singly. 'Buck up, Flick,' they had said, and when she cried because Dottie told her the decaying apple tree had fallen down at last, Mark had said, 'You want to pull yourself together, old girl, you really do.'

'They wanted me to go home for Christmas,' she hissed into Tim's ear, 'so I did something bad, so Doctor Max wouldn't let me go.'

'What did you do?'

'Guess.'

By her face, he knew it was something rude. He giggled.

'Gently dear.' Mrs Fletcher stopped by their table. 'This is a quiet place, remember.' Crash, scream, as one of the goons who helped in the library dropped a whole pile of books on the foot of a man who was reading a crime story standing up, as if he were eating it. 'Ah, I see you've finished these.' Mrs Fletcher believed in letting chaos sort itself out. 'I'll bring you this week's *Life*.'

'No thanks.' Felicity finished turning the last magazine page and stood up. 'I've got to go.'

Round the corner from the library, there was a place they knew where brooms and pails and great drums of scouring powder and floor wax were kept in a sort of big cupboard. Sometimes the maids forgot to lock it. Felicity pulled Tim in there and they squeezed and pressed each other and gasped in the tiny space between the scrubbing board and the shelves.

'Do it.'

'No.' He was afraid.

'You're afraid.'

'I'm not.'

'I'm not afraid of anything.' But then she jammed her face against his, her mouth stringy and wet with tears. 'Yes, I am, yes, I am. I was always afraid at home.'

'What of?'

'That they would find me out.'

'What had you done?' He held her off. She was taller than him. She had to sag at the knees to make their bodies fit.

'Nothing. I couldn't do nothing. It was them, them, always them, don't you see?'

Tim did not know how to hush or comfort her. 'I don't see what's so awful about a family,' he began. 'I think I—'

'Who cares what you think?' She pulled away from him, knocking down a broom, and was gone in an instant, leaving Tim crouched behind the rubbish bin for a full five minutes in case anybody had heard the noise.

He did not tell anyone about Felicity. Not Doctor Ling nor the great Doctor Vandenburg, whom he hardly ever saw, except striding by with a cheery wave. Not Mr Podgorsky, who was the only one he talked to in the carpentry shop. Not anyone on the ward, because he hardly talked to anyone on the ward. Not even much to Olive, although she knew something was up, and that was why she was jealous.

When Felicity did not turn up at any of their meeting

places for days, Tim began stacking plates again one evening. Olive never said, 'Look who's helping,' or, 'Well, we *have* missed you.' She handed him the plates out of the sudsy water, smooth, smooth, smooth, working like an oiled machine together – 'a peck of method saves a bushel of time' – chattering comfortably away about nothing.

Why, she was not jealous at all! Tim should be spanked for thinking it.

After the lunch with Tim at the Appledore Café in the town which lay under the hill where Highfield loomed, grey and battlemented, scheduled so long ago for urgent rebuilding that it was no longer top priority, Paul felt rather encouraged. It was the first time the boy had talked to him at all about his family. Such terrible damage seemed to have been done to him in his childhood and boyhood years that it was no wonder that he had become, as Doctor Vandenberg categorized him, 'an inadequate personality'.

Paul saw the doctor when he brought Tim back after lunch.

'Get anything significant out of the boy?' he asked.

'He talked a bit about his parents.' As a Samaritan, Paul could not pass on anything without Tim's permission.

'The father was in gaol, I gather, and the mother on the streets.'

'Oh?'

'Isn't that what he told you?'

'Well – he didn't say much.'

'There's a lot of fantasy, of course, with a boy like that, but we're really quite pleased with him. With antidepressant drugs and the regular work programme – I think we may get him back into the swim quite nicely. Your help, as usual, invaluable.' He sketched a bow.

'I should come more often. It's been chaos at school. Everyone's got flu.'

'It's all right. He's too dependent anyway. That's one of the main problems of these institutionalized youngsters.' He stood up. 'And a happy Christmas to you, sir,' he said, as if Paul had already begun to take his leave.

At Singleton Court, happy Christmas was in progress. Laura and her husband had arrived before Paul got home.

'Daddy, where have you *been*?' She galloped down the hall like a child and flung herself against his stomach, lifting her feet off the floor as he hugged her. She always greeted him with a surge of her old childish joy, then ebbed back to where he was not completely at ease with her.

'Out to Highfield to see a boy I'm befriending. Didn't your mother tell you?'

'She said she had no idea where you were.' Laura did not frown or look puzzled. Her young face had a smooth, static quality like a china dish. Not secretive or wary. Composed. Controlled.

'I suppose she forgot.' No point in confronting Alice with 'You knew I was at Highfield.' He had given up those tactics long ago. Let them just get through Christmas without a fight.

Laura and Nigel could only stay one night, so they were having the turkey this evening. Laura was wearing an apron. 'When we got here, she hadn't even put the thing in the *oven*,' she whispered to Paul as he took off his coat. 'There were no potatoes, nothing for a vegetable, she hadn't done a thing except make hard sauce for the pudding. Mountains of it. Jeff has gone out to get what I need.'

'I'm sorry, pet.'

'Don't worry.' She brisked off his guilt, his regret, his pity for her homecoming. 'I'm coping. But dinner will be pretty late, I'm afraid.'

'Laura turned me out of the kitchen,' Alice told him.

'Were you in it?'

'No, but she insisted on taking over. She thinks she is a better cook than me, so we'll see.'

'I am,' Laura said quite fondly. Alice smiled at her in what would have been a friendly moment, had not Laura's husband, a specious, unsubtle man, much too old and used for her, cut in with, 'You all talk as if Alice was a mental defective. I object to that.'

Alice did not particularly like him, but he behaved as if he and she were in some sort of league together. He thought Alice was 'fun' and Paul rather dull. He made his special martinis for her, with a minim of whisky and the lemon peel twisted clockwise, never the other way.

When Laura said to him in the kitchen where he appeared with the empty martini jug and that clubbable smile on his face, 'Please don't make any more,' he wagged his finger and told her not to nag.

'It's Christmas, dearie. Your mother and I are going to pin one on.'

'Please, Nigel.'

Nigel did not believe in people being alcoholics. You either drank or you did not. You got drunk, rather drunk, merry, or you stayed sober. Alcoholism as a disease had been explained to him by Paul, by Laura and even by Jeff. He still wooed his mother-in-law with his extra special Nigelinis.

To marry him, Laura had said that she was going to have his baby. Perhaps she had really believed that. Perhaps, as she had told them, the laboratory had really mixed the tests and given her another woman's positive report. Perhaps Nigel would have married her anyway. Perhaps he would not. Paul did not think that Laura would stay with him after next year when she got her degree and left London University. Nigel would hardly notice her going.

He paid very little attention to her, except physically. He was the sort of pseudo-virile man who felt the need for constant innuendo. When they stayed at this flat, they had Laura's tiny room and narrow bed. Saying goodnight, he would add something like, 'Off to the virginal couch to see who I can deflower,' or, 'Tight squeeze – like my wife.'

It was reasonably sickening, although Alice pretended to find Nigel comic. The simulated bond between the two of them was as much to provoke Paul as to please themselves.

Jeff came back through the cold wet slush of dirty melted snow in sandals and a pair of short wide cotton trousers flapping round his bony bare ankles. He had bought imported new potatoes, beans, spinach, carrots, mushrooms, much more than he had been sent out for. Not having enough money to pay, he had entered into a complicated deal with the shopkeeper, who did not know him in this amorphous part of town where shops and tenants changed hands constantly, leaving his watch as security over the holiday.

'You'll never see that again,' Alice said. 'Go back at once and redeem it. Here's the money. Nigel, someone, give him ten shillings.'

'I'm not going out again.' Jeff poured a wineglassful of cherry brandy and sat down, sticking out his dirty frozen toes towards the pulsing electric fire.

'Come on, old chap, do as your mother says,' Paul said, so of course Alice retorted, 'Don't make him. Look at his poor feet.'

'Go and put on some shoes,' Paul said, heading doggedly towards the difficult evening.

Dinner was very late, although Laura had the oven turned up high enough to fill the flat with fumes from the burning grease her mother never cleaned. In a splurge of Christmas spirit yesterday, Alice had bought a bird that was much too big. Also presents that were expensive and unsuited, some of them to the recipient and all of them to her bank balance.

For Laura, who slept in the top half of Nigel's pyjamas, a frothy, elaborate nightdress. She said, 'Thank you very much' and folded it carefully back into the tissue paper nest of the box. She would perhaps give it to her mother-in-law tomorrow.

For Nigel, a bottle. He shook the parcel and said, 'Gurgle, gurgle, that's the way I like my presents to sound.' He had brought Alice a bottle of Beefeater's gin, done up in a special package the shape of an old ruffled and skirted yeoman at the Tower of London.

'Bath salts!' cried Alice. 'Just what I wanted.'

Paul had a wry mental vision of Jane and Phil, two ex-friends from the A.A. days, toasting each other in Coca-Cola and toddling off to a meeting tonight, and Christmas night, and every blooming night.

Alice gave Jeff quite a large cheque. He asked for that. She gave it to him. For Paul, she had bought a very beautiful, very expensive brocade waistcoat, red watered silk shot through with threads of all colours. He could think of no occasion on which he might wear it.

'Put it on.'

'Not now.'

'Don't you like it? I went to ten shops looking for it, and now he won't even wear it.'

'Put it on, Dad.'

It was too small for him. That was why he had not wanted to try it on. Alice burst into tears of dismay and ran out of the room, falling over Jeff's feet. She was halfway to being drunk, and by the time the turkey was ready to carve, she was three-quarters of the way there. Nigel had taken the martinis to her room and they had stayed in there drinking and watching the television in a miasma of smoke and cheese crumbs among the orange-stained cigarette butts. Paul read, and Laura told Jeff about a programme she was in at college to devise a revolutionary system of physical and mental education for vitamin-deficient children, while Jeff picked at the dead skin round his toe nails.

'Do you want me to put shoes on?' he asked when he saw Paul watching him.

'I did ask you to, hours ago.'

'I thought that was only repartee to my mother.' He always referred to her as that. To her face, he had not called her by any name for a long time.

'What are you going to do, Daddy?'

'About what?'

'You know.' Laura nodded towards the bedroom.

'Oh—' he shrugged, and she said, 'Don't hedge,' looking at him with the steady eyes that did not seem to need to blink.

'Nothing much I can do, Laura, She won't go back to A.A. I can't drag her there. Anyway, it doesn't work unless you want it.'

'The clinic?'

'It costs the earth and she goes happily back on the bottle as soon as she comes out.'

'Why do you stick with her?'

He might say, Because she's my wife. Because of you two. Because it's the right thing to do. Because she needs me. Laura would have accepted none of those answers, so he said, 'Nowhere else to go.'

'I wish you wouldn't talk about me when I'm not in the room.' Alice came back, blurred in face and voice. 'Did I miss anything interesting?'

'We were asking Dad why he stuck with you,' Jeff said cruelly.

It was going to be a splendid Christmas. What a splendid family, in which something like that could be said, ingested, digested, and excreted by Alice, 'You heard him – nowhere else to go,' without rancour.

But Jeff had not done with the evening. At dinner, when Nigel asked him if he would be a prefect next year, he said calmly, bolting great quantities of unchewed food, 'I shan't be there next year.' He did not look at his father, but he was speaking to him.

'Where will you be?' Paul asked mildly.

'Abroad somewhere, I don't know. I'm leaving at the end of the summer. I've told the Beast.'

'Before you told us?'

'Well, it's his concern more than yours. He'll want to fill my place.'

'What if I say no?'

'To saving the money? Why should you?'

Laura said, 'You won't get into University without A levels.'

'I don't want to. Nothing in that for me. Any more than there is at Burlington. Shocking waste of time and money.' He reached for the bread, broke off a chunk and chewed it round his small even teeth with his mouth open. The school had done nothing for his table manners.

'You should have thought of that,' Paul said, 'when you made such a fuss about staying when I left. Why did you?'

'Laura knows.' Brother and sister exchanged a glance, their faces closed to everyone else.

'Laura knows – what?' Alice leaned her wasted breasts across the table, believing that she was articulating very clearly. 'What does Laura know?'

'Oh – how I feel about schools. Public schools in particular. The worst criminal folly in British sociological history.'

'Oh listen here.' Nigel by some fluke had been at Winchester, and had never got over it. 'Our public schools – I consider that our public school system . . .' He spoke ponderously, with a royal We, as he did when he was drunk, starting stories that would never end. 'All things considered, and when we take the alternatives – when we consider that our experiences – impressions of those years are the most very deep and lasting of our lives . . .'

'I suppose you think Winchester made you a gentleman,' Jeff said chattily, and plunged forward like a starving animal to stuff a loaded fork into his mouth.

It was horrible, horrible. When Paul apologized to Laura, exhaustedly finishing in the kitchen long after Nigel had gone to bed, she shrugged her square shoulders and said, 'Standard family Christmas.'

'Why did you want to come home then?' he asked miserably.

'Because I loved you.'

'Did love or do love?'

'Don't analyse, Daddy. Just get on with the job.'

'Is that what you do?'

'Day to day.'

'That's the A.A. method. One day at a time.'

'Good. If it comes out in me, I'll know.'

They were both too unhappy to help each other.

After Christmas, Jeff took off for Bristol to stay with a friend specified only as Someone I know at school.

'What's his name?'

'It wouldn't mean anything to you.'

'What's his name?'

'Bernard Grimbell.'

'I haven't heard of him.'

'I told you.'

He left home wearing a reefer jacket and a pair of fisherman's boots he had picked up in a shop near the harbour.

'Aren't you going to shave?'

'I thought it might be fun to grow a beard while I'm away. Well – goodbye, you two. Better be going.'

'Wait a minute and I'll drive you to the station.' Paul was dressing. Alice was still in bed.

'Don't bother, Dad. There's plenty of time.'

'What time's your train?' Alice asked.

'In about an hour. I forget exactly.'

'Have you got enough money?'

'I cashed that cheque you gave me.'

'Let me help you with the fare.' Paul put his hand in his pocket. 'It will be quite a lot.'

'No, it's all right, really it is. I'm perfectly all right. See you in about a week.' He sidled himself out of the room and away.

When Paul shut the front door and came back to the bedroom, Alice said, 'He's going to hitchhike, isn't he?'

'God, I hope not.'

'I know he is. He's spent that money I gave him. He owed it.'

'When you went Christmas shopping,' Paul asked, 'did you have any idea what your overdraft was?'

'It's yours too, dear. I generously share it with you. Would you rather have separate bank accounts?'

'We shan't have any bank accounts, Alice, if it goes on like this.'

'You mean...' she put on the throbbing voice. 'You mean it ca-hant go on?' She tousled her hair forward and looked up through it tragically.

He put on his jacket and went out. He would not play.

He was not on Samaritan duty today, but he went up to the Centre anyway and heard about different Christmases from Peter and Ralph and ugly scarred Nancy, who was not an acute Samaritan client any more, but came in regularly, as if it were a club.

Nancy had spent her Christmas in hospital. 'Accident prone, they call me.' She had brought a large cake and was cutting it and handing it round among Samaritans and clients. 'Not the stove this time, no. I've given up frying, it's everything boiled, no wonder my sister stays away. Struck from behind on that same corner I've been crossing for years. You should see my legs. That's why I wasn't in here over Christmas.'

'We were worried about you,' 200 said. 'Diana went up to your place.'

'It was company anyway, and we had a nice dinner. The Lady Mayoress came. Did you have a nice time?' She turned the plate round for Paul to take the largest piece of cake.

'Very nice. Quiet, with my family.'

'Treasure your family,' said Nancy, old at fifty, battered by life and loneliness. 'That's where it lies.'

Paul went across the hall to sit with Ralph at the big scarred desk which held the 4000 telephone. He listened to Ralph's end of conversations with a man who could not find his wife, a girl who was afraid of her father, a Pakistani woman who was being persecuted by the neighbours.

At noon, Ralph went out for a sandwich, and Paul moved into his chair. He sat with his elbows on the desk, his chin heavy in his hands, and watched the mysterious telephone. He was sleeping badly. He was very weary. He did not want to think, or open the newspaper, or read through the log book. He did not want anybody to come in and talk. He did not want the telephone to ring. If he wanted anything, it would have been to take a magical draught and be put away unconscious somewhere by gentle hands until it was all over. The accidents that plagued Nancy usually happened when she felt especially blue. Ambulance men were her flights of angels. Penicillin and bandages and novocaine sprays her rest.

If Paul got an emergency call now, he would not be able to handle it properly. It was not fair to make a promise to people that you would never let them down, and then place by the telephone a dead, empty man with nothing to offer. He felt so numb that he could not even remember how the telephone's ring was pitched, although he had heard it hundreds of times. He felt stupid, thick-headed in the warm little room, the panelling boxing him away from the world outside where phantom figures wept and fought and wrung their hands. Where Alice was sullenly into the afternoon's soak. Where Mrs Frost, in the cool cameo in which he still thought of her, would be clearing up after the directors' lunch, neat-handed and at peace, her expectations unstirred by any remembrance of Paul Hammond.

The telephone rang. He jerked up his nodding head and picked it up, surprised to hear his normal voice. 'Samaritans – can I help you?'

'Oh yes. Oh yes, I think you can. Please help me.'

Instantly the close panelled walls of the study dissolved into life and he could see the woman, gripping her telephone hard, youngish, faded, strained. He saw the house, one in a row, bay-windowed villas, smoke-sick plants in front, washing and broken tricycles behind.

'I'll try. Tell me what the trouble is. I'll try to help.'

'I've not told anyone. I daren't. If my husband found out, he'd kill me.'

She had bought some things at the door. Children's clothes. A watch. A transistor radio. 'And now that doesn't work and they tell me at the repair shop they never heard of the make, or a battery that would go in it.'

When she began to miss payments, the salesmen's visits

became more frequent. Last week one of them, 'the one I thought was the nicest', had said, 'I'm afraid the next step will have to be a letter to your husband.'

'No, I'll tell him.'

She could not. The letter came when he was at work. She hid it, unopened. When the man came again, she was able to give him half the outstanding money.

She paused. Paul waited. 'It's all right,' he said then. 'Go on, my dear. You can say anything you want. It's just you and me. What's your name?' he asked, to get her talking.

'Jenny.'

'I'm Paul.'

'It's having no one to tell that kills you. I sit in the room here with my husband and a dozen times in the evening I sort of begin to open my mouth, and I'm going to tell him, but then of course I can't. He wouldn't understand.'

'He might.'

'Oh no, he couldn't. No one could. I don't know why I thought *you* could.'

'I'll try.'

She had taken the money in a shop. A knitwear sale. Throngs of women picking things over. A handbag had been left for a moment on a chair by the counter. In a dream, she had taken out a wallet, and half fainting with fear, gone away in the crowd. 'There was ten pounds in it. More than half what I owed.'

'Was there a name in the wallet?'

'A driving licence, yes. I didn't look at it. I didn't want to know. I burned it. I burned the whole wallet. I—' She gave a short laugh. 'Funny, I feel better now I've told someone, even though I suppose you'll have to tell the police.'

'If you really thought that, you wouldn't have told me, would you? Look, Jenny, could you come in and see us? I think we ought to talk it over, don't you, and decide what's best to be done. Don't worry, my dear. Everything is going to be all right. We'll help you.'

'You won't tell my husband?'

'Perhaps we can help you to tell him. That's what you want, isn't it?'

'Yes.' A whisper. 'He really isn't as bad as I've made out. He's very kind really, that's why I—'

'Don't cry, Jenny. Lots of women get themselves into this kind of fix.'

'Do they really?'

'Of course. Thanks to those unscrupulous doorstep artists. It can be worked out. Do you think you could come in tomorrow?'

'Will you be there?'

'There are plenty of people who would help you, but if you want to see me to save going through the story again, I'll be here after two.'

'I'll come at two.'

'Good, Jenny. Ask for me. Paul. I'll watch for you.'

'God bless you.'

When he first started to work as a Samaritan, Paul tried to take home to Alice something of the distress and sorrow and anxiety that he found. Drinking and quarrelsome, he would not have attempted to tell her anything, but even during dry and amiable phases, she would hear nothing of it. She was jealous of this second life where somehow he was able to be nicer, wiser, more patient. Once in the days when he still joined battle with her, after a bitter fight in which they had said unbearable things to each other, she had said, 'If I rang 333-4000 and told you about us, you'd be very nice to me.'

He would have liked to spend the afternoon at the Centre, but since it was the holidays, there were extra students about, and when Ralph came back to 4000, a new young Samaritan, Ronnie, came to sit with him to listen and learn.

Paul went away. The sun was out and up. There would be an afternoon glitter on the sea that aped its summer look. He should take Alice somewhere, drive miles along the coast, have dinner, ration her drinks, stay at a hotel, make love. Instead, he turned the car left and headed towards Royal Bridge, negotiating the hopeless traffic of this cumbersome town that had so planlessly multiplied. In the old factory district under the hill, there were still tramlines in some streets, appearing and disappearing like messages from the past as the old square paving stones went under to the macadam, came lumpily up again, to be smothered once more by the black surface, already sundering into potholes.

The dirty district, where the impenetrable windows of wholesale houses still dustily proclaimed beltings and feltings and spring grives, ran itself under the railway and emerged to better things. A Blitz-like demolition awaited the builder, children footballing in the mud, bulldozers stranded below ground level in the puddles of excavation. Mesh fences guarded a dorp of pre-fabs, and then the road straightened its shoulders and headed wide and white for the Butterfields Industrial Estate, flags flying, even the smoke cleansed and hygienic.

Paul walked from the car park across the tailored winter grass and went briskly in past the doorman at the main entrance, as if he had business with Unitech Electronics. 'Look in again any time,' Upjohn had said. Well, he was looking in.

Mr Upjohn's secretary, as cold and blank as her telephone manner, with a bright jungle talisman dangling invitingly between her sharp uninviting breasts, said, 'I'm sorry, he's out to lunch.' She looked at her watch to show it was an odd time for Paul to expect to find him.

'Give him my regards. Tell him I was passing. I hope we can have that game of golf soon. Paul Hammond.'

'I'll tell him.' She did not write it down.

Like a burglar, like Jenny at the knitwear sale, Paul went round the back of the lift and walked up the stairs on his toes. Mrs Frost was at the stove in the little shining galley, scrambling eggs. When he greeted her, she turned with a smile and put her hand up to her hair, although it was not untidy.

'I came to see Mr Upjohn, but he wasn't here. So I thought I'd just—'

'How nice of you. Wait a minute while I finish these.'

He waited while she spooned the creamy egg on to rounds of toast in a silver dish, and neatly crisscrossed them with strips of anchovy. Paul's mouth was full of juices for the fluffy yellow egg. He had not wanted breakfast after Jeff pounded off with the turned-over tops of his boots flapping. As she took the pan to the sink, Paul almost asked, 'Can I scrape it out?'

Good thing he had not. The steward came through the swing door, raised a pair of black matador's eyebrows at Paul, picked up the dish of savouries and went back to the dining-room.

'You're not lunching?' Mrs Frost was wearing a white woollen dress, its front covered by the long red apron. Her legs were straight, rather undeveloped, but good. Feet small. Back of neck clean under short petals of hair.

'I don't always. This is a business lunch.'

'Is Upjohn in there?' What if he came out napkin in hand to say, 'Where's the mustard?' or 'The lunch was splendid'? 'Are you allowed followers?'

'No.' She grinned.

'I'll help wash up.'

'No.' She sat him down with a cup of coffee. The matador came in and out a few times, bringing out plates and glasses, taking away the coffee tray.

'That's it then,' he said. 'That's their lot. All on diets, the half of them. You're wasting your talents here.'

'If you're in a hurry to go,' she said, 'I'll finish clearing. Walter's wife is ill,' she told Paul.

'I'm sorry.'

'It's all right. Thanks, Barbara.' He hung his white coat on a hook in the steel cupboard, put on the jacket of his dark suit and left, taking a pocketful of cigars.

Paul sat on the stainless steel stool which was cold to be on for more than a few minutes. As Barbara Frost ran hot water into the sink, he said, 'Tell me about your husband.'

'He's dead.' Paul let out his breath on a sigh. 'He's

been dead for almost fifteen years. My children were quite small.'

'Why didn't you marry again?' It was easy to ask direct questions. She did not look at him, and her back did not stiffen.

'No time, I suppose. The boys. And I was working.'

'Have you had lunch?'

'Not yet.'

'Would you like to come and have something to eat when you've finished? It's a lovely day. We could drive along the coast a bit, if you've got time.'

Jackie's mother did not really believe in Christmas, although there was no doubt it was very good for business. It might be an old wives' tale to suppose that Jesus was born on December 25th, but as the date grew near, the sale of slippers and handbags was marvellous to see. Shoe dyes moved well too, as the ladies got last summer's whites coloured up to match their party dresses.

Jackie was not allowed to make sales, but as he came through into the front shop with heels for waiting customers, he watched the people turning the revolving stand of slippers, puddling the green Duralon carpet with their umbrellas, and listened to his mother's selling voice.

'That's a top-quality bag. You've only to look at the lining. That's where you can always tell, the workmanship inside. You see the label? That's a Dorolee bag.'

'Oh yes?' said the customer, as if she had ever heard of Dorolee.

When the sale was made: 'Thank you, madam. You've made a good choice. If your daughter doesn't appreciate it, you send her right back to me and I will show her the difference between quality merchandise and your run-of-the-mill goods.'

Miriam, who came every day to help as Christmas approached, had a different style.

'That?' she would exclaim in her half scream. 'Who are

you buying it for, your sister or your grandmother?' She dangled the big pouchy bag by the handle, making a face as if it had forgotten itself. 'Let's face it, these went out with Queen Victoria.'

When Muh and Miriam were together at the cash register at the end of the counter, Muh muttered, 'Please don't denigrate the stock.'

'Ha!' Miriam flung back her abundant head. 'It does that for itself.'

Muh was a bit dubious about taking the morning off to go to the Play School Christmas party. 'She's getting very slapdash, that Miriam,' she told Dad the night before, accusingly, as if it were his cousin, not hers. 'I doubt she's good for trade.'

'Nonsense, Ena, everyone loves Miriam.'

'I luh Mim.'

'Not with your mouth full, Jack,' his mother said, and his father said, 'Of course you do. So do I. She's very good to all of us.'

'Hmmm ... yes ...' Muh drummed her pebble-hard fingertips on the table and looked at Dad, as Malcom said afterwards, as if she thought he had Miriam laid out on the cutting bench with her skirt up as soon as her back was turned.

'Oh, ho, ho,' Jackie chuckled to that.

'Want to see something, old Jack?'

'Yeh, yeh.' He nodded his head so violently that his eyes rattled.

'What'll you give us then?'

'A fag?'

'Two.' Malcom clicked his fingers, and after Jackie pulled out the cigarettes Miriam had stuffed into his pocket and fiddled two out of the crumpled packet, Malcom showed him the picture he had hidden in chapter six of his chemistry book.

'Whee-ew.' Jackie's whistle was full of breath and spittle.

Later that night, he crept downstairs to dial the Samaritans and tell Helen that he was going to a party.

'Ring me up next week and tell me all about it,' she said. 'OK, love? Happy Christmas!'

'Ha-ie Iss-uss!' He went upstairs on hands and knees like a silent night cat.

But next day when Miriam arrived and Jackie went to get his coat and his bag of gifts, his mother said, 'Where are you going, young man?'

'Going a party.'

'I told you, Jack.' She tried to steer him back into the workshop, but he stood firm. 'I don't believe we should go, with all there is to do here. Work-a first, then play. You know the golden rule.'

'You told him he should go to the party!' Miriam plunged into the scene before she had even taken off the fur hood which made her look like a wolf, all nose and teeth.

'Don't interfere.'

'Sometimes I wonder who's bonkers in this family.' Ignoring two women who came suspiciously into the shop with faces prepared to say, 'That's too dear' at the first price-ticket, Miriam began to button Jackie's coat. As fast as she buttoned it, his mother undid the buttons and there they were, the three of them, swaying back and forth against swing doors between the workshop and the front shop, so that Dad got up from the stitching machine with a cordovan brogue on one hand to say, 'Here, here, what's up?'

'You may well ask.' Willpower vanquished brute strength, and Muh had Jackie through the door and into the workshop, his coat half done up in the wrong button holes, his carrier bag of presents for the children bumping round his ankles.

'What's the matter, son?' his father asked, for Jackie's face was working, the tongue wandering about with a life of its own, making spit.

'You heard me say last night we shouldn't go.' It was only with Dad that she relaxed into shrillness like any other woman, and did not bother how she formed her words.

'Ah – let him have a bit of fun.'

'You spoil him rotten.'

'How can they have the party without *you*?' Sometimes Dad was keener than you'd expect. He sat down again at the stitcher, a relic of the days in Camden Town, a little old treadle machine so low that he sat on a child's iron chair bolted to the floor. With a sweep of his hand, he turned the wheel towards him and began to treadle away for dear life, his head glistening, a goblin running up toys for Santa Claus.

'All things to all men...' Muh said. 'Sometimes it's hard to see where one's duty lies.'

'You're a good woman, Ena.'

'Thank you.'

As she took Jackie out through the side door and past the window, pretending not to see Miriam pointing at the cash register which had rung up an £11 sale, he realized that she had meant to go all along. Her bag and gloves were under her coat on the hall table. She had her rainboots on. How could he and Miriam and Dad not have noticed?

Jackie had bought a Christmas present for Sarah. He had toy whistles and trumpets for all the children ('My stars, what a shindy!' Harriet seized a tootler and joined in) and a harmonica for Sarah, as if he did not class her with the grown-ups.

Sarah had brought a toy for each child and a cigarette lighter for Jackie, with his intials on it. She knew that he smoked, since they had had a serious conversation with their heads in the refrigerator, getting out the milk, about various brands of cigarettes. She did not know that he was not supposed to smoke. When he began to unwrap the present, his jaw fell, his eyes slid quickly to his mother and he dropped the lighter into his jacket and clamped his hand over the pocket.

Sarah caught his eye and they winked. What became of a boy like that? What would happen when his mother grew old and died and he himself carried his child's brain about in a middle-aged skull? What happened about sex? Sarah was still at the age when she visualized herself going to bed with every man she saw, postmen and waiters and concert pianists. She imagined it without much variety, an endless procession of heavy bodies thumping down between her legs.

The presents were distributed from under a Christmas tree in the middle of the room, made of aluminium strips and hung with coloured glass, glittering and fantastic. The children could not keep away. Hands reached out. The glass bubbles broke. You did not scold after something had happened. You watched and tried to prevent it happening.

'No, no, Mara. It's to look at. Pretty. See? Pretty Christmas tree.'

Mara shot out her arm like a dictator and crushed a golden ball carefully in her fat fist. She opened her hand and watched the eggshell pieces sprinkle to the floor.

By the time Jackie's mother gave out the presents, there was as much glass as wrapping paper on the floor round the tree. She called out names and some of the children came forward. Most of them had to be propelled by Harriet or Sarah or a rosy young medical student called Bill. Mrs Manson, the mother of the mongoloid boy was not here today, and Bill spent his morning with Charlie, working his arms, talking to him, picking him up and swinging him, winding musical boxes and waggling puppets in front of his face. When he paused, Charlie went to his chair and sat with his arm on the back of it and his head on his arm until Bill came and swept him up again.

'We usually leave him alone,' Jackie's mother said, pronouncing it 'yews-yew-alley' with a niminy mouth. 'He gets on much better, if he's not too excited.'

'He's *not* excited, that's the problem,' Bill said. 'Don't you think that everything should be done to try and get through to him?'

'Hear, hear.' Harriet, hot and panting, came up from under a bench with a child who had gone to ground, and carried him off to the basins, holding him well away from her, like a tray.

'Last week I got him to hit me,' Sarah said, and Jackie cried, 'Char-ie hit Sair!' and bent double with his feet planted for balance like the tinies, slapping his knees and laughing himself into a choking fit. He coughed with his mouth wide open, thick tongue out, eyes bolting.

'Where's your hand?' his mother asked.

Before the end of the morning, Sarah found some carol music in the stool of St Barnabas' jangling piano. She played some of the tunes and everyone sang. Sarah and Bill and Harriet and Jackie and his mother sang. Some of the children made noises. Some waved arms. Beth wandered away, blowing mournfully on the only tin trumpet that was not smashed. Charlie had fallen asleep in Bill's arms. Neddy, the child with the taped ears, sat on Sarah's lap and stretched out tiny tentative fingers towards her moving fingers on the keys.

When she stopped playing, he twisted round and looked up, his face very close to hers. His breath was sweet, like a baby. He was the ugliest child she had ever seen. Strange slitted eyes, horribly squinting. Flattened nose and top lip crusted with sores, oozing yellow through ointment and powder, scattered teeth like grey cobwebs.

Since Sarah had started to come to the Play School, she thought often about having a baby.

'Put you off, I'd have thought,' Brian said. But it was the other way. Was there one of these somewhere waiting for her? She hugged the child close until he shivered, poor, botched, unbearable face, victim of something crueller than mere human sadism.

With his chin on her shoulder, Neddy chuckled. Jackie was standing behind Sarah, making extraordinary faces.

'Look out there,' chortled Harriet, 'The wind might change.' Her hair was on end. Her blouse was rucked up, with a tail of moth-riddled vest coming out over her skirt. She had ice cream and orangeade all over her front.

'Don't talk to him as if he was a baby.' His mother

came out of the cloakroom with her sleeves rolled up, brisk and immaculate, although she had given two children a bath.

'Once in *Roy*-al Da-ha-vi-hid's ci-tee,' carolled Harriet. There would be a fight one day. Sarah prayed she would be there to see it.

The Front Royal Hotel was full over Christmas, with a dinner dance and a fancy dress party and balloons and funny hats, like a transatlantic cruise. All quite archaic.

Different kinds of people came. Middle-aged men and girls with long glossy switches the wrong colour for their skin. Families who had more money than sense and a mother who refused to cook a turkey. Girls with excess sebaceous secretions who had had no luck last summer on the Costa Brava. Long-necked men in spectacles, equally out of luck, more likely to end up in the dock for exposure than in bed with one of the sebaceous girls. Barrel women in mink capes. Grey, gastric-mouthed men who had been told it would be good for them.

Some of the regulars, Mrs Stoddard, Lady Tredegar and the Colonel, had visitors. Children and grandchildren, getting away as soon as they could. Some of them went to stay with families or friends. The ones who remained, the Formans and the Dutch couple and the lady whose hip would not knit and the old man with the mad nurse, withdrew into themselves on the overheated veranda and waited Christmas out.

Brian, the most junior, had to work on Christmas day, so Sarah went home to her parents' farmhouse out in the country beyond the University. They were housing a lustrous Venezuelan Law student, who, whether or not she had designs on Sarah's father, was apparently the object of some design of his.

As a barrister in court, he had always been a showman, using his voice dramatically, making stage business of the smallest gesture; thumbs inside edges of the gown, glasses off, glasses on in order to look over them with incredulity for a witness's stupidity, glasses polished with a silk handkerchief to prolong the suspense of a pause. For the Venezuelan girl, as local friends drifted in and out for eggnog, he put on the roaring-good-host routine, taking centre stage, forcing the conversation his way, even doing the imitation of the Queen getting plastered before her television speech, which he had stolen from one of his students.

In the kitchen with her mother, Sarah jerked her head towards the laughter and said, 'He carries on so.'

'People like it.'

'Does Maria? She looks a little detached.'

'She's constipated, I think. But your father's giving her a nice time. It saves me having to think up things for her to do. She likes him.' She blinked mildly and smiled. She was only fifty, but increasing deafness was blanking her out.

'He needs to be liked.' Sarah raised her voice over a small clatter of plates. 'Why does he need reassurance all the time?'

Her mother nodded agreement. She had not heard the question.

Was this where Sarah derived her own need? As she grew older at home, she had realized that her father, even when he was leaning back on the end of his spine murmuring sage counsel, never stopped working for popularity. It was not until she had married and gone away that Sarah began to recognize in herself the same anxiety.

She did not put on acts like her father, who tried to turn every lecture into a *tour de force*. She did not tell stories brilliantly in dialect, or suddenly recreate herself as landed gentry, as he did every year at the Agricultural Show, with a pork-pie hat and drinks for all in the boot of the car. But she began to see what she had not recognized in her few feckless spinster years, that there was a wagging spaniel in her nature that would turn somersaults and lick hands to get approval. She began to hear herself saying not what she thought, but what she thought people wanted to hear.

She began to catch herself doing it with Brian, working

too hard to please him, not always succeeding. What did he want her to be?

When she asked him, he naturally said, 'Be yourself.' But had she ever quite been herself with him? What was herself? She did not think he knew. At times when she found herself drifting this way and that in the breezes of other people's estimation, she did not know herself.

To live as much in fantasy – remembering, looking forward – as in present reality was what kept people sane. Sometimes she felt as though she and Brian were in a fantasy most of the time. Making up dialogue, funny. tender, irritable, sexy. Playing at being a boy in a mono-grammed blazer who people saw as a reception clerk because he was behind a high polished counter. Acting a long-legged, big-eyed wife with a shopping basket, chat-ting up the tradesmen. Masquerading as a swinging young couple with hosts of friends and a life of charm and gaiety.

The day after Christmas, they went to a screaming, clawing party in the basement of a house in the old part of town where two or three couples they knew lived in convivial squalor, the men emerging somehow each morning with clean collars and rolled umbrellas to sit at office desks.

The noise of their parties did not usually trouble Sarah, but tonight she found that her glands were swell-ing, her whole neck tight and her mouth dry and aching in the effort to talk above the racket of people and music. She could tell by the face of the man she was talking to that even the part he could hear was not worth the effort.

'Don't talk then,' Brian said. Slightly drunk, he pinned her in a corner for a while.

'Let's go home.'

'Not yet.'

He danced with one of the girls who lived in the house, who was dressed above the waist only in her long pale hair, crossed over her breasts and tied behind. When she danced, her nipples showed through, purplish brown from having babies, not very attractive.

Sarah sat on a rolled-up rug on the floor and listened to some people arguing, without hearing what they said. She was Brian's boring wife, not gay, not sexy. She looked at her stuck-out legs in green tights. There was not enough shape to them. The tights wrinkled unless you washed them every five minutes. Would Brian like her to be intense and brilliant like Tilly with the hair shirt, who was now singing with a guitar, her face beatified, the people round her listening rapt to the secret message of her repetitive words, her nipples parting the swags of ivory-coloured hair?

Down at the dark end of the basement, among bedding and tin baths and stacked pictures, a man and woman were preparing to copulate. Sarah could see white limbs begin to move less spasmodically and more rhythmically.

Brian came back to her. He did not want to go, so she did not ask again. She held his hand while a man with lank dirty hair and elliptical drugged eyes began to play the drums. He looked like the boy she had seen at the Samaritan Centre, waiting lustrelessly for help.

Only a week before she could go back there to take the test with Meredith and Richard Bayes and the rest of them. All this Christmas time had been an abeyance, waiting to go back to the Samaritans.

Victoria's mother lived in Scotland. 'Are you coming up for Christmas?'

'There won't be time.'

'Can't you ask the editor for an extra day?' She never could remember Willie Fisher's name, or the name of the paper.

'I mean the Samaritans. I signed up for extra duty.'

'Oh well, that's different.' Her mother felt rather holy about the Samaritans. She had no idea what they did, but visualized them as a sort of missionary order, with her daughter as a lay preacher, converting people through the telephone Word.

Telephone words from Billie took up part of Victoria's

Christmas duty. Billie and Morna had been to a party.

'You remember the night that bugger made me work late and the girl went down the pier without me?'

Down the pier referred to the derelict café where the pier ended in the muddy channel of the estuary. It was refurbished every summer, and torn apart every winter by various groups.

'Don't you remember? What's the matter, you stopped listening to me, like everyone else? I thought that was what you lot were there for, listening.'

'When there's something worth hearing.' Often Billie would not come out with it until she had stirred Victoria to comradely repartee.

'Well, do you remember or don't you?'

'I think so.' Victoria talked to Billie several times a week. It was hard to separate all the traumas.

'Told you I didn't trust her, didn't I?' Billie said, although at the time she had protested that she did. 'I know that sort. Any girl with hands like that, the end joint of the little finger longer than the others, you can never trust them, did you know that?'

'No, I didn't.'

'There's a lot you don't know, Victoria, if you don't mind my saying so. Sometimes I think it's me should be by that phone telling people how to do away with themselves, and you here sweating it out between Fettiche and that perverted little tramp. You couldn't bitch it up worse than me, that's for sure.'

'Wasn't the party fun?'

'It was all right. I didn't mind it, as a matter of fact, though normally I don't go much for that kind of thing. There was this fellow there, I didn't like his looks. He knew Morna, though she pretended at first she never saw him before in her life. Lana Turner: "I never saw you bee-fore in my life—" *slap*! That was because she'd met him that other time, you see, and got up to God knows what without my restraining influence. Very sweet, she was, such a well-behaved little girl, stayed by me most of the time. Bill this, Bill that, are you having a nice time,

Bill, let me hot up your drink. Yvonne, she'd brought some of the food — sausage rolls the size of a pillow, you couldn't get your lips round them, and that ham was off, I found *that* out afterwards — even Yvonne remarked on it, though she's thick at the best of times. Like her rough puff pastry. "What's up with you?" she says to Morna. "Trying to get Billie to remember you in her will?" That's how they talk about me, that lot, as if I was already dead. Times I wish I was.'

'Oh come on, Billie dear, I thought you weren't going to say that any more. Tell me what else you've been doing.'

'That's just it. I bloomin' worked, right up to yesterday. Parties for the kiddies. Not to mention the old folks. Those professors' wives are full of the milk of, but my legs can tell you who does the work.'

'I thought you were going to see the doctor.'

'So did I, but it's Mondays, the vein clinic, and that's not my best day, or anyone else's. You get more suicide calls on a Monday, don't you?'

'Not really. Perhaps it's because a lot of other people are fed up too, on Mondays. Some time like now, when everyone else is being jolly, that's when we seem to get more calls. If you're a left-out sort of person, something like Christmas just rubs it in.'

'You're telling me. And when everyone else is off work but you. You know what we're going to do next week? Wash down the walls with sugar soap. "You'll have the Union to reckon with," I told him. "Look at your contract, Camilla Cripps," he says . . .'

Victoria's ear was Billie's most useful possession.

4000 rang. Victoria said goodbye quickly to Billie and pulled the emergency telephone towards her. It always seemed bigger, blacker, heavier than any other telephone, weighted with distress and need.

'Samaritans – can I help you?'

'You always say that.' A disgruntled man. 'And then hang up.'

'No, we don't. We never hang up on people.'

'On me, you do. They're all sick of me because they've

heard it all too often. I haven't had you before, have I?'
It was a querulous Germanic voice, like a violin teacher
who has listened for too many years to sulky untalented
children.

'I don't think so. I'm Victoria.'

'Look here, Victoria, I don't want you to tell me,
"There's a call on the other line," when I can hear quite
well the other telephone is not ringing. Tell me how
long I can talk.'

'How long would you like?'

'You tell me.'

'Well – five minutes?'

'I'm timing it. Don't cut me short.'

'Of course I won't.'

'It came to me last night. This was the dream. Listen,
Victoria, listen.'

Victoria listened. The dream was grandiloquent, meaningless, like the dreams you turn enthralled to tell a bed
partner and find them slipping into nothing. He talked
without pause for nearly five minutes. 'Now do you
understand?'

'It's a bit complicated. I don't understand it very
well.'

'I don't understand it at *all*, so how could you?' A
buzzer sounded somewhere. 'My egg timer,' the man said
briskly. 'Five minutes. Thank you,' and rang off.

Victoria stayed on the emergency telephone all afternoon. It was exhausting, compulsive, satisfying, because it
drained you of yourself. It drained you into simplicity.
Nothing existed except this contract between two people.
A cry of despair. An answer of love.

'Tell me ... tell me.' When she had picked up the
telephone and heard the old lady sobbing, Victoria had
felt the usual second of panic: What shall I do? How can
I help her? Then remembered. You don't have to do
anything. You just have to be there. If all she can do is
weep, you are just there to listen to her weeping.

She listened for an hour. People came in and out of the
study. Betty brought a cup of tea. Ralph came to find a

file in the bookshelves. Someone else came to take away the log book. A new girl, Polly, like an owl, came in bare feet, listened for a while, staring, and went noiselessly away.

Unselfconscious, hardly aware of them, Victoria clutched the telephone as if it were the old lady herself. 'It's all right, darling, it's all right. I love you.' Tears fell down her own face for the pity of grief.

No one bothered her. Peter came in to ask her something and stopped to listen, as he did sometimes with Samaritans, but not in judgement. He sat down at the other side of the desk, his face sad, his soft golden-brown eyes considering Victoria, while she hung on to the old lady as if she were drowning.

'Come in and see us,' she said. 'Do please come in whenever you can get here. We'll be your friends ... Don't say that, May darling, you've got us now. You're not alone ... Oh, I'm so glad you did. We wouldn't have known ... I know, I know, he must have been ... all right, love, all right. Yes, you do that. Any time. Or ring again. Don't be afraid ...'

She put down the telephone and looked at Peter, stretching her tear-filled eyes. '*God!*' She shook her head and blinked. 'I'm sorry. Too emotional?'

'Why get self-conscious now? Can you only be really yourself on the telephone?'

'Perhaps.'

Perhaps May could. Things that she had said to Victoria she never would have said to her children, if she ever saw them, to neighbours, if they ever came, to friends, if she had any.

'She lives in one of those rotten papery bungalows the other side of the estuary. She and her husband bought it to retire to. He had a heart attack the week they moved in. It was the time of the floods. A man came in a boat and took him away out of a window. Her carpets were ruined. Some men pumped her out later. No one else comes. A couple of women called after he died, but she was so shocked, crazy with loss, she was rude to them. She gets up. She goes to bed. The tide in the river rises and falls, she said. That's all that ever happens.'

'She's coming in?'

'I think so.'

'Good. Would you like to befriend her, if she wants that?'

'Yes, I will if you think I—'

'All right.'

She wanted his approval, wanted it terribly. She was slightly in love with him, in the way it is possible to be in love with a saint or a legendary hero. But as a Samaritan, you were seldom praised or thanked. You would be told if you did wrong, but not admired for doing right. If you wanted that, you had better get out.

The inter-office buzzer sounded. Victoria picked up the other telephone. 'There's a personal call for you,' Ralph said. 'Can you take it?'

She glanced at Peter. You were not supposed to have personal calls, but Robbie considered himself exempt. 'Tell him I can't talk now.'

She sensed that 4000 was going to ring. You could feel that sometimes, your spine on edge, like waiting for a gunshot on stage. It rang just after Peter said, 'Go ahead,' and she picked up the office telephone. Peter picked up the other line making his 4000 face, jaw out, eyes half closed, absorbed.

'If you can't come out to dinner,' Robbie said. 'I'll never speak to you again.'

'Speak on.'

'You can? Oh great, darling. I've got your present. What time shall I fetch you?'

'There's just one thing.'

He groaned. 'Don't tell me.'

'Well – it's Jean.'

He groaned again. 'At Christmas?'

'Especially at Christmas. I promised her I'd go. Her husband has bought a bottle of sherry.'

'I'll fetch you there.'

From Peter's grunts and monosyllables and thoughtful,

gentle comments, his call sounded fascinating. Damn you, Robbie, I could have had that one.

The client's good luck that she had not. When you found yourself getting greedy about emergency calls, hating to miss anything, wanting to be a super-Samaritan, it was time to knock off. She went out to ask Ralph if someone could take over 4000.

Jean's husband, Harold, a loose-jointed, nonplussed man who did television repairs and tried to keep some kind of home going for his two daughters, had bought two bottles of sherry, and had another idea, which was not so good.

To cheer Jean up, a cause which he had not abandoned even after nearly two years of her fears and depression, he had invited a family of friends to come in. Jean had been all right all day. She had been to church and cooked a big chicken and tidied away Christmas toys quite equably before the guests came. She had changed her dress and taken the rollers out of her hair and brushed her small daughter's hair into ringlets round the handle of a wooden spoon, and set out cheese straws and nuts and a bowl of peppermints. She sat by the window with her hands in her lap, and it was not until the car stopped and doors opened all round it, front and back, that her heart leaped in a panic surge of adrenalin and she ran upstairs to her room and locked the door.

When Victoria walked down the street from the bus stop, a quarter mile of identical twin houses with Christmas trees in the downstairs windows and the back of a dressing table mirror upstairs, Mr and Mrs Jefferson and their son and daughter-in-law were conducting a polite, uneasy party, as if nothing was wrong.

'Where's Jean?' Victoria asked Harold. He looked blank, as if it was an unfamiliar name.

'Poor Jean has a headache,' Mrs Jefferson said, too indulgently. 'We're hoping she'll come down and join us in a little while.'

'She won't.' Jean's elder daughter was a solid veteran of eleven. 'Not when she's like this, she won't. She was all right all day, but now she won't come down for ages, will she Victoria?'

'Victoria is Jean's friend.' Harold answered the unspoken curiosity of all four Jeffersons. 'She and Jean—'

'We've known each other for ages.'

Harold tried, perhaps mistakenly, to minimize Jean's problem. If the story ever got out that she had turned on the gas oven and sealed the windows and cried out to the Samaritans before she sealed the door, he would be hard put to it to hold up his head. His daughter was more realistic than he was.

Victoria sat for a while and drank sherry and exchanged with the Jeffersons the sort of innocuous conversation she was not very good at.

'Can I go up?' she asked Harold quietly when he came to refill her glass.

'She'll come down.' He did not want to be left with the Jeffersons wondering what on earth was going on upstairs, as if Victoria were a doctor or a midwife. But Jean was her client, not Harold, so she excused herself and asked Sally to go up and tell her mother that she was there.

She waited in the hall. Sally appeared at the top of the stairs, long pink legs in ankle socks, jersey knitted and hair cut square by Jean in a good period. 'She says you can come if you like.' She licked her fingers and wiped a smear off the banister. Her childhood was passing in unsurprised acceptance of a situation that had aged her into a substitute housewife.

The bedroom door was locked. 'Jean? Please open the door. It's only me.'

'I can't.'

'What are you afraid of?'

'I don't know.'

'Then open the door. You needn't come down. The people will go in a minute.'

They talked through the door for a while, and at last Victoria heard bare feet on the floor and the key was turned. Jean was already scuttling back to her bed as she opened the door. She sat high up on the pillow, the eiderdown drawn round her, her pale spectacled face wary. She had put the pink rollers in again, as a sort of protective armour.

Things had begun to go wrong for Jean after she had her younger child. She had not wanted to repeat the pain and unreasonable depression of the first. Her second pregnancy had been full of fear and resentment. After the Caesarian operation, the depression had come back, much worse, and it never went away. Even the fear of the anaesthetic had not gone away. 'Every time I lie down to go to sleep,' she told Victoria, 'I believe I will never wake. That's why I can't sleep.'

'Are you taking the tablets?'

'I'm afraid to.'

'Jean, you must see Dr Hunt.'

'I can't. Harold doesn't like it. He thinks I'm going mad.' She paused, twisting the edge of the eiderdown. 'So do I.'

'Oh no, Jean, don't ever think that, but you do need help. I'm not going to pressure you, but I'd love to go with you. I could make an appointment for my free day, or get off early some afternoon. We could go in a cab if you—'

'You want to unload me?'

'No Jean, I've told you no, but you need more help than I can give you. Come down to the Centre at least and talk to Peter, or one of the counsellors.'

'You give me all the help I need.'

'I know I don't.'

'I feel you understand. You understand how awful it is. When I was a girl, I thought it was all going to be such an adventure, with me as the heroine. It isn't like that at all, is it? You know that. You know how awful it all can be. That's why you haven't married, isn't it?'

'It wasn't that.' Victoria was sitting on the end of the bed. She stroked the blanket. 'I was engaged twice. Once when I was too young. Then there was someone else, and he died. Then I was in love with a married man.

That took up almost three years, off and on.'

'When?'

'About a year ago.' Only a year? It seemed that Sam had been gone for ever.

'You've had more life than me,' Jean said.

Victoria did not say, 'You've got a nice husband and lovely children.' That was no help.

The husband put his head round the door, turning it left and right as if he expected spies in the woodwork. 'There's a car come for Victoria. A green Jag. Last year's model.'

'Who's that?' Jean asked quickly.

'It's only Robbie. You know him.' Once when Victoria was going to the cinema with Robbie, she had brought Jean along. Jean had sat stiffly, shrunk narrow in the seat, although Victoria was between her and Robbie. Afterwards she would not discuss the film. Victoria did not think she had watched it.

'Does he still want to marry you?'

'I think so.'

'Don't do it,' Harold said, the sherry fermenting him into unwonted wit. 'Nothing in it.'

Jean looked at him in surprise. Then she laughed, and slowly, one by one, began to take the rollers out and pile them in her lap.

After dinner, Victoria and Robbie walked in the main shopping streets to see the lights and the window displays, hand in hand, full of wine, watching the families in from the country, the couples who walked together, arm in arm, hand in hand, not seeing that they looked like them.

Weinberg's windows were full of moving scenes from fairy tales, animals and little people nodding and jerking and dancing and sawing. Mrs Bear endlessly stirred an empty porringer. Humpty Dumpty slid down the wall on a wire, disappeared under it and reappeared on top.

'It's as good as Selfridges,' a woman kept marvelling. 'I say, it's as good as Selfridges.' Her family pushed her on to the next window, with no better luck. 'It's as good as Selfridges...'

Staring into the Humpty Dumpty window, for it was compulsive to see the egg come over the top of the wall just once more, Victoria saw herself and Robbie in the glass, almost the same height when she wore flat shoes, the same build, slim with narrow shoulders, the same long necks and small heads, hers wound round with smooth hair, his clean and glossy, with highlights on his Camelot fringe.

'Look at us. We look like brother and sister. Your older sister,' she added, to hear him deny it.

'If so, it's incest. Victoria—' Robbie kneaded her fingers painfully, pressing the ring that she had taken out of her coat pocket in the car. 'Let's go. Come on. Come back to the flat.'

'No.'

'Then yours. Why not? You never used to be so frigid.'

In the first dead misery of Sam, she had turned to Robbie (hovering patiently like a fireman with a blanket), in a lunatic attempt to show herself that Sam did not matter.

'I know. I don't know what's happened to me. Do you think it could be the change of life?'

'At thirty-five?' Robbie put on a womanish mouth. 'I doubt it, dear.'

Humpty Dumpty slid down the wall and went under. 'Let's go, quick, before it comes up again.' They ducked as if the egg were after them.

The car was parked in Marsh Lane, that narrow interminable street which dragged a trail of sleazy shops and pubs and failing projects zig-zag through the middle of the town, following the wanderings of some ancient bell wether. Where it crossed the middle of the town, it picked up a rash of coffee bars, foreign film houses, Indian restaurants, male boutiques, cellar clubs, hairdressers and betting shops. Robbie's car was opposite a black screened window in which a Gothic lettered sign told of the Brethren of the Judgement and the times of their meetings within. Farther down, in the gutter, an old man shuffled, wearing over his shoulders like an *Alice in Wonderland* playing-card a board that said '*Repent ye sinners, for the end of the world is tomorrow.*'

As he shambled closer, his eyes on the ground, his broken boots weaving through the Marsh Lane litter, Victoria saw who it was.

'Michael!' She ran to the old man. 'Hullo, Mike.'

He stopped, raised his head and blinked at her.

'I was at the Samaritans last time you were in. What are you doing out so late?'

'Well, I'll tell you.' They were by a lamp-post. He rested against it, leaning on his back board like a coiffed Japanese, and shifted the weight of the front board up, moving his shoulders feebly under the worn leather straps. 'It's Christmas, see.' His mouth was a toothless cavern. 'They gimme five bob extra to keep the board out till nine.'

'But it's long after nine. Time you went home.'

Robbie had come up, light and springy in his suede ankle boots. 'This is Michael,' Victoria said. 'He comes to the Samaritans sometimes for a cup of tea and a warm. Where are you living now? Are you still with the students?'

He nodded. 'Got a fag?'

People were passing back and forth on the neon-lit pavement. Robbie had taken Victoria's arm to lead her away, but when he saw heads turn to look, he stayed, intrigued, not by Michael, but by the image of himself stopping on Marsh Lane to chat with a derelict sandwich man. He took out a cigarette for the old man and lit it. After two deep drags, Michael was choked by a bubbling paroxysm. He could not bend double because of the boards. He leaned against the lamp-post with his legs sagging in the baggy trousers, his chin hanging over the edge of the front board like a man in a noose. The cigarette stayed on his lower lip, smoking up into his streaming eyes and the dirty grey mat of hair that covered most of his face.

'Ta,' he said, when he recovered breath. He wiped his nose on a tattered scarf and held out his hand for Victoria to pull him upright.

'Are you all right? Is there anything you need?' 'Shall I try and get you some shoes?' His boots were grotesque lumps, bearing no relation to the shape of feet. 'I'll look in the Director's office. Perhaps I can find a coat too. Shall I bring them here?'

'Yes, darling.'

'Come on, it's time to go. Let's take him to the hostel, Rob. Please. It's miles to walk, right up by the old factories above Royal Bridge.'

'What about the boards?' The Brethren of the Judgement were sealed up with a padlocked grill. 'Do you take them with you?'

'That's right, mate. Slept on 'em before now, an old man like me. Been through two wars. Lost half my ribs . . .'

'We'll never get them in the car, Victoria.'

'Let's try.' She began to lift off the sandwich boards. Michael gave a yell as the edge caught on his head. A few people stopped to watch.

'Victoria, don't be childish. They're wider than the door.'

'You could at least try.'

'You're making a scene.' A man and a girl ran up from a noisy cellar like rabbits, and stopped to stare. While Victoria and Robbie were arguing, the old man resettled the boards and weaved away from them along the gutter at a fairly good pace. The board on his back said, '*Salvation from Doom, Tues. & Thurs. 7.30. Brethren of the Judgement.*'

Robbie drove Victoria to the house in one of the stucco squares whose top floor was her flat.

'I'm coming up.' Usually he asked, 'Can I come up?'

'No, Robbie.'

'Why not?'

'Because you didn't want to have Michael in your car.'

'That's stupid.'

'So were you. Those boards would have gone in.'

'He didn't want to go in the car.'

'You didn't want to take him.'

'Well then, everyone was happy. Good night, dear love.' He surprised her by crossing the pavement on his quick neat feet, getting into the car and driving off – Beep-beep! A light snapped on in the Berridges' window. Everyone in this square was a member of the Noise Abatement League. They had forced the Council to change the route of a yodelling dustman.

FIVE

ON THE SECOND day of the New Year, Sarah went up to the Samaritan Centre to take the telephone test. She met Meredith at the door in a white Austrian coat, miraculously clean in this dirty town. 'I'm afraid,' she said. 'Are you?'

'What the hell.' Meredith made a face. 'I didn't want to be a Samaritan in the first place.'

Upstairs, two telephones were rigged up to a loud-speaker, so that everyone could hear the calls. The volunteers crowded into one of the interviewing rooms partitioned off from the loveless rectory bedrooms, and went out one by one to pretend to be a Samaritan.

The smiling lady, who sported a soft little fur hat today and looked like the sort you would be glad to own as your mother, was called first.

'Oh!' She gave a yelp. 'Not me.' She had wanted to sit with her head on one side and listen to the others make fools of themselves.

'Why not?' Peter was brusquer tonight. 'That's what you came for.'

She twittered out to the next room, and Meredith was chosen to make the call.

'I can say anything, right?'

'Our real clients do.'

Meredith pressed a buzzer. The lady in the fur hat said, 'Hullo?', although she had been told to say, 'Samaritans – can I help you?'

'I'm going to kill myself,' Meredith said in a gruff, mulish voice.

Long pause. Dead silence.

'Did you hear what I said?' Meredith asked irritably. 'I'm going to kill myself.'

'Oh look here' – a gasp – 'You can't do that.'

'Why not? It's my life.'

'Yes, but I say, it's against the Law.'

'What'll I care if I'm dead? I'm on the windowsill. I'm going to jump now.'

'Oh no!'

'Why not?'

'What's your name?' the lady asked sharply.

'None of your business.'

'Tell me your name and where you are.'

'I don't want anyone to find me.' Meredith began to cry, simulating dry sobs.

'Now listen to me, you must pull yourself together—'

When Peter called her, she came back, not smiling any more, very flushed and flustered, breathing rapidly through cut-back nostrils.

'I know I was terrible,' she began, and Peter said, 'Yes. Perhaps it's a good thing. You made every mistake in the book.' He was not nearly so nice tonight. 'Who's next – Jillie?'

'I'd rather wait till the end.' There was only one student now. The fat one had dropped out, with a few other people, before the end of the lectures.

'I'm as likely to insult you then as now,' Peter said, 'I've got to be tough, don't you see, because of the clients. It's their feelings that matter, not yours.'

Sarah had planned that she would pretend to be an unmarried mother of forty, but when she began to talk to Jillie, she was somebody else. She was a terrified girl, alone in a cold quaking house with haunted attics – her grandmother's house in Wales – waiting for her husband and knowing that he was not coming back. She gabbled and gasped and stammered. She was unwanted and alone. It was her fault. She would be alone for ever.

When Jillie came back from the struggle, she said to Peter, 'I didn't say enough, did I?'

'You didn't get much chance. Good act, Sarah. It's odd.

Volunteers always make better clients than Samaritans.'

'Because they air their own problems?' Meredith suggested.

'Perhaps.'

Richard Bayes pretended to be a college student, desperate about exams, and letting down sacrificial parents, and not having made any friends. Was that the story of his own recent youth? 'People think I'm a bore,' he said. And it was true. Richard Bayes was a bore, a humourless person without colour, tirelessly plodding after the same issues, like an ant rebuilding its labyrinth each time it is kicked over.

'I don't think you're a bore at all,' Meredith said, much more warmly than she spoke to real people. 'I think you sound like fun.' She activated him into a conversation that became subtly charged with sex. Richard Bayes actually tried to make a date with her.

'Samaritans don't have sex with the clients,' Peter said when she was finished. 'That's about the only thing they don't do. Symbolically though, as Meredith was doing – sometimes that's just what's needed.'

Sarah's call was made by the bald grandfatherly man in the soft heather tweeds. He turned himself (his life's secret fear – or desire?) into a respectable bank manager who had gone mad in a jewellery shop and pocketed a diamond bracelet.

'How can I face the trial? Everyone will know. I'll lose my job, my friends – what will I tell my children? I can't face it.'

He spoke slowly, heavily. Sitting on a high stool, her feet tucked through the rungs, hugging the dummy telephone on her knees, Sarah could see him exactly as he would be. Not the kindly man with the freckled scalp and the well preserved stomach under the tweed, but a stout red-faced man who had been drinking. She could see where he lived, a decent small house out Haddington way, with dahlias and a wife called Evelyn. He had locked himself into his room to make the call, terrified that Evelyn would come and rattle the knob. He had opened the drawer where his old Service revolver lay. Loaded?

'We'll stand by you,' she heard herself say. 'You're not alone – really. We'll help you all we can. Whatever happens, we'll be your friends.' She saw herself outside a great studded door like a medieval gaol, a bag of food and books on her arm. *Are you his daughter?*

'I've forfeited my friends.'

'Not us. Oh please believe me—'

She would not have been surprised to hear a shot from the other room.

When they were leaving, Meredith said on the stairs, 'Your left eye is smudged. Were you crying?' She asked it with bald curiosity, like a schoolgirl.

'I made a mess of it.'

'He said you sounded like a natural Samaritan.'

'He didn't say anything to me.'

'I don't think they do. They only say nice things to the clients.'

'They've taken me.' When the letter came, Sarah could not help telling Mrs Wrigley, who ran the Mens Sana. 'The Samaritans have taken me.'

'I think it's very splendid of you to do that, dear. A wonderful thing for a girl of your age.'

'But you don't understand. It's splendid of *them* to take *me*.'

The usual depressing customers were in and out. Sarah tried to be convinced by Mrs Wrigley's faith in the health breads and herbal creams, but they did not visibly improve the clientele. Most of them were regulars, for the Mens Sana, with its bunches of dried herbs in the window and stacks of stone-ground loaves which either were or looked like cardboard, did not usually attract impulse shoppers.

'How are you, my dear?' they asked, and some inquired after her cats. She barely knew what she answered. I am going to be a Samaritan, her mens sana sang. They took me.

'They've taken me!' She did not go home, but panted up the wide marble steps of the Front Royal, across the veranda and through the lounge to where Brian was behind the reception desk, putting letters into pigeon-holes. She grabbed the counter, her legs weak. 'They've taken me.'

'Where to?'

'The Samaritans. They want me.' She felt her face alight, provocative, stunning him with joy.

'Of course they do, darling. Who wouldn't?'

His smile devastated her. Their eyes clung, staring, as they did in bed, their faces changed.

A woman in a stiff fur coat put down her room key with its phallic wooden weight. 'What did Mr Postman bring me today, young man?'

'Just a moment, Mrs Quiller.' Brian did not turn quickly to her. He moved his head round slowly from Sarah in a way that would have been quite insulting if Mrs Quiller had not been immunized by a lifetime of disparagement.

He completed the turn and drew a letter out of the honeycomb behind him.

'But that's a bill!' she protested, pouting in a manner that had captivated the late Mr Quiller half a century ago before he made his money and began to destroy her. 'I ordered a nice long letter.'

'Sorry, Mrs Quiller.'

'I'll write you a letter some day, telling you all the things I think about in my room up there with only the wild wet sea for company; then you'll have to write back.'

'Yes, we will,' Sarah answered for him, but Mrs Quiller did not register that she was Brian's wife. She rotated and went on to the door like a walking toy, as if Sarah had not spoken.

SAMARITAN LOG BOOK. NIGHT DUTY.
05.40 Agnes rang from South Station, distressed and exhausted. Wants help with some trouble (unspecified) and will come here. (Ralph, 255)

Long before dawn, when the empty milk-cans began to clang about, they kicked out the people who had been sleeping on the benches and under the arches of the old goods shunting.

When the man came shouting round, Agnes did not wake, since she had not slept. She had held herself in a tight ball under her thin coat, curled like an unborn baby, rigid with cold. If she did not move, she could survive.

She opened her eyes. 'Come on,' the man said, not unkindly, but not looking properly at her, as if she were not a person at all. 'You've got to get moving. Shouldn't be here at all. The police are round almost every night now. You were lucky.'

Lucky. She sat up, still holding herself clenched tightly, as if her soul would leak out if she let go. She ran her tongue round a rank mouth and pushed back her hair.

'Got change for a cup of tea?' She did not look at him. He pretended not to hear, moving away grumbling among the black brick pillars.

Hot tea and bread and butter. Agnes could feel them falling into the hollow well of her stomach. Water came into her mouth. Being sick on nothing was worse than bringing up your dinner. She had found that out.

Somewhere at the back of her head, in a cavern of demons, the wailing and mewing never stopped. Faces pressed against a grimy window. The baby rolled about on the strewn floor, naked, red and screaming.

It had been too easy to go. All the time she had thought about it, all the times since John disappeared, that she had shrieked, 'Shut up – shut up! I'll walk out of this room and never come back!' as if they were old enough to understand, the twins and the baby, wet, stinking, the three of them, crying night and day. And then, day before yesterday, day before that, last week – how long ago? – she had just put on her coat and gone. It was so easy.

The sun was out. At the bus station, naming a town, the first that came into her head, she had wanted to tell every woman in the world, Get out, get out. You don't have to bother with it. When she climbed down at the noisy, crowded bus terminal, as strange as a foreign land, she had used almost the last of her money to ring the Police at home. She told them where the children were. 'It's not locked. Someone must take them away. I'm not coming back.'

'Just a minute. Wait just a minute. Hold on . . .' And be caught and dragged back? No thanks.

There was nothing to do and nothing to do it with. If she went for work or money, they'd get her. She walked about the town, two days, three days. A man gave her a meat pie at a stall somewhere. She grew as frozen as a walking corpse. The children wailed ceaselessly in her empty head.

In the market, where she picked among the cabbage leaves for something to see her through, an old man told her about the station, and she had dragged herself over the bridge. The oily black river looked soft and welcoming. Her mind climbed on to the railing and tumbled easily over. She had no strength to climb, barely to walk. In the station entrance, she staggered and was almost knocked down by a weaving line of boys. The end one caught her with his elbow and she spun round and clutched the wall.

'What a piece of 'uman wreckage,' one of them said, and the others guffawed and pranced out singing.

In the middle of the night, people came, young ones, and a line of human wreckage straggled out of the shadows. They brought soup, bread which Agnes could not eat, but she swallowed the soup, without wondering about the hands that gave it.

'Are you all right?' A girl's face like a white flower leaned to her between skeins of soft hair. 'Do you need some help?'

Agnes shook her head. When she went back to the bench, she had cried for the first time.

She pushed herself up from the bench and began to walk. She would walk about until she dropped. Dented into the jelly of her brain with her mother's finger, an old image of hospital hands undressing her. She dragged herself across the empty station and pushed at the door of the Ladies'. They had forgotten to lock it. She leaned over the basin with her mouth under the single tap. The cold water splashed into her stomach and came right up again. She hung over the basin, her hair among the grimy hair combings, and wailed with her children.

She washed her face and stood vacantly, wringing her hands, since there was no towel. She would not look in the speckled mirror. On the wall next to it was a notice about a VD clinic, the usual ... 'If you are desperate.' It wasn't the VD. It wasn't the usual ... 'If you are at the end of your tether.'

Under the entrance arch, she stood against the wall, trembling. A few people were about, walking briskly, not loitering. This town had as bad a name as any other. One of the bums who had slept in the station came out, shuffling and muttering, lips red and wet in a tangle of beard. No good trying him, but she stepped forward.

He groped a sixpence out of a pocket somewhere among his clothes and shuffled on faster when she tried to thank him.

'Samaritans – can I help you?' A man's voice.

'Yes ... yes, I need help. I can't go on.'

'Tell me?'

'I can't.'

'You can tell me anything.'

It was years since anyone had spoken to her like that. She felt like a child. 'Come and help me.'

'I can't leave here, I'm afraid, but we can talk for as long as you like.'

'I want to see someone. I want someone to help me.'

'Can you come up to us?'

'Where is it?'

He told her, gave her a bus number.

'I'll have to walk.'

He told her the way. 'Do you want to tell me your name? All right Agnes, we'll watch for you.'

* * *

Sarah was to work two afternoons a week at the Samaritan Centre. Going to hang up her coat the first day, she found Meredith putting hers on.

'Oh – did they take you?' she was going to say, but it might sound rude. Meredith said it to her, and it did sound rude.

In the reception room, there was a young medical student called Andrew, friendly and casual, sporting a staple-shaped moustache, talking in jerks and hesitations, leaning on the lesser parts of speech.

'Don't be nervous,' he told her, '*because*, it's all quite – you know. Look, Sarah, *when* people come in, what you do – chat 'em up a bit. See what they want. May only want to sell us paper clips, but don't leave them, you know, standing.'

When the door opened and a woman looked in, waxen, drained, no stockings, her thick legs blue, Andrew broke off in mid-sentence and jumped up.

'Hullo, come in. Here—' He grabbed her arm and caught her as she staggered, and put her into a chair. 'Poor dearie. It's – oh yes, it's Agnes, isn't it? We've been expecting you.'

'I couldn't—'

'Look, it's all right. Sit for a minute. Then we'll talk. Sarah will get you a cup of tea.'

Sarah jumped up as if she had been asked to go to the top of St Saviour's tower and pull someone in off the ledge. When she came back, the woman thanked her weakly. She looked as if she had been walking all night, all day and all night. Andrew sat beside her, not looking at her, not not looking at her, just being with her while she drank the hot tea and sighed.

'There's some bread *and* – something or other in the kitchen,' Andrew told Sarah. 'Could you make, like – you know, a sandwich?'

14.10 Max Legge, a father looking for his missing daughter Jane, came in to ask if we knew anything. Nothing in files. (Sarah, 589.)

'Aren't you going to the office, Max?'

'I can't. Phil and Olive will have to manage.'

'Don't worry so. Why do you worry like this all the time? It doesn't do any good.'

'My daughter's been gone four months. Your daughter. Don't you worry?'

'Not any more. *I hate her now.*'

'Margaret – don't!'

'Why not? After all we've done for her...' The old tune.

'Did we do it to get gratitude?'

'I don't know. All right, yes. What's wrong with parents wanting that from their children?'

'If there were something I could do...' His old tune.

'You've tried everything. Police. Hospitals. Church Army – you must have rung every agency there is. Janie is probably hundreds of miles away.'

'I think she is in terrible trouble. That's why she won't come home, or write to us. I'm so afraid, Margaret.'

She looked at him, her face drawn down.

'I keep thinking she might be dead.'

When Sarah was in the hall, a tall woman with a head of swathed sandy red hair cupped in the turned-up collar of her coat came in at the front door and stood looking at her.

Don't leave them, you know, standing. Sarah went to her, smiling shakily. 'Can I help you?'

'Oh thanks.' The long mouth curved into a friendly smile. 'Are you new? I'm Victoria, 422. Don't worry,' she said. 'Everyone does it till they get to know people. My first day, the Director came wandering in looking exhausted in a jacket I wouldn't give to the Salvation Army, and I rushed up and almost killed him with sympathy.'

As they went to the back of the house, the unlatched front door was pushed open and a middle-aged man with an astrakhan hat came in. He looked at the notice which told him to go to the reception room, then looked uncertainly down the hall at Victoria and Sarah.

'Try again,' Victoria murmured. 'That's a genuine one.'

'No, you.'

'I've got to take off my coat.'

'Can I help you?'

The man was tall and stiff. His overcoat was a black tube, too long. He took off his hat and looked down at Sarah as if it was not what he had expected to see. 'I doubt it,' he said wearily, 'but I thought I'd better try everything.'

'Would you like to come in and sit down?' Sarah asked, like a polite child at a grown-up party.

'I only want an answer, yes or no.'

His daughter had been missing for four months. Had she been here for help? He believed she was in some trouble.

'How dreadful for you.' Sarah stared up at him, transfixed by what she now saw was sorrow and pain in the lines of his grey face.

'What shall I do?' She went to ask Andrew.

He told her to look in the files for the girl's name. 'But if she *has* been to us, we'd have to get in touch with her before we could tell him anything.'

'But her father?'

'Anyone. You never tell.'

There was nothing. Two or three cards in the file identified as 'Jane', but too long ago.

'I'm so sorry.'

'It's not your fault.' The father put on his astrakhan hat dead centre over his sad face and went away.

Later, when Sarah had dealt breathlessly with the office telephone, 'You talk too fast,' Andrew told her. '*And* too much. Got to learn you know, to shut up in this place.'

'At least she's articulate,' Victoria said. 'She doesn't call everyone Whatsaname or Thing.'

'Doesn't talk like a secretary either.'

'Do I still?'

'Once in a while. A bit too official.'

'Oh God, that's my office training. "*Courier*, good

morning. Mr Fisher is in conference. Can I take a message?" Thanks for reminding me, Andrew.'

They criticized without rancour or affront. 'People don't do that anywhere else,' Sarah said.

'They would if they were all after the same thing. It's like – well, there is this Unanism thing. A sort of non-religion. The most significant human relationship is when people do something in the same way and for the same what's-it. Kon-tiki. Doctors and nurses in an operating theatre. Even a football team. Unanism. It's why grown-ups go on playing schoolboy games.'

'Or become Samaritans,' Victoria said.

'Yeh. Boy from London came in here the other day, on the – you know – on the run. Wild with me, though I spent all morning trying to find him a room. What was I doing here, why wasn't I up there chucking bricks through the windows of the American Embassy?'

'What did you tell him?'

'Too busy. Nothing I can do about Viet Nam. Something here I *can* do. What got you in here, Victoria?'

'Unoriginal reason. Someone I knew killed himself. Someone I thought I loved.'

'With me—' the reception room was empty now. Andrew was lounging on a sofa in his jeans and torn sweaters; Victoria was writing a report about her talk with Agnes – 'with me, it was someone I detested. My first year at University. I shared a room with him, till I could find some kind *of* – you know – to move out. The world's bore. He still came to my room all the time, talk, talk, all his problems, I stopped listening. One day, he hanged himself. Sorry? Yes, I was, *but* – you know? – for myself. Cheated. He cheated me of the chance to do something for him. Not that I ever did, but he was sort of – filed away. I might. Now I couldn't. Make you sick? It did me. I came up here and learned how to listen.'

And Sarah too, as the weeks went by, Sarah learned to listen. For some of the people to whom she listened, nothing could be resolved; it was part of an endless quest for what they could not find in themselves. Listen, Sarah, listen, you have nothing to give but your ears. She did not think she was much use.

One evening, leaving late, she met David, 520, getting out of his shuddery car.

'Hullo?' He peered through his thick smeared glasses. 'Oh, *hullo*. Are you one of us now?'

'Yes, I am. Sarah, 589.'

Sarah King. Warm. Alertly young. Eager. She will make a better Samaritan than me, Victoria thought. I'd like to meet her husband, and know the rest of what she is.

Sarah had looked at Victoria's left hand, then curiously up at her face, seeing – what? Would she evaluate me differently if I were married to Robbie? The Hon. Mrs Robert Fielding. Lady Roundswell. Who would even *speak* to me?

'If I were married to a Lord,' she asked Peter, rummaging through the boxes in his office to find shoes for Michael, 'could I still be a Samaritan?'

'You could still be Victoria, 422,' he said. 'Why are you so neurotic?'

'I'd be an anachronism.'

'We've all been anachronisms since we were born, to the babies that come tumbling after.' He was reading her report. 'Did Agnes ask you to find out where her children were?'

'Oh yes. I talked to the Children's Officer. She wanted me to do that before she would tell me anything.'

With an old Army overcoat and a pair of shoes and thick socks to stuff them with, Victoria went down to Marsh Lane that evening. Michael was not on his beat. The Brethren of the Judgement was open for business, however, and she went in.

In the small room behind the black glass window, there was a counter, shelves of books and leaflets, and a few chairs and low tables, like a carrot-juice cocktail-bar.

'Have you come to read?' The woman behind the counter wore a tam o'shanter and a black overall pinned tightly across the chest as if Marsh Lane were full of rapists.

'It was about the old man with the boards—'

'You are interested in the Brethren? You're early for the meeting. Are you going to wait?'

'It's really old Michael I want to see. He's a friend of mine.'

'I see,' said the woman, not seeing anything. 'Well, it's nothing to do with me. It's Mr Naylor who pays the old gentleman, for not very much, if they want my opinion, but Mr Naylor is like that. Man or beast, he'll not see anybody go in need.'

'Is he here?'

'On a Thursday? No, my dear. He's in the field.'

'Where is that?'

'Wherever he sets down his stand and banner. Street corners, car parks, the zoo. He spoke on the pier one Whitsun. It was quite nice.' Her eyes glazed over.

'You haven't seen Michael?' Victoria tried to bring her back. 'I've got some shoes and a coat for him. It's cold.'

'Don't look at me.' The glazing slid back like shutters. 'If he chooses to traipse up and down in the gutter, it's no affair of mine.'

Victoria went on up Marsh Lane, which became increasingly shabbier and more downhearted, until it died among a huddle of condemned houses and abandoned workshops near the coalyards. Under the railway, the arches dripped and stank. On one side of the street that ran along these sluggish reaches of the river, warehouses and garages and blocks of prosaic flats had been raised out of bomb ruins after the war. On the other, many of the old factories still tottered on the river bank, windowless shells, chimneys standing alone, blackened timbers fallen across burned-out floors.

Rusted chain fencing topped with spikes locked these sad relics from the street. A hole clipped out of the wire and replaced by an old door led through a puddled yard to the two-storey building where the students ran their house of last hope for the jakies and junkies and rejected derelicts, the carrion of the town.

'But we don't really run it, you know,' a streamlined Jamaican girl, like a dark greyhound, told Victoria. 'We are just working here with the men. This is their place. That's why they come. They help each other, whatever they can do, even if it's only sharing their last quarter-bottle of meths. They can go away when they like and come back, no questions asked. That's what old Mike does. Leave the clothes here. If he doesn't come in, we'll find him some night on the soup run.'

'Where do you go?'

'The stations, the derries, the camps, the skipper behind Caxton's bakery where the hot air blows out. A whole sub-continent. You ought to come out with us some night.'

'Could I?'

A body that had been swaddled on the floor in a corner of the room unwound itself from the blanket and stood up, wild-lipped, and began to shout.

'It's all right, Donald.' The girl went to him, a man with a nest of hair like snakes, tatters of cloth you could hardly call clothes, the smell and filth of him stronger than the fumes of the rusted oil heater.

He shook off her hand, and stood balanced on wide unsteady legs, trying to focus where he was. She put up her hand again to his shoulder.

'Donald? It's Hattie.'

He lurched out of the room and thudded down, screaming in the passage.

Feet on the stairs. Through the doorway, Victoria saw a stocky young man with bare feet jump down. 'Come down and help, Nosey!' he called.

A tall top-heavy person with a bashed-in nose came down the stairs two at a time, long arms swinging like a chimpanzee, and together they dragged the bellowing man upstairs.

'Nosey is a marvellous stong man. He can fight two, three people even when he's drunk. Jack thinks he might go dry if he could get away from the others who are stuck with meths, keeping them alive until it kills them.'

'I think it's marvellous what you—'

'It's not enough. We can't cure anyone. We can only *be* here. Most of these people have nobody anywhere, you see.'

The banging and shouting upstairs subsided. Jack came down lightfooted. 'I'm going to start the sandwiches,' he said to Hattie. 'Dick's got a bottle up there and it's no good waiting for Doris when she's gone as long as this.'

In the passage, Victoria and Hattie stepped round a yellow puddle of vomit. Outside in the wet yard, pocked and hillocked with years of shifting coal dust, an old man was sitting on an upturned tank.

'Mike?'

He turned his face round under a mushroom hat. It was not Michael, but another old man, wasted, toothless, his face no different from what it would be when he was dead.

'Are you coming in?'

He turned his face away again.

'He hates being indoors. I'll bring you out a mug of soup.' Hattie went inside. As Victoria walked past the old man, she saw the hands that lay on his scarecrow knees, bone white and bloodless. One had only three fingers. The other had only stumps.

There was nothing she had to do tonight. Why did she not go back in to the shabby smelly house and cut sandwiches and clean up the vomit and go out with Hattie and Jack in the little daisy van to the derries and ramps and skippers? She walked on to the end of the chain fence. A boat in the river hooted jadedly at the bridge, dragging a string of covered barges like coffins. At the corner a taxi passed with its roof light on. She stopped it and got in. The last woman had left a flower scent behind. Victoria was instantly removed from Hattie's subcontinent. Ahead of her, a drink, a bath, meat to cook in her easy kitchen. A new dress to try on. A book she was enjoying. The lonely self indulgence of her white bed.

She paid the taxi and went up. Robbie had sent his week's flowers. Mrs Edgar from downstairs had arranged them with care and propped the card proudly, as if it were from a new exciting lover. Victoria made a drink and sat for a moment, thinking about the black greyhound girl and Jack and how they did not have to force themselves to conquer revulsion. It was never there.

She sighed and turned to the telephone by the fireplace. Dialling Billie's number made her feel suddenly very tired.

Billie – how are you?

Grumble, grumble. She always started off negatively to disguise any positive pleasure.

Let's meet somewhere and go to the cinema. Have you seen the Space thing? They say you hate it or love it but you can't not see it.

Don't do me any favours, Victoria. You've got something better to do than go out with me.

Not home ... not home ... not home ... Victoria let the telephone ring for quite a long time before she hung up.

'*Barbara. Barbara. When are you going to sleep with me?*'

'*Wait, Paul, we must wait.*'

'*Why wait? What for?*'

In this town, which was full of odd pockets of different variegations of society, it was easy to conduct a discreet affair without anyone knowing or caring. What was happening between Paul and Barbara Frost was not yet an affair. They met often, discovered each other, discovered their love. She had cooked dinner for him in her small ivy-swamped house where the suburbs relaxed into country, but he had never stayed. One son was still at home. The married son's room was let to a student who shook the house with wild piano music.

'When are you going to sleep with me?' Paul began to ask it very soon. A sense of urgency plagued him. The world would end. He would be too old. One of them would die. There was no time, no time for gradual growth of love. He was afraid, not that they would be found out, but that something would happen to take this away.

'Wait, darling, we must wait.' More passive, her sexuality for a long pause asleep, for Barbara it was enough that they had found each other.

'Why wait? What for? There's no time.'

'Because we're both so old?' She was six years younger than he was. He had been feeling used and finished at fifty. He did not now think of either of them as anything but in their prime.

He told her she was beautiful, and after a while she gave up denying it. 'And I don't look in the mirror so much. I used to force myself to look in a strong light, because I thought that you must face the truth of what Nature does to your face as the price of using it. Now I think it's better to imagine you look all right than to keep reminding yourself you don't.'

Alice was drinking very heavily after Christmas. That was not an excuse, but it was a cause perhaps. It made this more necessary.

'It also makes it more possible.' Barbara was endowed with a rueful commonsense that stood her in good stead of wit. She was calm, accepting, un-volatile, very peaceful and lovely to be with.

They were able to be quite often together. Alice spent whole evenings at the club by the harbour, returning sometimes in a taxi after midnight and waking Paul to rail at him. Sometimes not returning at all. Paul thought she stayed with some raffish friends who lived in the harbour village, but one morning when he rang them, she was not there.

If she was not at home when he left for the Butterfields school, he pencilled a message on the refrigerator door: 'Back about five,' or, 'I'll bring something in for dinner.' He did not write, 'Where have you been?'

By the time he came home, especially if he had a late

detention class, Alice would be several drinks into the evening, and would not remember where she had spent the night out, nor even whether. Often when he came home, she was already out again, with a rude addendum to his refrigerator message.

'Ought we to feel guilty?' Barbara asked.

'What about?' In Paul's imagination, they went to Bahama Cays, to Scottish inns, to a hotel he knew in a farming village in the Perigord, where the water meadows nudged the white-washed walls.

'But Alice—'

'Laura says I owe her nothing.'

'Do you believe that?'

'Of course not. Laura sees everything black and white. If your marriage doesn't work, you drop it, as she will, and shut the door on the ghosts. Only for her there won't be any ghosts, and she won't wonder about Nigel's.'

And then there was a weekend when Barbara's son was going away and Alice announced in the middle of the night that she was going down the coast to stay with Hazel Rencher.

'You're a glutton for punishment.' Paul was wide awake now, trying not to sound pleased.

'Hazel has been a good friend.' Alice had pulled off her girdle and she fell into bed in a pinned petticoat, her stockings wrinkled round her ankles. 'But I'd go there anyway,' she humped her bony back to Paul, 'because it's obvious you don't want me here.'

'You hardly ever are here.'

'Why should I be when you don't want me?'

She could keep that sort of thing up for hours. Sometimes Paul got up and made tea or a drink and sat reading until she fell asleep, her mouth open, snoring stale alcohol.

'I want you here, of course,' he said. 'The flat isn't the same without you.'

'As if I was a sofa repossessed by the Hire Purchase people. At least you can sit on a sofa. Remember when—'

'Oh stop.'

'You haven't slept with me for months,' she whined, 'do you know that?'

'You're always drunk. You'd fall alseep.'

'You're past it, I expect, dear,' Alice said comfortably. 'Hazel thought you were looking awfully old the last time she saw you.'

'Hazel can go and screw herself.'

'I daresay she does,' Alice said equably. 'Who else would?'

In the morning when Alice woke fairly cheerful, which could either mean that she had drunk less last night, or that she was still slightly drunk, Paul offered to drive her to Hazel's after school.

'That would be getting rid of me too fast. I shall free you of me more slowly, in a bus.'

'This is improbably easy,' Barbara said when she got into the car. She was wearing a coat with big red and white squares like a horse blanket. She always wore very good shoes on her narrow feet. Her silk scarf was French. Her bag was the kind of leather that costs a lot to buy, but well kept, lasts for years. Short locks of hair lay softly over each other, like leaves. She looked like the best kind of Burlington mother setting off for the Burlington–Stowe rugger match, the social event of the Spring term. She looked like Mrs Watts, mother of the star forward in Paul's time. Except that no one would ever take Mrs Watts to a hotel they knew of which looked, and treated its few guests, as if it was still a comfortable shabby manor house in a park with a walled fruit garden.

Mr and Mrs Harding. Barbara did not blush. Her skin and circulation did not work that way.

Before they got home, Paul asked, 'How are you going to feel about this?'

'All right, I think. Surprised at myself. I always thought I was so cautious, but – yes, all right,' After a pause, she said, 'I'd forgotten what I'd been missing.'

There was a yellow bar under the front door of Paul's flat. He had left the hall light on. Chronically worried about money, the electricity bill flipped through his mind's letter box. He could not even light the grill for steak without seeing the gas roar through the pipes and burn away.

He carried his suitcase down the hall. As he passed the open door of the sitting room, his eyes registered something before his mind and body. He had gone past the doorway before he realized that Alice was sitting on an upright chair with her feet neatly crossed, ironing.

He went back. 'I thought you weren't coming home till tomorrow.'

'I couldn't wait to see you. Have you been at the Samaritans?'

That was one alibi he would never use. 'I was playing golf with Upjohn. The father of that boy Stephen. You remember.' You remember that day at Archway when he came to tea with Bluey Morgan and you were sloshed.

'Carry your clubs in a suitcase?'

'I spent the night with them.'

Now it began. It had been too easy. Now the lies must begin. He looked at Alice. There was something wrong. Not just that she was ironing a shirt, but it was six-thirty on a Saturday evening and she – he went closer and looked at her prominent pale blue eyes – yes, she was sober.

'Don't say anything. Please don't say you're glad, or it's about time. Please don't laugh. It's bad enough without that.' She pressed firmly on the iron, but when she stood it on its heel to turn the shirt, he saw that her hands were shaking. She was smiling with her teeth closed. Tiny beads of sweat spattered her lip. 'Hazel's been working on me. You're right. She is a damn bore. To shut her up, I said I'd try again. That's really why I came home. I want you to take me to A.A. tonight.'

For weeks, they went to an Alcoholics Anonymous meeting almost every night. There were several groups in the town. There was always a meeting somewhere. Alice could only hang on to sobriety if she went among the people who fought the same battle. She did not beg Paul to go with her, but she would not go without him.

Occasionally Paul could see Barbara on his way home from school. Brief times together, not happy, not properly talking, because there was no time. Alice could hardly survive the day without his support.

'For how long?' Barbara asked.

'It depends. There are people who've been going to A.A. meetings for sixteen, twenty years. It replaces social life, church going, everything. It's like being on an artificial kidney. They can't cope without it.'

'What are we going to do?' Barbara was the one who asked it.

'I don't know. Don't ask me yet. I can't see ahead. I only know I have to do this now. All the times I've begged her, nagged at her, even threatened her, had A.A. people round to talk to her, prayed for it, God knows, it was the one thing I wanted.'

'And now you don't want it?'

'Of course I want it for her.'

'But not for us.' Barbara looked at him candidly. 'It was better for us when she was drinking.'

Barbara could voice the forbidden things, the things he hated himself for thinking. She was willing to understand, but not to pretend.

Alice's group had been asked to put on a meeting for another branch in a town fifteen miles away where the river ran under green willows and bungalow gardens came down to the bank. A place where you would not expect to find alcoholics, but there were just as many there as anywhere else. Alice and two men called Leslie and Scott were to speak.

'Are you going in Scott's car?'

'I said we could go in ours. Scott's good eye is getting worse.'

'Doesn't Leslie drive?'

'Paul—' Alice's eyes were instantly full of tears. She cried more easily now than when she was drinking. She was under a great strain. Every waking hour of her day was a conflict. It tired her, made her weaker than her nature. 'I've got to speak.'

'Yes, I know. I'm glad.'

'I can't do it.'

'You've done it before.'

'But you were there.' She was forced to say it. 'Paul, I—' She looked at him with eyes that the years of drinking had paled and bleared, now with drops quivering under the stubby lashes. 'I can't do it without you.'

'You never used to need me so much.' He said it lightly.

'I'm asking too much of you, aren't I?' She wiped her eyes, and her mouth trembled into a smile.

'I was the one who wanted you to get sober.'

'God, what will the children say!' Alice veered into a laugh. 'It will kill Jeff when he comes home at Easter and finds me wholesome and sweet-breathed as a dairy cow.'

'He isn't coming home,' Paul said. 'He's going to Sweden. Don't you remember?'

'I forget things. My brain has been rotted by years of alcohol.'

All the way in the car, she and Leslie and Scott made terrible crude jokes about booze, things that Paul would never dream of saying to an alcoholic, but they did it with a sort of spontaneous compulsion. It was part of their need for alcohol that they must talk about it endlessly, set it up and knock it down, deride it, nostalgically lament it, take it out and shake it, worry it, chew it into tag ends of old jests, as if by constant onslaught they could wear away its power.

After being with a group of dry alcoholics, the one thing Paul wanted was a drink.

And before. 'Oh good,' said Leslie, getting into the front seat of the car. 'I can get drunk on your breath. No – forget the peppermints. I like it.'

The meeting was in a parish hall, bare wood and iron-rod rafters, bleak with the memories of ill-attended jumble sales. When they went in, Leslie and Scott slid into the small crowd like fish into their own element, greeting several people by name. Alice hung back, her hand on Paul's arm. He pressed her wrist, feeling how little substance there was between flesh and bone. Her cheeks were flushed, her nose white and shiny. She used less make-up when she was not drinking.

'Don't be afraid, Alice.'

'How can anyone be expected to stand up and talk cold sober?'

'Inhuman, isn't it?' The evening's chairman came up, a mop-and-duster sort of woman on whom an actress might model herself for a margarine commercial. 'You must be Alice. I'm June.'

'My husband, Paul.'

'On the programme too?' June asked.

'Practically, he's been with me to so many meetings. I think it's putting him off not drinking.'

Alice was smiling and pleasant, but Paul could see that her whole body was trembling very slightly. A faint sour smell of something like fear came from her. They drank black coffee out of paper cups and stood about exchanging bright harmless small talk – to Paul and Alice the hardest part of alcoholism – until June called the meeting to order.

'My name is June and I'm an alcoholic. I'm conducting the meeting tonight, but I'm not going to talk for long, because I know you all want to hear our three fine speakers who have come from Town to be with us.' She sent her margarine smile to Alice and Leslie and Scott sitting beside her at the table. 'All I'm going to say, and you've heard me say it before and you'll hear me again, is that if it wasn't for A.A., I wouldn't be here tonight. I would probably be dead. Or in prison. I've been there, and if by any unlikely chance any of you have not,' (laughter) 'let me tell you it's no fun.'

Although he had listened to many horror stories from many perfectly ordinary people, Paul had never quite got over the surprise that a woman like this – short curly brown hair, lipstick too bright, green knit suit straight out of a woman's magazine, right forefinger that peeled potatoes every day – could have descended into hell and been dragged out of it with so little outward blemish.

When Leslie began to speak, the surprise was the same. He was a youngish, beaky man with thin fluffy hair and a way of clearing a non-existent obstruction in his throat that must drive his wife up the wall if he did it at home. He wore a grey suit and a striped tie and he worked for the Post Office as a telephone linesman. He had only been in the A.A. programme for two years. Before that, he had been in hospital five times with DTs, he had lost his job, his money, his wife, his children. Sleeping rough in a derelict house, he had talked to another drunk who had been in and out of A.A. like a needle through a hem. Next day, the police took him to hospital with a raging pneumonia. When he came out, he went back to the same derry, but the drunk had disappeared.

Leslie disappeared too – 'run-down metal polish this time' – until one night, desperate, cynical, belligerent, he stumbled into the house on Flagg's Hill where every Saturday at midnight an A.A. meeting was held for anyone who could drag themselves in from the gutter.

'I don't remember any of it. I don't think I heard anything that was said. But next day, I found a card in my pocket that a chap I'd talked to had put there. I phoned him. He left his office and came to me. That was the day I was born.'

Leslie got back his job, and eventually his wife, 'though she keeps a suitcase packed,' he grinned, 'in case I take a drink again.'

He had been drinking since he was eleven, sneaking sherry out of a bottle in his father's sideboard. 'I see now that with those first secret nips, I was on my way. I can't drink. I'm an alcoholic. I give thanks every day that I came to A.A. That A.A. found me, rather. I wouldn't have had the sense or the guts to get in on my own.'

When he finished, the running commentary of racking coughs among the rows of chairs before him broke into a storm. Saved from cirrhosis of the liver, the alcoholics were all furiously engaged in smoking themselves to death, almost everyone with an ashtray or a saucer on their laps, burning little troughs in the plastic, a chest surgeon's dream.

It was Alice's turn. Paul, sitting in the second row, trying to smile encouragement to her, was almost as nervous as she was. If she failed at this, actually or in her own mind, if she showed up worse than some of the normally inarticulate people who were so incredibly articulate in describing their lives in hell, he knew she might go back to the bottle from one day to the next.

She knew that too. When June introduced her, she got up, wringing her knuckly fingers, and then she gave a little gasp and said, 'Do you mind if Scott speaks next? I – it's ridiculous to be so nervous—'

'What you need is a drink,' Scott said, getting heavily to his feet. He was a stout blockbuster of a man, a boxer in his Army days, his girth in a double-breasted blue suit immense.

'Excuse me. I'm nervous too.' He unbuttoned the jacket on an enormous expanse of white shirt like the side of a marquee. He was a lovely genial man, kindly and full of inherent wisdom not gathered from books. A man of whom the lady who drooled, 'I wish I was blind so I could have one of them lovely dogs' might say, 'I wish my husband was an alcoholic so he could be like that when he was reformed.'

Scott wore a patch over one eye. He told the audience, as he had told other audiences over and over again for almost five years, how a lifetime of drinking and fighting and losing his Army career and everything else since had culminated in three months' oblivion, ended by a shot through the head and the loss of one eye.

'I can see why I did it,' he said, 'though I don't remember doing it. I only remember I woke up in a hospital somewhere and I couldn't see, and when they told me what I'd done, by God, I yelled and fought them. To have got so near to getting out of the whole bloody mess and just missed ... There was an A.A. group at that hospital. I fought them too, but they fought harder. One of the nurses, he was an alcoholic. I don't think he took any off-duty while I was there. There was a pal of mine, Freddie, his name was, my old boozing pal. He sneaked me in a bottle one day under his coat and this nurse kicked him out of that ward like a drunk out of a bar.

'I've been sober now for about five years, grace of God who would have been within his rights for not troubling about me. I've still got a chip of metal in me brain,' he ended chattily, 'just to remind me.'

Applause. Volcanic coughing. Scott looked at Alice and nodded, and she stood up, resting her fingers on the edge of the table and licking her lips.

'My name is Alice.' She was wearing one of the old tailored dresses Paul used to like on her before she began buying neon-coloured brief vulgar things much too young for her. 'I'm an alcoholic.'

She began the story that Paul knew so well. But told like this, it sounded different, as if it were a stage play in which he had no part. When she talked about, 'my husband', it did not seem to be him. 'My son' was not Jeff, sobbing once to Paul, 'Mummy's ill, what's wrong with Mummy?' 'My daughter' was not tough, unsentimental Laura at fourteen telling him, 'I don't want to have a birthday party if *she's* going to get drunk.'

Alice was not concealing or embroidering. She was telling her story simply and coherently, giving it a pattern of descent, whereas at the time, it had been a shapeless chaos of wasted years, quarrels, crises, tears, false hopes, despair, and all the sordid episodes of living with a drunk.

'And then, towards the end of the time when we were at the school, my husband started on the serious drinking. You could hardly blame him. I was polluted most of the time and when he was drinking too, it was the only thing we were doing together, the only fun we ever had. We pretended it was fun, but it was a hideous business of two or three drinks before we could even dress for those awful parties the other masters used to throw, and coming home stumbling and paralytic and scared to death one of the boys would hear us. It was a wonder we weren't kicked out long before. But my husband was popular and they made allowances. Until I got stupefied enough to start sleeping with a randy Australian who still smelled of sheep. He was the cousin of the Assistant Headmaster's wife. I think she'd had a bit of a go with him herself.'

Alice was quite relaxed now. The release of being able to tell everything to people who had been there themselves was working in her, as it did on all the speakers. People who did not know anything about A.A. called it exhibitionism, and said they could not bear to sit and listen all evening to squalid confessions, not understanding the two-way therapy of release and reassurance.

'After we left, my husband stopped drinking. He's not an alcoholic.' She smiled down at Paul, 'So it was easy.'

Easy! A private joke, because she knew about the Paul who had pounded and howled outside the door of the Samaritans in the middle of one night.

She told her audience how he had persuaded her to join A.A. 'It didn't work. I hated it. I cheated. I had a bottle in my bag. I used to sit at meetings sweating like a pig till I could get out and have a drink. I put the story round that I had chronic cystitis to explain why I kept popping out to the Ladies'. I hated the whole thing. It sickened me. I thought everyone was so smug. If that was what sobriety meant, I'd choose boozing.

'Now I've come back. I'm sober today. Tomorrow I may wake up dead drunk in the flat of some man whose name I don't even know. That happened to me two months ago. Gives you a bit of a fright. Your only hope is that he was drunk enough to be just as non-operative as you.'

She did not look at Paul as she joined the laughter, and the coughing that it brought on.

'I'll stop now,' she said breathlessly, 'because I'm dying for a cigarette. I'm dying for a drink too, of course. But I haven't had one today. Not yet anyway. I can only say I haven't had a drink today as I'm falling asleep. And then I still might get up.'

'You were marvellous,' Paul told her in the car.

'She's a good speaker,' Scott said. 'I think I'll take her to London next month. We've been asked to take part in a three-day thing.'

'No,' Alice said. 'Don't ask me.'

'Thought you'd be flattered,' Scott grumbled.

'I don't want to get hooked on A.A.'

'You must.'

'I'm not a joiner. I don't want to be identified with it. I want to use it my way and not be a part of it.'

'Won't work, Alice,' Leslie said.

'You don't know it all,' she rounded on him, biting her nails. 'I'm sick of making jokes and pretending all's well with me under the A.A. umbrella. All's not well. I hate the whole thing. I want a drink.'

After they had taken Leslie and Scott home, Paul asked Alice, 'Did you make that up – about the man whose name you didn't know?'

'Mm-mm.' She shook her head. Her nails, which once she had spent hours grooming into refined claws, were chewed into sore stumps below her fingertips. 'Funny. I was able to tell it to that rabble. But not to you.'

'I knew you weren't at Bruce's one night.'

'I'm sorry,' she said ungraciously.

He could not answer anything that would not be hypocrisy.

Later when they were going to bed, the telephone rang. Paul was on Flying Squad call tonight. He was so sure that he would have to go out that he stepped back into the shoe he had just taken off before he picked up the telephone.

It was Scott. 'Alice all right?'

'She's in the bath.'

'She all right?'

'I think so.'

'Tell her she can ring me any time she wants. Make sure she knows that. Any time in the night. I can come round if you need me, Paul.'

But why wouldn't *I* do? Why is it that I can go dashing

out to rescue a man in a phone box who has taken half a dozen Seconal and yet I can't rescue my wife?

'Thanks, Scott. That's good of you.'

He could tell none of any of this to Barbara. They had both told each other everything of their lives before, and it was a betrayal of their closeness that he could not betray Alice now.

After the New Year, Dr Ling went from Highfield, or went to another section, which was almost the same as going away in that rambling, overpopulated place.

He was replaced by a blank smiling person called Dr Marjorie, who did not bother Tim very much. Plump in a white coat, she appeared in the day room, looking vaguely round over people's heads as if she wanted to hang a picture.

'Alec – yes, hullo there – Alec Brand, isn't it? Would you like to come and have a bit of a chat?'

Alec came up with that smile like an unselective dog, and Dr Marjorie looked mildly round to see what next. A nurse opened the door of one of the side rooms, and the doctor ambled in with her white coat strained across her hips, Alec following as if he were on a leash.

When the door opened and Alec came out, scratching his head, the doctor looked round at the men reading the paper, or watching television, or knitting (Dick's great talent, endless tubular works like airfield windsocks, growing down the wheel of his chair), or just sitting and waiting for the world to end.

'Timothy – Timothy Shaw. Do they call you Tim? Yes – hullo. Would you like to come and have a bit of a chat?'

'No, thanks.' Tim was at a table polishing silver for Olive Barrett.

'Come on, old chap, won't keep you a minute.' She had evidently been ordered by Dr Vandenburg to see all his patients, so Tim took pity on her, and after warning Ernie not to touch the polish, and telling Mr Podgorsky to watch him, he went into the side room.

The doctor had his folder on the table between them. If Dr Ling had written down everything that Tim told him, it must be quite a wonderful tale. Tim did not remember much of what he had said, so he decided to keep mum, lest Dr Marjorie catch him out and start up the business about fantasizing.

Idea. 'Could you' – Tim tried to think himself paler – 'I feel funny all of a sudden. Could you get me a glass of water?' Golden opportunity to look into the folder and see if Olive had told any of the things that he and she had talked about.

Instead of getting up, Dr Marjorie leaned her chair back, lifting her blunt feet off the floor, and pressed the wall buzzer.

Rajah Bill looked in. 'Timothy feels faint. Could you please get him some water?'

'I'll get it. I can— I'm—' Tim managed to get out of the room.

'What is the matter with you?' The Indian orderly hissed and gobbled at him.

'Just a joke.'

'Ha perishing ha.'

Tim had told Olive Barrett things that nobody else knew. Even at the House of God's Angels, he did not think they had known much. When he was a boy, asking questions, Mrs Pfister used to put on what she thought was her kind face and say, 'Don't worry that little noodle about all those bygone things. What's done is done. We must think about what's to be.'

Yes, but what had been done? A lot of it had swirled away in fog. Tim could remember fear. He could remember the scalding water going over his shoulder, because his skin bore the scars of it, although he could not remember how it had happened.

He could remember the stove blowing up in Auntie Ruth's face and how surprised she had looked with her brows and lashes all gone to frizzled crumbs.

'That must have been after we left London, because it was in that house where the trains went over, higher than the roofs. Serve her right. She hated her.'

'Hated who?' He and Olive were making beds. Tim liked to do those kind of girls jobs. When he was sweeping the floor one day, Nobby said, 'Sissy,' as he shuffled by, and Tim had kicked him in the crotch.

'Her that came.' Tim stopped the blanket in mid-shake, and stared past Olive, right through the wall.

'Who?'

'Her.'

'Say it.'

He looked back at Olive and his hands began to shake the blanket again. 'My mother. She came and they yelled at each other. I run under the settee. She hated Aunt Posy too. "You'd not say that if my man was at home," Aunt Posy told her. "Why don't you take the kid then and have done with it?"'

Sitting with Olive on his bed when the dormitory was empty, memories were wrung out of him, with tears, as if he were a dishcloth. Buried things came so painfully to the surface that he would moan and clutch his chest as if he were trying to have a baby through his mouth.

Olive hugged him close. 'Poor Tim, poor Timmy boy. Olive's here. It's all right. Don't you fret, love.'

When she asked him, he could not remember how many aunties there had been. He remembered bits of gardens, furniture, different kinds of bread, a striped cat, the smell of his mother that hung in the hall – she seldom got much further. Two steps from the door and she was into a shouting match.

'What did she look like?' Olive asked.

'I dunno. I never saw her. I hid. Hid in the toolshed once two days. They passed me cake in under the door. Fruit bread. There was some rotten apples in there. I licked the boards where they melted. Auntie got a fire-man to break down the door. Laugh! There he was with his axe and me sitting on the coal with the pruning knife. At the Home, when Auntie took me, we was walking by the hedge that smelled of cats and she said, "I have tried Tim, I'm sorry." I didn't know what she meant. I didn't know I wouldn't see her. She had my picture in her camera.'

'It's a shame,' Olive said. 'When I think of the good safe childhood my four have had—'

He got up off the bed, so that the mattress went down where she was sitting. Who wanted to talk about her rotten kids? She babbled on sometimes like rinse water about her family and her house and how she was going to start training to be a State Enrolled nurse and make more money so she could do something or other to the house and send her stupid son somewhere or other.

'Why don't you take me home with you?' Tim asked her once.

'Hush dear.' She looked round as if the walls were bugged, as well they might be. 'It's against the rules.'

'Ho ho, if you knew all the rules I break,' he said darkly.

'What dear?' She was washing Uncle Fred's crêpe bandage, humming, her sleeves rolled up above the dough-dimples of her elbows.

'Fliss and me,' he hinted. 'Places we go.'

'It's so nice for you to have a little friend.'

'She's prettier than you.' Tim darted it in, watching her, but she was purring over the sudsy bowl as if they were talking of the weather.

'I daresay she is, dear. She's thirty years younger than me. But you should have seen me in my day.'

Who cared? Tim walked off, telling himself a string of ugly words that Arthur Callaghan had taught him.

Olive thought she knew all about Tim, but she did not know about the maids' cupboard, and she did not know about the air-raid shelter behind the boiler room where the folding chairs were kept, and she did not know about the sheltered place behind the hedge behind the student nurses' dormitory. Out of bounds to all patients, that bit of the grounds, but Mr Semple had once seen a fat girl taking a bath. The story was legend.

That would make Olive sit up, if Tim could tell her where they went, but Felicity threatened him with freakish tortures if he breathed a word to a living soul. Or a dead one. She had once got into the mortuary, and seen an old man and a new-born baby. She was so wild. There was nothing she had not done.

She drove Tim wild, and then laughed at him, because he could not wait.

'Do it, do it,' she begged, and he was so mad with excitement and terror that someone would come, that it was done before she could open his trousers. The problem of his life was taking care of his clothes before he was found out. They wore brown overall coats in the carpentry shop. After recreation time, he often came back to the ward wearing his overall.

'Why don't you go to bed in that, you're in such a hurry to get to work?' Mr Podgorsky asked, his sad face heavy with the joke.

The rules of Highfield allowed Tim and Felicity to be together in the library, the common rooms, or walking about the paths that criss-crossed the frost-beaten glass between the turreted buildings. Felicity did not care to be in any of those places. One evening, just as it was getting dark and the bells were ringing for visitors to leave, they were caught coming up from the air-raid shelter by no less a person than Mrs Purchase, matron of all the women nurses, with a row of war medals across the top part of her grey egg-timer dress.

'Just a minute—' as Felicity began to whistle and stride by on her long thin legs. 'Who—? It's Felicity, isn't it? Felicity Gretch.'

'In one.' For a girl who had been so put down by her family, Felicity could be quite insolent.

'And who are you, young man?'

'Tim Shaw. Ward C2.'

'And where have you two been?'

Tim raised a rifle and picked off the medals, ping, ping, ping, and then her nipples – fff-lofsh.

'Exploring. This is a funny old place, isn't it?'

'Very funny.' Mrs Purchase did not disclose what she thought. She went on her way like a person in a Noah's

Ark, but the following day, Felicity's recreation time was cancelled.

Tim waited in vain at the end of the long corridor that led to the block where she lived. Doors swished at the far end, and a nurse ran down the stone corridor towards him, her hair flying up as she passed each open window, pulling off her apron as she came.

She recognized Tim and stopped. 'Are you waiting for Felicity? She must stay in for a few days.'

'Why?'

'Dearie, I don't make the rules. Run!' she told herself. 'Run for your life!' Tim went slowly after her.

When he next saw Felicity, they sat in the library for an hour and read *Good Housekeeping* and the *Sunday Times Magazine* cover to cover, all the advertisements, while Felicity wet Tim's ear with her whispers. She looked even thinner, greenish bruises under her eyes, her teeth more prominent, the salt cellars in her neck unfathomable.

'They can't make me eat if I don't want to,' she boasted.

'They put a tube down you.' Tim had seen it done to old Simon after he blacked out and lay like dead for days.

'I went one better,' Felicity giggled, and Mrs Fletcher said, 'Softly, softly,' without looking up from her desk.

'What?'

'You know.'

'Tell me.'

'No.' She shook her head till the metal clip on the end of one of her plaits swung into his face.

'Tell.' He pinched her thin thigh.

She suffocated with giggles, stuffing the side of her hand into her mouth, her shoulders shaking.

'Are you all right, dear?' Mrs Fletcher got up and came over.

'Just a joke.' Felicity's eyes were watering.

'I'm glad you can always see the funny side, but remember that Louise is trying to study.' Louise was in an unlit corner wearing thick dark glasses and making out she was reading the tiny print of the Encyclopaedia, so that Mrs Fletcher would tell everyone else to keep quiet.

'No more talking now. Remember.'

Felicity raised the magazine and lowered her head. 'Shoved it – you know where.' She looked sideways at Tim behind a two-page colour-spread of Ways and Means with left-over Lamb and Mutton.

'What?'

'Daffodil stalk. Spoon. Cork. Anything.'

'Why?' He goggled at her. His brain was on strike against picturing it.

'They have to get it down.' Felicity collapsed help-lessly, and Mrs Fletcher led her to the door, stopped a passing student nurse and had her conducted back to her ward.

Dr Max decided that Felicity needed more to occupy her time than the cookery school and the sewing shop, where she had caused a lot of trouble by stitching one of her hangnails down on to the machine. She was sent to one of the geriatric wards to learn how to take care of the old folk, which gave her different hours, so that Tim could hardly ever see her.

He wrote letters, which Olive delivered – or said she did – but there was no answer.

One day when he was strolling with Mr Podgorsky through a misted March morning to the carpentry shop – he no longer had to go with Alec and Arthur Callaghan and the rest of the chain gang – he saw Felicity ahead, pushing a wheelchair. She was wearing an unfamiliar pink uniform, but there was no mistaking those legs and the way she turned her feet out, and the two braided snakes of hair down her narrow back.

Tim ran to catch up with her. 'Hey!'

She jerked the chair to such a stop that the old lady nearly fell out.

'Hullo, Fliss.' Now that they were together, Tim did not know what to say. Felicity said nothing. Her treacle eyes shone with amusement, looking him up and down as if he were somehow freakish, her tongue showing between her teeth.

'Where to then?'

'Industrial therapy. The old faggots make little bows all day. Don't you, dear?' She bent down and yelled. The old lady sat and gazed back into her past, since she could not have much future. 'Did you know, Timothy, that all the little bows on all the ladies' underwear in all of Europe are made here at Highfield? Did you know that?' She put her head on one side, rocking the chair as if she had a baby.

'No. I didn't know that.'

It was a stupid conversation. When Mr Podgorsky came up with his bent knees and his little paunch and his one strand of hair so carefully over the top of his head, they had got nowhere.

'You like it then, up there?' Tim was not even quite sure where her new ward was, so he could not jerk his head in any direction.

'They like me.' The mist coiled the front of her hair into wispy springs. 'I've done very well,' she said prissily. 'Sister says I might go out and work at the nursing home some day.'

It was not the old wild Felicity. Where had that one gone? Tim stood staring after her with an ache like heartburn. Mr Podgorsky took his arm to pull him along. 'Wine, women and song, Timothy. And work for the masses.'

Tim went down the same path at the same time every day, but he did not see Felicity again for a long time. Olive Barrett had gone off on holiday, and Tim lapsed into a listless boredom.

'In affairs of the heart,' Mr Podgorsky said, 'I am the laughing philosopher.' He tried to teach Tim to play draughts, but Tim could not rouse himself to more than throwing dice for Snakes and Ladders, which Mr Podgorsky despised, although he was kindly enough to play, and let Tim win.

Paul found Tim playing against himself one evening,

and mistakenly played a round or two, thinking that this was what Tim wanted to do.

'What do you want to do?' Paul asked, when Tim overturned the board. 'Want to come down to the cafeteria? Like to come out? It's too wet to walk, but I could get you a pass to go into Town. There's almost an hour.'

Tim shook his head.

'Anything the matter?'

'I feel rotten.'

'That's a shame. You've been going so well. They're very pleased with your work in the shop, I understand, and the way you've picked up generally.'

'I don't feel no better.' He didn't. Since Olive and Felicity had abandoned him, he was beginning to feel as lost and direction-less as when he came in.

'You've forgotten what it was like for you before. We couldn't have sat and talked like this. I think it's wonderful, Tim, how you've got yourself going again. You'll be leaving pretty soon, they seem to think.'

Tim had not thought about it. 'Where would I go?'

'We'll work something out. I'll help you, of course. The Medical Social Worker here will help you to find some work you like, and a place to stay. Perhaps you could go on with the carpentry, get some more training, since you seem to be good with your hands.'

Tim looked at them, palm down on his knees. As he looked, they began very slightly to shake. Under cover of the table, he felt his pulse. It was quickening. When Paul asked him a question, he began to stutter.

Paul lit a cigarette and began to talk about something else, telling Tim a story about a fight at school in which a boy had broken a leg, and the teacher in the playground had called the police because he was afraid to interfere.

Tim scarcely heard what he was saying. His thoughts were stopped behind a gate. A gate that said, 'You'll be leaving,' and swung slowly open on a great unknown plain where the wind howled in terror, and there was no shelter, and no horizon.

The next morning was Sunday. He humbled himself to Rajah Bill and asked him to take a note when he went off duty and try to find Felicity Gretch on one of the geriatric wards.

'What about me?' Rajah Bill had a fierce face like an eagle. 'What do I get for my trouble?'

Tim went to his locker and took out two packets of cigarettes, went back and added a third. What if the canary lady had been marking the fags on the trolley to find out who was knocking them off? Rajah would swing.

'Come to Himms,' his note said. 'I'll wait at the back of the hall.'

On Sunday evenings, there was community hymn singing in the assembly hall: rows of folding chairs from Tim and Felicity's air-raid shelter, and everyone singing *Abide with me* and other such dragging melodies. It was quite sad. Tim put on the bright blue pullover that Paul had given him for Christmas, and asked Mr Gilbert's permission after tea.

'I didn't know you went in for that sort of thing.'

'Give it a try,' Tim mumbled. 'Can't do no harm.'

'If you're going, you can take Mr Pargiter and Norman along with you, save someone the trip.'

Tim was in good standing on this ward. He was entrusted with people like Norman and poor Mr Pargiter whose head was permanently twisted round, like a knob, so that he had to come at himself from the side with his food. Tim pinned bulletins on the board. He fetched stores, and went to the record library, and bought stamps and toothpaste from the shops for those who could not navigate. As Olive said, it was a wonder how they had ever run C2 without him.

He got Norman and Mr Pargiter going early and sat them somewhere near the front. 'Don't move till I come back for you after.' He gave Norman a fresh paper-napkin for his tap of a nose. Then he hung about at the back while the hall filled up, and at last, when Dr Stoneman was already striking bold chords on the piano and the doors at the back were being closed, here she was sauntering round the corner from the main lobby as if there were all the time in the world.

Tim nipped out and let the doors close behind him on the first surge of song. 'You came, Fliss.'

'I always come to Hymns.' She must mean that as a joke, because she knew he knew it was a lie.

'I've got to talk to you.'

'Go ahead.' She sat down on a bench by the wall. He sat beside her. People passing back and forth, hospital staff, patients, visitors, glanced towards the music, but did not look at them.

'You didn't answer my notes.'

'What notes?'

'Didn't you get them?'

She shook her head. Who was the liar – Felicity or Olive? He did not trust either of them.

'I wanted—' He could not say, 'I wanted to see you. He could not say anything. 'Fliss—'

'What's up, Shorty?' She hardly ever used to call him that. 'You look like death not warmed up.'

'They may send me away from here.'

'Lucky.'

'I d-, I d—' His mouth opened and shut like the goldfish on Mr Gilbert's windowsill. He was getting lock-jaw.

'Is that all you wanted to tell me?'

He wanted to cry on her neck, to be with her in the broom cupboard, close, safe, just them in the world and the world no bigger than a cupboard.

'I don't know why you should think I care,' Felicity said rather grandly. She got up, smoothing down her short skirt and picking off a thread that was not there. 'I'll be gone myself pretty soon.'

He stared.

'I'll be at the nursing home next month. My people are *shocked*. Such rough work! But it's a nice bit of pay and a room of my own—'

'*Flissa*—!'

But she said gaily, 'May as well get grooving,' pushed

the swing door into the hall with the flat of her hand and was gone from him.

Olive would be back on Monday. All night to get through, but she would be there in the morning with her pudgy smile and her warm smell and she would listen to him properly and understand. She would not let them kick him out. He hardly slept all night. He lay with his hands behind his head, staring into the half dark, while shadowy figures went past him towards the bathrooms, stubbing their toes and cursing.

In the morning, he made an excuse not to go to carpentry. When it was time for Olive to come on duty, he sat watching the door. A stubble-haired woman in Olive's blue uniform walked in like a duck, looked round, tutted, as if she found the C2 dayroom the mess it was when Olive was not there, and waddled on into the office.

She came out. 'Are you Tim? Staff Nurse says you will help me with the dinner tables.'

'Where's Olive?'

'Who?'

'Mrs Barrett. She's the Nursing Assistant on this ward.'

'Not any longer, whoever she is. I was sent here. You can call me Mrs Dominic.'

I'll see you dead ... He charged into the office, which was not allowed without knocking. Mr Gilbert looked up from the dispensary slips and stood up when he saw how Tim looked.

'What's up, old chap?'

'Where's Olive?'

'I meant to tell you. She's taking her State Enrolled course. She got the chance to start as soon as she came back from holiday.'

'She's got my money.' That was not what he meant to say. He did not care about the money. His voice just came out with that.

'No, no she hasn't.' Mr Gilbert's strong freckled hands caught hold of Tim by the upper arms and held him firmly. 'It's all in the bank. You can get it any time you want.'

Mr Gilbert sat him down and stuck a thermometer in his mouth, because he had said he had a headache, to get out of carpentry. 'I thought you were shamming, Tim, but you do look a bit rough.'

When Mr Gilbert turned his back, Tim ground the thermometer between his teeth and caressed it with his tongue, trying to make it warm up.

'No problem there,' Mr Gilbert gave it a quick look. He sent Tim to bed for the rest of the day (a tray of food with the tea all slopped over brought by Uncle Fred), and the next morning, sent him off to the wood shop as a matter of course.

Tim was dead, a walking mummy case. He was working on a flap table. 'You can finish chiselling out that joint this morning.' An unreal man who looked and sounded like Bob Bamber.

When the chisel slipped and all of a sudden there was blood all over the table and a jagged piece of finger skin hanging, Tim felt nothing.

It was Arthur Callaghan who yelled. 'He's chopped himself!'

'Very brave. Good boy, very brave.' Bob came quickly with the first-aid box, and kept saying, 'Bad luck, Tim,' and, 'What a good lad.' But it was a stranger who went with one of the instructors to the surgery and had his wound dressed and a shot of something for his nerves. Not Tim.

At dinner time, when the men came back on the ward, Arthur Callaghan sidled into the chair next to where Tim sat waiting, like the Good Lad he was today, for his fish.

'Tried it on again, eh?' Arthur said.

Tim was holding up the dollied finger of his left hand to ease the throb. 'History repeats itself.' Arthur put his slimy fingers on the wrist, touching the raised scar.

Was *that* what he had done? The blood spilling over the table, soaking into the wood, the same blood that had welled into the dirty basin under the stairs. Was that what he had tried to do?

He thought that Olive would come to see him now that he was hurt, but she didn't care. He lay in bed and cried into the hot pillow. Aunt Posy used to come up when he called out that it was too dark, or he wanted a drink, so he called every night, two or three times a night, so she didn't come up any more. She did not even stand at the bottom of the stairs and yell, 'Waddayawant?'

Olive didn't care. Her fault, her fault. He'd get the chisel and find her.

They did not let him go to work for a few days. Then the doctor in the surgery looked at his finger, put a plaster on it and sent him along to the carpentry shop.

'Welcome back to the mines,' Mr Podgorsky said cheerfully, ruling a meticulous line on a piece of plywood, his spread hand holding it steady. Tim picked up a small saw and brought it down as hard as he could across the splayed-out fingers.

SIX

'THERE'S A SCHOOL Board dinner tomorrow.' Paul was not very good at lying, but to see Barbara, he had to lie, and if he could not see Barbara at all, he could not go on. 'Some new schemes are coming up for the English Department and they want all of us there.'

Alice was quite good at being lied to. She did not question the lie, she questioned what it said. 'You mean, *all* the English teachers?'

'All of us who work with the seniors.'

'I thought you might take me out to dinner.'

'Sorry, Alice. Day after tomorrow.'

'Day after tomorrow I'll be dead.'

In the middle of a class next morning Glenn Brimmer's moon face appeared behind the glass top of the door. He watched for a moment, turning his eyes from side to side, until Paul told someone near the door, 'Tell that boy to come in or go away.'

He came in. 'You're wanted on the phone.'

Calls were forbidden during classes. 'Look at chapter ten,' Paul told the room. 'Try and see why the jury arrived at that verdict. No rioting.' He hurried down the stairs and along the hall to the office, past a group of girls who said, 'Walk, don't run, Mr Hammond.' Alice was under a bus. Barbara had burned all the skin off her freckled arm at Unitech. Jeff was in a Swedish gaol. Laura was having a miscarriage. Scott had found Alice dead drunk on the floor.

'I just talked to Jane. She sent you her love.'

'Look, Alice, I'm not supposed—'

'She's putting on a meeting tonight, in the South End.

One of her speakers is ill. Or drunk. She wants me to do it.'

'You'll be all right.'

'Only if you come with me.'

'Can't you go with Jane and Phil?'

'Not without you.'

'You know I've got to go to the Board dinner. If you really won't go without me, you'll have to tell Jane you can't do it.'

'I told her I would.'

'Ring her back.'

'She's out for the day. Don't groan, dearest. I do need you, you know.'

Paul telephoned Barbara at Unitech to tell her that they could not meet that night, and went back to his class. They were not rioting. They were perching on the desks, lying on the floor, talking in groups. Stuart Jenkins, sitting at Paul's high desk, flicking a cigarette neatly through the window.

Barbara had said, at Unitech, 'It's all right. I do understand,' but without fondness, as if she did not understand, or did not want to.

After school, when he was in the library choosing sonnets from anthologies, one of the cleaners huffed up the stairs to call him to the telephone accusingly, as if he were responsible for her emphysema.

It was 200. 'Sorry to bother you at school. There was a call from your boy, Tim Shaw, from Highfield. Something has happened, I think. He wouldn't tell me, but he sounded pretty rough. Can you go to him?'

Ward H was no different from C2. The same sort of furniture. The same kind of people sitting and staring, or shuffling about, or doing jigsaws, or lying in bed with their toes turned up in the little rooms off the long corridor. The meals were the same. The orderly brought the same kind of medicine round on the same kind of a tray, and the same music came out of the earphones when you put them on your head.

The same – but with two differences. The window in the little bedrooms had bars across them. The door at the end of the main corridor was locked.

After tea on the first day, when a lady had come in and tried to organize some game or other, Tim had made off down the corridor. Time to go back to C2 where they had given up trying to organize games because no one would play. Time to go and see Norman and Uncle Fred and them. Mr Podgorsky would have the Snakes and Ladders board set up. He would not like it if Tim did not come.

On Ward C2 there were two knobs on the outer door. They turned different ways, the idea being that if you were bright enough to figure out how to open the door, you would not be run over by a bread van if you found your way outside.

On H there was only one knob, and it was stiff. Tim tried it both ways. He wrenched at it, hurting his bad finger, and let out a wail. A hand came from behind and lifted his hand off the knob and turned him round.

'You'll be able to go out soon, Tim,' the strange man said, the man who had stolen him from Mr Gilbert. 'Come and sit down and I'll find you a book.'

It's locked, isn't it? Tim did not need to ask it. He had not spoken to anyone since they brought him to Ward H. They would not get a word out of him, even under torture. Even if Dr Marjorie spent all day and all night with her 'Like to have a bit of a chat?'

It was not until the next day that he found out where the telephone was. He heard someone talking, gabbing away to himself, nothing odd in that. Nobby did it all the time. When Tim went round the corner to see if it was Nobby come to keep him company, he found a very short elderly man standing on his toes to speak into a telephone on the wall, his free hand gesturing elaborately, talking in some foreign language, or some sort of Nobby language, whatever it was, it made no sense.

Tim walked on casually. Later when everyone was at tea, he got up and made as if to go to his locker, then doubled back through a side passage and round past the baths to the visitors' room where the telephone was. He knew a thing or two, you see. They did not reckon with Tim Shaw.

'I want to speak to Paul.' It was the first time he had used his voice for two days. It was weak and cramped, like a leg too long in one position. 'Paul, 401. It's Tim. He'll know. Tell him . . . tell him . . .'

Outside the room, rubber soles squeaked on the linoleum. They were coming for him. 'Tell him to come,' he gasped. 'Tell him I—'

He crashed the receiver back on the hook as the rubber footsteps paused outside the door. Panting, he flattened himself against the wall, his heart like a piston. The footsteps squeaked on, grew faint, a door banged.

He went to sit in the main corridor. He sat on the floor with his book jammed against the wall and watched the single knob of the door. He sat there for hours. One or two people tried to persuade him to move, but it was like trying to get periwinkles off the rocks.

A key turned in the door. An arm in a white coat opened it, jangling more keys, and Paul came in. He always looked larger than ever at Highfield. In this place where people either scurried or crept like moles, Paul's shoulders were wider, and he stood straighter and moved more deliberately.

'Hullo, Tim.' If he had said, 'What on earth are you doing there?' Tim would have stayed on the floor. He did not say it, so Tim got up and they went into the visitors' room and had a bit of a smoke, and after a while Paul said, 'Do you want to tell me what happened?'

'Don't you know?'

'I had a word with that lady doctor. She was a bit vague.'

'What did she tell you?' If Tim could find out just what had happened, he would know what to say.

'Only that there was an accident in the carpentry shop. One of your mates got hurt, wasn't that it?'

The chisel slipped and Mr Podgorsky got chopped.

'*Tried it on again, eh?*' Arthur Callaghan said, his mouth like slugs, like snails without shells.

'It wasn't my fault.' Tim said. His eyes blanked, and all of a sudden, clear pictures moved into his brain like slides. He saw Mr Podgorsky's fingers splayed and waiting. He saw again the colours of his sick flashing rage, and doubled up, clutching himself.

Paul stayed with Tim for a long time. The boy would not let him go. He clung to him, wept, fell into a dumb depression, staring blankly at the floor, got up once and beat his head feebly against the wall. One of the few coherent things that came through was his fear of being sent away from Highfield.

'We talked about his discharge, last time I was here,' Paul told the staff nurse, after Tim had been given a sedative and put to bed. 'Could that—'

'It's possible.' The nurse had been down for his supper. Remnants of it were eluding his tongue. 'Sometimes when they've been on this closed ward, I've even known them to do a violence so as to be put back in. Safe, you see. Gets too institutionalized, a boy like young Shaw.'

How do you get him back into the world? Paul felt depressed and discouraged. Tim seemed to have slipped back a long way.

It was late. He would be late to fetch Alice. She would be late for the South End A.A. meeting. She would have to go into a crowded hall after the meeting had started, and it would panic her.

He stopped at a garage to telephone.

'Don't bother,' Alice said. 'Don't bother to come home. I'm not going to the damned meeting.'

'You must. It won't matter, the others can talk first. I'll be there in half an hour. Be ready and we'll go right away.'

'I am ready.' She laughed that hoarse nicotine laugh, and then Paul realized.

Punishing his small car, taking chances, he drove home as fast as he could, and left the car in a forbidden place, its end sticking out into the traffic. The lift was stuck with the doors open on the top floor. He ran up the stairs, seeing himself collapse there, turn blue. 'Heart,' they would say as they turned him over. 'What a wonderful way to go.'

His unsteady hands fumbled with the key. He crashed in, shouting. Alice was sitting calmly at the kitchen table with a bottle and a glass, quite civilized, quite ladylike in the oatmeal dress ('the colour of sick – so suitable') she often wore to A.A. meetings.

'For God's *sake* – after all you've been through! How can you be such a damn fool?' He was furious with her. He smashed her glass into the sink, took the bottle and poured the whisky on the broken glass.

Alice half rose to get at the cupboard, but he pushed her back into her chair.

'I'm through with you. All the chances you've had, and you chuck the whole bloody thing away—' He shouted at her, chanting abuse as if he were speaking dialogue in a play.

'That makes us even then,' Alice said rather gleefully. 'I'm really glad I found out about your fancy lady. It would have been too sad to have missed such a watertight excuse to have a drink. Though I've thought for some time you must have someone. I mean, you'd be pretty silly if you didn't, all things considered, but it's a pity she was lying on your shirt-tail tonight. It's bad luck on Jane.'

'I went to Highfield to see Tim.'

'I mean, *I* didn't mind. I didn't really want to speak at the meeting, but it's a bit hard on poor old Jane. Eight years sober, and St Paul lets her down. Who, as they say, is she?'

'God, this is ironical, Alice, I was at Highfield, I told you. Tim Shaw is in trouble. I had to go to him.'

'Don't lie, you fake Samaritan.'

'Call the Samaritan Centre. Ask someone to look in the log book and see if Tim rang for me.'

'That would give them a laugh, wouldn't it? Poor old

sozzled Mrs Hammond, checking up on the old man.'

Look – Alice, I'll make coffee. We can still get to the meeting. You'll be all right.'

'No thanks. I'd rather stay here.' She got up and took another glass and a bottle of something from the cupboard under the sink.

Paul went to the telephone.

'Want me to come round?' Scott sounded very tired.

'Not much good tonight. Perhaps tomorrow you could talk to her?'

'I'll try. It's going to be tough, if I know Alice.'

'She say's it my fault.'

'Oh, of course. It's always someone else's fault. God damn acoholics, they'll do this every time,' Scott said disgustedly, as if he were not one himself.

On a Saturday afternoon in spring, when Brian had gone cursing to the Front Royal to 'wait on people who aren't fit to wait on me,' Sarah King was in the small panelled study at the Samaritan Centre, listening to Paul on the telephone.

'Of course, Jim. Come up right away ... Bit of a sit, of course, as long as you like. Do you want to talk to someone? Yes, I'm sure he will. Don't worry, Jim. Come on up. I'm glad you rang.'

He wrote in the log, *'Jim Baxter rang, distressed. Will come in for a sit and poss. talk to 100.'*

'Why is he distressed?' Sarah asked.

'He mucks about with young children. Got about twenty convictions, been in and out of mental hospitals, it's hardly helped at all. He comes in here when he feels it coming on. Bit of a sit. You can go and chat to him when he comes in. He likes a new ear.'

'What shall I say?'

'He'll do most of the saying. Don't worry. I've heard you talking to clients. You're doing very well.'

'Am I? Am I really?' She snapped at it like a dog biscuit.

'What's the matter, Sarah? Why are you so unsure?'

Paul looked very tired. When Sarah had first come like a magnetized sleepwalker up to Church Grove and this old stone house, Paul had seemed strong and wise and unassailable. Since then she saw him sometimes looking older than he was, his hair greyer, his face more deeply lined, his voice lower, his broad shoulders not stooped, but carrying some burden which he only set down when he turned with his slow smile to take up the burdens that were brought to the Samaritans.

When he asked her, 'What's the matter?' Sarah wished that she could give him back the question.

'I don't think I'm unsure,' she said, 'Do I look it?'

'Only if you feel it. People take each other at face value. That woman who went into the bank after the thief had locked up the staff, she saw him as a bank clerk because he was behind the grill. A client who comes in here sees you as a Samaritan, existing just for him. Your funny chopped hair and the nothing skirt and that damn dangly thing my mother used to swing like a lasso in the Twenties. You are there for him.'

'I always feel he thinks, "What's *she* doing here? I came for help." '

'So he sees you as someone who can help.'

She got up restlessly and went to the window, moving the curtain. Nothing in the road beyond the brick wall. In the garden, the lush green weeds that had devoured the vicar's lawn steamed in the surprising sun.

'Brian calls it playing angels, coming up here, a drop-out from reality. I go home excited, wanting to tell him what happened, but he wants to tell me about Colonel Sebastian and the Spanish waiter, and I think *that's* unreal.'

'Do you fight?'

'Sometimes. No, not really. That's unreal too. We throw things carefully. He shouts. I cry. As if it were expected of us.' She came back to sit opposite him. 'Do you fight with your wife?' She felt secure enough with Paul to ask it.

He laughed instead of answering, and then said,

'You'll find out that being a Samaritan here doesn't make you one at home.'

'It ought to.'

He shook his head. Rachel, number 350, pearls and aqua cardigan and undulated dated hair, came in with a bottle and a cloth.

'My weekly sanitizing.' She wiped round the mouthpiece of the telephone. 'This phone must be loaded with germs. No wonder we all get colds. I do mine at home every day in the flu season.'

'Do you get flu?' You were supposed to give tolerance to the other Samaritans as well as the clients.

'My Robin, you know,' she perched a rubbery haunch on the desk to prattle to Paul, 'I thought he would never pick up after last time. Cough – it would break your heart. He came back from school with a note. "Please, Mrs Drew, keep him away." But he's so behind with his maths, it's such a worry with exams coming up. He could pass them on his head, but he—'

4000 rang like a sharp rebuke. Paul picked it up at once, glad to cut Rachel off in mid-flight. A click, then nothing. The burr of the dialling tone. He wrote 'Dud call' in the log book.

'—because you see,' Rachel went on as if she had never stopped, 'if he doesn't pass enough subjects this year, he'll miss his chance at Grenoble. And with my cousin so near ... I wish you could see her house. Last summer when I—'

Paul picked up the strident telephone, listened for a moment, and wrote again, 'Dud call.'

SAMARITAN LOG BOOK. DAY DUTY.
15.30 Dud call. (Paul, 401.)
15.35 Dud call. (Paul, 401.)

When Gretchen had ironed the flax of her hair and gone out, Carrie heaved herself clumsily out of her bed nest and padded into the other room, narrowing her eyes to see, because her glasses were lost. The piece of furniture they pretended was a settee still looked like Gretchen's bed, unmade, magazines and underwear and toast crusts among the rumpled sheets. It was a two-roomed flat, with a bathroom on another floor and a niche across the passage to cook in, a cold tap on the half landing.

'It's a slum really,' Gretchen told people. She was proud of it, in an irritating, unnecessary way. Her mother pronounced it 'fascinating, atmospheric,' jangling the jewellery she crafted out of bits of old cars. Carrie's parents had never seen it. Her young brother had been there once on his way to a motorcycle rally, and been ordered not to tell.

Carrie was taking a teachers' course. Gretchen, who was a Sociology student unfitted by temperament or desire for any kind of sociological career, had only asked her to share because she was no threat. They were both dislikeable girls. Gretchen was bossy and coarse, with tombstone teeth. Carrie was sullen, heavy-jawed, her major talent the giving of offence or taking it. When they had people in for spaghetti, or the sticky mass of rice which Gretchen said was paella, Gretchen made a lot of noise and ill-informed argument, while Carrie 'The Carrier' slouched round with coffee and some kind of wine which you could not get drunk on before you brought it up.

At home in the spiritual wastelands of Bucks, where her parents grew vegetables and various smaller livestock with edible flesh or products, she had always been called Caroline, with the O pronounced to rhyme with barrow. She had changed it to Carrie when she won the scholarship ('Were they *sorry* for her, or what?' her brother marvelled) and escaped to the University. Gretchen's name was not Gretchen. She had changed to that when she discovered how to make her hair this colour.

The water jug was empty. In her pyjamas, Carrie went barefoot down to the tap that dripped out of the wall into a stained metal basin like a urinal.

'Not dressed yet?' Mrs Mason was climbing the stairs with two loaded string-bags.

'I didn't feel well.'

'You girls.' Mrs Mason wagged her head as if Carrie were hung over or pregnant, and turned up the next flight.

I was the last one to see her, she would be able to say. The last one to lay eyes on her and she said to me, 'Mrs Mason, I don't feel well.' If I had only – if I had only – wouldn't you think that ordinary human kindness would have led me to ask what was the matter? But that's the way we all are now, sir, everyone so caught up in the pace of life, men on the moon, hydrofoils across the Channel, we don't look close and see our brother.

Carrie brought the water jug back, treading heavily on the large feet that were never completely clean, since they were bare most of the time or with the thong of a cracked sandal hanging between the toes, like everybody else. She had let her hair grow, like everybody else, but it was so thick, with those tight corrugations which used to cause strange ladies to exclaim when she was little, that it would not hang in curtains, like everybody else. It stuck out all round her shoulders in a sort of pyramid, and with her heavy face and large bumpy nose, people thought she was a boy. She hung weights on the ends of it. She ironed it into a dry frizz, burnt hair stopping up the steam holes on Gretchen's iron, then chopped it off quite short and someone said, 'Kinky! My cousin brought one of those Afro wigs back from the States.' It was now cut completely short, like an American footballer. Carrie's father, as short-sighted as she was, might have difficulty identifying her. Her mother would not be able to come, if the pigs were farrowing.

She poured a glass of water and sat down amid the fusty chaos of Gretchen's bed. Unfair to die in here? But if she was in her own room, Gretchen might not come in for a long time. Carrie hated anyone in her room. At home, she locked the door whether she was in or out of it. Here at the flat, she had only agreed to share the rent if she could have the inner room.

When Gretchen came back, she might have Teddo with her, if she was not at the restaurant. Her globular eyes would bulge, stretching the blood vessels. She would stare, her lips dropping away from her outsize teeth. A scream. 'Carrie – oh my *God!*' Carrie's life meant nothing to her. Carrie dead would be another thing.

'Don't look, Gretch. Don't touch her.'

Teddo would not look or touch either. He would probably run shrieking from the building, and Gretchen could begin to give interviews. Carrie was doing her that favour, at least, but she would only be a supporting player. Carrie would be the star.

She sat for a while, swirling the water round in the glass and sighing. This seemed to need a lot of oxygen. The telephone was on the floor under the bed. With her feet flat on the floor and her knees apart, Carrie bent down like an old woman and dragged it out. She listened to the dialling tone as if it were telling her something.

Sorry to be so long, her mother would say. I was in with the baby chicks. What is it – what? I don't understand. What do you mean, Caroline, what do you mean – fail? But I don't understand. you've always been able to work at your books.

Carrie put down the telephone and stood up, went to the window and drew the curtains. She went into her own room and pulled the lopsided blind as far down as it would reach. In the front room, she pressed the catch on the lock so that Gretchen's key would not turn it, sat down, got up again and released the catch, then wandered about the room, touching things, running her hand along flat surfaces, the table, the fretted shelf above the tiny Victorian grate, the top of the bookcase, 'environmental surfaces', as it said in *Orientation of the Child's Visual Experience.*

The feel of the room meant nothing. It had no power over her. The flat was just an ugly place where she had been unhappy, more unhappy than in the dormitory building, since she was more alone. At the dormitory, she could walk among the people in the halls and downstairs rooms quite briskly, as if she were going somewhere.

She took the bottle from the pocket of her pyjama

jacket, and read the label for the hundredth time, with one eye shut. 'Be careful,' the doctor had said, but she had not taken any of the pills. If she could sleep, there would be no excuse for failing. If she got another pair of National Health glasses, there would be no excuse for the print to swim before her aching eyes. Staring at words without seeing them, prowling round her room in the night, smoking, weeping, once she had opened the window and sat on the sill, her thick bare legs dangling over the Mortons' coal shed. When she slept, she could not rouse herself. She missed morning lectures, hiding in her bed. Her mole eyes were drawn back into their lairs. Bruised shadows marked her puffy skin. *That girl is ill.*

She put the bottle on the table beside the glass of water. Still life. Something was missing. If she could call up to Mrs Mason – bring someone in from the street to stand in the doorway like cab-drivers conscripted into a wedding – 'I'm going to kill myself. Will you watch me?'

Mummy! Mummy! Watch me, I'm going to dive!

Yes dear, I see you.

Back at the window, Carrie opened the curtains and thrust her blank face against the glass. A woman pushing a baby smothered in groceries. A man with a briefcase. Running children, squinting at the sun. Cars, bicycles. Two half-empty buses, torsos staring straight ahead, newspapers up. They would read it in tomorrow's. Except there would be no tomorrow. She could stop the whole thing, blot it out. No me, no world.

Turning from the window, she peered into an endless succession of tomorrows, mirrors within mirrors, empty of hope. She dropped to the floor and crouched by Gretchen's bed. She was as cold as if her blood had stopped running. At this hollow core of loneliness, she was abandoned even by herself.

The torn telephone book was under the bed with shoes, an apple core, a cigarette packet. She could not see numbers.

'Operator – those people – I want the Samaritans.'

One ring. A click. 'Samaritans – can I help you?' She banged down the receiver. He can't change it. It's nothing to do with him.

What would he have said? Would he use the doctor's word, neurotic? Would he say, like her father, 'Go out and get some friends', as if they were to be had in shops?

She tried again, listened to the man's deep patient voice for half a minute, then hung up quietly. Nothing was changed. There was no way of changing anything.

She put the telephone on to the bed among the disordered sheets and the purple shawl that Gretchen had found in a street market. She knelt up to reach the bottle from the table and shook out all the pills into her cupped hand. One by one? All at once? The pills were very difficult to swallow. She took four and put the rest back in the bottle, then she sat on the floor, leaning against the bed, and pulled down the shawl to wrap round herself like a shroud.

'Next time it rings,' Paul said, 'you answer it, Sarah. They may have rung off because they want to talk to a woman.'

'I can take it,' Rachel said.

'Let Sarah. She's got to start some time.'

Rachel looked at her doubtfully. 'I will if you like.'

'It's all right,' Sarah said, but after Rachel had gone out, she told Paul, 'I'm scared.'

She had talked to many people who came into the reception room. She had talked to regular clients who rang the office telephone number so as to leave the emergency line free. Free for what? The instrument that Paul pushed across the desk to her was a black mystery, charged with the dynamite of the unknown. She stared at it. I can't—

'So you're one of us now,' David, 520 had said. Sarah, 589. If she were one of them, she must do this, or go away and never come back, and they would give her number, 589, to someone else, and Peter would say, 'A pity about that girl, I thought she was the type,' and then no one would say anything, and they would forget her.

'I hope they ring again,' Paul said. 'It's worrying not to know. It might be a joker, it might be a wrong number, but it's more likely to be someone whose trouble is too bad to talk about.'

'Suppose I don't know how to help? I haven't learned—'

'All you have to learn is just to listen.' The constant refrain. 'No instant salvation. Just humanity. Let it come through in your voice. Let your love come through, Sarah,' he said gently, smiling, looking at her as if he liked her very much.

He was about the same age as her father. He had come into her dream once, not as a father figure. Her father was an old goat, capering in front of girls like Maria.

The telephone rang. Sarah jumped, and was paralysed, staring at it.

'Pick the damn thing up,' Paul said quite roughly. 'Do you want them to think no one cares?'

When George came out of the station, he had asked the way and been told, 'Turn left, turn right, take this or that number bus. Get off at the last gate of the football ground, you can't miss it.'

He had taken the wrong bus. The football ground never came. They never even went over a bridge. When the conductor came to the top deck, he laughed and told George he was miles away and going in the wrong direction.

'What's the joke?'

'Got to laugh, mate. Keeps you from going mad.'

George swore at him and clumped down the stairs and dropped off as the bus swung round a corner. He did it clumsily, stumbling, grazing his hand to save himself. Shouldering his way through the clowns who had nothing better to do than saunter in the Saturday street, he thought, bad omen on this job, he never should have gone for it. Why did Linda want him to? Only gone half a day, and he was angry already for what he imagined about her.

He took another bus and it stopped in some wide square with new white buildings and a clock made of flowers and announced that it would go no farther.

'You're supposed to go to the stadium.'

'Circus only, dear.' The conductress pointed to the sign above the back step.

'Why did you take my whole fare?'

'I didn't. Just as far as here. Don't you know what the fares are?'

'Look. I've never been in the cruddy town before.'

'Some people.'

'. . . stranger here.'

'I'm a bit lost myself.'

'I'm sorry, I'm hopeless at directions.'

'Hainh – hyunh – anna – hyi – angya . . .'

George's luck to get them with no roof to their mouth. George's perishing luck that caused matchboxes to catch fire in his hand, strange towns to declare Early Closing Day as soon as he arrived, telephones to be always engaged, when they were not wrong numbers. Watch him get to the Exhibition Hall, if he ever did, and find the job had gone five minutes ago to someone else.

He growled down some steps in the middle of the road, expecting to find the Public Convenience out of order, flooded, or full of queers.

'*If you are in despair,*' the notice said. Well, if that's what they want, here I am.

'Samaritans – can I help you?' A young girl's voice. Things are looking up.

'I'm in despair, darling.'

She made a sympathetic noise.

'I'm lost in this bloody city and I'm late and I'll probably lose that job and what the hell do you care?'

'What can I – can I help you?'

'That's what I'm asking you,' George said patiently. 'How can I get to the Exhibition Hall?'

'Where are you?'

'If I knew, I'd not be lost.'

She laughed then, and George laughed, and finally she

said she would look at the map, and then she told him some streets and bus numbers, but he was not really listening. He had seen a clock in a bank window and realized how late it was.

'All right now?'

'*All right?* I'm an hour late. I'll have to get a taxi.'

Mrs Latimer turned the telephone dial with a special gold gadget for turning telephone dials. She had a device for lifting sausages out of the frying pan and ejecting them on to a plate. She had a pair of tongs on a long extending handle to pick the dog's mess off the lawn, and another extending handle with a scoop at the end to get cans off the top shelf. She had brushes with disposable pads for cleaning toilets and baths, a little hook on a ribbon for pulling up zip fasteners at the back of dresses, and a button in her car which made the garage door go up and down. When a certain kind of plane flew over, the door went spookily up by itself in the middle of the night.

'Samaritans – can I help you?'

A young voice. She had expected someone cool and mature. A nice young voice, quick and a little breathless, eager, like the voices of the daughters of her friends. Like someone she might know. It might even be someone she knew.

'This is Mrs Charles Latimer,' she said, as if she were going to give an order at a store where she had an account. 'It's on behalf of my son. You do help people, don't you? Yes, oh, how nice ... Well, he would, I think. He wanted me to ring you. He won't see his doctor any more, but he said he might come to you.' With iodine painted round his mouth to make them think he had swallowed it?

'Of course, he can come in any time and talk to someone.'

The young voice was warm and interested. Not official. Perhaps they could make Gordie see that he did not need the gestures.

I did it. It was easy. First that man, then Mrs Latimer. I did it, I coped. I didn't panic. I was able to help them. They thought I was a Samaritan. Perhaps I am. One of us. Sarah, 589.

When the telephone rang again, she stretched out her hand without glancing at Paul, and picked it up quite confidently. Omnipotent Sarah. The saviour of the world.

In a dream or awake, Carrie saw the sea. She saw herself walking out straight-legged, her hands at her sides, walking far out at low tide, and walking on, along the bottom of the sea. A deep regretful sadness lay over her like the water. Was this what dying was?

Sighing, she raised an arm to pull the shawl round her shoulders, and knocked the telephone clattering off the bed. The receiver was split, but the dial still worked.

'Samaritans – can I help you?' A young girl spoke quickly to her as if she had been waiting.

'I want to kill myself.'

The girl did not say anything. At last she whispered, 'What – what's the matter?'

'I can't tell anybody.'

She waited. The girl waited. It was as if they were staring at each other across a chasm of death. Carrie fell asleep.

Sarah burst into tears. Paul tried to comfort her, but she would not be comforted by him, or Andrew, or anyone who tried to tell her that they had all been paralysed by their first shock call, that after that it was all right. She did not hear them. She heard only her own useless stupidity, repeating itself over and over.

'I want to kill myself.'

'What – what's the matter?'

'She'll try again,' they said, but the telephone was mute for the rest of the afternoon. When Sarah went home, she said nothing to Brian. That would be flagellation, masochism, confession, all the things he hated. In the stories that Brian liked, the narrator was the hero, not the villain.

Gretchen came stumbling in, rather drunk, and kicked her awake.

'Get out. Get out of my room.' There was a foggy shadow in the doorway that might be Teddo.

'I was going to kill myself.' Carrie rolled up her eyes.

'Oh, belt up,' Gretchen said, 'I'm sick of it.'

Still clutching the purple shawl, Carrie waddled away and fell on to her bed. Gretchen banged the door between the rooms.

She slept for a day and a night and half another day. Waking like lead, she rolled off the bed and groped her way to the telephone. The split in the receiver was wider. Screws showed and a piece of flat copper wire. It still worked.

'I talked to someone there on Saturday. Could I – would she be there now?'

'Who was it?'

'*I* don't know.' Her mouth was lined with some kind of furred sacking, like the bottom of a poultry feed bag. 'She was quite young.'

'Let's see – Saturday. Was it Sarah?'

'I don't know.'

'Have we got your name?'

'No.' *And* you won't.

'Would you like to speak to Sarah and see if it was her?'

'All right.'

Carrie was in the middle of a massive yawn when the breathless 'Yes?' came through.

'I'm the one who rang you Saturday.'

'Oh, thank *God*. Thank God you rang again. I've been sick with worry because I—'

'I was asleep.'

'I was stupid. I'm sorry. What you said – I was afraid—'

'You were more afraid than I was,' Carrie said. 'That's why I rang again.'

They talked for half an hour. It was surprisingly easy when the other person could not see you. When Sarah asked her to come across the river and up to Church Grove, Carrie refused, and then she thought, oh, what the hell. Gretchen will be coming back in her sickening leotard.

'Is it Monday?'

'Yes.'

Gretchen in her Eurythmy leotard, her thighs swelling like torpedos in the blue acetate tights.

What did Sarah expect to see? She greeted Carrie like an old friend. A man with a beard called Ralph took her upstairs to what might have once been part of a bedroom – Coo, look at Carrie, in a bedroom with a man – but she was too tired to talk to him.

'Come back,' he told her. 'Come back, Carrie,' Sarah said. Everyone said 'Come back any time.'

You've got to laugh. Where have you been, Carrier Pigeon?

Been with my friends.

Didn't know you had any. (Those teeth were like shin bones.)

Made some today.

Who?

The Suicide Squad.

Oh belt up, I'm sick of it.

If Monday was physically the vilest day of the week, Wednesdays at the student cafeteria ran it pretty close, because of the sausages.

Hot Fried was always sausages on a Wednesday. They came from the kitchen soaking in grease, their skins pale and papery like the skins of old ladies, their accumulated aroma at the end of an hour thick with memories of the cast-off meats that went into their making.

As Billie ladled them queasily out on to plates for dim-witted students who had been raised on bangers and chips and were not going to risk anything else at this late date, her stomach rose up and fell like a lift, the back of her throat the top floor, her bowels the basement.

With the sausages, it was usually kedgeree or liver.

'Take it or leave it,' Billie said when they grumbled. 'No, Fido, egg mayonnaise is off. The rest of the eggs went into the kedgeree.'

'That's criminal waste in a world where millions starve.'

'Criminal waste sending you to university, if you want my opinion.' Billie seethed at the boy in the dusty tight black trousers, his privates as offensive as a stallion.

Some of them joked with her.

'Old Bill.'

'Look at old Bill.'

'Who spat in the soup, Billie?'

'What died?' as she forked out liver.

She was getting to be a fixture here. Students who had left looked for her if they came back for some reason. 'There's old Billie. Still wiping your hands on the bread?' The world moved onwards, taking these furry delinquents with it. Billie was left behind on the fly-paper.

Last night, she had walked in unfamiliar streets, alone, watching, peering into cars, leaning in doorways. She had spoken to a girl who was waiting at a street corner, quite nice, nothing offensive, but the girl had spat abuse at her and said she would call the police.

'Hardly, in your trade,' Billie said coldly and walked on, watching the people who moved in and out of the neon shop lights, their faces changing from death to hectic colour, watching for Morna. She had come out with the vague idea of searching for a girl. Any girl, a girl who was lonely and strange. The faces went by like moons and flowers and precious gems, but none of them was Morna.

As lunches slacked off, Billie and Tontine, who tended the urns, took turns to go back into the kitchen for their own meal.

'What's this?' On the table in the corner, one of the cooks had put three sausages like the turds of an anaemic dog, chips flabby as macaroni, a sliced tomato flaunting a mildew mark.

The cook was Polish, conveniently not learning any English, but Billie told him where he could put it anyway. Back on the counter, she knocked off some rolls and squares of cheese and a few Bakewell tarts into her uniform pockets on top of the two spoons to replace the ones that went out with the garbage. On a nice afternoon like this, she used to fetch Morna at the laundry and they would have a picnic on the hillside park, sit on the fallen blossom and hear the speeches, the anarchy and the guitars.

But Morna was not at the hospital laundry any more. 'My friends think I should better myself.' She had got a job in a hosiery shop, but Billie could not remember its name. She did not answer the telephone at her rooms. Billie did not know where she was.

In the cement yard of her flats, which, like the whole area, looked much the same, spring, summer and winter. Billie stopped to speak to Gary Peace, on the see-saw with another child, too dirty to recognize. She gave them two of the Bakewell tarts.

'Gary Peace!' A window shrieked open four floors above. 'I told you to come straight in from school.' Gary see-sawed on, his mouth ringed with crumbs. 'Come up here and I'll tan you,' Olive Peace invited.

'Come on then.' Billie held out a hand and he went up with her, plodding up the stone steps like two old people, spiked with a blast of wind at each turn of the open stairway. On the fourth floor, a peeling green door opened, Olive Peace's bare washday arm came out and plucked young Gary inside.

Billie opened her front door quickly, as if the note or the chocolate bar or the postcard of bathing ladies with fat red cheeks both ends might scuttle away. Sometimes on her way to the hospital, Morna used to stop by the flat and shove something through the letter-box (a piece of raw tripe once, done up with ribbon). She had not done that for a long time.

On Billie's kitchen window, something like a flayed skin hung. It was the cat Thing, waiting to be let in. She opened the window and he dropped down to the sill and came huffily inside.

'No need for that, I brought you some kedgeree.' It was in a paper cup in her handbag. 'Never doubt my love.' She put it on the oven shelf and the cat jumped in, balancing on the grid. Last winter, she had lit the oven with him inside, for a joke, and he had crouched there purring, cave cat.

Poor old Victoria. Billie had not talked to her for three days. Better have a word with her now, in case she was wondering what was up. She worried, did Victoria. She was one of the world's born worriers. That was why she had taken on the telephoning bit, so as to get some more things to worry about.

Ronnie answered the telephone. '. . . yes, I'll tell her. Is that Billie? How are you? All right? All right.' She was quite a regular. A lot of Samaritans knew her voice. Good old Billie. Old Bill.

Victoria rang her back almost at once. 'Mr Fisher has gone to play golf. I'm typing letters. Very boring. How are you, my old Bill?'

'Up yours, me old Victoria. *I'm* all right. I thought I'd better find out how you were.'

'In a rut.'

'That's bad. You ought to get out and about more, like me.'

'What have you seen?' It was always movies, movies, like two Englishmen meeting in the jungle and swopping their own language hungrily, among the natives.

Billie had seen *Charly*. 'The mouse was better than the fellow. Just making faces isn't being mad. I look like that all the time.'

Victoria had gone with this dreary boyfriend of hers to see an offering called *Secret Ceremony*. 'Nothing secret about it and no ceremony that I could see, except Mia Farrow having an orgasm on the floor, if you call that a ceremony, it certainly wasn't a secret.'

'Ha ha.' Billie produced her rusted laugh, because poor old Victoria was trying.

'Is everything all right?' Victoria's casual voice.

'Why shouldn't it be?'

'I mean, well—' She knew enough to stay off Morna unless Billie brought her up. 'You're all right then?'

'Don't be so nosy, of course I'm all right. What's the matter with you? You poke about like some fucking gynaecologist. My business is my business.'

'You rang *me*.'

'Never again.' The whisky was spreading its tentacles through the roots and branches of Billie's system. 'You can whistle for it.'

When she had banged down the telephone, she sobbed and howled, staring at herself in the crooked mirror, strands of saliva bridging her mouth like a broken harp. She did a forbidden thing, the only thing Victoria had told her not to do. She knew where Victoria worked, because it had come out in a conversation about film reviews, and now she rang the *Courier* and asked for Mr Fisher's secretary. After all this time, she did not even know Victoria's name.

'Mr Fisher's office, good—Billie! What's the matter?'

Like the luxury of diarrhoea, she poured it all out in sobs and wails, the whole bloody insulting mess of it, from the time when Morna started to tease her, 'When I get married, will you come to my wedding?' No harm. Just teasing.

'You'll never get what we've had from any man.'

'That's right, Bill, that's right, Bill dear ...'

And then ... it was on the pier. 'I went down the pier' (the soft wet wood and the mud smell, the muffled old gentlemen left out to rot on the damp benches). 'Yvonne and them had got some booze down there and I knew Morna had gone along.'

The windows were all out on one side of the octagonal café at the pier's end. As Billie drew near – 'Barricade the doors!' someone yelled. 'Here comes that lezzie friend of Morna's.'

And Morna's shrill squeak like a castrated rabbit, 'Quick, Phil, pull the table across!'

As Victoria listened, people were in and out of the waiting-room, banging through the door of the reporters' room, leaving things on her desk, passing through on their way to the stairs, coming in with things to sell, questions to ask, the tea trolley trundling through like a mechanized convoy. Victoria put her elbows on the desk and held the telephone close, to keep Billie's misery locked in to her ear.

'Poor Billie,' she said. 'Poor girl. I'm sorry . . .'

'Who the hell was that?' The doorman had been waiting by her desk for a signature.

'A friend of mine.'

'They bring you all their troubles? That's like me. One look at my face and I hear it all. Marriage, childbirth, grand delusions, the lot. But I'd not have thought you had that kind of face.'

'This friend has never seen me.'

'Blind, eh? There's trouble for a starter. I'll tell you what it is, Victoria. There's always someone worse off. I find that quite a comfort.'

Old Michael had still not turned up, at Marsh Lane or at the hostel. He had gone off somewhere with his sandwich boards, for which the Brethren of the Judgement intended to charge him eleven-and-six if he came back without them.

The students had seen him once or twice at the railway station or on one of the ramps – the demolition sites where the skippers and drinkers gathered – so Victoria went with them on the soup-run one night to look for him. He seemed to have become her responsibility. She could not forget her last sight of him, weaving away along the gutter like a turtle, his head bent below the top of the board on his back, '*Salvation from Doom*'.

With Jack and soft-eyed Sheila, Victoria went in the van to the dried silt bed under the old dock where the river had receded, to bombsites where fireweed had been growing for twenty-five years, down stinking alleys and into boarded-up houses with no floors, where the rustling in the corner might be rats or the remains of a man rousing himself from his torn wrappings of newspaper.

The town was being 'spring cleaned', so the men and women who slept on the station benches had to get up every three hours and shuffle about until the police had gone.

Jack stopped the van under the archway in the long brick wall behind the goods sheds, and soon figures began to drift out from the dark areas, like walking dead. As Sheila handed out the soup which she had made from vegetables begged in the market, the soft wings of her hair swung forward round her serious face. Jack cast jokes out with the sandwiches, but the girl was very solemn, ladling out the hot soup with the concentrated face of an artist, going to look for those who would not come out of the shadows, touching the untouchables, as if they were her Christ.

Behind the giant bakery which was swallowing shop after little independent shop and breeding a generation of children in this town who had never tasted real bread, there was a small, cat-stunk area of mud and rubble, stuck about with the skeletons of prams and bedsteads. Low down in the bakery wall, warm steam came periodically from a grating, and here behind a pile of broken bricks, half a dozen people were crouching or lying.

Victoria was dressed like the students in jeans and an old sweater, her hair in pigtails, but she felt too clumsily bountiful, handing out the broken pastries which the pie factory contributed, bending down to hear the cracked whisper of a man who could not get up. He had only one leg. No stick or crutches.

'Fetch us something then.' He was not a man but a woman, wearing an ancient suit too big for her, the sleeves over her hands, a felt hat stiff with dirt pulled down on her head like a bag, a face grey and pitted like an old-time coal miner.

'I thought they gave you some crutches.' Jack came over.

'I lost them.'

'You sold them again?'

'Yes dear.'

Jack grinned at her. 'Any idea where Michael is? We've been looking for him.'

'He was taken last week.' The woman sat on the ground with her one leg stuck out in front of her. The smell of spirits that came from her was strong enough to ignite.

'To the Spike?'

'The bogeys come with guns that night and drove them into the vans.'

'With *guns!*' Victoria could not believe it.

'Water guns. Toys.' The woman opened the cavern of her mouth into something like a smile. Her head wagged and bobbed constantly. She could not hold the mug of soup steady enough to drink it. Victoria crouched down and held the mug to her dark crusted lips. The woman drank. They looked into each other's eyes. When the woman had swallowed all the soup, she vomited it up over Victoria's hands and the knees of her trousers where she knelt before her.

After consulting with Peter, Victoria went to the Government Reception Centre to see what she could do for Michael.

The hostel was a square grey block, slate-roofed, moated with an asphalt yard on the worst side of Flagg's Hill. It had once been a workhouse, then a casual ward in the days when there was a string of them within walking distance of each other all over England for the thousands of vagrants who tramped the land. Now it was the only Government hostel in the town, crowded, understaffed, unjustly disliked, both by its customers because it imposed some discipline, and by its neighbours because it 'dragged down' a district which was already no pleasure garden.

On the high wall round the yard of the Spike, various offensive messages had been scrawled in chalk or faecal matter. *'Burn the bums'*, *'Piss off you freaks'* were among the most civilized. The steps of the buildings were strewn with gravel and small stones, as if someone had been assaulting the door. Broken windowpanes were patched with cardboard.

'You find us under siege.' The Warden was a round wheezing man with a face squeezed choleric by a tight shirt collar.

'Who sieges?'

'Boys mostly. Egged on by their parents – not discouraged anyway. They've been breaking windows faster than I can get anyone in to repair them.'

'Couldn't some of the men—'

'My dear,' the Warden had a touch of the homosexual in his voice and finger movements, 'watch your talk. The Glaziers' Union.'

Old Michael was in one of the dormitories, sitting on the side of a neat narrow bed with an unlit cigarette stub wetly between his lips, his eyes closed, swaying gently back and forth. There were about twenty beds in the long room, with a locker and a worn strip of carpet, which was each man's kingdom.

'Hullo, Mike.'

'You've not to be late for mumble-mumble.' The bleared eyes saw something far back beyond this place and time. Knots of yellow tissue partly obscured the whites. The iris was faded and watery.

'It's Victoria – from the Samaritans. Remember me?'

'I know you,' the old man said quite sharply. 'Where's them boots you were going to fetch to me?'

'Oh Mike.' Victoria laughed, and a man a few beds away, crouched over a minutely folded newspaper, looked up at her as if she had shouted in a library. 'I've been trying to give them to you for weeks. I couldn't find you.'

'Can't feel me feet.' He stuck them out and seemed

surprised to find them covered in a fairly decent pair of brown boots.

'Can't you walk?'

'Not much. I couldn't go back up the Lane, that's why, and get my money.'

'Where are the boards?'

'Eh?' He put his hand behind his ear and screwed up his grizzled face. 'Eh?'

'The sandwich boards.'

'Eh?' He was quite cross. 'They got my money down the post office,' he grumbled.

'Your pension? You can get that if you're going to stay here. You must go there and give them an address.'

'With these feet...' He lifted up the brown boots as if they were wooden blocks and put them carefully down again.

Victoria found the Warden. He was cutting meat for stew, scarlet in the face, although the kitchen was not hot.

'Can't get the help,' he wheezed apologetically. Three or four men were in the kitchen, one at the sink, one mopping the floor with grey water, a bald man with albino eyelashes crouched on a chair without a back, very slowly peeling potatoes with a knife that looked as blunt as a wooden spoon. 'No one here with a steady enough hand.' The Warden savaged the meat, wearing a plastic see-through apron with a psychedelic heart centred with the word LOVE.

'Can I help you?'

'My dear ... You get down to the post office for the old man. He'll be able to feel his feet all right when he has something to buy a drink with.'

'I'll come back.'

'You do that, Missie.' At thirty-five, Victoria was usually glad not to be called Madam. From this man it could be a veiled insult. The back of his trousers was like the Marble Arch. His eyebrows were half hoops, very black as if he had dyed them, although his thick hair was white.

The post office was in one half of a tobacconist and

newsagent's shop, rather quaint, with an old rubbed counter that had seen better days when this was a better district. A man and his wife were behind the grill, their pig-faced daughter across the shop with the sweets and cigarettes. Victoria had a note from the Warden and what passed for a signature from Michael.

'Mind how you go,' the man said, when he gave her the money. 'We've had some of the old people robbed. It's a bad neighbourhood. I come from Nottingham.' He disclaimed responsibility.

It was a nasty street of cut-price groceries, stalls selling bacon and cheap underwear, a sour-looking pub on every other corner, a grudging chapel, its door boarded across, its iron gate chained. Victoria clutched her bag and watched loiterers and pretended she was Rita Hayworth moving on stilt heels through the press of a New York sidewalk, trying not to look as if she knew a bit player was going to pounce when she reached the chalk mark.

When Tim went back to Ward C2, Mr Podgorsky had gone. Tim wondered if he was dead.

They sent Tim out to work in the vegetable garden, and they changed the colour of his pills and said that he was better. They sent him to the Resettlement Officer who found him a job at a grocery in the town at the bottom of the hill, and they put him to live in the Highfield hostel across the road from the main gate. Tim allowed all these things to happen to him as if he were a doll.

The hostel was called Halfway House. It was a modern building with big windows and bright plastic flowers on all the tables. Tim had his own room on the men's floor, with a wardrobe and a mirror and a basin and a plastic lace cloth on the table by his bed, where he put the transistor radio he bought with some of his money from the carpentry shop.

It was the nicest room he had ever had. It looked out on a field with a pond where two small boys came every evening to catch tadpoles and eat them. It had curtains which moved all night at the open window. The floor was slashed and scarred by some former desperado, but they had waxed it over and put a blue rug on it, which Tim shook out of the window every day.

When Paul came to see him, one of the women made them a pot of tea and they sat in the comfortable chairs in the window of the lounge. Paul said that it was like being in a good hotel, which perhaps it was.

'I had the devil of a job to find you,' Paul said. 'No one on the ward seemed to know where you were. I wish you'd write me a letter next time you move.'

They laughed because Tim did not write letters. That was known between them. When Paul had brought him paper and envelopes, Tim hid them for a while, and then gave them back to him.

'I didn't know where this place was, so I asked a nurse who was walking by the car park, and who do you think it was?'

Tim scratched his head. Dolores? ... Rajah? ... Bett? ... The Strangler? ... He had known so many nurses.

'That nice Olive who was with you on C2.'

'Oh her.'

'She was glad to know where you were. She was worried about you.'

Tim stuck out his lip. 'She never come to see me. She went away.'

'To start her training, you know that. She was going to come back and see you, and then she heard about the accident, and she was afraid – no, of course not of you – but she told me today, "I was afraid they would say I spoiled him."'

'She coming here?'

'Perhaps. Shall I ask her?'

Tim shook his head. If you kept yourself secret from people, they could not get at you to hurt you. It was that simple.

'What about that girl you told me about?'

'Who?'

'The Smasher. Felicity, wasn't it?'

'Oh her.'

'Have you seen her again?'

'She's gone to that place where they put the old people who can pay to die.'

'A nursing home?'

'Just down the hill. I go by it every morning on my way to the bus.' And stare at all the windows. One day she will be standing there pulling a blind and she'll see me and stick out her tongue.

Nearly all the residents of Halfway House went out to work. Tim took a bus down into the town and back every day. 'How does it go?' Mr Perry, the Warden, asked him the same question every evening, and Tim gave him the same answer. 'Same old game.'

The same old game was pushing cartons of groceries out into the shop, unpacking them, stamping the tins and boxes with a price and putting them up on the shelves for customers to take down again. It was a demanding job, but Tim was trying quite hard to learn it, because he did not want to be sent back to the carpentry shop.

One morning, when he was mooning about in the white apron that was too long for him, with the tapes going three times round his waist instead of once round Jumbo Dodd's, trying to decide whether to risk one more layer on the soup cans, she came round a corner of the cereals and stopped dead.

'You could knock me over,' she said.

'Hullo, Fliss.' He stood there with a grin all over his face, a tin of mushroom soup in each hand. She pretended to be surprised to find him, but something about her manner made him say, 'You knew I was here.'

'I know everything that goes on,' she said darkly.

They stood for a while swopping words like Well and I dunno and Small world. She looked stronger, less spooked.

'You all right then?'

'Been worse.'

'What's it like then,' he watched his toes, 'where you are?'

'Stuffing food in one end and cleaning it up when it

comes out the other. I can come and go though.' Her voice went up into a question. The old Felicity invitation, pale mouth parted, tongue tip running along her teeth, her eyes sliding about under the smooth shiny lids, looking everywhere but at you.

'So can I.'

'Nights?'

'If I ask Mr Perry. I'm at Halfway House.'

'I know.'

Did she? You could never tell her anything. 'I can stay out till nine-thirty. You – you want—'

'Meet you tonight.' She began to gabble and whisper rapidly, her eyes darting. 'I can get out after supper. Wait by the bus stop. I'll meet you there.'

Tim polished his shoes in the laundry. Martha, who was quite ugly, with a lump on her neck in which it was said there grew teeth and hair, sang out spitefully, 'Someone's got a gir-irl!'

'No harm in that,' said Mr Perry, fiddling with taps and knobs, trying to get the washing machine back into cycle. There was some nice equipment at Halfway House, if it wasn't for the people who used it. 'You have a good time, Tim, and be home by nine-thirty because that's when I lock up and Mrs P. doesn't enjoy gravel thrown at the window.' The Warden worked very hard at making things sound like sensible arrangements rather than rules.

Tim and Felicity went down the hill on the bus and stood in the line outside the cinema for ten minutes before they conveyed to each other that this was not what they wanted to do. They walked on through the broad main street of the old market town to the other side, where the houses and pubs and shops grew smaller and the pale street lamps were the only light. Every so often they went into a doorway. Headlamps of cars swept over them like a policeman's torch. By the door of a public house called the Waggoner's Arms, there was a sign that said it was a commercial hotel. They stopped. By now they did not have to say things.

'I've not enough money,' Tim said.

'I have.'

'They'll know us. It's too near the hospital.' Everybody in this town was on the lookout for Highfield patients. At the shop, when he had toppled a hundred packets of cornflakes, women had stared and said things to each other.

'Let's go to a lodging room.' Felicity was sweating heat, as if she were feverish.

'It's too late.' The lights were out in many of the houses. This end of the town was dead by nine. 'We've got to get back.'

She dragged him on, and they went beyond the houses and into a place that was used as a dump. There was a car standing there without wheels or doors. She pulled him inside and on top of her on what was left of the back seat.

'Wait...' And this time he could wait, just long enough. He exploded inside her, and she held him close, rolling about on the broken cushions, and would not let him free.

'I'm good at this, aren't I?' She whispered in his ear, like gnats.

The moon was in and out of clouds. Struggling away from him, she sat in the corner of the car and undid her hair and took off all her clothes. It was the most fantastic thing that ever happened to Tim, far far beyond any fantasy dreamed up by Dr Ling.

She lay in his lap, and he stroked her. She lay with her head back, her long throat moving as she talked. He listened, hardly hearing, while her voice moved on, her body breathless under his moving hand.

'When I was quite young,' she said. 'I was quite young...' She used to get out of the house almost every night and go with a boy. 'They treated me like a child, because I was no good at anything. Then they found out there was something I was good at.' She laughed, and Tim put his mouth over her mouth, because of the dark houses.

'How did they find out?'

'How do you think? I was pregnant. I was fifteen, so they said I should get rid of it. You can, you know, if you get a doctor to certify your nerves.'

She knew so many things that Tim did not know. She knew she would not have a baby now, because she had starved herself long enough to get rid of her monthlies.

'I didn't care,' she said, 'but after, I cried all the time. I was in such a state they sent me to some kind of school, I don't know. I wouldn't stay there. It was miles out in the country and there was a lake. I was going to throw myself in it, but it was so deep and dark, they would never have found me. I went in the kitchen one morning before anybody got up.' She turned towards him, her small pointed breasts dropping downwards like the fruit of a tree. 'I got a knife.'

'Is that why they sent you to Highfield?'

'And other things.'

'Tell me.'

'No.' Sometimes that meant she had nothing more to tell. She fell back across his legs and flung her arm over her eyes. Perhaps it meant that she was crying. When he pulled the arm away, she sputtered into a laugh and twisted round and grabbed him, and again, he could do it again, while her laughing became an exultant cry – 'I'm good at this! I'm good at it! I'm good at it!'

SEVEN

SPRING UNFOLDED GENTLY into all the surprises of summer. The grocery put Tim to riding round with Ted
Dace in the mobile shop. He left Halfway House and went
to live in a brick cottage with half a dozen other ex-High-
field patients. They did their own cooking and shopping
and cleaning, and were just like a quarrelsome family,
with no one to boss them except Miss Ogden, the Social
Worker, who dropped in now and then because they
usually had some port.

Mr Perry had been quite upset about Tim staying out
all night (no one knew about Felicity, because she had
climbed in over a roof). He sent him up to Dr Vandenburg. Tim felt physically afraid, as if he were going to be
beaten. The doctor merely said mildly, 'Goes to show
how ready you are to step farther out into the world,
young Tim,' and sent him to Diddlecot, with Larry and
Vernon and the old man, and silent Gussie who was a
maid at the hospital, and old Mary Tolliver, who cooked
for them and washed their shirts and told tales on them
to Miss Ogden.

Tim planted peas and carrots and beans in the strip
of garden at the back. Vernon put in some geraniums.
Gussie bought a big beach hat and sat in a chair outside
the back door with the cord of the gramophone strung
through the kitchen window.

The hedges foamed with green and white, and pats of
yellow turf flowers appeared on the side of the hills. Tim
rode round with Ted Dace to the little villages and housing estates and the outlying farms, covering fifty miles a
day over the back roads, the tins flying off the shelves as
Ted took the hump-back bridges.

Spring bloomed hopefully into the hopelessness of Paul's summer. Alice had refused to talk to Scott or Jane, 'or any of those sober swine'. She had cast off A.A. for ever, with the same horrid glee as she had emancipated herself from her school nuns.

'Free at last.' She toasted Paul. 'Thank God Almighty.'

They did not speak much now. She talked intermittently, in clauses of abuse. He sheltered mostly in silence. When she could not rouse him to a fight, she found other fuddled ways to attack, ringing up the Headmaster of the school to pour a stream of anonymous scandal into his hairy and astonished ears. In the middle of the night, she rang down to the Steiners on the ground floor to say that Paul was drunk and beating her up.

'Hullo there – I say!' Mr Steiner in sagging pyjama trousers hallooing through the letter-box.

'It's all right. I'm so sorry.' Paul opened the door. 'She had a dream.'

'Some dream.' Mr Steiner ducked his head right and left to peer past Paul's broad shoulders for a view of something shocking.

Alice was becoming the scandal of Singleton Court. She would not cook meals, but if Paul took her down to the restaurant, there was usually a scene, small or large. Even Phyllis had stopped relating. She had bribed the other waitress to take the Hammonds' table.

Alice, who had not written to Jeff for months, wrote him long letters complaining about his father, with anecdotes of his unfaithfulness which she had to invent, since she did not know about Barbara. Paul had tried to tell her the truth, but she preferred her wildest fancies. He had read some of them when he opened one of the letters she gave him to post.

'Did you post it afterwards?' Barbara asked.

'Would you?'

'I would have burned it.'

'I did.'

Alice got herself on a train to London, arriving at Laura's flat after midnight with no money for the taxi.

She stayed three days, drinking and weeping so continuously that Laura could not go to work.

She brought her home. 'Daddy, I'm sorry. She's not my problem. Why do you go on letting her be yours?'

'She won't even talk about a divorce.'

'You could divorce her.'

'You can't divorce someone for being drunk.'

'You can for cruelty,' Laura said. 'Jeff and I have talked about this. We both think you're insane to stick with her. Even Nigel sees that now.'

'Don't bring him into our family crisis.'

'He is family,' Laura said stubbornly, 'whether you like it or not. Perhaps I shan't like – you have got someone else, haven't you? She didn't make that bit up?'

When Paul went to Burlington to see Jeff, staying this last term only because they were doing *Lear*, Jeff said, 'Look, for God's sake, I'd be *glad*. What's it matter to me? The State will take care of my mother. Go off with what's-it. That's you taken care of.'

How hard they both were. Hard and direct. Paul went to his lawyer to talk about divorce.

The decision edged out guilt. The summer began to be a time of increasing hope. He and Barbara could look far ahead, instead of just to the next dinner, the next weekend. They began to plan where they would live, where he would look for a job, what kind of dog he would have. In a street market one Sunday they bought the dog, a fair fat puppy obviously stolen. Barbara began to buy clothes less like a Burlington mother. Paul was light-hearted at school, a breezier, less pedantic, sexier Mr Hammond. Caroline Fulmer gave up cricket to fall in love with him. Puberty, her friends told her, the dawn of a new you. But it was the dawn of a new Paul. The hottest puberty on record would not have inflamed Caroline with the old Mr Hammond.

Barbara told her sons. Paul told his children. The indifferent approval of all four was transparent with relief.

'I'm moving out, Alice.'

'Oh – why? I thought you didn't mind this flat.'

'You must face this. How can I make you understand? I want a divorce.'

'I don't.' She clamped her mouth in the toothless, jawless shape to which drink leached it.

'You know I can divorce you.'

'Funny how long it took you to find that out.'

Paul began to pack some things.

'Where will you go?' she asked with polite interest.

'I've got a room.'

'Tell me where.'

He shook his head.

'That's what I thought.'

His escape made safe the way for pity. Damn pity. But he had to turn from the cupboard and look at her. She was gaunt and unkempt. Her hair was receding from her bony forehead and she did not bother to curl it forward. She was usually in a dressing gown now. She only dressed to go out in the evening, in clothes that were stained, a hem undone, a coat without some of its buttons.

He tried to look at her as a stranger. If she came stumbling in as a Samaritan client, would he reach out to her? Would he talk to her, love her, try to understand, try everything he could to help, begin the long war of drying out, stand by her and fight the demon with her?

He could no longer fight on her side. Alice herself had become the demon.

He went back to the flat for the last time to get some books.

'Alice?' He had not called from the hall for a long time, but all the lights were out and there was a smell of gas from the kitchen. Samaritans were well known for seeing suicide everywhere. On the stove, something that might be soup had boiled over, putting out the flame. Sad that the one time she cooked something for herself, she went out and forgot about it.

He went across the dark sitting-room to turn on the lamp by the bookcase and fell over something on the floor. Alice was lying near the fireplace on her back, snoring drunkenly. He pushed her with his foot quite roughly. She did not even groan. He switched on the lamp and saw that her eyes were open, staring at the ceiling, as if some horror was there. Her face was flushed dark red. He went quickly to the telephone.

Several weeks after the stroke, Alice could be propped into a chair, with her hands curled upwards on her lap like the claws of a dead bird. She could not speak, and no one knew if she could hear or understand. Her face did not move. Her mouth hung slightly open. Whoever was with her, or passing by, wiped away the saliva.

The doctor suggested a nursing home, and talked of the place that was run by Highfield. It sounded familiar. Tim. Tim's girl Felicity, the Smasher, was working there.

Paul went with Alice in the ambulance to the nursing home which was just down the hill from the gates of Highfield. A sign swung over a little box of geraniums: 'Extended Care Facility'. Euphemism for 'The only way out of here is feet first.'

The lady in charge was a certain Mrs Laidlaw, no wedding ring, the 'Mrs' a prerogative title to go with the autocracy.

She held absolute sway over the shrunken bodies in beds and chairs and dumped in a row on a sofa in front of a flickering television set they did not watch. They could and did complain, about the food, the nurses, the heat, the cold, the draught, their bowels. That was expected of them. They did not complain about Mrs Laidlaw. She was all smiles, so kind, worked day and night for them, rolling up her sleeves when the nurses were busy, baking a cake for ninetieth birthdays.

Paul had been pleased with Mrs Laidlaw and her smile when he first came here to make arrangements for Alice. Now when Alice was in bed in a room with two other logs and he was writing a cheque for the first month, he caught a hint of ghastliness. The smile assured him that she would do everything to make his wife comfortable. He asked her about the other women in Alice's room. One of them had terminal cancer. The other had been in the Home for ten years without ever getting a visitor or even a letter. As she told him this, *she was still smiling*. Kindly Mrs Laidlaw behind her polished desk with the cut-glass bowl of roses was suddenly a grinning death mask.

The coming of summer, for anyone who had their life or livelihood down by the sea, meant the coming of the rabble. On weekends and surprise sunny weekdays, the visitors began to push inexorably in until they crowded each other off the land and into the sea, the pebbly beach a writhing mat of flesh, the bathers shoulder to shoulder.

From Sarah's red front-door, she could see a bristle of masts in the harbour at the foot of Salt Street. The Yacht Club ran up its flags and opened its gin locker. Boats big and small were tethered to the finger piers. Easels came out, and the man in the beret who painted the same picture every month: sail, gulls, rocks, cliffs and a sea made of whipped green jelly.

All the little hotels and boarding-houses began to open up, window box pelargoniums and cinerarias challenging their fresh paint. Peter stayed away from the Samaritan Centre for a week to help his wife open the Baytree, and came back with paint under his fingernails and a new knowledge of plumbing which he applied to the old lavatory at the back of the rectory where clients dashed to empty out all the tea pumped into them by zealous Samaritans.

The big hotels put up their awnings, and the huge circular bed outside the portico of the Front Royal was planted at great cost in a zodiac design which could only be seen from the top floor or from an aeroplane. The reception staff were outfitted in white trousers and pale blue jackets, beautiful on Brian. He was tanned from lying with Sarah in the sun and wind of a tiny rock-circled cove they knew below the cliffs. His brown arms were cobwebbed with bleached hair, and the hair of his head was white gold. The side whiskers grew and grew and almost met in a fringe of silken beard before Mr

Rattigan let out a yell of agony and ordered them away.

The Front Royal filled up, the winter dwellers scathing from the veranda like cruise passengers lining the rail at each embarkation port. Hours were longer. Overtime was paid. Brian and Sarah were saving to buy a boat.

The waxworks opened with a set piece of the murder of Martin Luther King, sold off by some more topical museum. The Aquarium poured in some more fish and gaffed out the dead ones. The dance hall was closed for three weeks for decorating and re-opened looking exactly the same. Shops and restaurants and bars mended their broken windows. The café at the end of the pier was repaired, although the pier itself still rotted quietly into the stinking bed of the estuary. Champions of the pier, who never went on it, claimed that the water level had dropped since it was built some seventy years ago to commemorate the marriage of George V. Others said that the mud flats had always been there, but the site had been chosen at high tide.

When the sea was in, lapping under the landward piles, where small boys called and fought for pennies thrown down by people who came through the turnstile with change in their hand, the water at the far end was deep enough to drown yourself. One raining, blowing afternoon, when there was no one on the pier except the wind-flung sea-gulls screaming round the café garbage, Roland Mead, father of three, petty embezzler, went over the rail with a gull's cry.

'Why did he ring us?' Sarah asked Andrew. They had sent the Flying Squad to the pier, but it was too late. 'Why, if he really meant it?'

'Oh God, I don't know.' Andrew looked battered. He had answered the call from the telephone box on the pier. He would wonder forever whether there was not something he could have said ... 'Perhaps it's like, you know, when they struggle in the water.'

'One last fight of a losing battle?'

Paul was with them. He nodded, brooding. 'Sometimes,' he said heavily, 'I think it's just that suicide is just too damn lonely to bear alone.'

Paul's wife was very ill. She had suffered a stroke. She was dying, paralysed, witless – no one knew much about it. Paul did not want anyone to ask.

He asked Sarah, 'How is it going with Carrie?'

'All right, I think.' With her first client, she was not going to say it was difficult.

'Is it tough?'

'It's all right.'

But Carrie was quite tough. Befriending sounded so simple – to be a friend to someone who needed one – until you realized why they were short of friends.

At first, Carrie seemed to resent Sarah. 'Why do you always ring up after I've gone to bed?'

'You go to bed at such funny times.'

'I go to bed when I'm tired. What's the matter? You think I'm going to kill myself again? Look, I'm not a child. I'm older than you as a matter of fact.'

But if she did not hear from Sarah, it was 'I waited in all afternoon. I was sure you'd ring.'

Once when they were out together, on the way to the oculist, Carrie plunged forward as if she were going to throw herself in front of a car. Sarah grabbed her and pulled her back. The driver shook his fist, mouthing behind glass.

'What's the matter?' Carrie brushed off Sarah's hand. 'Can't I even cross the road?'

They went to the sea and sat under a breakwater, sharing Sarah's coat. Carrie always came out with too few or too many clothes. The coat was turned sideways across their shoulders, the skirt of it round Carrie, the big collar round Sarah. Carrie smelled a little. Her hair was never very clean. To get a warm bath in her building, you had to go up and down the passage with kettles. But she said jerkily to Sarah, after a long time of saying nothing, chucking pebbles rather savagely at the sea. 'I'm not going to try it on again, you know. It's not so bad now. I'm not on my own any more.'

'Oh Carrie!' Sarah hugged her. 'What a marvellous thing to say.'

Carrie shook off the coat and stood up, trampling her big feet in the gritty sand. 'Let's go and get something to eat.'

Lumpy, small-eyed, her nose like a Jerusalem artichoke, she was sadly unattractive. Because she knew it, she deliberately made the worst of herself, so that nobody should imagine she was trying to compete. When Sarah invited her home to supper, Brian looked out of the window and said, 'There's a rather dirty fat boy pounding on the door.'

Carrie was wearing dirt on her feet instead of shoes, trousers that managed to have one bell bottom and one straight leg, a man's khaki shirt with the tail out. To please Sarah, or to shut her up, she was letting her hair grow. It hung in greasy jags over her ears and eyes, not an imitation urchin crop like Sarah's, but the urchin itself. Her skin erupted all over her face. When Sarah suggested make-up, Carrie said it would be unhygienic.

She came upstairs on her unhygienic feet and greeted Brian warily, sticking out her hand without moving it from her side, so that he had to cross the room to shake it. She would not eat much. She pushed at her food, and nibbled as if her teeth were bad. She drank wine fast as if it were medicine. She was very shy.

Watching Carrie so ungracious at the table, watching herself so graciously bringing food, chattering and smiling across at her, Sarah thought busily, I love her in the way God loves people – if he does. Safely superior. Unthreatened.

Brian was good, but not good enough. He had expected a wan, dramatic figure of tragedy, rescued from disaster by his brilliant wife. Carrie's tragedy was being Carrie: her disaster was still with her.

'But I can't ask her once and then never again. That's worse than not asking her at all.'

'If she comes again, I go out.'

'She'll know why.'

'Who cares?'

'I hate you.' (Paul's voice, 'Being a Samaritan doesn't make you one at home.')

They slid into one of their formalized fights, words and objects flying about as if the room were a stage, ending dutifully in bed, as if the fight were ritual foreplay. In the morning, they did not speak about making love, as if it had not happened, or they had been drunk.

One evening when Brian was working, Sarah and Andrew took Carrie to the theatre. Carrie fell asleep in the second act. She fell asleep everywhere she sat down. She was past insomnia, but she had a lot to make up.

They took her back to her flat and met Gretchen, who stared and said, 'I thought you made that up about having new friends. What did you mean, the Suicide Squad?'

'We ride a motorbike on the Wall of Death,' Andrew said.

'I've never seen you.'

'We're in the hospital a lot.'

'Oh belt up,' Gretchen said. She stuck far out in front and behind, her back hollow. She had enormous healthy incisors, like a blunted vampire. They had bruised the mouth of her boy friend, an etiolated Italian, who remained lying on the sofa bed when the others came in.

It was a wretched place for Carrie to live, two stuffy rooms in a slum street not even near the University. She came out to light Sarah and Andrew down with a torch, since there was no bulb on the staircase.

'I told you it was a dump,' she said.

'I could help you look for something else.'

'Gretchen wouldn't let me. She needs me.'

Andrew drove Sarah home. She liked being with him. He was uncomplicated, enjoying being young, not striking attitudes, eagerly voluble, or easily silent if he did not want to talk. He was the sort of man you could go round the world with. He was not beautiful like Brian, assured and spoiled, a shining stranger; but when he kissed her lightly outside her house, the unfolding vistas of the kind of man she might have married quite unnerved her. She got out of the car quickly.

Brian was turning into Salt Street at the top of the hill. 'Who brought you home?'

'Andrew. One of the Samaritans. I told you about him.'

'Oh God.' For some reason he took off his shoes to climb the stairs, as if he were a sneak lover in Sarah's girlhood home. 'I'm jealous of that spotted girl. Now have I got to be jealous of Andrew too?'

Rape and pillage and drug raids. Tot kidnapped by babysitter. Thirteen nude teenagers arrested in Edgewater cottage. Seasonal licences must be slashed, says Alderman. As the summer teemed in, the *Courier* increased in size and heat.

'Better take a quick holiday, Victoria, while there's still time.' Uncle Willie, chaotic and unpredictable, one of his pockets smouldering.

'When?'

'Tomorrow. Mrs Start can come in. Order up some Guinness.'

Victoria stayed with friends in London, and bought clothes and went to the cinema. If she married Robbie, as he still thought she might, they would have his parents' flat when the Bank moved him to London, and what the hell would Victoria do? Not much point in being someone's secretary if you were richer than they were.

She would join the London Samaritans at the old City Church. She went to look at it, walking past the door in the corner of the church tower, too shy to go inside.

Those who were chosen to become Companions, the inner core and lasting spirit of the movement, went to a service here in this lovely church, to dedicate their lives to the work of the Samaritans.

200 was a Companion. So was Ralph, and Betty. Helen had recently been chosen. 'Why me, for God's sake? I'm a bigger mess than most of the clients.'

Peter had once told Victoria that the instinctive 'Why

me?' reaction was a sign that they had picked the right person.

Leaving the church, she went underground at the Bank station. She had come by bus. She would force herself to go back in the Tube, although even as she went down the steps, the anxiety was there.

Seven, eight years ago, quite a long time after she and Joe had seen the last of each other after wasting years of pretending they would marry, he had fallen under a train. Her hatred of the Tube had been one of her reasons for leaving London.

She sat solemnly in the train opposite the solemn faces, without recognition on her part or theirs. Here eyes could only look at eyes, not into them. If crowds of strangers were to smile and greet each other, it would be too exhausting, like being at a perpetual cocktail party or soul gathering.

At the no-man's-land of Earl's Court, nobody's home station, everybody's junction, she waited for another train at the end of the platform, looking at the other people, as all Samaritans did, as potential clients. A little scrum of boys charged down the steps carrying a football. With vacant, wordless jokes, they pushed each other forward and stood at the edge of the platform, windmilling their arms as if they were losing their balance. The live rail gleamed back at them. Cold steel, but if you fell on it, you would fry instantly, bubbling like batter. The tallest of the boys threw the ball over the line, and as Victoria watched in horror, he jumped down, bent over the live rail, stretched his long arms for the ball, swung upright and was back on the platform as the train swayed racketing in.

Victoria still stood transfixed. If I had been there when Joe fell forward on to the line, I would have stood and watched and done nothing.

The train slid away without her. She turned and went back to the escalator. She felt sick and faint, very ill. Her heart felt swollen, beating thickly. It was hard to breathe. Past the advertisements of all the offered crotches in swim suits, panties, Y-front shorts, she was carried upwards, drooping over the moving black handrail. Something would happen. Something dreadful was going to happen to her, while the people glided up and down and did not see that she was there.

Was this what Jean meant? Trying to go into a crowd: 'I was in a panic that my heart would stop, would in some way explode. I was moving in a nightmare...'

I am going to have a heart attack. Victoria could not reach out to the coat of the woman standing two steps above her. Bodies don't touch other strange bodies. *Help me*, she said silently to the woman's broad back, not loudly enough to see her swing round a face impatient with suspicion.

Victoria's heart was pounding, her mouth dry, her legs would hardly carry her over the top of the stairs as they rolled under. She went to a little hotel and took a room and lay for a long time on the bed until the terror quietened and at last left her. She had lived with Joe the horror of his death. Unable to cry out or to have the cry answered, he must have known that panic aloneness as he fell forward from the staring people.

She left her friends and London the next day.

'You should see a doctor,' the woman said, when she told them something of what had happened. 'That's really neurotic, Victoria.'

The man said, 'I tell you what it is, sweetie. I've told you before. It's time you were married.'

Her rose-and-white flat was a shell.

Soon after she came home, she went up to the government hostel to see old Michael.

'He's scarpered, dear.' The Warden was tending a small patch of onions in the unlikely soil of Flagg's Hill.

'On those feet?'

'He'll be back. He's signed on here. He'll come back to get his money.'

'Could you telephone me if he does?'

'Why all the interest, Missie?'

'I don't know.' Victoria laughed. 'He's such a pitiful

old man. I think: if it were my father ... I find myself worrying about him.'

'Save your energies. Here, you can have these green tops if you like. Quite a lift to your salads. There's not much you can do for that old sport. They go their own way, that kind, you know, and die alone.'

EIGHT

'AND SO WHAT are you going to do now, Dad?' Jeff, taking refuge behind the plain glass of his huge wire spectacles, asked it as soon as they left the nursing home.

He had come with Paul, but then would not look at his mother, nor touch her. He had wanted to come, perhaps to assure himself that what his father had told him was true.

Alice was in a chair, tied round the waist with a soft binder, because she could push herself forward and fall out. Her short hair was cleaner and paler. Her slipped face knew nobody. From time to time, she wept.

'It doesn't mean anything.' Mrs Laidlaw's grin sugared the scene. 'There's some liability of the emotional control mechanism. It doesn't mean that she is sad.'

'How do you know?'

'Mr Hammond, we don't, but your wife is in a vegetable state. She cannot feel or understand.'

'Will she ever?' Jeff's voice from where he hung back in the doorway sounded unused and creaky, as if it had never broken.

'We can only hope.'

'And so what are you going to do now, Dad?'

'About what?' They got into the car.

'The divorce. Barbara.' He had met Barbara and liked her, but he drawled her name as if he found it ridiculous.

'Nothing. Nothing can be done now. I was too much a coward to say that to Barbara, but she said it first anyway.'

'Yes, that's very noble.' Jeff thought for a while and then he asked, 'What's the point of being noble?'

'It's preferable to being bitter. It's also the Law, when

someone can't speak or make a sign, can't prove they understand what is said to them. I can't divorce your mother, Jeff.'

When he went back to see Alice, he sat in front of her and held the dead claws of her hands and said over and over again, 'I'm here, Alice. It's Paul. It's all right, dear, it's all right. I'm here.'

'It's a pity she can't hear you.' Mrs Laidlaw, a woman of much wiry energy, roamed ceaselessly through all the rooms of the home, checking to see who had died, dusting off table tops and lockers with a paper towel and a can of aerosol deodorant instead of spray wax.

'Sometimes I almost think she knows me.'

Mrs Laidlaw shook her head, grinning from ear to ear. 'That's a good girl!' She patted the old lady, curled up like a foetus on one of the beds, a bright orange bow tied round the few hairs that were left on her pink scalp.

When she had gone out, the young nurse who was in the room feeding the other patient stuck out a narrow pointed tongue automatically at the doorway. She was thin and pale, with dark shifting eyes that settled no-where, hair piled carelessly up under a rumpled cap, straggling round her sharp face.

'Don't give any notice to her,' she told Paul. 'Alice knows more than you think, Alice does.'

Alice sagged into the binder, the dressing gown fallen open over her bony chest, the bags of her breasts.

'It's me. It's Paul. It's all right, Alice.' He stared at her to force understanding into her eyes. He squeezed her hands. '*Alice!*' Her mouth drooped. Saliva ran. Tears ran gently and he reached out his fingers tenderly to brush them away as he had when she was young and stormy.

'She knows *me* all right.' The nurse shoved a spoonful of baby food into and around the cracked mouth of the patient, wiped it on the edge of the sheet and came over.

'Alice.' She bent forward and clicked long bony fingers in front of the empty eyes. 'Wake up, dear. It's me – Felicity.'

Felicity. The Smasher. Skinny and sallow, with long

sticks of legs and an evasive, head-tossing manner, she did not in the least fit Tim's admiring description, but if she had, she would hardly have bothered with poor little Tim.

'I know a friend of yours,' Paul said. 'Tim Shaw.'

'He's no friend of mine,' the girl said quickly.

'He told me you went out with him.'

'Did do,' Felicity said, 'doesn't mean I do now.' She bent over Alice, who did slightly turn her face upwards, though without expression. 'She can't speak, you see,' Felicity said bossily, 'so I'm teaching her to wink. Once for yes. Two for no. You understand that, don't you Alice? There. You see?'

'No. Nothing.'

'You've got to look very closely. You've got to know. Are you a good girl, Alice?' She raised her voice. 'Of course you are. Not going to pee the chair?'

'Stop that,' Paul said, 'I'll tell Mrs Laidlaw.'

'You do that,' Felicity said, 'and see where it gets you. Alice likes me. Perhaps that makes you feel jealous. She likes me because I'm very good to her.'

Paul got up, bent to kiss Alice lightly and went to the door.

'You're Paul, aren't you?' Felicity said. 'Paul, 401. Yes, that's right. I know a lot about you.'

Mrs Laidlaw was in her office, telling a visitor a story about a patient who became so swollen with cancer that the skin of her upper arm burst like an overblown balloon.

'Excuse me.'

She turned the skeletal grin to Paul.

'The nurse – that girl Felicity. She – she's good with the patients, is she?'

'I'm quite pleased with her. She's nice with the old folk, and they like to have a young person about.'

'She seems to think my wife can communicate with her.'

The smiling headshake. 'There's too much motor damage, Mr Hammond. Even if she could possibly take anything in, she's not able to put out. I'm afraid,' she added, not for the benefit of Paul, who was a known quantity, but for the visitor, who was a prospect.

The mobile shop of which Ted Dace was driver and manager and Tim was boy ('Here Tim boy, come on boy!' as if he had a tail to wag) was a box on wheels, with shelves all round and a counter near the back door for Special Offers.

'And you watch that like a hawk, Tim boy,' Ted warned, 'Because that's where the bloody kids knock off the stuff when Mum asks for something from out of the cab.'

If the kids were at school, Mum would argue the change, or say she had been overcharged last week, or shorted on the weight of plums. Some of the women on the housing estates would cheat anything on wheels.

Ted Dace was a youngish, unsmiling man with a thin mouth notched back between nose and chin, a great thinker and talker, with or without an audience, since he had long been driving about these deserted roads alone, before the grocery dreamed up the job to help boys like Tim. This suited Tim, who sometimes did not say a word from the start of the day until they coasted on their last egg-cup of petrol into the garage.

The mobile philosopher. 'Stay around, Tim boy,' Ted said out of the side of his mouth that did not have the match stuck in it. 'You may get an education yet.'

Jouncing down the rutted lane that led to Castle Farm, Ted wrenched the wheel round, but too late. They were into a pothole and out of it, and they knew what they would find back in the van, even without the noise of fallen angels.

He stopped the engine and opened his newspaper, while Tim went round to the back. Each time they went into a pothole or a deep rut, the tins on the shelves flew into the air, and as the van bounced back under the falling tins and boxes and jars, it caught them one shelf lower, with the things that had been on the bottom shelf all over the floor.

Tim had an idea. It was an afternoon of driving rain. They were both fretting to get home, Ted to a new wife, Tim to give his owl-hoot on a blade of grass under Felicity's window. He left the goods where the shelves had caught them, and put the stuff on the floor up on to the empty top shelf.

'You been quick,' Ted said when he climbed back into the cab. Tim nodded. He did not need to speak. Ted did the talking for both, and knew better than to ask Tim a question that needed an answer.

Castle Farm was a dilapidated stone house on a windy hill, built of the remains of an ancient fortress, and haunted by fettered monks. Ted Dace had seen them on a dark winter afternoon, walking through the pig yard, right through wall and sties and all. The bachelor farmer who lived there left out a list for the mobile in a hole under his doorstep. It was a two-mile drive from the nearest house. Sometimes the list said, 'Marg. 1 small white. Bit of soup.' Sometimes it only said, '1 small tin baked beans thank u.' Ted had tried to cut this farm off his route, but the manager of the grocery said, 'The outlying farms are the life-blood of the mobile trade.'

'If so, we've got anaemia.' Ted thought of that afterwards, and said it, going backwards up Pea Hill when low gear was slipping.

Tim got out of the van and walked through the wet manure and straw of the farmyard to the back doorstep. The list was written over a printed page. The farmer's departed father had had a few books, and he was using them up for grocery lists.

Tim collected the goods and carried the box back to the step and covered it with a sack. On the way back to the van, a cow swung its head down and began to come at him. Tim ran, fell in the mud, climbed the gate, fell again. His hair was plastered over his eyes. His hands were filthy. Ted made him wash them in a watering trough before he would let him into the van.

Lecturing about the contamination of food, with particular reference to his aunt, who had been a typhoid carrier in a West End hotel and had finished off half a dozen people after a wedding banquet, Ted went into the same pothole with the other wheel and out again with the same sound of the heavens falling.

He stopped and jerked his head. Tim got out cursing, all his words in the right order, and sorted out the jumble of sweets and jelly packets and biscuits and cake mix on the floor on to the top shelf where the soups ought to be. When they reached East Cross, the brakes announcing them like an ice cream bell, and Ted went round to the back to fill orders, he could not find anything.

He was angry with Tim. 'People who are bloody feeble-minded got to follow directions,' he raved. 'Follow directions, or we're all in the queer. Look at this.' The familiar old mobile did look odd, with all the soap powders and bleaches up where tinned fruit and veg. ought to be, and fruit and veg. down on the meat and fish shelf, and meat and fish all jumbled in with big bags of flour that had not fallen.

'Look at this, and tomorrow my stocktaking.' He began savagely to rearrange the shelves, while two or three housewives stood outside with coats and aprons over their heads and invited him to knock it off and get out their orders.

'Feeble-minded ... Welfare State ... honest crust ... week's work for a day's pay ...' grunts and snarls flew out of the van as Ted slung the goods back where they should be like a speeded-up old moving picture. Tim climbed in to help him, but he elbowed him out of the way.

'You shouldn't treat the poor boy like that,' a round woman like suet said. 'That's not very nice.'

'Sick to death of it ... always some bloody loony ... have us all inside before we're done ...'

Tim stood at the back of the van with the impatient women, listening to Ted without properly hearing. 'Never you mind, dear,' the pudding woman said. He did not mind. He liked to ride about the countryside, as he had when he used to drift round the Lincolnshire villages with the subsize vegetables and hyacinth seconds. He liked to earn six pounds a week, and he liked to live at Diddlecot, where he had the room under the roof because he was the shortest, and could go out every night as long as Felicity agreed.

He did not mind Ted Dace. He was not afraid of him, as he was afraid of Larry, who had a chopper under his mattress and would one night have all their heads.

Tim told Mary Tolliver. She wagged her large head, which was said to have a plate in it the size of a florin piece, and said, 'Don't make up stories, Timmy. I turned that mattress yesterday.' He told Miss Ogden, the Social Worker, and she made an excuse to come back after Larry had gone out to the pub, and sneaked upstairs like a thief.

'No, Tim.' She came down shaking her head. 'You must have dreamed it.' She looked embarrassed, as if she felt silly to have believed him.

Mary Tolliver and the old man were always quarrelling. She cooked a lot of mutton stew, because the meat was cheap and she was salting away some of the food money for her old age. The old man did not like mutton stew. He would come into the kitchen in his long underwear when he smelled the onions starting up, and he and Mary would hit each other with anything handy, spoons, the newspaper, a saucepan, a cushion, nothing hard enough to hurt. Thwack! Thud! You could hear them at it all over the little stucco house.

The old man should not be in Diddlecot, because the Highfield cottages were supposed to be for ex-patients who went out to work and could contribute towards the housekeeping. He had got a job as sweeper in the local box works, and as soon as they moved him into Diddlecot, he had officially retired. He cried if they talked of moving him out, because it would be back to the Gerry ward at Highfield, so Miss Ogden let him stay, with his pension and his foul tobacco and his cat which spent the day on the exact middle of the dining-room table, like a great white icing cake.

Tim was glad to find him and Mary always in the house, even when Ted Dace went on strike against the farthest farms and they fetched up early at the garage. It was like it must be to have a gran and a grandad nattering about the place and whacking each other and telling him, 'You young lads don't know the meaning of a day's work.'

Every night after tea, or after washing up, if it was his turn, Tim put on his suit and walked the mile and a half to the road where the nursing home was. He picked a blade of grass and holding it between his hollowed thumbs, blew gently on it like the ghost of an owl.

Sometimes with no result. The light in Felicity's back room would be out, which could mean she was working, or watching television downstairs. Sometimes the light was on, but the blind was down and it never moved. Sometimes the blind flew up and she flung up the window and leaned far out, reaching down with her arms as if she were going to hurl herself on to the laundry lines.

With Tim's wealth, they could take a bus into the town and have something to eat, or go to the cinema, or go to the Town Hall if there was a dance or a concert on. Tim could not dance. He stood and shuffled in a corner, getting an erection while Felicity pranced and wiggled round him, throwing her body about in extraordinary ways as if her bones were put together backwards.

Sometimes they walked far out to the other end of the town for sentimental reasons, and tumbled about a bit in the back of the junk car. Once, she made him sit in the front, and compared him unfavourably with the gear lever. After that, he would not go to the old car with her any more.

Although he had some small power over her at times, when she begged him, 'Do it, do it, I can't stand it,' behind the bushes of the cricket field, or in one of the punts pulled up on the river bank by the boathouse, he usually had to do what Felicity wanted. She was quite changeable. If he wanted to do it, and she didn't, they didn't do it. 'I'll have you up for assault,' she hissed, 'and they'll put you in the nick, Tim Shaw, and I'll come and laugh at you through the bars and throw peanuts.'

Once, when she gave the same excuse three times running, he said, 'I thought you didn't see your monthlies,' and she said, 'Don't talk dirty,' and hit him hard across the face, wearing a sharp ring.

Being with Felicity was the thing he thought about all day as the mobile shop careened up and down the narrow lanes, or rolled among the new brick Council houses with an eye out for dogs and toddlers. Ted Dace talked about his wife a lot. Her name was Doreen and she was going to have a baby. That was why the stealing and trickery were so bitter, since Ted's commission could mean the difference between this or that cot mattress, a play pen, a painted swing to hang in the doorway. He was always buying things for the baby. Tim and Felicity agreed that it would be a laugh if it was born dead.

When a tin of peaches or a half-dozen of the Finnish sardines went missing, Ted would chew on the match and mutter, 'Child murderers,' as he drove away. He did not know about the cigarettes that Tim slipped into his pockets for Larry, to keep on his good side, or the sweets he took for Felicity, and the little silver balls she loved to tip into her mouth, pop, pop, pop, catching them on her long tongue.

All day he thought of her, and the evenings when she would not come out, he sat about the lounge of Diddlecot, biting his nails and kicking the old man's cat.

'Want a game cards, young Tim?' Vernon was always pleasant, a plump, fresh-featured young man who worked as a post office sorter and had somehow got the authorities to promise they would never send him back to his mother.

Tim shook his head.

'Play Old Maid if you like.'

'OK.' He did not speak much more at Diddlecot than he did in the mobile. He did not need to. Vernon was nice to you whether you talked or not. Gussie never said a word. Larry told dark tales of the injustices of the railway yard, and Mary Tolliver and the old man kept up their cackle and whack all day and half the night if the fit was on them.

One evening he had hooted for half an hour outside the back of the nursing home before walking the mile and a half home. The next evening, Felicity accused him, 'Why didn't you come? I waited and waited. I had my new dress on.'

'That one?' She was wearing a very short orange skirt, just a square of stuff, with her long skinny legs in patterned stockings, like snakes going up.

'This old thing – you've seen it hundreds of times.'

'Where's the new one then?' They were in the café, spooning custard ice cream from plastic bowls that had got bent in the dishwasher.

'I gave it to one of the girls.'

'Mad—'

'I didn't like it.'

'Why d'you buy it then?'

'I didn't. Somebody gave it to me.'

'Who?'

'Guess.'

'Mrs Laidlaw?'

'Her.' Felicity laughed, spraying yellow ice at him. 'She wouldn't give you the crust off her corns.'

'Who then?'

'That old man.' She bent her head, so that her loose hair fell forward, and looked up at him through it with one glittering eye.

'What old man?'

'Mr Sissons. I told you about him.'

'The one who's always after you to fetch him in the special food and that?' Mr Sissons had been put into the nursing home by his children, and he could not stand the food, nor the life, nor the other patients, who urinated into his bottle of lemon squash.

'Mm.' Her head was still down. The long finger which he liked to suck like a sugar stick traced puddles in the melting ice on the table. 'He likes me, Mr Sissons. He's always giving me things. Money sometimes. You get me this, you get me that, Felicity. Felicitations. Felicitous girl. That's how he talks. Get me some chocolate peppermint creams, he says, Oh Felicitous young lady.'

'That where the cholcolate peps went I give you?' Tim scraped back his chair.

Felicity looked up and shook back her hair. 'Yeth.' She lisped it. 'Yeth, Timothy. I'm thorry for poor old Mithter Thithonth.'

Tim would not talk to her any more. He went home to Diddlecot without seeing her back up the hill to the nursing home. She did not mind. She was laughing and waving as he trudged away.

On the country road, a car slowed and offered Tim a lift. He shook his head. There was a man and two women in the car, kidnappers all.

He felt very unhappy for a few days. He fumbled with groceries, spilling a packet of lentils, and dropped a two-pound tin of apricots on Ted's toe. He would not go out in the evenings. He would not play cards or work at the big communal jigsaw. He would not eat Mary Tolliver's toad-in-the-hole.

'Why don't you go and see your young lady?' Vernon asked. 'That would cheer you up.'

Tim shook his head.

'Had a tiff? She a bit tricky, eh?' Vernon knew a lot for someone who had never been anywhere or done anything or had anything to do with women except his mother, in whose bed he had still slept when he was fourteen.

'Messing about with old men.' Tim could say things to Vernon that he would not tell even to Paul. Paul was kind and wise and dependable, but he was one of the All Rights. When you felt yourself a human wreck, you needed another human wreck, like Vernon.

'Whore,' Vernon said. That was not the word the men had taught him to use at Highfield, but he preferred it.

'Kill her,' Tim muttered. And then, 'Remember I told you, Vernon, if she messes me up, I'll shoot myself.'

'Oh, yes, yes, we've heard all that before. If you was to

shoot yourself every time you said, we could strain the spinach through you.'

One day when Sarah was sitting by the emergency telephone, hoping that it would not ring and yet that it would, Peter came in to talk.

He stood by the desk, hitching his trousers out and up, as he still did, although he had given up smoking and regained all the weight he had lost.

'How are things at the bran and carrots shop?'

Sarah made a face. 'Some of the complexion creams are going off. It's the weather.'

'How long are you going to stay there?'

'I don't think I can stick it much longer. Mrs Wrigley is making bio-chemical pickles in the back store-room. I'm going to look for something else.'

'You wouldn't like to come down to the Baytree for a bit?' He said it diffidently, not looking at her, his large hand fiddling with something on the desk. He was a shy-confident mixture, very strong and sure about clients, talking only with difficulty about himself.

'As a maid?' She would get a blue check gingham dress, no make-up at all, just her brown face and legs and very pale lipstick. Good morning, here's your tea. It's a lovely day. Rattling the big curtain rings back to show the morning beyond the promenade, sparkling and fresh before the tourists used it, herself sparkling and healthy because she had been up and about with mops and brushes while the holidaymakers frowsted.

'We need some help in the office. The cook broke her leg, so my wife has to spend most of her time in the kitchen. Can you type?'

'Two fingers.'

'Enough.'

The office was a small hutch separated from the hall of the Baytree by a partition covered with photographs of guests, and postcards they had sent from other places, saying it was not nearly so nice. On the first morning when Sarah went there early to catch up on the accumulation of letters and bills, everyone who came past the office window stopped to speak to her and ask her name. The staff at the Baytree never changed. Sarah King was a small event on a cold misty day, with a fire at each end of the lounge and nothing to do with the children that would not cost money.

One of the men who came down the stairs and stopped to speak to her on his way to breakfast was Mr Reynolds, the American in the bar of the Front Royal who had shown her the pictures of his wife and children.

Remembering that he had told her he must bring his wife to the Baytree, Sarah asked, 'Is your wife with you?' She had asked him something like that before, and regretted it before he answered. She regretted it now, knowing, even as she asked it, what he was going to say.

'She couldn't make it.'

'I'm sorry.'

'We've been taking the kids to Maine the last few years. They made her take them again. Well—' he smiled, 'not *made*, exactly, but she wanted to, I guess.'

'She's not missing much in weather,' Sarah said brightly, because he looked glum. 'Are you having a nice time?'

'It'll do. I'm hoping a friend may join me at the end of the week.'

He went into the dining-room. When he came out, he put on a green hat and a short, very British raincoat and went out.

What did he do all day? He talked very little with the other guests, many of whom knew each other from other years, or became easily friendly, because it was that kind of hotel, with children everywhere, and Peter's wife roasting beautiful meat, and evening regulars coming in to hear Peter playing the piano in the bar.

Every morning, Mr Reynolds stopped by the office for a little conversation with Sarah about nothing.

'Why do the British keep talking about the weather?' he asked, leaning his elbows on the ledge of the window, nothing to do and all day to do it. One day soon he was going to ask Sarah to go out to lunch, she could see it coming.

'You have to say something. If you say something that means anything, people back away.'

'Why say anything then?'

'I don't know. To sort of – reassure each other? Like making familiar noises to babies and animals. Like Americans asking people where they come from.'

'Where *do* you come from, Sarah?'

'I don't know. Nowhere special. You see – that always stumps the English, because why does it matter? It tells you nothing about a person.'

'Nor does the weather.'

Sarah did go to lunch with Mr Reynolds one day. When she told Brian, and he began to work himself up to object, she said, 'You don't have to. He's a homosexual.'

'He tell you that at lunch?'

'Yes.' He had told her a lot of things. He told her that his wife had left him. He told her about the boy he had picked up on a New England beach – 'Two solid miles of queers, Sarah, you've never seen anything like it, and me one of them.' He told her about the friend in London. 'I don't know whether to hope he will come here, or hope he won't. Anne might come back, maybe, if I could lick this thing.'

'Can one?'

'I've tried. Then I get a couple of belts in me, and there's always some kid, some boy...'

The friend from London did not arrive, although Mr Reynolds continued to tell Peter's wife every day that he was expecting him. He was quite unhappy. He wandered about on the pier or the seafront with his badly cut hair and his too-thin suit and his air of slight seediness, his slight smell of failure, of not being liked. In an era when ninety-nine per cent of opinion was visual, he had the bad luck, like Carrie, to have a physical presence that was somehow repellent, the shape of a burgundy bottle, the tedious face of a yak.

His wife did not write to him. No one wrote to him. He

showed Sarah some more pictures of his children. He told her they were beautiful and brilliant, although the pictures belied it. Walking part of the way home with her along the hard wet sand, the sea far out, their footsteps spreading and filling, he told her that he had thought of killing himself.

In the morning at the Baytree, she went through to the flat where Peter and his wife lived.

'I've found a client.'

'They're supposed to find us.'

Peter was having breakfast in a rough blue shirt with the top buttons missing, large and bulky in the small room which was overcrowded with useless gifts from guests which they could not throw away, not remembering who had given what.

'It's Mr Reynolds.'

'Oh yes,' he said, as if he knew.

'Do you know about him?'

'Not much. Do you?'

'He needs help. He's terribly unhappy.'

'So are lots of people. We can't help anybody unless they ask.'

'He won't. I told him about the Samaritans, but he jeered, He called it exhibitionism. He told me yesterday he had thought of suicide.'

Pete went, 'Mm-hm,' as he did when he was listening on the telephone.

'Can't you talk to him?'

'Not unless he talks to me first.'

Sarah had hardly slept for worrying about Mr Reynolds. She had exhausted Brian by talking about it obsessively. Now Peter only sat there eating a boiled egg that looked too small for him.

'But he said that, he said, "I've thought about killing myself." '

'Try and get him to ring us.'

'I told you, he won't. Can't you help him?'

'Look, if we went charging in every time we saw someone unhappy, we'd be accosting half the population of this town. All I can do is try and help you to try and help him.'

'What can *I* do?' Sarah said miserably. 'A middle-aged queer who doesn't know if he wants to be queer or not, who doesn't like himself or anyone else—'

'You can like him. You can do that.'

'It's not *enough*!'

'It's all you have. Try and persuade him to look for proper help. Meanwhile, be his friend.'

'I don't like him,' Sarah said rather sulkily. 'I can't.'

'Did you think being a Samaritan was going to be so easy?'

It was not easy. It was terribly, defeatingly difficult. The harder she tried with Mr Reynolds, the further he withdrew.

'Leave me alone,' he said, when she found him huddled on the blustery beach among a few children with macintoshes and sou'westers who had been brought to the seaside and by God were going to build sandcastles even if they could hardly keep on their feet.

'It's cold. Come into the hotel and I'll get you some coffee.' The wind blew her short hair into her eyes and her words away.

'Leave me alone.' He threw stones. 'Stop being so bloody nice.'

'You bastard!' If that was the way he wanted it—

He still sat in his British raincoat that was made in Hong Kong, throwing stones at the sea.

'OK,' he said. 'OK.'

Two days later, he asked her quite formally for his bill, gave her some travellers' cheques and went to London. On his receipted bill, she wrote the telephone number of the London Samaritans. He put his green hat on over his long dull face and went away.

She tried to help Carrie. She tried too hard perhaps. Too bloody nice. Nobody had ever been as nice as this to Carrie. She knew when she was on to a good thing, and she was not going to let Sarah go.

She had become very dependent on her. They were friends. 'Be my friend,' a girl had once said to Sarah at school, and they had gone overboard into a claustrophobic relationship that shielded them from the assaults of the hockey-playing world.

Be my friend, Carrie was saying, with every telephone call, every meeting, every insistence on planning the next meeting before they said goodbye. The dependence was not one-sided. Nobody had ever needed Sarah as much as this. Nobody, not even Brian when he showed her off, encouraging her to be witty, mod Sarah, had ever made her feel so clever and so kind, so excellent.

'You can do anything, can't you, Sarah?' They had been swimming in the public gardens pool that rivalled, successfully, the sea. Sarah in a bikini had performed on the diving board. Carrie floundered in the shallow end, getting water up her nose, capsized by tots on rubber sea-monsters.

'I've always been able to swim.'

'But you do all that pottery, and you know how to play tennis, and ride horses, and type, and play the piano.' Carrie could not do anything. She had not been brought up that way. She played no games. She had no talents. She could not even cook or sew, because her mother had never had time to teach her. She had won the teaching scholarship because there was nothing else to do at home but study, if you wanted to avoid the pig pens. Now she was discovering that she could not teach.

'You'll learn,' Sarah said.

'Never.' When she went out for her first sessions as a student teacher, the children had practically broken up the classroom, and Carrie had to be rescued by the principal. 'I'm not going back to college next year,' she said. 'I don't want to finish the course.'

'What will you do?' Sarah was secretly glad that Carrie was not going to have the chance to mould young minds.

'I may go home. I can get a job in the town. There's a shop I was in before.'

'I thought you didn't want to go home.'

'Don't take me up on everything I say!' The mildest remark could set her off. 'I wanted to get away where nobody knew me. In the village, I was Caroline who went to University, Caroline who won the scholarship, tuppence to speak to you now, I daresay. They thought I had such a wonderful life. I've never told anybody about failing that last exam. I wanted them to think, there's that Caroline who's gone up in the world. That's why I – you know – I wanted to take those pills, because I wasn't going up and I couldn't go back and I wasn't going anywhere. I did go home before that, just for the day, just in case. It was the spring. You can't imagine what spring is like at our place. Everything was pregnant or hatched out, seedlings coming up all over the place. The blossom was out, the cat was stretched on the doorstep feeding eight kittens. To top it all, my mother told me she was going to have a baby. At forty-two! After eighteen years. Can you imagine anything more disgusting? I wouldn't speak to my father.'

The next time she went home, she took Sarah with her. They went unannounced. Carrie would not telephone or write. They drove in Brian's car between fields of cabbages and beans to a small brick and flint house surrounded by sheds and sties and henhouses, and trampled yards fenced in with barbed wire and bedsteads.

They walked round the house and went in to the kitchen where her mother and father were eating. A row of boots stood by the door. A chicken was dying in a box by the stove.

'Well, you are a stranger, Caroline!'

The father continued to eat bread and cheese. The mother's greying hair was cut in a square round her weather-pickled face. She wore trousers and a man's jersey several sizes too large as a maternity jacket.

'You told me to bring home a friend,' Carrie said defensively, 'so I've brought one. This is Sarah King. My friend.'

When she told them that she was going to leave the

University, they did not seem to mind. They were not sinister, dominating people, but a quite complacent couple who worked hard on their land and had no time to bother about anyone else, or even their own relationship. The baby must have been conceived in the few moments between falling exhausted into bed and falling exhaustedly asleep.

'You must do what you want,' they said. 'You must do what you think best.'

'I thought I might come home for a bit,' Carrie said. 'Would you mind?'

'Mind?' Her mother was at the stone sink, standing on a carrot box because she was so short. The father had gone out to kill a chicken for supper. 'Why should we mind, Caroline?'

'You wanted me to be a teacher.'

'You wanted it. It's your life. If you go back to Benting's, you'll be earning good money, I daresay.' She stepped off the box and turned round. Although she was only about four months gone, her initial shape and stance exaggerated her pregnancy, but her seasoned face and hair made it seem more like an ovarian cyst than a baby.

'Well, I—' It was difficult for Carrie to say anything real to her. 'I'll not be so crabby, I don't think.'

'Oh my yes, you were a misery.' Her mother's smile spread her tanned lips to show her cheap false teeth, unnecessarily yellow. The father had them too, cavern meeting cavern in a big bed that filled a little upstairs room. 'Growing pains.'

'It wasn't growing pains.' Carrie pressed on, as if it were possible to get through. 'I was very unhappy.'

'Oh well, some folks can be unhappy anywhere.' Her mother hung the torn wet dishcloth on a nail and went to the door, wiping her hands on her trousers.

'I was unhappy at the University too.' Sarah reached out and squeezed Carrie's hand, wanting her to stop. The mother had trodden into boots and had her hand on the door knob. 'They didn't like me.'

'Oh come on yes, of course they did,' the mother said.

'But they put a lot of fanciful nonsense into your head, if you ask me. You're all right. You look better than I've seen you for years, even though the hair's a fright.'

'Sarah's helped me.'

'Well, that's nice, I'm sure. I'm very grateful.' She gave the impression of bobbing her head, as if Sarah were a tyrant social worker.

That's not the point! Sarah wanted to shout after her as she went down the cinder path, clucking to the various animals pecking and rootling about. You've got it all wrong!

While the chicken was roasting, Carrie took Sarah round the village, introducing her to people as My friend Sarah, and ordering her about – 'Pick up your feet. Look at Mrs Daniel's roses. Don't touch that dog' – to show that she had not only a friend, but one she could control.

After the chicken, they had apple pie. 'I was saving it for Sunday,' the mother said, 'but you can have it if you like.'

The napkins smelled of gravy. No, it was the apple pie. No, it was the spoon. Sarah could never again eat apple pie without the taste of gravy coming unbidden into her mouth.

Because Sarah enjoyed doing things for Carrie, she thought that Carrie might enjoy doing something for somebody. There were some extra children at the Play School, two of them in wheelchairs and one of them almost blind, and the student helpers were mostly tied up with exams, so one morning she took Carrie with her to help.

Carrie went along, not so much to please Sarah as because Gretchen was at home, doing what she called swotting, which meant one pound of apples and glass after glass of buttermilk, gurgling down like bathwater. When she went into the basement room of the church, she hung back behind Sarah.

'This is my friend Carrie. She's come to help. She's worked with children,' Sarah said hopefully.

'Splendid, splendid.' Harriet welcomed Carrie as if she were another Special child. 'Another pair of hands, hooray!'

Jackie's mother went on building a house of blocks with Beth – 'And-a now a beeg one for ower corner' – and did not look up.

Neddy crawled over to clutch at Carrie's knees and squint up at her, trying to smile, trying to laugh, with his terrible sore stretched face. He had had another operation on his ears, and still wore a bandage round his head, covered with a plastic shower cap.

'This is my Neddy.' Sarah bent to pick him up.

Carrie said, 'Ugh,' and would not touch him. She stared appalled at Charlie, who was lying on the floor in his underpants while Harriet tried to find dry trousers, head lolling, fists in his slobbering mouth.

'I wish you hadn't made me come.'

'I thought you wanted to.'

'To please you. I'm going.'

'I can't drive you back till twelve.'

'I'll get a bus or something. These children – my *God*.'

'Your friend is leaving?' Jackie's mother looked up when Carrie went to get her coat.

'She doesn't feel well.'

'I have some bicarbonate tablets.' Jackie's mother's bag was always stocked with pills and Band-aids and little bottles of breath sweetener which she had been known to offer to people, like cigarettes or a bag of toffees.

'It's her sinuses.'

'She could have asked for my inhaler.'

It was going to be a special day. Even this morning Jackie had known it, when they started out late for the school because of Miriam, and then it came down hailing and they had to take a taxi from the Broadway to Saint Barnabas Church, and Muh had begun to gasp because she could not get the window open.

'Here – you pay the man.' She gave Jackie her wallet – a thing she would never have done when not in distress –

and he got a look at the money she had in there before he picked out the five shillings for the taxi.

Seven or eight pound notes. Now let her say she could not afford to stop for ice lollies on the way home!

'Huh-o Sair.'

'Hullo, Jackie. How does it go?'

'Swi-ing.' He hopped his feet about and flapped his hands. Sarah had been teaching him to dance. She had a friend with her, a great ugly girl like the statue on the corner of the Bank, all spots with white heads on them you would be able to squeeze if they were yours. Poor old Ned was making up to her in that bathing hat. She went, 'Ugh!' at him, Jackie heard her. She and Sarah whispered, frowning. Would there be a fight? The friend went away. Muh was not very pleased, although a girl like that was not much use, staring at the children in the room as if they were all idiots.

Sarah and Harriet were trying to teach Charlie to read words, as a surprise for Mrs Manson when she came back from her holiday. Jackie was helping. He held up the big cards before Charlie's empty eyes while Sarah clutched him on her lap and Harriet repeated the word over and over. 'Ball . . . ball . . . ball.'

Jackie turned the card round to look. 'Baw.' he said, to show Charlie how easy it was.

Charlie made a noise. Sarah bent her head to hear it, then she gave a little cry and hugged Charlie, laughing. 'He said it, Harriet, he said it! Read it again, Charlie. Ball, ball, ball.'

'Bah-h-h!' Charlie expelled a lot of breath. Sarah and Harriet looked at each other with sparkling eyes. Jackie, who had been squatting with the card, lost his balance and fell over, kicking his heels in the air.

'Get up, Jack, that floor is dusty.' His mother had looked over to see what the commotion was.

'Charlie read the card,' Harriet called excitedly. 'He said ball. Oh Sarah – oh frabjous day!'

'Anyone would think the boy had recited Shakespeare.' This was not Muh's day for rejoicing. She had one of her heads when she got up, but when Miriam suggested lying down instead of going to the Play School, she had said, 'Those who have much to offer, can-a not withhold it.' Miriam blew a raspberry. 'Besides,' said Muh, ignoring that, 'I have to think of Jack.'

'He won't mind not going, just this once.'

'That's not the point. It's very important for him to go to the Play School and see others worse off than himself.'

She told Sarah and Harriet, 'I'd be obliged if you two would get on with the job in hand.'

'This is the job in hand,' Harriet said. 'Everyone is playing quite happily. We're teaching Charlie to read.'

'You know that child has a mental age of about two.' Muh came over, her mouth buttoned, her eyes like coloured glass. 'And you're trying to make him *read*?'

'They're teaching them with cards like this at a year old,' Sarah said.

'Not mongoloids.' Muh looked at Sarah as if she were dog mess. 'I studied this at College. A child like that can't possibly begin to learn anything until he's ten, and then he may only live another few years, if Mrs Manson is lucky.' She meant unlucky. 'You're wasting your time, and the time of everyone else.'

'Don't you believe it!' Harriet flung herself at Charlie and picked him up and swung him to the ceiling. 'This child can *learn*.'

Muh made such a rude pooh noise that Harriet turned on her with a face Jackie had never seen, teeth bared in anger instead of in a grin. 'So could Jackie,' she said, 'if you'd only let him.'

'You leave Jackie out of it.' Muh drew him to her. She was so much shorter than he that her arm went round his hips instead of his waist. 'He knows all he needs to know.' They glared at each other, Muh holding Jackie, Harriet holding Charlie, flopping like a rag doll, dribbling all down into her front. 'You leave him alone. He can read numbers and write his name. He helps in the shop. He contributes to society.'

'Mending heels – oh ha ha.'

It was thrilling. Jackie stood with his mouth open, enjoying the fight as if it was about somebody else. Sarah was staring and grinning. When Harriet said, 'When you were at College! Centuries ago, my dear. Ideas have changed since then,' Jackie and Sarah wanted to cheer.

The whole morning went to pot. They never had Circle Time. Half the kids wet themselves. Jackie had to take the rest to the toilet by himself. He and Sarah had to manage Table Time as best they could, because Harriet stayed with Charlie, who was bawling, and Muh had shut herself in the storeroom. She had shut herself in with the biscuits, so the children had to have stale potato crisps.

When Charlie let up and Harriet came over, still panting lightly, Jackie heard her say things to Sarah like, 'Bloody fool woman,' and, 'Should be a Law against.' He could not wait to get home and tell Malcom. 'Should be a Law' could be one of their jokes to mutter without moving their lips across the dinner table.

Muh was still shaken so wordless when she came out of the storeroom after the great and famous row, that Sarah and Jackie decided to ask her if he could go home with Sarah for lunch. They had planned this, but neither of them had yet dared to ask his mother.

Surprisingly, she said, 'I don't mind.'

'I'll bring him back to the shop. I think I know where it is.'

'Jackie can show you the way,' Muh said and added crisply, getting back on the tracks, 'He's not an idiot, you know.'

Jackie had hardly ever been in a proper car. He had been in taxis, and once in a big black Daimler to his cousin Delia's wedding. There was a little silver trumpet in that, with a flower in it, but no water. He had stuck his finger in to see.

Sarah's car was sporty and red, with the top down. She tied him in and away they went, leaving Saint Barnabas far behind, leaving Butterfields, leaving the river, flying away from all the people who went about their business as if this was only an ordinary day. They drove along by the sea with their hair on end, and people in other cars waved to them, the young ones. Sarah and Jackie waved back.

She showed him the hotel which belonged to her husband.

'We ha' 'unch there?' he asked.

She laughed. 'Dreams. We're going home to my house and we'll have bacon and eggs and fried bread and fried tomatoes.'

'And beer,' Jackie said. He was not allowed beer.

She lived in a little house on a hill not much wider than the staircase that led up to Jackie's flat above the shoe repair shop. They went into her kitchen and he sat and drank beer out of a gold can, while she fried a tremendous panful of all the things his mother said were bad for his gall bladder. Afterwards she took him into the small shed at the back where she made pots and bowls and vases to put flowers in.

The clay was marvellous to handle. She let him mould up a bowl, rolling a long smooth snake and winding it round. His hands trembled with love for it as he worked.

'I'll get it fired and then you can come back and glaze it with a colour and give it to your mother.'

Bugger that, Jackie thought, but he nodded and grinned, because he was too excited to bother with words.

'Do you think she'll let you come again? I'd love to work with you, show you how to make things. You'd like that, wouldn't you, Jackie? You could be good at that.' She was as pleased as he was.

When it was time to go home, he asked if they could go on the pier. He was not allowed to go on the pier because of the crude-a element. They went on the pier and he spent three shillings playing the machines. They went to the little zoo because Jackie was not allowed to go to the zoo. He stood for quite a while making faces at the monkeys, but Sarah did not like it, so they went on a bit and when they got to the shops, there was a car pulling out to make a space for them. Sarah parked the red car and they went into Woolworth's to buy a comb for

Jackie, so that Muh would not know he had lost his own down a crack between the boards of the pier.

Inside the shop, while Sarah wandered, looking at all sorts of things except combs, Jackie found a few things that he could give to her in exchange for the lunch and the pots and the pier and the zoo.

Sarah paid for the comb, and they were crossing the pavement to the car when the man spoke to them.

'Excuse me, Miss.'

She turned, thinking she had left something in the shop, or been given the wrong change.

'I'd like you to come to the manager's office for a minute.'

'What for?' They were standing in the middle of the crowded pavement, like a stone in a stream, with the flow of people parting round them and coming together again.

The man coughed into his hand. 'It's about the young gentleman.'

'What's he done?' Jackie was smiling beside her, stretching his upper lip like a frog.

'If you'd just step upstairs to the office.'

'What's he supposed to have *done*?'

'He was seen, you see, Miss. No fuss. We don't want any fuss. If you'll just step up to the office and we'll see what he has, the whole matter can be straightened out with no fuss at all, no unpleasantness. It's up to you, Miss.'

'Did you take something, Jackie?'

'Yeh.' He put a hand into his jacket pocket and pulled out a posy of artificial flowers. The trouser pocket was smaller, and he had difficulty fishing about in it with his large hand. He brought out string, pebbles, chewing gum, a golf-tee, a few small nails, sticky pennies. With his other hand under the pocket, he twisted and contorted his long legs to find what he had for Sarah.

Between them, she and the man got him up to the office. The manager was quite friendly and human, but humanly suspicious. He thought that Sarah was using Jackie to steal for her.

'But no – no!' She was almost in tears. 'Look what he took. It was nothing – just little things.'

'They often start small. Your husband? All right, I don't mind you phoning him as long as it's a local call.'

It was hard to tell Brian. She thought he would swear and rage, but he understood quickly. He was not angry. He sounded – almost pleased. Pleased she needed his help.

'Come and help me.'

'Darling, I *can't*. I want to, but I can't. I'm alone on the desk. Oh God, this is torture. I love you, my darling.'

'I love you too. Please talk to the manager.'

'All right. Yes. Of course.' He put on a deeper, responsible voice.

'I see,' the manager said. 'I understand ... Yes, I'll tell her.' He put down the telephone and told Sarah, 'He wants you to ring his solicitor if we decide to take this further.'

'Are you going to call the police?'

On the manager's desk were the flowers, a tiny jar of cream rouge, a bar of chocolate, a loop of red ribbon, some packets of gum which might or might not have been taken today. Jackie was frowning and fidgeting, his brows working, his mouth and tongue fighting each other.

'We can't have this sort of thing going on. The young man should not be in a shop without supervision. He should have some treatment, you know.'

'Oh, look, he's – I mean, Look at him. You can't—'

'Stealing is stealing, Mrs King.'

He played with them a little while longer, until he had them both on the edge of tears, Jackie not quite knowing why, his eyes filling because Sarah's were filling. In the end, he let them go. He had meant to all along.

Sarah took Jackie home. He did not speak. He closed his eyes and sagged into his seat belt like a dummy, as if the episode had totally sapped him.

They went through the shoe shop. Some relation of Jackie's greeted them breezily, slapping him on the back hard enough to make him stumble and choke. His father was in the workshop, running a battery of machines. He saluted as Jackie walked through, slumped like an ape man. His mother was upstairs. Sarah had to tell her.

'It was my fault,' she said. 'I should have kept him with me.'

The mother, on her own ground, with no Harriet to strive against, was surprisingly relaxed. She took Jackie to his room for a nap. 'Cheer up, old man,' she said, 'don't look so blue. Nobody's angry with you.'

That was not why he was sad. 'They too' away my hings for Sair.'

'Yes, yes, it's all right,' the mother said, not hearing, as she led him away.

'I'm really sorry,' Sarah said when she came back. 'I wanted it all to go so well.'

'We can't always get what we want,' Jackie's mother said tritely, but with feeling. She made tea and they talked about Jackie and how she had had to leave College when she found that she was going to have him.

To get married? She allowed Sarah to believe that if she liked.

'If I had known what he was going to be . . .'

She would have got rid of him and not had to marry?

The other son Malcom was in and out, pestering. When was supper? Where were his plaid socks, his compass, his pocket money? What was wrong with old Jack? Could he go down to the playground and look for Terry?

'You must be proud of Malcom,' Sarah said. 'He's so bright and quick.'

'He's adopted.' She said it like a denial. 'I wouldn't risk another child. We adopted Malcom when Jack was nine. He said to me once, "Wasn't I enough?" Droll, wasn't it? He doesn't understand, of course, about the adoption. He doesn't know. Nor does Malcom.'

'Aren't you going to tell him?'

'No.'

'Why not?'

'His parents were – well, I don't want to talk about that. I wouldn't want him ever to have to know that he was not-a my child.'

NINE

THE WARDEN of the Reception Centre did not telephone Victoria. She had not expected him to, whether
old Michael went back there or not. She collected some
socks and handkerchiefs and some cigarettes and soft
sweets and went up to the Spike on Flagg's Hill, because
the old man was on her mind.

'Oh yes, he came back,' the Warden said. 'I told you he
would.'

'You told me you'd let me know.'

'Ah no.' He wagged a fat red finger close to her nose.
'You told me to let you know. There's that difference.'

Michael had gone to the post office to draw his pension. It was evening. 'The post office must have closed
long ago.'

'It takes him a long time to get back.'

Victoria went to meet him. She walked through side
streets where the town's unfortunates were supposed to
think themselves fortunate to live twenty in a house,
three or four in one room. It was a warm night. Children
out on the steps, women leaning incuriously out of
ground-floor windows, groups of boys on corners ready
for trouble, if not looking for it. At a cross roads she
paused, and looked along the streets, not knowing which
way the old man would choose to creep on his ruined
feet.

'Lost something?' A boy with long sidewhiskers like a
chinstrap leaned in the doorway of a guitar shop.

'I'm looking for one of the old men from the Reception
Centre. He's very lame. Have you—?'

The boy hawked and spat. His eyes did not follow her as

she crossed the road. She walked past a dump yard, partly fenced with old doors. Through a broken door, she could see someone moving about in the dark yard, boys jumping round like cats, something on the ground, a boy running from the alley at the far end of the yard with a can.

Without thought she pushed the broken door hard. It split and fell and she ran in, stumbling over the broken ground, stones and bits of iron, calling out something, she did not know what it was, just a noise.

The old man was lying with his face on the stony ground, his arms spread and his feet turned at a strange angle. He looked as if he were dead. The boy was pouring petrol over him. Victoria crashed forward, shouting. A stone flew at her head. Her skull exploded in a thunder-clap of pain and she fell, still shouting, screaming at the boys, but they were running away.

She was in a small quiet room, bare and shadowed like a cell. A nun sat by the window, sewing.

'How can you sew in that light?'

The nun got up and came over, 'You're awake, that's good. How do you feel?'

'Is my skull broken?'

'A very bad concussion. It was lucky for you and the old man that someone heard you shouting.'

She lay hardly moving, wandering in and out of sleep. White nuns came in and out and gave her drink and food and said kind boring things. More life was going on in her dreams than in the room.

In a dream, a man wandered into the Samaritan Centre. He had thick tawny hair and a strong sweet face which thinking had made sad, a coarse blue shirt with missing buttons.

He said, 'I am the angel of God, and you are my messengers.'

She was waking as he said that. When she was awake, she thought that Peter had said, 'I am the *agent* of God.'

'I am the agent of God, and you are my messengers.'

Billie found out where Morna was. She was living with this Phil, you wouldn't credit it, but that was what she was doing.

This Phil made his living buying up property that was to be condemned, filling it with desperate coloured families, and then not being available when the roof fell in or the tenants were turned out. He lived in various places and under various names. Billie had first met him as Phil at a bungalow party in the good old days when she and Morna went everywhere as a couple. He was a burly, curly fellow with coathanger shoulders and a quick way of moving, and women's hair spray all over his wiry head. He was said to have been a boxer, but in Billie's and Morna's estimation, that first time they had met him, the nearest he had ever got to the prize ring was in the corner with a bucket and sponge.

And now, she ... she ... Phil and she were in that crummy bungalow with the brass bells that rang in the draught and the carpet damp enough to cultivate mushrooms. After weeks of ringing Morna's old place and finally going round there and being repulsed by a homicidal Syrian, Billie had met her by chance on the street.

'Morna!' The fair bubbly head was bobbing in front of her like a star among the walking mortals. Pushing past people, Billie pounded after her.

'What do you want?' Morna did not even have to turn round to see who had clutched her.

'I've been looking for you everywhere.'

'What for? I owe you money?'

'Morna – look baby, meet me this evening. I've got to go to work now. Meet me outside the Odeon. It's *True Grit*.'

'I've seen it.'

'You can't have. It's only just on.'

'I saw it in London.'

'Who with?'

'With Phil.'

So it was true. Billie dropped her hand from Morna's arm and dropped back among the walking people, staring, craning and staring until the babydoll head could no longer be seen.

Somehow she dragged herself through that day's work, and the next, and the next. She moved like a drugged person along the cafeteria counter, ladling out food without even seeing it, answering quips automatically, good old Bill, her green bow stuck somewhere in her stiff hair and her heart an aching deadweight too heavy to carry about much longer.

She would not ring Victoria. What could Victoria do? Or care. She had heard enough of Billie's saga. You wouldn't blame her if she was glad that it was over.

On the fourth day, a voice came to her in the ladies' room behind the kitchen, which smelled as bad as some of the food they put out.

'Get out there and fight,' said the voice. 'Do something.'

It was a long journey out to where the colony of bungalows and caravans and tenting sites squatted on the flat foggy land at the far side of the estuary. There was only a chance that they would be there, but, 'Do something', the voice had said, and this was the only thing to do.

She got off the bus and walked down a long straight road to the water, lined with identical coloured boxes, each one of which looked like the one where she and Morna had gone in Ray's car and met this Phil. She remembered that the bungalow was painted in whitish yellow, because someone had said, 'The colour of pus', and there was a plaster gnome on the edge of a tiny dry pool. Someone had knocked off his head with a bottle.

There it was. Pus, pool, gnome. Billie trudged up the path and turned the handle of the musical bell genteelly, though she felt more like pounding on the door.

Phil opened it. Naked to the waist, he looked somehow more obscene than if he had his trousers off.

'Is Morna there?' Billie could see her sitting in the room beyond. Morna looked at her, but said nothing, just stared with those round eyes that did not blink.

'I want to talk to Morna.'

'Well, she don't want to talk to you.'

'Tell her to come out here.'

'Oh piss off. She's with me now.' Phil began to close the door.

'Don't you know what she is?' Billie shouted. 'Don't you know what she bloody is?'

'Oh shut up, you old butch,' he said and slammed the door in Billie's face.

It was Victoria's night at the Samaritans. When Billie got home at last, somehow, some time of the night, she pushed her pudgy fingers wearily into the holes of the telephone dial – 333-1000.

'Samaritans – can I help you?'

'Where's Victoria?'

Hospital of Saint Olaf and Saint Jude. Well, if Victoria had really gone and got herself mugged, there was nothing like doing it somewhere where the nuns could take care of you.

'Billie? Oh, I'm glad to hear your voice.'

'I wanted to talk to you last night.'

'What's up?' Victoria's voice was strange. 'You sound rather low, me old Bill.'

'I am low.'

'So am I. Come and see me, and we'll mourn together.'

'At the hospital? No thanks.'

'Oh come on. This one is nice. It's small and old and no one is in a hurry.'

'I hate all hospitals.'

But that afternoon after work, she put on her cracked leather coat over her green overall and trekked over to Saint Olaf's and Saint Jude's, a convent hospital that had been expanded during the war, with long Army huts running out behind the original white building where the nuns had been for years.

In the hall, the sickly drugging smell was there, in spite of all the flowers and floor wax. If her need for Victoria were not so great, Billie would have turned and walked out.

'Twenty-nine? I'll take you there.' The nun moved without feet, her young shining face narrowed by stiff white blinkers.

In a tiny room, there was a woman in bed, with long reddish hair plaited over her shoulders and the whole of one side of her face swollen black and blue, the eye almost closed.

'Victoria?' Billie did not know what she had expected to see.

'Hullo, Billie.' She could only smile and speak with one side of her mouth. She looked as if she were in pain.

'My God – *Victoria*.' Billie stood by the door, too stupidly shaken to come into the room. Victoria put out a hand and patted the chair by the bed, and Billie came in, feeling huge in the little room.

Victoria said, 'Oh, I'm *so* glad you came. They won't let me up, and I can't read, and I'm getting lonely and depressed.'

Of course. Of course. Billie sat in the chair, hot in her coat, because she would not let Victoria see her in the stupid green overall with C. Cripps woven on the top pocket, and it all became clear. It was not her need of Victoria that had tugged her unwillingly across the river and through the worst parts of Flagg's Hill to the hospital. Victoria needed her.

Victoria could not talk much, so Billie did most of it for both of them. She chattered on about the cafeteria and Mr Fettiche's niece, who he had put over everybody at the cash register, and about a Norwegian film that was either not as dirty as they claimed, or so filthy that Billie had not understood what they were up to.

She did not say anything about Morna and Phil, and by the time the young nun brought a tray of tea for both of them, she knew she was not going to.

'Oh Billie,' Victoria said. 'I do like you. Why didn't we meet before?'

'The unseen voice,' Billie said. 'Mysterious, tantalizing. No man knew her face.'

Victoria clicked her fingers. '*Far Caravans?* Yes, I remember. Stewart Granger.'

Billie shook her head smugly. 'No dear. *They Walk By Night*. I like you too, Victoria.'

There had been times, when she was lonely, or bored, or sick of the newspaper or of being single among married friends, when Victoria had almost thought she had better marry Robbie. This was not one of the times. He sat in her room looking a little petulant. He thought this whole happening was very unnecessary of her. Other people did good works without being so obsessed and childish. Other Samaritans stayed by the telephone. Victoria had to get involved in the stupidest possible way.

'You need a keeper.' He leaned forward and took her hand in his gentle friendly hand. 'You can't go blundering about on your own. You need to get married, Victoria. You could still have a baby. I'll find another flat, a house if you like, we'll go anywhere you want.'

'But Uncle Willie—'

'You can give up your job. Give up this slumming thing. Give up the Samaritans, I wish you would. You've done your bit.'

'I've hardly even begun.'

'My God, Victoria!' Robbie was quite angry. He got up and paced what little floor there was to pace. 'Stop trying to save the world. Try saving yourself.'

Not that way. She shook her aching head. Her face was very sore. Her blurred eye felt as if it would never see properly again.

'It's Sam – is it?' He stood with his back to the window so that she could not see the detail of his familiar, brotherly face. 'You still love him. Is that it?'

Oh – love. What was that kind of hopeless fantasy love? Jealousy? Regret? Humiliation? You could think yourself into or out of it. But she said, 'Yes, I think so,' to avoid telling Robbie that she did not love him.

She had never seen Peter except at the old rectory. She had not expected that he would come to the hospital. Except for Sarah, who had worked for him, he did not see any of the Samaritans outside the Centre.

Victoria had been dozing when he wandered in, as he had in the dream when she thought he had said, 'I am the angel of God...', and stood with his hands in his trouser pockets, holding them up because they were baggy and old.

He told her that he had seen Michael. 'They've got him down at the Chater Home. He seems all right. Whether he fell or was knocked down, he was too drunk to get hurt. When I told him you saved his life, he said, "Victoria – who's she?"'

Smiling was still painful. Laughing was impossible. 'I always have to tell him.'

'And I came to tell you that at last night's meeting, the Companions decided to ask you to join them.'

'*Me?* Because of Mike? But that was nothing. I stumbled into it. I wasn't brave or anything. All I did was get knocked out.'

Peter said, 'Not because of what you did. Companions aren't chosen that way. It's because of what you *are*.'

'Oh no, not me. Why me?'

'Yes.' He nodded his tawny rough head from which the barber thinned 'enough to stuff a sofa' without any appreciable difference. 'You.'

'... and so I rang Dr Strong and told him. "Mrs Potter is extremely ill," I told him. "I believe it's a heart attack."'

Paul had come to see Alice, but Mrs Laidlaw, grinning behind her desk, had snared him on the way in.

'"How old is she?" he asks. I tell him, "Ninety." "Then she'll probably die anyway," says this good Doctor Strong of whom they think so highly. Two hours later, I ring him back and tell him, "Mrs Potter has expired," and he says, "I told you so." ' Paul could not detect whether she thought this was funny or not.

He went to the room where Alice sat with a piece of blue ribbon tied round her hair, which seemed to get whiter each time they washed it. On the way, he passed Tim's girl Felicity, arm in arm with a rather sprightly old man on a cane.

She stopped and said, 'Hullo, Mr H.' in her vaguely insulting way, jaw tipped, as if inviting you to sock it. 'Meet Mr Sissons.' The old gentleman was wearing a fairly decent light-grey suit with a flower in his button-hole and a shine on his shoes. A soft grey hat was arranged over the wens and brown patches of his head at a carefully rakish angle. They were going for a walk.

'Mr Sissons is my very special patient,' Felicity said, giving his arm a little squeeze.

'And she's my special girlfriend,' the old gentleman said, a white moustache covering his upper lip, the lower one impotently lascivious. 'You know this felicitous young lady?'

'Oh yes, she takes care of my wife.'

'I take care of everybody, don't I?' Felicity led Mr Sissons away, cackling and besotted.

Alice had not changed in the weeks she had been here, but when Felicity came into the room after the walk, she began the finger clicking and the winking. She told Alice something that the old gentleman had said, and she told her a story about another patient who had fallen out of bed. Alice stared, her sad face unmoved.

'You see?' Felicity said. 'She knows. She understands everything I say.'

What if she could? What if Alice was still Alice behind that dribbling mask, suffering without succour the tor-ment of hearing without being able to speak, of not even being able to tell them that she heard?

If that could possibly be so, then Paul's 'I don't think so' would be another nail driven.

'Listen, Alice.' He bent to look full into her faded,

meaningless eyes. 'If you can understand, forgive me for not understanding. How can I know? I want to help you. Don't be afraid.'

The girl Felicity was standing just behind him. He felt aware that she was laughing at him, but when he turned, her face was only bored.

His car was parked in the side street at the back of the building. Barbara had got out and was walking with the leggy puppy, trying to teach him not to drag on the leash. He was pulling ahead of her, legs spread and striving, choking himself. Paul picked him up. 'Don't torture him. He'll come to it.'

'He's got to learn if he's going with me to London.'

'He's not. Don't start that, darling. You're not going away. You can't go away. Stay with me. It will be all right. Everything will come out all right.'

She shook her head. She was a lovely and gentle and patient woman, but the events of her life had not taught her optimism.

'Don't be sad.' Paul put down the dog and kissed her as he pushed her gently towards the car. He went round to the other side and opened the door. Before he got in, he looked up for some reason. Felicity was at the window of Alice's room, watching him.

He had not seen Tim for quite a long time, so on his way back to town, Paul stopped at the village where the boy lived in one of a group of white cottages built for Highfield patients who could take care of themselves.

Tim was in the garden at the back, 'hoeing his salads', the old lady who opened the door told Paul, but he found Tim sitting on the ground, with his back supported in an upturned wheelbarrow. He did not get up. Paul sat on the ground beside him, and they smoked without saying much. Tim had not seemed particularly pleased to see Paul, but did not want him to leave.

'It's getting cold,' Paul said. 'If you're not going to work out here any more, let's go inside.'

'Nah.' The wheelbarrow was like a turtle's shell. Tim

sat inside it and plucked bits of grass and chewed them dry.

After a while, Paul went into the cottage and talked to old Mrs Tolliver, who was sensible enough in a slapdash way.

'Is Tim all right? He looks a bit—'

'He's off his food. Don't look at me. They all complain about the meals, I don't pay no attention.'

She and two other men and a tiny pinched woman like a fieldmouse were in the front room watching television and sucking peppermints.

'He don't like the telly.' From a rocking chair, Mrs Tolliver looked up at Paul, her slippered feet taking a flight off the floor as she tipped back. 'That's why he likes to be outside. Someone was reading the News, and old Timmy starts fancying they're saying something about him. Daft, innit? He's no trouble.' The commercials came on with a blaring shout and she lowered the slippers on to the floor and gave the set her whole attention.

All of a sudden, Felicity wanted to go out with Tim again. When he got back from the garage late one evening after a gruelling day of extra deliveries before the bank holiday weekend, she had written him a letter. It was in the middle of the dining-room table, propped against the old man's white cat. It had been opened and licked shut again.

'Meet me Friday night,' it said, so since this was Friday, Tim went out again without supper and trudged the mile and a half to whistle under Felicity's window.

The room was dark. The light did not go on. The blind did not go up. He waited almost half an hour, and was turning to go when a wild beast leaped on him from out of the syringa bushes and bore him to the ground.

They rolled over and over and she moaned and whimpered and said, 'Yes-yes,' but he had only got his hand inside her blouse when she pushed him away and jumped up, brushing down her skirt in a very prissy way, and tut-tutting at him.

'Men are all the same,' she said. 'Disgusting.'

Tim raised his eyebrows, waiting for her to make sense.

She said that she was hungry, so they walked down the hill and went into the narrow café like a railway carriage, where the bacon had bits of string in it and the iron feet of the tables were crusted thick with dirt, like castors.

'I saw your friend yesterday,' Felicity said.

'Who?'

'Paul.'

'I seen him too. He come to the house.'

'He came to see his wife. I suppose as he was out this way, he thought he might as well drop in and see if you were still alive.'

'He likes me,' Tim said. 'He comes to see me. He helped get me put on the mobile.'

'Some treat,' Felicity said.

'It's all right.'

'For those that know no better. There's people out at Rowton works making twenty pounds a week.'

Tim stared. What would you do with such money? Tonight he had all he wanted. A home, food, clothes, Felicity. He fidgeted on the bench. In a bit, he was going to say, 'Come on down the boats then?'

'There's blood on your coat,' she said.

He looked down. He had not had time to change his working jacket and trousers. 'Bloody sow broke a bottle of ketchup.' In that last house at the end of the lane, not worth the bumpy trip for a packet of matches and two wholemeal. And then she had said, 'You'd better clean that up, young man, before Ted cleans you.'

'Come on down the boats, Fliss,' he said urgently.

'Not tonight.' But she was smiling. 'I'm too tired.' But the yawn was artificial.

'Tomorrow?'

'If I don't work late. I have more on my back now that I have everything to do for Mr Sissons. He won't let anyone else near him, not even Mrs L. "I want Felicity," he grumbles. "She's the only one I can stand near me."

He's dreadfully particular, you see, on account of always having been looked after, on account of his money.'

'Tomorrow?' Tim stuck to that thought.

'Do you know what he said to me the other day?' Felicity went on as if he had not spoken. Perhaps he hadn't? 'He said, "If I can get out of this hell hole will you come and take care of me, oh felicitous one?"'

'They wouldn't let you.'

Tim sucked the last of his sticky drink up through the straw. His fair hair flopped in his eyes. He bubbled up air as she said, 'I can do what I like now. No one can stop me.'

No one could stop her going out the next night, although she was not supposed to go out without permission. 'If I don't work late,' she had said, finishing her artificial yawn with a smile.

Her light was on. The blind was up. Tim whistled and waited. He waited for a long time. Then he saw her come to the window. She did not lean out with her long plaits hanging down. She pulled down the blind, and he stood in the garden and watched her undress behind it, moving slowly back and forth behind the blind with nothing on at all.

Paul was back to see him in a week. They sat in the dining-room and looked at the fan of paper in the grate. Tim did not think he said very much. Sometimes there was no way of knowing whether he was speaking or thinking, because thoughts that were in his head could be heard out loud.

Paul began to ask him questions, as he used to do long ago when they first met and Tim had to be so careful. He was very careful now. When Paul asked after Felicity, he looked into the corners of the room before he said, 'All right, I suppose.' Paul knew how Felicity was. He saw her at the place where she worked.

'Don't you like her any more?'

When Paul looked at him like that with his kind and

serious eyes, Tim's hands began to tremble. 'I – I—' He could not have spoken if he wanted to. His mouth was going like a baby. He got up and spun out of the room, stumbled up the stairs and on to his bed under the slanted ceiling.

Paul came and knocked at the door, but he had bolted it. That was the best thing about Diddlecot. No one locked you in. You could do it for yourself.

'Could you come out of the room for a minute?' Paul asked. 'I want to talk to you.'

'I'm busy with my patient.' Felicity fiddled and fussed with the curled-up old lady, tucking in the sheet and untucking it, so Paul said curtly, 'Come outside,' and she left the bed and came quite meekly.

'It's about Tim.' It was very hard to talk to this girl. She changed moods rapidly from belligerent to sly to malleable to pert, and swiftly back to belligerent if you said anything she could interpret as an affront.

'Tim Shaw?' she asked innocently, all eyes and ripe mouth.

'I think he likes you very much. Don't tease him. He's a very sensitive boy, you know. He's been through a rough time. You can help him so much by being his friend.'

'What's in it for you?' The innocence was quickly gone, the eyes long and scheming, the mouth twenty years older, and shrewd.

'I'm his friend too. I like him. I'm interested in what happens to him.'

'Because you saved his life? He told me that. And he told me, "Sometimes I wish he hadn't interfered."'

'He asked for help.'

'He won't next time,' Felicity said, watching him.

'There won't be a next time.'

'What's the matter?' Felicity leaned against the wall and rubbed the back of her head against the paint. 'Afraid of losing a customer?'

'You watch your step.' Paul was infuriated with her. 'Or you're going to find yourself in a lot of trouble.'

For the next few weeks when he came to see Alice, Felicity kept out of his way. He sat in front of Alice and dried her slow tears, and wondered how long it would go on like this. In the end, if she was never going to come alive, would he stop visiting her?

If divorce was never possible and Barbara agreed that they should live together, perhaps abroad, how would he manage to live without the Samaritans?

Being a Samaritan was his hold on hope, his clutch of treasure. The Samaritans was an obsession, a disease for which there was no cure.

'Why does my wife weep so much?' he asked Mrs Laidlaw.

'I told you, it's because there is no control of the emotional mechanisms,' she said. 'Of course, we can't know whether Mrs Hammond is suffering or not, since she cannot tell us.'

Paul was distressed enough by this pleasant shaft to ask Felicity, when she came nonchalantly into the room with sheets, 'Do you think it means anything when she cries?'

'Poor Alice.' Clutching the sheets, Felicity came and stood thoughtfully in front of the chair with her head on one side and her flat stomach thrust forward. 'It's hard for her, of course, but it's better she knows the truth. I think she's sort of glad for you, in a way.'

'What the hell are you talking about?'

'Well, I asked her if she wanted to know something and she winked once. That means Yes.'

'She can't wink.'

'She can for me. So I told her not to worry about you. Because you were very well taken care of. "Do you mind that, Alice?" I asked, and she winked twice, didn't you dear? That's a clever girl.'

Paul went quickly out of the room, to keep his hands off her throat. He did not go to Mrs Laidlaw. He went to Highfield, since the girl was still under their supervision.

'If the sick woman can speak, and be proved to under-

stand what is being said to her, then it could be possible for divorce proceedings to be instigated.'

If Felicity was right about Alice, then he and Barbara . . .

If Felicity was right about Alice, the cruelty was already unbearable.

When Paul left the solicitor's office, he went up to the rectory on Church Avenue to find Peter.

'What am I going to do? For God's sake tell me what to do!'

Felicity had left the nursing home.

'Got fed up,' she told Tim on the telephone. 'Got browned off cleaning up all those shitty old women.'

'Where are you?' She would not say. 'What are you going to do?'

'Oh – I don't know. Might get married one of these days.'

'Fliss!' They had talked about marriage sometimes. It had been their secret dream when they were at Highfield, clinging together in the broom cupboard, planning what they would have to eat and what colour the curtains would be. 'I'm getting a raise next—' he began, and her laughter cackled through the wire like static.

'Be able to give me a nice wedding present then, won't you? Not that I'd want you to spend your money if I'm going to be so well fixed.'

'What are – what—'

'He's asked me before, as I told you.' Her voice was airy and ladylike, teasing him, as so often before, to make him say, 'Come off it' and grab her where it mattered. 'He shouldn't be in that place, and he won't be much longer, because I'm going to take him out of there, poor old gentleman, and live with him for the rest of his life, if it doesn't kill him sooner.'

'Fliss, you—' He could think of only one thing. 'You mean you'd *do it* with him?'

'Well . . .' Her laugh was a silver bell. 'I'll be his wife, won't I?'

330

'I want to speak to Paul. 401, Paul. Is he there?'

'He was here earlier. I think he's gone. Wait a minute, and I'll see.'

Tim leaned against the glass of the telephone box. He felt sick and faint. He could hardly stand. Sagging, he waited for the strength of Paul's voice to shore him up.

'I'm sorry he's gone. Shall I try and get hold of him and ask him to ring you?'

'Yes.' Tim hardly knew whether he was speaking or not. 'Tell him—'

'What? Sorry, I can't hear you.'

'Tim.'

'Does he know the number?'

'Yes. No. I'm not at home. Here's the number. I'll wait here.'

'I'll miss you, my Sarah.'

'I'll miss you too.'

'You won't. You love that place so much, you've got to be there all night now, as well as half the day.'

'It's my first night duty. I can't help being excited. Do you think that's childish?'

'It's a funny thing.' Brian held her off and looked at her, making a face as if she were revolting. 'I think you're growing up.'

'I think perhaps we both might be?'

'That's a pity.' Brian's beautiful face became grave, as if he were going to say something serious. 'I'd much rather stay childish and spoiled.'

When Andrew handed over the 4000 telephone to Sarah, he said, 'I've been trying to get hold of Paul. Keep trying him and ask him to call Tim Shaw. Here's the number.'

Tim waited for a long time in the telephone box. Twice someone came to make a call, and when they saw that he was not using the telephone, they tapped on the glass with a coin, and he waited outside until they had finished.

He waited for hours. A church clock kept striking, the quarter, the half, three quarters, nine, ten, eleven.

Some of them were still up at Diddlecot. He could hear the set going in the front room, and the clink of tea-spoons. They did not care whether he was in or out. They didn't care. Paul didn't care. He was in league with Felicity, the two of them, meeting at the nursing home and laughing about Tim, he knew that now.

Well, he would show them. He had known for days how he would show them, ever since he found Vernon's sleeping pills in the bathroom cabinet, mad thing to do, leave them there where anyone could get them.

'Anyone seen my capsules?'

'I'll help you look.' Tim had helped Vernon to look everywhere but in his own pocket where he had the little bottle hid.

'One tablet at night, as necessary.' Standing under the light in the middle of his room, Tim read the label. He opened a bottle of Coca-Cola and took five of the pills. They went down tasteless, like jelly. It would be Vernon who found him, coming up to tell him he would be late for work.

Tim – oh Timmy! How would they find his mother? She would have to be told. They would all have to be told, gathering in this room, a weeping crowd of them, like doves.

Tim began to feel dizzy. He blinked away tears and sat on the bed to sample his dizziness, watching the floor tip and the door handle swell and recede, swell and re-cede. It was like the time when he was drunk, in the pub with Frank that time when the sailor had bought their drinks, and the table-top came up and smacked Tim on the nose.

He pushed himself off the bed and walked to the door, swaying from foot to foot, feeling the air with his hands. Giant steps would carry him down the stairs, floating along the road until he came to her lighted window. Crash! A stone as big as a football. She would poke out her head through the jagged glass and the blood would run all down the bricks where the tight braids of her hair hung down.

In the mirror on the back of the door, he saw his white face, aghast. He put his fingers on his wrist and felt the blood throbbing under the little ridge of scar. Under the stairs when the glass went in, the blood had welled quickly without pain and Paul had come and put his hands on him and shouted, 'Here he is!'

'No one can tell you what to do,' Peter had said. 'Don't ask for answers. The only answer to your life is you.'

'I don't know what to do.'

'Wait. Be yourself. Don't listen to anyone else. Listen to yourself.'

He got into his car and drove away from the town. He stopped by a telephone to tell Barbara to come with him, but when he heard the beeps, he hung up without putting in the money. He drove far out along the top of the hills where the trees were stunted flat on top and blown away from the sea. After a long time, he followed a narrow white road down into a cleft of the cliffs and when it became sand, he got out and slept on the dry turf.

He woke stiff and heavy. The day at school hung before him like a sullen threat. Tim had once said, in depression, 'You can't stand to look at how long the day is, but you have to keep looking.'

Sighing, looking at the day, Paul drove more slowly back. Before the town, he turned off the road and went round by the village where Tim lived. The cottage and the lane before it were in commotion. Tim had taken some Seconal and then slashed his wrist and bled to death when the drug blacked him out.

Helen's employer had been kicked by a Shetland pony that ran through her first-aid tent at a horse show, so Victoria was taking Helen's Thursday night duty.

She still looked rather battered. One side of her face was grazed and discoloured, and she wore dark glasses because of her eye. She and Sarah switched the telephone through to the bunk room quite early, and turned on a small lamp, so that Victoria could lie down and take off the glasses.

'Samaritans – can I help you?'

'Helen? Oh – Sair!' Jackie chuckled. 'I come your hou make pots?'

'I'd love it.'

'Next week? Munnay?'

'Will she let you?'

'I don't care.'

Sarah began to rehearse fighting words. Somehow, in spite of the trauma of Woolworth's, it was going to be easier to talk to Jackie's mother.

Quite late, they heard a key in the front door and Peter called to them from the hall. 'Not burglars. I've come to try and find some slippers and stuff for that drug man. We're going to the clinic and his feet are all swollen.' He came up to the doorway of the bunk room. Sarah got up. 'First night duty? How nice you look in jeans. No hips.'

He went down to his office at the back of the house. The telephone on the shelf between the bunks rang. Sarah looked across at Victoria. She shut her eyes and said, 'You.'

The man had left the girl he had been living with. 'I'm no good for her. When I'm drunk I don't know what I do. When I get sober, she's gone sometimes, but she always comes back. Why?'

'She loves you?'

'It's useless. Why shouldn't I kill myself? There's ... well, it's like ... there's nothing ...'

'You feel life's got nothing for you?' Sarah sat on the edge of the bunk and clutched the telephone, crouching over it, alone in the world with the man's slurred voice. 'What about the things you have to give to life?'

'Like what?'

'Yourself. Work to do. You said you wanted to be a journalist. A story to write. Someone who needs you.'

'I'm no good for her. Oh look, why am I telling you this? You don't care.'

'I do.'

'Why? Why do you? Have you got time to talk? Do you mind if I talk? I know I'm not making much sense, but I'll go off my head if I can't talk to someone...'

Sarah came out of the call as if she were coming out of water, shaking off the concentration. Peter was standing in the shadow by the door with an armful of clothes.

'All right,' he said. 'One thing, Sarah. Don't say, "*You feel* there's nothing to live for." Say something like, "There's nothing to live for." See the difference? It identifies you with him. It shows him that you know it might as well be you, suffering what he is suffering.' He bent to kiss the top of Victoria's sandy red hair. 'Good luck.'

He only kissed Companions. Questions stormed into Sarah's head, but she did not ask them.

'Who is he?' she asked when he had gone. 'What is he? I worked for him for two months and I don't really know him at all.'

'I don't think anybody does. I think he's what each one of us needs him to be. When I was in hospital, I had a dream about him. He said, "I am the agent of God, and you are my messengers." '

The telephone rang, and one of them picked it up.

'Samaritans – can I help you? Oh, I'm sorry ... I'm sorry. Don't cry. It's all right ... Yes I know, it's terrible when you can't sleep. I know ... I know ... It's all right ... Yes, I'm here. I'll wait. I'm listening...'

Monica Dickens

The author of ONE PAIR OF HANDS